QUEST FOR AN ISLAND

QUEST FOR AN ISLAND

BY

VASSILY AKSYONOV

PAJ PUBLICATIONS
NEW YORK

Library of Congress Cataloging in Publication Data
Quest For An Island
Library of Congress Catalog Card No.: 87-81201
ISBN: 1-55554-020-1

Printed in the United States of America

Publication of this book has been made possible in part by grants received from the National Endowment for the Arts, Washington, D.C., a federal agency, and the New York State Council on the Arts.

CONTENTS

QUEST FOR AN ISLAND

Destruction of Pompeii
(A Story for Bella)

Translated by Slava Yastremski and Joel Wilkinson

EVERY TIME YOU APPROACH POMPEII YOU THINK: "NOW HERE'S a little corner of paradise." The platitude is inescapable, for prior to plunging down into Pompeii from a high point on the road above the city, you catch sight of the marvelously chiselled shoreline and white houses rising from the bay in terraces interspersed with the eternally verdant flora. The eye is captivated: greenery swirls above the city with abandon and climbs the steep gray-white wall of the mountain range that shelters the town and the shore from the north winds. And each time "all these things" (as modern idiom would have it) loom before you, you sense a powerful uplifting of the soul, some half-forgotten moment of ecstasy, and the expediency of your own presence here. And inside the car, in the space between the windshield and your own forehead that little platitude flashes by: "now here's a little corner of paradise."

In early spring that year I set out for Pompeii with the most serious of intentions. I had made detailed preparations to spend no less than a month here, far from the frantic noise and dirty slush of Rome, in the hope of bringing a three-year project to completion, that of polishing off a major opus in my specialty. I had meticulously selected books and manuscripts and loaded them into the trunk, which also contained the clothes necessary for the "sundry occasions in Pompeiian social life." Now with respect to these "sundry occasions in Pompeiian social life," well, I must confess that I was jerking my own knee a bit there, for as I packed the suitcase, I kept saying to myself sternly—now none of those "social occasions in Pompeii." Only a jog in the mornings, work in the afternoons, a walk in the evenings and a bit of listening to the radio before going to sleep. Track shoes with thick soles, a typewriter, and the transistor. Oh, the times I'd become entangled in the so-called romance of that seaside resort! The number of totally scandalous escapades had been so huge that I tossed into the suitcase most of my classy threads (the distinctive hallmark of our circle) for the "sundry occasions in Pompeiian social life."

In our circle the thing to do in those years was to be taken for a foreigner at first glance, but absolutely not a second glance. You were supposed to be slightly scornful of both your own (those long since recognized not to be foreigners) and of foreigners (those who were obviously not your own).

So, as I was tossing various kinds of silk shirts and sweaters from London into the suitcase, I was tacitly allowing the idea that Pompeii nonetheless would "suck me in" to slip through the net of all my strictures about serious intentions. However, since I was tossing all the stuff in haphazardly without sorting it out, I was more or less telling myself that if I should get sucked in it wouldn't be for long and that it would just be for a momentary diversion from my righteous labor.

I booked a room in the old Intourist hotel "Oreanda" which faced onto a row of palm trees. In among the palms, almost obscured from the view along Shoreline Road, stood a plaster of paris statue of Historic Titan painted bronze. By some strange fluke he had been dragged here to the inner courtyard of the hotel, where the masses could take no pleasure in contemplating him. To tell the truth, even if you could detach yourself from thoughts of what he represented, the figure itself still looked rather strange: a fake bronze patrician in a thick coat who stood under the shade of palms, in the midst of magnolia leaves and the purple flowers of a Judas tree; he held his right hand outstretched, palm upwards, as if he were weighing a small watermelon or bolstering up some dairy maid's tit.

It's funny that I was in no way annoyed by having it for a neighbor! Quite to the contrary, this figure hidden from everyone except me and several other patrons of the "Oreanda" suddenly struck me as being a rather likeable and, to a certain extent, even congenial fellow. I made a distinction between this Historic Titan of mine and all his other millions of replicas, and I pretended that he was a hypothetical consultant, adversary, and evaluator for my righteous labor.

The "Oreanda" is situated on Shoreline Road, directly above the sea. Having stashed my suitcase in the room, off I went to acclimatize myself in the way creative types have traditionally "acclimatized themselves" in Pompeii: you sit on the pebbles three meters from the Mediterranean Sea with a manuscript of your cherished opus in hand, gaze at a page on which something has been inscribed, like "one can also reach this conclusion, based on the theory of disturbances, from yet another point of view once focus has been centered upon the collapse of the system which takes place under the influence of certain disturbances, when the system's energy level is expressed as Eo and there is a total disregard of any possibility of the system's collapse." You repeat these expressive, carefully coined lines and, at the same time, attune yourself to your primeval and primordial homeland as you listen to the waves reshuffling the pebbles and deeply inhale the smells of boundless courage and joy.

Try to steer clear of Shoreline Road with its idle crowd of vacationing barbarians, the façade of the hotel covered with a scaffolding where devil-may-care painters are idling about. Don't be tempted to drop in at the café, either, where that familiar company of Romans convenes by the window on the second floor.

It went without saying that there were two or three Georgians in this company, too, who oversaw and paid for everyone, proposing toast after toast to Arabella.

"Ara-bella!" one Georgian would say, holding his wine glass high above the table.

And everyone gazed at the glass as if it were a fortune-teller's hypnotic crystal ball and repeated: "Ara-bella!"

It's funny that in the Georgian tongue "ara" is a negative particle and that Georgians, in toasting our famous Arabella, almost seemed to be consecrating their drinks to a sort of mysterious Non-Bella.

Arabella rose up from one of the small café tables and extended her glass of wine to me. She and I had been slightly acquainted, so she was holding this beverage out to me, the one luxury which she possessed, in a kind of mute gesture of welcome. Her hand stretched through the glass, and, exposed to the wrist, was now offering me something pleasant.

Should any speculative talk arise as a consequence of this, I will certainly explain that at that moment it was simply impossible for me to have had either Arabella or, what's more, the wine glass in my line of sight due to the obstructions in my plane of vision caused by my position.

Meanwhile, a painter had calmly climbed down the scaffolding to the café window, taken the glass from her hand and bowed spryly to thank her. He had just about positioned his little pinkie on the glass stem so that he could partake nobly of this noble beverage when he suddenly interrupted his enchanting ritual and hollered at someone in a powerful voice: "Nikolai! Lie the brick down! I order you, lie the brick down! Lie the brick back or I'll shoot!"

There was absolutely nothing around from which he could have fired a shot. In discussions later, this fact was echoed far and wide along Shoreline Road. Why would he shout "I'll shoot" when there wasn't a weapon to fire?! He bellowed "I'll shoot," you understand, but what did he have to shoot with?! These people are really something: they shout "I'll shoot," with no firearm at hand, but what can you do about it, they're such braggarts?!

Passersby looked to see whom this painter was shouting at so loudly and they all spotted another painter in splotchy overalls who was standing on the scaffolding and painting a third-floor balcony. He was painting away to his heart's content, sluggishly and sloppily; he blew his nose on his sleeve, not suspecting a thing. Above him, the second painter; there likewise stood on the balcony a third painter, who had a brick in his hand aimed at the crown of his co-worker's head.

A long, drawn-out second:
1)The first painter was still holding the glass of fine wine. The second painter was holding a brick aimed at the third one's head. The third painter was holding his brush with a shaky, drunken hand.
2) The second painter smashed the brick against the third

painter's head. The third fell from the scaffolding onto the asphalt, where he lay sprawled out. The first painter drank from the glass of wine.

3) The painter with the empty glass in his hand dashed off somewhere—either to save the victim or nab the criminal. The second painter, his face bathed in a dazzling smile, finished off the third painter with a second brick. And the third one, with a violent twitch, flopped onto his back and once more sprawled out, spread-eagled and motionless.

A dark puddle began to collect.

Shoreline Road burst into a babble of shouts. "He did it for his broad, his broad, his own wife."

Some brave individuals tore through the door leading to the balcony. The murderer, still bathed in a dazzling smile, scrambled across the railing, and his body flew head over heels, struck against the second-floor balcony, and plummeted like a sack down to the asphalt right beside the first victim; immediately a second dark puddle began to collect.

As in Bizet's opera, over a woman, a whore—the hairdresser Svetka—and out of jealousy, two skilled workmen perished in broad daylight. They hadn't even had a lot to drink.

From the crowd of vacationers under the surveillance of the voluntary militia came a steady hum of voices. The appropriate vehicle drove up and individuals designated for such tasks removed the corpses. Slowly, the vehicle moved away.

The person responsible for what had happened dashed out of the hairdressing salon on Shoreline Road. The dazzling bright polyester-clad body under her white work-smock, now flung wide open, glistened with the delightful chimera of unruly flesh.

It's been reported that they had even had two kids, and some people used the past tense in reference to them as if they assumed that Svetka's kids vanished together with their fathers.

The hairdresser lunged at the ambulance car with her hands; shocks of tufted red hair seemed to bounce across the roof of the vehicle. Her hands left black marks. And it's with hands like this that they shave us!

Later, I had the impression that the destruction of Pompeii began precisely from this moment. It was as if that fatal incident initiated the collapse of the resort town and all its sanatoriums, restaurants, and monuments to workers and to Historic Titan. As if the painter with the brick had given a signal to the volcano. As if only then the whiffs of smoke had begun to appear above the rocky spur suspended in the golden sky.

In actual fact, however, if there was any link between the two occurrences, it was more likely to have been the other way around: puffs of smoke began to appear much earlier. No one noticed it for a long time because, strange though it seems, the residents and tourists in Pompeii were not in the habit of observing nature closely. Generally, they observed only one another, for it was exclusively in the collection of individuals that they saw the source of their pleasures or, as it's fashionable to say now, *kaif*, their version of *la dolce vita*.

To be precise, the puffs of smoke were noticed only when they had turned into really thick smoke. However, the vacationers supposed that it was just a local tourist attraction and the natives thought it was just a case of some experiments or other being conducted in the mountains which had to do with nothing more or less, putting it as simply and bluntly as possible, than our armed forces. The military strength of our republic was such that the possibility of any natural disaster occurring could just be dismissed.

The thought didn't even enter anybody's head, of course, to search for a link between the pink smoke in the mountains and the wave of strange acts which, like a deluge, rushed ashore. The sudden flare-up of passion in the painters' guild was just one of the many ensuing episodes.

Stories like these began to circulate:

Early one morning a highway patrol inspector was supposedly seen at one of the major intersections. He was shaving, sitting on the roof of a patrol car in front of a huge round mirror installed there to facilitate traffic safety, but certainly not for the convenience of shavers.

Rumor has it that in the "Carthage" bar one evening black marketeering voluntary militia men sort of beat up a Dutch tourist. They were listening, you see, to the music of baroque and he, you understand, was disturbing them—either by trying to peddle some piece of merchandise or by asking them to fix him up with a girl. Yet if one takes into account the special relationships between the Dutch and the People's Voluntary Militia of Pompeii, this is probably the least credible detail in all of the many strange events which were reported.

And something else, too. One couple at a dance held in the Club at the Woodworking Plant shed all their clothes and gave a public exhibition of the act of coitus. What's more, they not only escaped being beaten up, but even enjoyed the loud applause of the other dancing youths. And, in addition, the club's director appeared before the City Council with a bouquet of wild poppies when he was summoned to undergo disciplinary criticism. What's amazing is that they accepted the bouquet.

The director of a film crew from Rome placed a call to the very same City Council and proposed, in conjunction with the film he was shooting in Pompeii about life abroad, that the whole town be converted into a film studio, that is, to restore capitalism, for all practical purposes, in Pompeii.

Also, some criminal types bashed a zinc bucket over the head of the pensioner Karandashkin who, as a free service to his country, was selling state lottery tickets on Shoreline Road. Of the hundred thousand tickets which the muggers took from him not one was a winning number. Subsequently, Karandashkin sent an open letter addressed to all honest people of the planet, only to have the letter published in the newspaper "The Furnace of Health." This led to a very absurd polemic which came to a halt only after the Ideological Commission issued a direct order.

Yet the record for mindless cruelty in those days turned out to be the attack on the circus tigers by some deadbeat tramps. They chased the beasts, frightened to death, out of their cages with fire extinguishers. These tigers had performed as circus entertainers for ten generations, so they now jumped through hoops simply because of genetic traits, not in response to any training. Once they had scattered through the town and come into contact with the strange lifestyle of the resort's inhabitants and tourists, they quite naturally ran wild again. The thunderous roars of these ill-fated creatures could be heard in Pompeii right up to the last day of its existence.

* * *

However, there were also occurrences of some questionably perspicuous acts of virtue. Once, late at night, a threesome grabbed Matvei Tryapkin, the chef at the sanatorium "Homeland," by his coat lapels and demanded: "You have fifty rubles?" Now where would a drunken cook get a hold of such a sum of money? The robbers frisked the poor fellow and, once they'd convinced themselves that he wasn't lying, gave him a gift of a fifty-ruble note.

What is the link between people's behavior and the action of fiery lava from the underworld—one of cause and effect or the opposite, a direct or indirect connection? No one knows, so everyone stays confused. The pink cap on top of the volcano grew larger with each passing day.

But oh how successfully my work progressed at the time! In the morning I would leave the hotel in my springy track shoes and begin to run up the asphalt-covered grade which led from the lower to upper level of the park. During the minutes just before dawn, when the dark-blue crest of the horizon in the East charts its domain with special clarity because the sun is about to burst out from behind it at any moment, my brains were teeming with all sorts of good ideas. I saw page after page of my opus, "Repercussions at the Quasi-Discrete Level," dance before my eyes. And my whole steam engine all warmed up quickly, skillfully and synchronically—the lactic acid in my muscles oxydized and broke down, oxygenated hemoglobin stretched my fallen alveolae, and my aesthetic gland, not to be caught napping in this burst of energy, gladly awoke and took in everything ecstatically: the tea-rose bushes which secretly and lovingly beckoned from under the stone walls where they had cornered a bit of light, the secret and slightly wanton swaying of the billowing Persian lilac, and the naively euphoric smell of the dew-drenched wisteria. What lines I managed to write then, what marvelous lines! "The system inclined towards collapse does not possess, strictly speaking, a discrete spectrum of energy. Particles which fly off during its collapse travel into infinity!" What lines!

I took breakfast right at my work table; I would eat a couple of cold, boiled eggs prepared in advance, drink some instant coffee, and read my new sentences through the window to Historic Titan. He would usually screw up his tiny barbaric eyes (a strange mixture of genes from a steppe nomad and a Swiss clerk) and stare at me in a thoroughly indecisive manner. Nonetheless, it was my impression that he condescendingly approved: write, I say, write on. What is there, huh, to keep you from writing with your swanky gold Mont Blanc pen on the pristine page? Write, but don't forget about the people who compensated for their passion to write with prison makeshift inkpot filled with skimmed milk.

The countless replicas of Historic Titan can be divided into two basic types: majestic images and lifelike images. Yet that Historic Titan of mine, secreted among Pompeii's blooming flora, was neither one nor the other. Some nameless sculptor had captured him in this emigré pose, it seems, while he was strolling casually and mindlessly. He'd probably had his quota of such empty days when he was making history: times when the movement falters and splits into stupid factions, the greengrocer's and butcher's bills pile up, but a ray of light, however slim, still glimmers in the kingdom of darkness—the "Knopf" publishers have promised an advance and in Rome the colonel of the centurions has been shot and wounded. A small matter, but all the same good news. At any rate, he could enjoy a quiet stroll with his neighbor, the tooth-extractor Gruber, and say, illustrating with his characteristically Volga palm turned upwards: well, well, Herr Gruber, you won't believe it, but it's a perfect archetypically round breast, such a compact and solid little watermelon . . . This HT of mine was really no titan at all, just a slightly perplexed and unhealthy patrician who bathed infrequently and talked a lot. A neighbor like any other neighbor, a regular *citoyen*.

I recited to him: "—. . . as a result of the effects of relativity the level represented by the variables L and S splits up into a series of levels represented by the new quantity J . . ."

He heard me out with no particular show of enthusiasm, but also with no strong reaction—as if he were making use of the pause to get a word in about his little watermelon.

On one paradisic morning (judge this epithet by what was said earlier), I noticed a thin crystal glass containing good wine on the palm of my Historic Titan. On the pedestal below, curled up like a pretzel, slept Arabella, her head on the historic shoes. My gaze woke her up.

"Good morning!" she said, "do you know that Pompeii is threatened with destruction?"

"When?" I asked.

"Will three days from now suit you?" she inquired.

I thought a bit and replied, "Three days? That's a long time."

"Maybe it'll be less. Make haste."

"How did you happen to turn up here, Arabella?"

"I stumbled onto his lordship here in the bushes quite by chance. He startled me, this poor abandoned child of history. He spent a long time telling me about Astrakhan watermelons and, as always, was grossly exaggerating. However, I listened to him the whole night through. After all, he's been unfortunate and isn't understood by anyone except his poor wife. If you trace the lineage of Polovtsian aristocrats, he and I even turn out to be distant relatives. It's sad that the European branch of our ancestors split off so long long ago. Their bough withered, but ours has borne fruit right up to the present. And who's to blame for that? I offered him all that I possess. The glass in his palm, you see? He's noble, you see, 'cause he hasn't touched it. He left it for me to have this morning. How sweet of him! No, no doubt about it—his private life was definitely misunderstood."

She stood up and stretched. Her white slacks and blouse were covered with bronze colored dust. The Titan was beginning to flake here and there.

O Rome's darling, mythical Arabella! Every time you encounter her you think it's just some trick of television photography or that newly invented holography. She scampered up the statue of Historic Titan like a monkey, securing her bare feet cleverly in the sculpture's defective spots, and took the glass.

"Good morning!"

Head tossed back. Large gulps. A huge neck muscle was adeptly pumping down the moisture which had stood out overnight under the starry fermenting sky.

"What's that? Something transmitted via enemy radio stations?" I asked.

"Oh, no! I myself put it in his palm," the pretender Arabella reacted in fright, "this is my wine, I swear."

"I'm not talking about wine."

"What about, then?"

"The news. Pompeii's destruction."

"Oh, that!" she remarked, dangling her legs gaily as she hung from HT's arms. "Yes, yes. It's either the song of an angel or blatant lies from the radio."

I began to put on my track shoes.

"How's the writing coming?" Arabella asked. "Read me a few lines from 'Repercussions.'"

I obliged.

"Bravo!" she exclaimed.

"And how's your singing doing?" I inquired.

"I'm fed up with it," she said with a laugh. "You've got it easy—you sit there like a lump and write. Performing songs on TV is desperately boring."

"But your fans . . . " I started to say.

"I know, I know," she said, dismissing the comment with a wave of her hand. "I'm trying to find a different way to get them to prop up their existence. Are you actually getting ready to jog? Take me with you."

We started off running together—evenly and rhythmically, with the intoxicating smell of wine from her puffs of breath. But when I later glanced to my side, I no longer found her next to me. I turned completely around and, in the distance which was growing more blurry with each step, caught sight of a truck vending beer. Painters and film people had gathered around it. Arabella, with her palms extended outwards, was encouraging our dopey citizens to prop up their existence.

That evening ash began to fall on Pompeii. A lackluster moon lit up the crest of the mountain range, above which there floated a rose-pink luminescence. Here and there, serpentines of fire crept along the wooded slopes.

Foreign radio stations were reporting Pompeii's destruction loud and clear. Our capital calmly but forcefully denied the rumors as slander.

That night I finished work on my monograph and set off for the hairdressing salon. For some reason I had a sudden urge to alter my appearance radically: maybe, to have them trim a bit off the temples or give my mustache a new twirl. In short, willy-nilly, my legs carried me off to the hairdresser's.

Picture me that evening: an enormous strapping red-head with a glint in his eyes! Good intentions forgotten. Forgotten, too, and thoroughly ventilated from my mind—the well-turned phrases in "Repercussions." Clearly realizing that Pompeii had "sucked me in" this time, I moved cheerfully towards the vortex of the "suction"—the hairdresser's. Flakes of ash flittered gracefully, swooped towards the lamplights of early evening and fell on the crowd of barbarians who, as always, were yearning for kaif.

A Greek liner had docked hard along Shoreline Road. Music drifted from that direction. They were playing the new hit record "Love Machine" over and over again. A teeming crowd milled around at dockside. Everyone except the most arrant lazybones was trafficking on the black market: young pioneers, pensioners, musicians, and even centurions in uniform. And just between us, there were even centurions in civilian clothes. It even seemed that the ultimate purpose of black marketeering had already been lost sight of; the primary goal of making money had been forgotten. Now it was merely a chaotic and greedy exchange: a hunt for clothes, drinks, various types of Japanese baubles, and tobacco.

Here I am at the hairdresser's: over the entry pre-revolutionary naiads hold aloft a wreath; on the left side of the door is a memorial plaque honoring the underground meetings of the Pompeii cell of our beehive; on the right a memorial plaque honoring the visit of the "great chronicler of the twilight era when public consciousness began to fade." There remains some question as to whether he spent a long time here and what he did during his visit, whether he ever had his mustache curled or the hair on his temples trimmed.

However, it seems that during the twilight epoch there wasn't a hairdressing salon on this site, but rather a sanitary house of ill repute. Of course, perhaps this, too, was nonsense—just a city legend told with a faint jeer. Uncouth boors usually spread only spiteful and bawdy stories about the chroniclers and it's impossible now to reconstruct the truth—archives have been destroyed and the historical record has been completely distorted through propaganda.

Anyway, I walk into the reception room and right away I see my reflection in two dozen mirrors. Quite an imposing sight: the arrival at the hairdresser's of a whole crowd of enormous, red-headed gargantuans. Two dozen armchairs and an equal number of hair-dressers, too—pudgy, skinny, busty, tushy ones, in creased and soil-ed smocks, and all of them in the same state of intoxication. A full load of customers. One is cackling insanely, twitching in the arm-chair with his arms and legs; another has bent his flabby body over and is moving his hands idly back and forth above the floor as if in search of underwater treasures; a third, having grabbed the chief hairdresser by the buttocks, is swirling around on his armchair and serenading her with the waltz song "He's shy—not bold." The rest are shaving, more or less.

What's the first impulse of the red-headed giant who's just entered? Why, he'd like to drive all this rubbish out of the broadway barber's temple with a whip and at one fell swoop plop down on all twenty-four chairs, because for some reason he is insanely pleased with all two dozen of the women. A most shameful impulse, of course.

Cut-down-to-size, I notice: here, it turns out, even the waiting line—five to seven other musclemen—has to hang around idling; in what way am I better than them?

There's nothing that can be done about that. This is the drunken rubbish you have to live with: a community of people stuttering and slurring words and poisoned by cheap disgusting port wines, that one-ruble swill with a slimy chemical sediment, the so-called "Mumbo Jumbo." With rubbish like us, not only Pompeii but, in a year or two, even Rome will topple. But we somehow have to live together with them, that is, with ourselves, and to face destruction with them. Emigration? No, that's just smoldering embers, both in-side and out.

The line rocked back and forth, drunken and pot-bellied, with mindlessly smiling eyes and faces smeared with volcanic soot. No one in the present company suspected that a short distance away, on the far shore of the dark, oil-slicked sea in the "lands of Capital," hundreds of hairdressers spend their time in charitable quietude, with the reserved assurance that they can expect only upstanding customers. On the other hand, I said to myself as I joined my com-rades on line, in a certain sense there is the same—if not worse—rot-ten smell everywhere.

"The same—if not worse—rotten smell is everywhere," I said out loud to boost the courage of my comrades.

"It's worse in our metallurgical district," said one smiling fellow.

"Why are you looking?" a second smiling fellow asked.

" 'Cause. I'm just looking," said a third smiling fellow.

"He waunts to look," uttered a fourth smiling fellow.

"Lat'm look," the fifth smiling fellow said.

"Look, if you waunt," the sixth smiling fellow said.

"Look, does no difference to me," said the seventh smiling fellow.

The red-headed giant looked at the group of port winos, not without a certain sense of horror. One of the smiling degenerates stood out from the others and made a definite impression on him: the powerful mold of a foolish old face—a retired colonel of the legion of honor. At least all these heirs of Caesarism have preserved something in their features, I thought, it may be the stability of an ungifted but majestic epoch. Should I stick with them, the last piers of society?

A peal of thunder slowly rolled over Pompeii. For a second the stormy sea was lit up. The floor of the hairdressing salon heaved violently. The pre-revolutionary Dutch tile cracked and shattered.

Perhaps all that's left is to join ranks with Caesarism, the red-headed giant thought. Theirs may be the only pillars which haven't begun to rot from the inside out. He offered the colonel a Marlboro cigarette.

"On television they're saying the overseas lands are putrifying," the colonel said, inhaling the pale blue smoke. "But actually, we've got the cesspool here and they've got the economic achievements. And what's the reason?"

"What?" the red-head asked.

"Ain't no decent organization," the colonel explained willingly. "They criticized Marshal Tarakankin and that criticism was right, I agree. However, they forgot that the Marshal had a brain. The kind of orders he gave? Why, to delay demobilization of all personnel with demerits for the same number of days as they had black marks on their record."

"Why is there no latrine here?" one smiling fellow asked in surprise. "The comrade here's pissing without the presence of a latrine."

"Every pencil wants to piss, but they hold their lead in silence," said another smiling fellow.

"Marshal Tarakankin arrived at our trireme," the colonel continued, "in time for demobilization. They saw the personnel off with an orchestra, but detained seaman Pushinkin for 105 days because in his three years of service he had chalked up 105 days in the brig. Everyone else returned to their productive civilian jobs, but Pushinkin roamed aimlessly through all compartments of the trireme and became disgustingly louse-ridden."

"Pardon me, but what link is there between this situation and the economics lag?" the red-headed giant asked.

"They've forgotten how to organize things right," the colonel explained. "Moreover, the campaigners fighting against cosmopolitanism seriously damaged the quality of our science. Just look around—no self-respecting tomcat will eat today's sausages."

"You've got sour aspic for brains," the red-headed giant mumbled as he moved away from under the pseudo life-jacket colonnades of Caesarism, not without some dismay.

Then, yet another blow. In one terrific burst, a gust of hot wind blew down all the palms on Shoreline Road. One of the prerevolutionary naiads toppled off the frieze and cracked into pieces. The glass door to the hairdresser's shattered with a loud bang. Flakes of ash and the vile trash of this public resort flew into the salon itself. Filthy smocks clung to the extremely enticing bodies of the twenty-four frightful tarts.

A second or two later and there was only the barren waste of catastrophe before our eyes: crimson flashes of sheet-lightning, palms bowed over by the wind's iron broom, a bloated sea with our naval fleet clumsily sliding down into its gluttonous mouth—had that poor fellow Pushinkin not served on one of those triremes?—and the torso of the naiad flung onto the street. Remember at least this, if all else is forgotten, remember at least this!

A group of youths walked past, guffawing and singing the song "Love Machine." In the process of stepping over the naiad, one of them propped his leg on her in order to lace his shoes. All's normal; life flows past, empty of memories; the organizations responsible cope with the ravages of natural disasters; the prognosis is good;

Rome stands firm, unshaken.

Suddenly, all at once seven closely shaven and neatly cut citizens came out of the beauty salon.

"Next!" boomed the voice of the chief hairdresser on the loudspeaker. The PA system, it turned out, was still working there.

The red-headed giant fell onto a chair, right into a woman's eager hands. How can they condone such filth when their guild's service is public beauty? Fingers with broken nails and chipped polish darted nimbly across the red-headed giant's chest, belly, and groin. A gigantic and eager mouth, smeared with lipstick, laughed above him. Tits were falling out of the unbridled polyester blouse. The wet hem of a skirt stuck to the protruding lower abdomen, and everything below brought to mind that deep-water Agave known for its passion for lurking, sucking in, and swallowing innocent fish. So, that's who's got the red-headed giant: Svetka, the disgrace of the city, the widow of the two painters.

"So, that's who's got me!" the obscene mouth laughed. "The red-headed one, red one, saucy one, shameless one! Let's get out of here, Red, let's get the hell out of here! I'll give you a shave on the beach! Take all this stuff! I'll do it to you 'deluxe' style on the beach!"

"Excuse me, but it seems to me that's against all the rules," babbled the red-headed giant. Nevertheless, he stuffed his pockets with boxes of powder, creams, and a rubber atomizer containing "Shipr" cologne, and helped Svetka to take down from the wall an ancient mirror with a special golden frame.

"Tomorrow, Senkina, you will be fired for laying the customers," said the chief hairdresser.

"Watch out or you'll be sacked yourself, Shmyrkina," Svetka shouted back. "It's not a private operation we've got here, it's a guild. You yourself fuck behind the partition and the customers aren't satisfied."

A bushy crack opened up in the ceiling. A volcanic wind whirled through the salon, lifting up a tornado of cut hair. Face to face, the two women rapidly snarled at one another, something completely offensive and incomprehensible.

The red-headed giant began dragging the mirror to the beach. Behind him Svetka was dragging spotted bed-sheets.

* * *

"Oh, momma dear! What a customer I've hooked, oh-ah-oh," moaned Svetka.

The red-headed giant gripped her thighs in his hands, but turned his head so as not to see her terrible face.

Waves of gray pebbles lay on the beach and in all their troughs there was grunting and squealing. Sin was being committed everywhere, and ashes fell onto all this carnal bestiality.

In our case the sin was aggravated by the stupid mirror, it stood at the heads of the copulating pair, and everytime the red-headed giant raised his head he could see in it his strangely undisturbed face.

Behind him, in the mirror, the crimson sea was becoming more and more luminous, the volcano was burning brighter and brighter over Pompeii.

Then two chicks in hip-hugging jeans appeared in the mirror. They stood with their horsey faces downcast, swaying back and forth. One of them held her hand on her friend's pubis, while the other squeezed her friend's breast.

"Here, Galka! Look how the pros work!" one of them said, sort of hiccuping in our direction. "But we are still trying to find our kaif."

Right then and there they tumbled down into some pit, where they expressed their ecstasy in real bawdy language: oh, I got banged sweet, ah, I'm all wet, oh, Galka, oh, Tomka, look how starry the sky is, look a star is falling a star is falling . . .

What they took for stars were falling volcanic bombs. The torturous and jolting eruptions began reducing the carnal bestiality's bellowing to an exhausted lowing.

"I tell you, Client, you made me rustle," Svetka uttered. "Since Nikolai and Tolya killed each other I haven't had a feast like that."

The soot was smeared all over her face; her eyes shone thankfully.

I looked at myself in the mirror. Where had the red-headed giant disappeared to? My balding head was melting away like a candle, my body was swelling up like yeasty-beasty, sour dough.

A scorching stone crashed onto the beach, cast up a fountain of pebbles, spun like a top, and rolled into the sea, where, with a hiss, it sank in a cloud of steam.

I got up and walked away, hardly moving my elephantine feet. Buttons on my shirt popped off and my hairy black stomach hung down, suddenly unbelievably swollen.

Roofs of the houses along Shoreline Road cracked under the pounding of boulders. Broken windows were raining down. Neon letters which survived here and there spelled out abracadabra. A powerful flame was raging inside of a little store with the coquettish name of "Sweet Tooth." However, next to it, people who had gathered in the morning were quietly standing on line at the neighboring grocery store. They were waiting for the delivery of some fantastic boiled salt pork, although there could be no chance of a delivery since all the passes above Pompeii were enveloped with smoke and covered in flames.

Orchestras were playing everywhere. The "Love Machine" thundered from basements, from under the canopies of open-air restaurants. People of all ages danced in a frenzy. It was freedom of movement unthinkable in the times of Caesarism: eyes bulging and mouths lusting; the eerie Pompeiian shimmy. Socialism which imitates capitalism is socialistic to the point of tears.

Of all the people who had it good in the burning Pompeii, the gloomy fat guy with dirty dark locks hanging down on both sides of his balding forehead had it the worst of all. The arrogant elephantine fat guy was meandering feebly and mindlessly through the crowd until he saw a telephone booth for long distance calls. From that booth he could immediately plug into the capital's telephone system, but, strangely enough, it was empty: apparently, nobody had any need at all to call Rome. The fat guy stepped into the booth.

"Do you know that we are burning?" he asked his colleague at the institute, the first person whom he managed to reach by phone.

"Old man, it's too late for philosophical questions!" playfully laughed his colleague—in principle, an okay fellow, who, as a matter of fact, was no different than me: the same kind of crafty slave of the communal system which swallowed us all up.

"No, not in the philosophical sense at all," said the fat guy. "Pompeii is perishing. The volcano has gone mad."

"Well, that's no topic for a telephone conversation," his colleague uttered angrily.

Everything is clear. Now they will put me down as a provocateur. I hung up the receiver and through the glass I saw Arabella who, dancing and waving her hands, headed up a very merry company. A calm herbivorous snake was lying softly coiled around Arabella's shoulders.

"Hey, come out of there!" Arabella shouted to me. "Why are you swelling up over there in the telephone booth? Look, gentlemen, how this character has swollen up!"

A couple of merry Georgians pulled the fat guy out of the telephone booth and offered him a bottle of wonderful wine.

"Where do you get such wine?" I was surprised. "And where, in general, do you find all these nice things?" I asked simpleheartedly. "How is it that you Georgians manage to live rather sumptuously in the midst of all this wretchedness?"

"No problem," the Georgians answered merrily.

A scorching piece of rock hit the telephone booth and instantly wiped it off the face of the earth. The face of the earth, in turn, slid apart under our feet and formed a crack half a meter wide. We jumped over the crack and walked along Shoreline Road passing lines of people craving kaif and those having a good time inside of burning cafés.

A small clever boy, a "young naturalist," was following on Arabella's heels and whining: "Lady, give me back my yellow-belly. I took it on loan from the zoological lab for some research."

"Child!" Arabella clasped her hands. "Do you really mean to separate us? Can't you see how your yellow-belly likes hanging around my neck? Child, the snake and I love each other!" She took the head of the yellow-belly in her palms and kissed it on the mouth. "Child, I confess that I myself am quite a yellow-belly and if you are truly a young naturalist, you must study both of us."

Something like a ball of lightning flew over Shoreline Road and hung over the main square of Pompeii, over the City Council building and over the most powerful and majestic sculpture of Historic Titan.

"We are all yellow-bellies!" enthusiastically shouted our entire company: Oh, that magnetic Arabella!

What was hanging in the distance over the square did not hang for a long time. It struck and scattered in a zillion sparks. Then, for a second, a phosphorescent light appeared and illuminated the main square. One could see the statues of various epochs falling: a border guard, a woman tractor-driver, a tank driver, an astronaut . . .—and how the principal, most powerful statue began to fall down. It became frozen in my memory just like that—in the state of leaning and falling—because the phosphorous disappeared and the crash of the statue's fall was muffled by the swelling uproar in Pompeii: orchestras, shouts, laughter, and the crackling of fires. A thought flashed through my mind—and how is mine, my personal HT doing there, what has happened to him?

"No victims!" exclaimed one of Arabella's retinue.

"An extraordinary phenomenon of nature, comrades! A volcanic eruption with no loss of life. It is the counterpart to the neutron bomb: material goods are destroyed, people remain whole. That's precisely what I reported to Rome on the hot line: no losses of human life; courage is making a stand against the elements!"

By his entire appearance, this man, dressed in an official two-piece suit, with our beehive pin in his buttonhole, was supposed to personify the stability of our all-embracing administration, but a small muscle was twitching in his face, and a bottle of cognac was sticking out of his jacket pocket.

Arabella encouraged him with her soft palm, caressing his neatly combed hair from one side of his head to another.

"Poor child, deserted in the midst of the fiery elements! This morning you were still reigning in your City Council office, and now you are all alone! We won't leave you! Take heart!"

"I am taking heart," the secretary looked trustingly at Arabella.

"That's exactly what I reported, I managed to say on the hot line: courage is making a stand against the elements . . . "

"Lady, give me back my yellow-belly!" begged the young naturalist. "It's time for it to eat."

Someone who appeared to have once had and lost some secret power approached, holding in his hands a bottle of Pepsi-cola and a glass.

"Your reptile, does it drink Pepsi-cola?" he asked the young naturalist, looking at him with his still penetrating eyes.

"It hasn't tried it yet," the young naturalist mumbled, "but I . . . I, personally, Comrade Colonel, drink Pepsi-cola with pleasure."

The colonel in civilian clothes, chief of the local department of centurions in civilian clothes, began to pour the bubbling Pepsi-cola into a glass and to treat the young naturalist and his snake to it. The boy swallowed the foreign drink greedily, while the yellow-belly hanging down from Arabella's shoulders only delicately sipped the brown moisture.

Our company was growing. It had turned into a crowd. The men and women and the young and old were walking; children and dogs were jumping up and down; cats were scurrying back and forth; and tigers from the local circus dragged along like sheep. The whole crowd was following the darling of all our people, the metropolitan area, and the barbaric regions: the television mirage, Arabella.

She once sang in an expressive voice in the attics and basements of Rome and was famous only among the attic-basement elite. Then, suddenly, this strange creature with the hypnotic voice appeared on TV in among all the mug-ugly peddlers, and all of our preposterously savage people, tired of hearing about their achievements, did not boo her; they fell in love with her. What miracle brought her into the tele-communication system? Wasn't it the first symptom of the present seismological storm?

Where were we going? For some reason, uphill—closer to the fire. Along the steep narrow streets of Pompeii, past the burning houses and closer to the scorching heat, we were ascending the Hill of Glory. In the houses, homemade vodka-distilling machinery was exploding, television tubes were bursting, and mirrors were melting, but the inhabitants for some reason didn't seem to take notice of the destruction of their property. Everybody was in a rush to get whatever kaif there was left and to join up with us.

"You've become younger again, pal," Arabella told me. "Where's your hairy belly? Where's your muddled look?"

Indeed, I felt a kind of strange youthful lightness. More and more easily, happier and happier, I was jumping over the streams of scorching lava which spread over the cobblestone road. Once, among dozens of other faces in a piece of broken glass, my reflection flashed out at me—this, it seems, is how I looked about twenty-five years ago, in my student days.

Strange transformations in age kept occurring during our entire procession: the young naturalist, for example, in his shorts was now resembling a very boring senior lecturer, and the chief of the secret service—a masturbating schoolboy, one of those who always hang about in school restrooms.

"Stop!" the secretary of the City Council suddenly shouted. "Here's the special-supplies warehouse!"

In front of us were the smoldering ruins of quite an ordinary house. A black "Tiber" limousine was ablaze next to it.

"Five minutes before the destruction of the City Council building I gave an order to Ananaskin to do a complete inventory," the secretary of the City Council explained worriedly. "Oh, no, Arabella, I assure you, I, personally, don't need anything: I'm just curious what the results were."

The gas tank in the "Tiber" exploded: a pastorale for the fire storm in the background. The door to the special-supplies warehouse fell off and Ananaskin appeared on the porch, hunched over from the weight of a huge smoked sturgeon that he was carrying on his back.

"Here's all I managed to save," he wheezed.

"Dear Ananaskin!" exclaimed Arabella. "Humble secret supplier! Gentle distributor with respect to labor! Are you shaking, Ananaskin? Take heart! Kiss the yellow-belly and join us."

Moaning, Ananaskin put his mouth to the snake's lips. Someone immediately came to his assistance, then a second and a third; they put their shoulders voluntarily under the beam of sturgeon, its weighty hulk.

We were drawing near to the top of the Hill of Glory where, among the destroyed bas-reliefs, there flickered a little ribbon of the Eternal Fire. So touching, in the raging of that Non-eternal Fire!

"It wasn't for us that this fish swam, and it wasn't for us that they smoked it, either," Ananaskin groaned. "They were expecting an important person. But now there's no point in keeping their secret—it was the Pro-Consul himself! Fortunately, he did not arrive . . ."

"What do you mean didn't arrive?" asked a man standing behind Ananaskin's back. "Who do you think is volunteering his help with transporting this beam of sturgeon?"

The little guy turned out to be the one who had been expected with such trepidation by the entire Pompeiian administration for two weeks already—the Pro-Consul from Rome. It turned out that his plane landed right in a puddle of lava and stuck there like a fly. No car was provided and the guards ran off in different directions to the barber shops. Now the Pro-Consul was walking among the people, trying to be inconspicuous.

Behind him, under the beam, the pensioner Karandashkin was walking with a zinc pail on his head. The procession of the four volunteers was brought up in the rear by my plaster-with-pitiful-remnants-of-gilt Historic Titan from the "Oreanda."

"Are you up to our sturgeon, comrades?" questioned Ananaskin.

"It's precisely labor like this that liberates people from those forms of exploitation which have become standard for them," Historic Titan spoke out.

"Just where is it we're going?" Karandashkin asked from under his pail. "Where will we eat this fish?"

"Don't you understand?" a Georgian dancer expressed his surprise. "Ara-bella will now sing to us from on top of the hill!"

"What a blast!" the pensioner shouted loudly.

"What a blast!" echoed the entire procession.

"How could I abandon them, these dear scarecrows?" Arabella thought with a quiet smile. "How could I deprive them of myself? What will they have without me? Sappho, George Sand?"

At the top of the Hill we all took our places. All around dry grass was burning, alabaster was melting, and the bas-reliefs of heroic deeds were tumbling down. Down below, to the thunder of its own jazz, Pompeii was collapsing.

Flaring up higher, growing more crude,
The feast is raging, the talk is rude . . .
My dear little girl, oh, Pompeii,
Child of Caesarina and of slave . . .

Arabella sang out and then cleared her throat a bit.

"I haven't sung for a long time, but now I will sing everything for you—from the beginning to the end, or from the end to the beginning, or from the middle in both directions."

The volcano was roaring like all the radio jammers of Caesarist times and of our days put together, but the feeble voice of the singer was heard all the same.

"Whazz she singing?" asked Karandashkin, knocked off his rocker by the sturgeon, which he had never before seen or eaten in his entire life.

"She's singing her own stuff, not ours," explained the Pro-Consul sluggishly, giving rare fish its customary tribute.

"It's amazing music, not human," croaked the Historic Titan pensively, quoting his own thoughts on classical music (Collected Works, Volume XII).

Flowing around the Hill of Glory, the streams of lava poured down onto Pompeii. From the top it seemed that everything was finished, but more new crowds of people still kept ascending the Hill.

There came our workers and vacationers, the crowd fishing for contemporary kaif, the advocates of maximum satisfaction of their own constantly growing needs. Everybody was sure that it was a live broadcast of Arabella's performance, so therefore nobody thought of the destruction of Pompeii. Television and the government know what they are doing; in this world there are no miracles.

Thus, with this faith in faithlessness, we all fell asleep on the Hill of Glory. Each of us was forgetting everything blissfully and ir-revocably. For example, as my brain began to go to sleep, it was forgetting stanzas from "Repercussions," my proud work designed to win the minds of humankind, and a thought about the vanity of vanities flashed through my head, but was immediately forgotten.

Nobody woke up, even when it started to rain. Streams of water descended from the merciful heavens on high and pacified the volcano. We were sleeping in clouds of hot steam, and then under the constantly increasing gushes of a pure north wind. The wind blew away the steam and cooled off the settling lava, but we were still sleeping.

When we woke up, a cool and bright new day had arrived. Thousands of light, clean creatures were sitting on the Hill of Glory and didn't remember anything. A quiet and unfamiliar landscape stretched all around us. We were all looking at each other—author of "Repercussions," tamed tigers, cats, dogs, painters, film people, musicians, Arabella, Georgians, Svetka the hairdresser, the chief hairdresser, the retired colonel, the colonel of the secret police, the young naturalist, the secretary of the City Council, Karandashkin, Ananaskin, the Pro-Counsul, the lesbians, Historic Titan, and all of yesterday's troglodytes of materialism. We were all looking at one another, not recognizing anybody, but loving everyone. Thousands of eyes were looking around with the hope of grasping the purpose of our awakening.

Finally, we saw a small tongue of fire at the top of the Hill and next to it there was a hot loaf of bread, a wheel of cheese and a pitcher of water. That was our breakfast. Then we saw a narrow path which ducked in between the cliffs and rose towards a pass in the mountains. That was our way. A second later and on the steep spur of the volcano appeared a snow-white, long-haired goat. She was our guide.

That's what happened in Pompeii that year at the beginning of spring. Later on during the excavations, scientists were surprised that no traces of human bodies were found in the destroyed buildings. In only one building, something resembling a school, they found a slithering emptiness in the lava which pointed to the fact that, probably, some time ago it was filled with the body of a small harmless snake. This allowed archeologists to make the suggestion that the inhabitants of Pompeii kept in their houses tame herbivorous snakes called ''yellow-bellies.''

VI-VII. 1979, Peredelkino

Written in the notebook which was Bella's gift in the spring of the Metropol year.

Looking For
Climatic Asylum

Translated by Mark H. Teeter

THE CLIMATE OF OUR CAPITAL CITY IS POOR. I HOPE I'M NOT giving away a state secret by saying that Moscow's climate is none too good. For it's true, in our city a rather nasty climate simply flourishes. It would be absurd, of course, to blame the government. What does the leadership have to do with it? We ourselves are guilty; there are no political machinations whatsoever in our unpleasant climatic situation. Even foreigners will confirm that. I can cite, for example, the case of a specialist from California who came over here recently and helped us install a technical device. The nature of the device, unfortunately, can't be revealed here; begging your pardon, but that *is* a state secret. Anyway, as I left the institute one day after work with this specialist, John, a grisly scene unfolded before us: trucks rumbled along one after another through filthy slush, making the street progressively narrower as the muck piled up on both sides. And how much more muck is there to come, I wondered: it's only December now, three and a half more months of winter lie ahead of us. Wet snow streamed down in thick flakes and the clouds hovered sullenly over the propaganda decorations. You couldn't even make out the slogan "GIVE THE FIVE-YEAR PLAN OF QUALITY THE WORKERS' GUARANTEE!" Professor John Bossanova didn't like all this. Well, perhaps I should say he liked it, but not a lot. He bundled himself up against the cold and mumbled "I don't understand how people can live here." Naturally, I took this as a political jape.

"And what in particular don't you like here, John?" I asked.

"The weather," he said.

"That's interesting, John," I replied. "You worked a good while in Copenhagen before coming to Moscow. Is the climate so much better there?"

"Not a whole lot better," he answered. "In some respects it's even worse. Between you and me, Popov, I can't understand how people can live in Copenhagen."

"Then where, pray tell, can people live?"

The answer came back immediately: "In California."

I won't hide the fact that I was deeply hurt and offended. Offended for myself, for my fellow countrymen and for the citizens of Copenhagen (in solidarity with the Danish working class). After all, the struggle of Marxism and capitalism is something one can understand; but climatic pressures on humanity are really beyond the pale of mortal wisdom.

I mean, look at me. I've lived forty years in a difficult climate, in a city with snow six months out of the year and rain the other six, where the sun seems like a rare manifestation of nature—and I'm okay. My limbs are limber and the bump between my shoulders keeps my hat on straight, as they say.

But allow me to introduce myself. My fellow workers call me simply Popov, although in truth I bear a rare, almost aristocratic double-barrelled last name Ivanov-Popov. I'm employed as an engineer in a scientific research institute, one of those establishments which are still called "boxes" from the Stalinist tradition of divulging only post box addresses for secret institutions. For many years our "box" was highly secretive indeed: a worker had to sign a form every time he used a slide rule. The institute had a whole Security Division, as a matter of fact, with a good-sized staff (which included some nice looking girls—one of whom, the attractive Galina Petrovna Koreshkova, I married). In any case, one day a disheartening discovery was made at the institute: we couldn't develop our pet secret any further without the help of foreign science. Since that time the place has been crawling with little Professor Bossanova types. The Security Division, of course, has been retained nonetheless. There is no unemployment in the Soviet Union. What else were they going to do with these people? And in particular, with my wife, Galina Petrovna?

Our situation at home is really rather good: besides our two children we have a two-room apartment in one of the outlying districts of Moscow, a district poetically named Warm Camp. The Camp may be *called* Warm, but when the wind blows in from the northeast we shiver in our 18th floor apartment. Last year around New Year's, Warm Camp registered a record 48 degrees below zero, Celsius—while the center of town was a good three degrees warmer. Around the local market several of our neighbors noted with surprise the appearance of some rather strange-looking dogs; it turned out they were wolves driven by the cold from their lairs in the idyllic countryside into the city for warmth. Then right before New Year's our heating pipes burst. We bundled ourselves up in everything we could get our hands on and greeted the New Year of the New Five-Year Plan in fine style, largely because our table was adorned with the contents of a "holiday basket" from the institute (which included those Russian favorites: dried salted fish and double-distilled vodka). Throughout the entire twenty-story build-ing a holiday atmosphere reigned in spite of the numbing cold—which people here call "Dr. Sussman" for some unknown reason. I have to admit that Muscovites usually reveal lively and endearing traits of character in catastrophic situations. You can't say the same under normal circumstances: all you generally see in buses and sub-ways are sour expressions.

Formerly Galina Petrovna and I had to put in ninety minutes every day commuting to work, what with two buses and two subway connections each way. On daily treks such as those, comrades, you really come to love books. We read more books than you can ima-gine! There I'd be, squeezed in from all sides on the bus, barely hanging on to the bar with one hand—while with the other I'd be clutching a book, imbibing the heady wine of Balzac. "Love books. They are the source of knowledge!" So the father of Soviet Literature, Maxim Gorky, instructed us. And Galina Petrovna and I, at Gorky's behest (and thanks to the commuting distance), really did come to love "the source of knowledge." Now we even sub-scribe to the Classics of World Literature series. Shelves of books grace our apartment. Along with the rug, the television and the refrigerator, our books give the apartment an air of particular in-timacy. However, we've been reading less since we bought our Zhiguli sedan. While driving a car you can only read propaganda slogans—which is also important, of course, since it serves to imbue one with party spirit.

One morning I gazed through the window at the endless snowy fields which stretch beyond our Warm Camp, past Moscow's Ring Road. Say what you like, we've got plenty of snow! "In winter, the celebrating peasant forges a fresh path with his sled," as Pushkin put it. And really, it does make a nice picture in your mind: riding along in your sleigh, cozy in a sheepskin coat with a bottle of the best moonshine close at hand. Romance of the first sort.

But at this point my gaze lowered and my heart contracted with pain as at the sight of an unfortunate relative or fellow employee: there she is, a little snow-covered, ice-encrusted hillock, my trusty steed, my Zhiguli. It may well be that some people in Russia like winter. I can testify, however, that the owners of Zhigulis, the Russian Fiats, do not.

They need cranking up. In my case, I have to sweep off the snow, chip off the ice, open the hood, unscrew the spark plugs, run up to my kitchen on the eighteenth floor, heat up the plugs on the gas stove and then race back down again, tossing the smoldering plugs from hand to hand in the hope that they won't get cold. They do get cold, of course, and manage in the process to burn my altogether innocent palms quite thoroughly. The wind from the countryside whips up my backside as I lean over to screw the damned plugs back in. About then, a line addressed to the Motherland by that great poet and patriot Vladimir Mayakovsky for some reason comes to mind: "I am not yours, you snow-covered heap!" I comfort myself solely with the knowledge that the poet didn't intend the slightest political commentary with this line. At all events, I generally get the Zhiguli going by the method known as "long range ignition": a truck and a tow line.

I am firmly convinced that this is the greatest service rendered the people of our city by trucks. Eighty percent of the trucks in Moscow rumble around the city totally empty the whole day long, burning up gas, blocking the streets and maiming great numbers of Zhigulis, to boot. I am firmly convinced that trucks do serious damage to the national economy. On the other hand, I don't maintain this conviction categorically. If someone cares to correct me, I'm entirely prepared to abandon the position altogether.

One way or another, Galina Petrovna and I got off to work in our car that day. All of a sudden a thought dawned on me and quickly emerged as a question. Why is it, I wondered aloud to Galina, that in our institute they never sell tickets for excursions to foreign countries?

"To capitalist foreign countries?" she asked, casting a vigilant eye my way.

"Well, warm foreign countries," I mumbled. "I mean, there *are* places in the world where it's always warm but never too hot, where ocean breezes blow and the leaves rustle on majestic palms. Can it be that no one from our institute will ever see Fiji, Hawaii or Bermuda, not to mention notorious California?"

That started it. You don't understand, said my wife, we work in a restricted institution. We have nothing to do with warm countries. You don't understand the international climate. But lots of people, I objected in turn, come to our restricted institution from all kinds of warm countries. Why can't *we* get around a little? You don't understand the alignment of power in the international arena, my wife returned sharply. You're the one who doesn't understand things, I shot back. And thus for the first time in our lives, our views differed on natural phenomena.

For the first time in my life I felt sadness as I cast a mental eye over our colossal city, covered with snow and blackened with truck exhaust, with its umpteenth inhabitant wearing the standard sour expression. For the first time in my life I looked at myself with bewilderment, at a forty-year-old Ivanov-Popov who had lived his entire life in a city with a lousy climate. I passed the entire working day in the shadow of this unsettling sensation. Somehow even the enjoyment of my labor in the restricted institute—where we worked so long to develop a secret that everybody found out—was diminished. This same sensation stayed with me, in fact, as I called it a day and went to bed.

It was either the next day or the day before (or sometime around then, in any case) that I saw the notice in the institute lobby: "Honored Comrades! All workers wishing to take trips to Lapland, Greenland and California should inquire at the trade union committee office. Tour prices, respectively: 50 rubles, 75 rubles and 1,500 rubles." Aha, Galina Petrovna, which of us doesn't properly understand the alignment of forces in the international arena?

I might note, in passing, that among the general populace of our city a number of mysterious anomalies of economics are at work. For example, a new Zhiguli costs 8,000 rubles, while a used one goes for 10,000. Or take the fact that a worker's average monthly wage is 150 rubles—but Moscow girls stroll around in boots costing 200 rubles the pair, boots you can't find in any of the city's stores no matter how hard you try. I submit that all such mysteries are connected with our forbidding climate.

Only the narrowest rivulet of the Gulfstream reaches our shores, which means, of course, that Soviet stores never have muskrat-fur hats on sale. Since they aren't available, muskrat-fur hats become a compulsion with Muscovites, who feel obliged to get them somewhere and then stroll around in them showing off. Every Muscovite, furthermore, dreams of getting a sheepskin coat; and though the dream has become a reality for many, the method of realization involved remains utterly unclear. Take me, for example, one of the satisfied dreamers. I attract no little envy from my contemporaries with my precious Canadian sheepskin coat; but even I can't piece together exactly how it came into my possession. I think the cycle went something like this: one of my card playing pals called up a fishing buddy who in turn called up a fellow he hunts with; the hunter called up his tennis partner, who got in touch with my card playing pal. Somewhere in there my wonderful little Canadian sheepskin materialized. The whole thing wouldn't have been so complicated if our climate were a little milder. Anyway, the official price of a sheepskin coat is 450 rubles. So the asking price, naturally is 1500—exactly the price, as you've no doubt figured out, of a trip to California.

Seized by an inspiration (born of literature, of course: fiction lies at the base of so many hasty actions), I headed out on my lunch break into the bone-chilling, arctic cold of the street, where I selected a passing citizen with a dream in his eye and sold him my sheepskin for the aforementioned price. Then off I went to the trade union committee office, where I plunked my money down on the table and told them to sign me up for California. I want to see and be seen, I said. The honor of Soviet man will be borne aloft. Be careful over there with state secrets, Popov, they told me. Relax, comrades, I said; expanding the horizons of the scientific worker makes for *better* state secrets.

Several wintry months went by as the requisite documents were assembled. I can't really say whether they went by quickly or slow-ly. For a man possessed by a dream, the boundaries of time become considerably blurred. But to make a long story short, ladies and gentlemen, on a wintry day in a wintry month the day of my depar-ture for California came around. At the airport, Galina Petrovna, in the great tradition of Russian womanhood, wailed over me: how on earth will you get along without your sheepskin, dear little Popov? You'll catch a cold on the way.

As usual a blizzard was blowing. Everybody was dancing about to keep warm. The clouds had almost reached the airfield and the general mood was one of discomfort.

We rose into the atmosphere, charted a course for California and *voilà*, there we were. And nobody, it turned out—not John Bossanova, not the fictional literature, not my cursed dream—has misled me. The sun shone, the ocean breezes blew and the majestic palms swayed gently. My immediate sensation was rapture.

The comrades in our tour group, of course, maintained a stoic front and observed my exulting countenance with a collective frown.

"Doesn't it strike you, Popov, that it's a little too damp here?" asked the comrades.

"No, it doesn't," I replied.

"You don't perceive the scowl of capitalism?"

"No, I don't." And with a sprightly step I approached the first handy policeman. "Mr. Policeman," I intoned," it is my desire to seek asylum in California." The first handy policeman turned out to be a good choice: healthy and apple-cheeked, he was obviously a warm-climate native.

"You're seeking political asylum, I take it."

"No sir, climatic."

"From Copenhagen, eh?"

"No, but you're close. Moscow."

"Okay, go to the right." He pointed, explaining "Political asylum to the left, climatic to the right."

So I went to the right and came upon a magnificent building which bore the words RECEPTION CENTER FOR CLIMATIC REFUGEES. I was met by a magnificent miss who clicked on an ap-propriate computer and monitored the data it gave out.

"Fine, sir, everything checks out," she said and led me through the appropriate seashore district to an appropriately wonderful little house under the palms. An appropriate wife—somehow resembling Galina Petrovna but with a nice tan and sparkling teeth—was already ensconced therein.

"This is where you'll live, Mr. Ivanov-Popov," said the girl from the center. The annual mean temperature is 78 degrees Fahrenheit; it never goes below 72 or above 84. Practically speaking, there's no change of seasons. The wind blows gently, grapefruit grows the year round, hummingbirds hover in the garden and your new family has a marvelous temperament. Satisfactory?"

"You know, I think it is," I said, glancing around. "This looks entirely acceptable."

"First off we recommend a good night's sleep," added the miss. "Take this pill and get in a healthy snooze. Otherwise you run the risk of climatic shock."

In a soft bed by an open window I dozed off in a state of bliss. The ocean murmured, the hummingbirds hummed and the television crooned a soulful song. Only one thought bothered me a little: how could there be no change of seasons? That meant there'd never be spring. I'd never get to wait for spring again. Then I smiled over the absurdity of my anxiety: if it's always summer, who cares about waiting for spring?

So off I dozed. The friendly stars twirled above me in the gentle breeze. My pretty wife, whose acquaintance I hadn't yet had the chance to make, cooed over the telephone. My picture-perfect children splashed in the swimming pool under the palms. How sweet to sleep in climatic asylum. Yet the thought bothered me all night: how can there be no spring, no waiting and hoping for spring? No, I decided, I'd have to get all that straightened out a little better. . . .

At length I awoke. My god, I'd overslept! The car had to be cranked up in a flash or we'd be late for work. With no time to shave, I pulled on my pants, my "Farewell, O Youth" boots, a sweater, a jacket, a scarf and my fur hat and was off.

"Put on your sheepskin coat!" shouted Galina Petrovna menacingly.

Without time for surprise—hadn't I sold that coat a good while back to some streetcorner dreamer?—I threw on the sheepskin and staggered down the stairs, disdaining the elevator as a lost cause. On the run I decided that if the damned car didn't start right up, I'd go for a truck first thing and get it going that way; there wasn't time to try roasting the spark plugs. I raced down the stairwell, the familiar snow-covered reaches glittering through the landing windows as I passed, when all of a sudden . . . all of a sudden a peculiar sensation startled me. I was so startled, in fact, that I stopped the race cold. Having put on the brakes somewhere between the ninth and tenth floors, I turned my attention more seriously to the familiar snow-covered reaches and began to sense in them, dear comrades, something out of the ordinary. For one thing, a sort of absence of the presence of a particular numbness could be noticed in the familiar snow-covered reaches. For another, I sensed that here amid our capital's endless accumulation of snow, soot, gloom and dreariness, a gentle call was ringing out.

I went out onto the porch of our residential behemoth and stopped. Something extraordinary was afoot in the district. I stood there in a strange and peacefully reflective state. The mad dash, which always makes me tremble, was suddenly over. I looked with new eyes at our neighborhood, which had always made me sick, and it seemed something marvelous. The hated snow suddenly took on the guise of a flowering lilac bush. The courtyard below was bright, crowded with pink-cheeked, playing children. A gentle snow flake landed on my lip and I felt a rush of unfamiliar good humor and affection. An Irish setter dashed about the courtyard like a will-o-the-wisp, now closer, now further away.

I climbed into my woebegone car, which didn't seem as cold and lifeless as on earlier winter days. A single turn of the key and the engine hummed lyrically like a bee. I got out to brush the snow off the windshield. The Irish setter bounded up to me and offered his head for a pat. I fulfilled his request with pleasure. What was going on?

The very air seemed like a tonic. I suddenly remembered my old neighborhood, long forgotten, where I first saw snow some forty years back: a little street lodged deep in the Arbat section of old Moscow with the endearing name of Bakery Lane. What, indeed, was going on?

Suddenly I understood what it was. On that day, in the midst of winter, the scent of spring had broken through. A distant, almost imperceptible feeling of spring touched our faces, was inhaled into in our lungs. No, I simply couldn't live without the expectation of spring. There lies the sole, yet powerful charm of our wretched climate: expectation.

On the way to work my wife passed along some news.

"You know, the Security Division at the institute has been abolished. They've turned it into a bureau for international tourism. But mind, that's between you and me for now—it's still a state secret."

January 1980, Moscow

The Hollow Herring

Translated by Valerie Borchardt

OUR FAMILY NEVER SUFFERED FROM A SURPLUS OF RELATIVES. Revolutions, wars and purges killed off quite a few of them, and we Shatkovskis were not known to be all that prolific. It's true there were rumors of a branch which had separated from the trunk of the family tree a long time ago (almost as far back as the period of the Stolypin reforms) and had moved to the Far East, to some semi-mythical mining town. Apparently that generation put down many roots into the Devonian layer of the soil there. The new tree bloomed and for many decades made noises with its branches. To this day apparently it is still making noises.

We had no communication at all, however, with these Far Easterners, and what this legend was based on is impossible to understand. Perhaps, alas, it was simply that a wish had been taken for reality. In our withering clan, during conversations about the Far Easterners there always existed one unspoken thought: even if we should all dry up, they never would. But, year after year, decade after decade, even this splendid myth grew faint. More recently, at our rare family get-togethers (most often for grandfather Vitaly's nameday) references to the Far Easterners had already begun to be considered in somewhat bad taste. Besides, after grandfather Vitaly himself set out on his eternal bureaucratically subsidized trip several years ago, the get-togethers ceased and very quickly everything froze up.

I stop myself short at the intersection of two deserted Moscow streets under the merciless holiday sky: stop, you lonely, empty being, look back in despair! Fifty years old, an ancient suede jacket, the absurd profession of basketball trainer, vegetative distonia . . . the threshold of old age, waning strength . . .

When I was young—even later, at the peak of my manhood—when I would smile at the thought of my old age, for some reason I always imagined a solid two-story country house with an attic, sort of a family estate (from where would I have gotten it?) full of life, swarming with children and animals, filled with music and humming. I would be the head of it, a rosy old man, a bit eccentric in a sweater and boots of excellent quality. People would laugh indulgently at me, but nonetheless respect and adore me. The source of this Connecticut idyll is quite unclear; I probably got it from some film.

My divorces, the first, the second and finally the third, completely exhausted me. Scattered somewhere around Moscow are women who hate me; among them is a grown-up daughter. The endless divisions of housing and the apartment exchanges connected with them brought me finally to a one-room apartment in a gigantic building a mile long and twenty stories high with no particularly distinctive features.

That evening the light of the sunset divided the complex into two isosceles triangles. I had just hit the top step of the underground passageway which leads from the metro to the microdistrict when suddenly I was seized by hopeless anguish. What sort of a world is it if not one secret, sweet sound remains? if there is not one historical, that is, living form to be found?

There is only the frosty sky, filled with smoke from the power station and the distant chemical plant, on whose gigantic façade is displayed the phrase, "Raise the banner of proletarian internationalism!"

Everything is over, nothing is left . . . Did my past really happen? In horror, as though gasping for breath, afraid of suffocating at any moment, or hurling myself screaming against the tile wall of the underground passageway, I began, confusedly, to turn back the black unread pages . . . the dark unread book, the dark . . . when suddenly I saw a crack of light, like a savior (but for how long?): the Pioneer camp "Hollow Herring." I'm lying on the grass on

Sviyazhsk after a soccer game. I look at the early stars over the pine forest, thinking for some reason of fantastic Venice. I feel an infinite well-being, the infinite presence of someone, a rejoicing in the life which lies ahead . . .

What came of it? What did my higher education in natural sciences and physiology reveal to me? Nothing. Not even the mystery of the cell, not even that tiny thing. So I'll just die here in the underground passageway from a suffocating anguish, insignificant and lonely, having wasted my entire life on ludicrous carryings on with a basketball. Just as it had suddenly appeared, "Hollow Herring" disappeared. A gray cloud engulfed me with a silent roar. I could neither move nor stand in one place. I wouldn't want anyone to have to experience that feeling, when you can neither move nor stay put.

A kind young man suddenly appeared out of the flow of people. He was obviously from the provinces; he looked like a seminarian with his long hair sticking out from under his fur hat. What's wrong? he asked. Are you feeling all right? What a strange young man. People will usually walk right past anyone, even over someone lying on the ground, and I was just standing there. Obviously, it was simply my vegetative distonia, which was pinching me or as Lev Tolstoy would say, I was enveloped in "Arzamasian anguish."

His light gray eyes were sensitive and relaxed. I forced a smile and gestured with my hand—it's nothing, everything is hunky-dory. He smiled, lightly touching my shoulder with his hand in its white knitted glove and walked on. But he turned around after he'd gotten about five feet away. This was such a strange thing, such a simple act—that question, that touch on the shoulder, that smile and that unprogrammed turn of the head—that it apparently revived me. It affected me like some kind of powerful injection.

There are people who are capable of communicating their prana to others. A friend who was fascinated with the East and esoteric theories recently handed me a xeroxed manuscript. In essence the saints were exactly such people, the manuscript said. Christ's miracles were not metaphor but reality, for He was granted the highest gift: the transmission of prana. Someone in a particularly painful state—say, in the grips of vegetative distonia—will perceive prana much more clearly than others. A simple smile from a passerby may well be enough to save him for a while.

I left the underground passageway, not without a touch of cheerfulness, thinking of the comfort to be drawn from that not quite legal manuscript. The supply of prana in the world is inexhaustible. Learn how to transmit prana. Master this so that in giving prana to others you don't waste any, but rather increase your own supply.

Before, when there were no such manuscripts in Moscow and when I was a good ten years younger, it seems that I knew instinctively how to give my prana to others. In any case, I was able to give it to the team. This sometimes happened during the most intense moments of a game: I would call time out, the guys would surround me, and I would find myself in some kind of special state. It was as if I would rise to the height of my giants. I would say the usual ''hold on to it tighter,'' ''aim your passes,'' ''go down the center,'' and the guys would nod, but at that moment it wasn't the meaning that they cared about. At such times everyone would say, ''Shatka is inspired,'' and now I understand that I was radiating mighty waves of prana. The players were charged by these waves. At those moments, I always knew that we had won.

Now it's not prana flowing from me, but anguished sediment that resembles stagnant piss. Now my team only beats those who are known to be weaker and even then by inertia. We've been losing for several seasons to the ''Tanks'' without a struggle. Before, even when we lost to this war machine, it was always boldly, and aggressively, and sometimes we would actually win.

Of course, I know this strange game, which has become my life, as few others know it. I've had enormous experience and the Federation values me, but in the heat of the game, the guys no longer surround me in a tight and passionate ring. Instead they stand limp like tired stallions and nod their heads weakly. My inspiration has dried up and everything else is freezing up . . .

An Indian yogi, Swami Krishnadevananda, is quoted in that manuscript. He declares that everyone should feel the permanent presence of the Omnipotent, with whom we are united by our eternal soul. The physical body is the temple of God and the astral body is the human essence, a little bay in the boundless ocean of world energy. It beats inside us and inside everyone to the metronome of the holy word *OM*, which is given to us from above.

Ten or fifteen years ago, at the height of my success, if I had heard the words of this yogi I might have simply smiled, but in all probability, I wouldn't even have heard them at all.

Now I think that I had already encountered this sacred metronome—there, at the edge of the forest at Hollow Herring, when I lay on my back in the grass. Nearby, a charming, green, fluffy caterpillar rocked on a stem. In the distance a charming gull flew towards Sviyazhsk. The wind didn't even touch the charming pansies as it blew through the ferns, the charming ferns. It got darker by the minute and the stars were washed by the invisible but distinct waves of some sort of enchantment, and each movement of these waves fully corresponded to what was going on inside me. I truly felt myself a little bay in a giant ocean and rejoiced in my incorporation.

Of course I couldn't have known anything about God then—there was only a fleeting picture preserved from my earliest childhood: Nanny on her knees before an icon which she usually kept hidden in her trunk. Religion was a subject of official witticisms, mass culture organization.

And here I am, an atheist, a member of the Party, a member of the Presidium of the Basketball Federation of the Soviet Union, and yet I always return to those happy days and think: did God touch me then or was it only my young body rejoicing at the peak of its metabolic processes?

Stop, Yasha Valevich says to me. This is the person who plays the role of best friend in my life and in whose life I play the same role. You shouldn't go on like that about God, Oleg. They'll laugh at you behind your back, even dump shit on you. Your metabolism was okay then but now vegetative distonia is acting up, male menopause. Take tranquilizers and wash with cold water. You'll get over this physiological hump and then you'll feel better. This is how he speaks, and I agree to translate all this into practical terms and, in fact, I do feel better. There must be some grain of truth in Valevich's advice, I think. I nod to Yasha and begin thinking of my Nanny Evfimiya Puzyreva and her nocturnal prayers. She's been on my mind often lately. More and more frequently, her face swims up from the past. I don't share these thoughts with anyone. Who is there for me to share them with anyway, except Valevich? But it would be absurd to tell him about Nanny's prayers.

The old woman must have been the same age then as I am now, though she had long been considered an old woman and I'm still considered a stud. In her case she probably was really suffering from menopause. Something was wrong with her vegetative system—she was tormented by fears and persistent tortures; life is a wilderness. Sometimes when I woke up in the middle of the night I would hear her turn over in the dark and mutter, "Holy Virgin Mary Queen of Heaven, save us and forgive us." Her whispers would fill me with comfort and tenderness and I would fall peacefully asleep again, with the promise of a new and happy day ahead. Now I understand how difficult it was for my unhappy Nanny, growing old without ever having blossomed into a young woman.

Once in the middle of the night I saw her on her knees. On the floor lay a square of moonlight and in this square Evfimiya knelt in her gray handwoven country nightshirt, her hair twisted in a short braid. She was bowing before the icon which she usually kept concealed in her trunk. Once I had looked in the trunk and asked Nanny what it was. An icon, she said compressing her lips severely, and she shut the trunk. Now she whispered in a passionate, loving tone: Lord Jesus, save and forgive this little child, his parents and Your sinful slave! Look down from heaven upon us tired as we are and give us strength! Defend us from the Devil and warm us in your bosom! Glory be to God, as it was in the beginning, is now and ever shall be, world without end!

She lowered her face into her hands and her shoulders began to shake with sobs but when she turned around, she had an expression on her face of amazing youthful joy. It was as though she had grown twenty years younger, as though she were once again that young girl from Vyatka arriving in the big city in search of her modest happiness. She bent towards her "little child" to kiss him and the "little child" quickly closed his eyes, pretending to be asleep. It seemed to me even then, though not quite four years old, I understood that some mystery was happening and that it mustn't be violated, and perhaps I understood this better then than I have ever since.

How can the basketball championship of the country, the continual traveling, the administrative affairs, training sessions, the conferences and the tournament nets, be related to God? Can you think of a profession that is farther from faith than that of a Soviet basketball trainer? All my life religion has seemed absurd to me, or rather I hardly ever thought about it. But now, my whole life's work, basketball, seems the strangest and most absurd nonsense to me. More and more often I remember Nanny's tear-stained face in the room full of moonlight; I remember the feeling which so powerfully possessed her, and I think: is it possible that such a powerful feeling can be inspired by something which, according to our wretched Marxist beliefs, doesn't exist. And then more and more often the fairy tale silhouette of Sviyazhsk floats up in my memory.

In that wretched year after the war, we went there one day to get bricks for a pioneer camp construction. We had a big long boat and we, the older Pioneers, did the rowing. You couldn't get to Sviyazhsk except by boat. The town was located on the island at the mouth of the Sviyaga river. It was washed from one direction by the quiet, muddy Sviyaga water which causes the Mordovian forests to blossom, and from the other by the steep waves of mother Volga. They were still as steep back then as they were transparent and clear, without any oil stains and patches of grease.

From a distance it seemed as though you were rowing to the city of Kitezh. A multitude of church cupolas and bell towers gave it a medieval silhouette which soared upward. Once on land, however, we saw that the cupolas were bent and broken, and the city was deserted: the remaining cobbled sidewalks were overgrown with tall thistles. The crumbling houses with broken windows and empty yards were silent, not a cat or dog or chicken in sight. It was as if the plague had passed through . . .

The Pioneers were bewildered in the midst of this vale without hope. Everyone fell silent. Even the director of our camp was quiet. Prakharenko was a one-armed war veteran who usually spewed martinet Soviet humor such as: "I'll teach you to love your homeland," or "We'll give the country coal—in small pieces, but a lot," or "No one's going to ride into Communism on someone else's ass," and so forth.

Soon, however, the Pioneer imagination came alive. The children were having visions of stores of arms in the cellars, perhaps left over from the fall of Kazan. In the aisles of the vaulted market you could imagine an ambush by the "Whites." The director came back to life, too, and began to snort and rumble through his impressive nose at Lydia the phys ed teacher. She was the only one, it seems, who was not affected by the abandoned city. She just threw off her skirt and blouse so as not to let the sun get away from her, as she was a tanning fanatic who caught every ray and had actually come to the Pioneer camp for that purpose, so that in the fall, ha-ha, she could astound the whole university department.

Suddenly sounds reached us. Not, alas, the click of a gun bolt or the ringing of spurs, but the most ordinary children's voices; a chorus singing, accordion music. We were obviously approaching some kind of institution for children. It seemed that there were ragged little Pioneers like us in these mysterious wilds too.

But the children's institution turned out not to be that ordinary; it was the Sviyazhsk home for the blind. We approached the only inhabited house on the island—a long two-story building with peeling plaster, and on the porch, cast iron railings that were bent as though some super-orangutan had tried to tie them in a knot. From the window came the smell of rancid wheat kasha, and the children, all wearing identical old-fashioned forage caps, could be glimpsed inside under the soot-covered vaults.

The director of the home came out. He was an invalid from the war too. His arms were intact, but he had a false leg. Both the directors sat down on the porch and began to smoke and talk about what they had in common—where they had been stationed during the war, whom they'd known. They looked at each other in a friendly way, and for the first time I felt sympathy for our Prakharenko with his mouth full of an endless supply of verbal chewing gum. For the first time I thought about how he felt with a missing arm. Maybe he was a clod and a martinet, but at times when he looked at his stump he must have felt a certain horror.

Having talked about the war, the directors, as leaders of neighboring children's institutions, went on to current professional topics. "How do you manage to live on this island?" our director wondered. "In the summer you can get along, but in the winter?" "In the winter it's much simpler in terms of supplies," objected their director. "There are sleds and horses and sometimes a truck from the Green Valley cuts across the ice, but in the summer it's almost impossible to get hold of a boat." "You must have trouble keeping your personnel here," our director asked importantly. He looked around furtively, searching for Lydia and then, having discovered her close by, he stretched his unattractive mouth in an ambiguous way.

Meanwhile the phys ed teacher wasn't paying any attention to anyone. She was tanning, leaning against the wall of an abandoned church. Eyes closed, her face was raised towards the sun. Her athletic legs and arms were turned out slightly so that not only their outside would be tanned, but the inner surfaces as well.

"Personnel?" The director of the blind was for some reason embarrassed by this question. "No, comrade, I have a full complement of technical personnel." "But how do you keep them in this rubble?" asked our director with surprise.

The director of the home for the blind was stumbling over his answer when suddenly there was a sound nearby like iron striking iron; it bore a certain resemblance to a bell. An old woman, a ragamuffin, sprang lightly from the children's school, wiping her hands and adjusting her kerchief as she went. Then she minced her way across the street and pulled open the creaky doors of the church. Surprisingly, the half-destroyed little church against which our sun-worshipper was leaning turned out to be alive inside. Candles glimmered and the dark gliding of the altar shone. Old people's voices were carried on the air, bringing something mysterious to the ears of the Pioneers—"Glory be to God, as it was in the beginning . . . is now and ever shall be . . . wor-or-orld without e-e-end . . ." And the smell of something like rosin came from inside . . .

"This is how we keep our local personnel," the one-legged director said with embarrassment. "There was only one small church left in a hundred-mile radius, you see, and only one half-alive priest left on Sviyazhsk. Science has triumphed everywhere, as you know. There used to be three cathedrals, two monasteries and about ten churches here. Trade was considerable, with a crossing to the Mari and the Mordva. Russian capitalism conducted colonial politics. Now, of course, there isn't anything because the people don't need this island. For the time being we still teach the blind here, but when they transfer us to the Green Valley everything will be completely covered with mud. It's a shame. But for now we are living here and the nuns who remain with us are considered to be 'technicians.' By the way, we came in first place in the region for sanitation and hygiene.''

After this, the director of the blind school invited our Prakharneko inside in order to fortify himself. Soon the gurgle of liquid and the loud voices of both directors reached us from the window of the first floor. Our director invited the blind musicians to Hollow Herring for the Big Bonfire of the Holiday of the Red Fleet. A heavy silence lay on the pier and the sea was shrouded in fog.

The Pioneers, understanding that it would be some time before they had to collect bricks, wandered about the town in search of treasure. Yashka and I quietly entered the church and stood in the shadow by the wall on which the contour of an elongated face with large yellow-brown eyes was vaguely outlined. ''Take off your hat, son,'' whispered a mousy old woman to Valevich, who hurriedly pulled off his forage cap.

Here there were not more than a dozen nuns, ''technicians'' as their director called them—that is, sisters—and one old man, a weak, dried-up priest. They were singing in unison ''We offer prayer to God, we offer prayer to God, we offer prayer to God . . . in the name of the Father and of the Son and of the Holy Ghost . . . '' and their faces were illuminated by a surprising peacefulness . . . complete calm, not a trace of anxiety. But they seemed to us like refugees, exiles, secretly performing some sort of suspicious ritual.

''Peace be with you,'' the thin voice of the priest proclaimed, raising the censer. And it suddenly seemed to me that this concerned me too, that peace was being bestowed upon my fate as well. And in my soul, that is somewhere inside me, I simply don't know where, there stirred something similar to ecstasy or, perhaps, a short sob of ecstasy. At that instant I, a tanned, muscular Pioneer and beginner basketball player, suddenly felt a sense of belonging, a complete unity with the leathery old Sviyazhsk women, and I experienced a total and childlike well-being as if I were under some powerful hand.

It seems that Yashka also experienced something unusual. Afterwards we never shared our impressions of the Sviyazhsk church and never even mentioned it, but that certainly says something in itself.

I must confess, however, that we very quickly forgot this brief unintelligible ecstasy. Upon leaving the church we discovered the disappearance of our phys ed teacher who was, after all, under our constant, secret surveillance. We rushed off through the burdock, past a rickety hut and the broken-down monastery fence, through which a misery could be glimpsed that was even more melancholy that the former streets of this former town. We raced off . . .

Now when I try to recall that day, as evening was approaching, I suddenly realize that I hardly remember anything. How far away it all is, how deep it has been buried! How little remains from the past life, almost nothing. As they usually say—details, details. Almost all the details are forgotten. Not to mention fleeting moments, some divine feelings which suddenly flare up, burn, and then vanish, so-called impulses. The feeling which visited me, a boy, in the Sviyazhsk church cannot be duplicated or remembered.

When you solemnly speak a certain thought, like my own recent maxim, something like ''if this, rather THIS, doesn't exist, then how can it, IT, evoke such strong emotions, emotions you have witnessed more than once in your life?,'' it means that you are sort of philosophizing; that your thought, like some photon ship, goes out into the abyss of the cosmos and suddenly turns into something bigger than a thought, and it seems to you that you have grabbed hold of something. But the waters of the cosmos close up, everything vanishes, and then, after the sense of revelation, banally, like radio waves, sensible scientific thoughts begin to take over about sublimation, reflexes, hormonal stresses and hypnotherapy . . .

How can I, an unchristened Soviet bear, come to have faith? Now all over Moscow people are carrying around various religious and esoteric manuscripts. Many of them wear crosses around their necks. Some even cross themselves at cupolas. I look at these people with a chill of awkwardness: aren't these stylish neophytes maintaining a new kind of atheism in opposition to our official Marxist-Leninist religion? For example, I will never raise my hand to form the sign of the cross. This is how our brains are turned inside out. Damn it, just because I don't recognize my own right to believe, why am I denying it to others? What if faith is only the lot of those who are weak and sick and, perhaps, for all of them this is enough? Everyone suffers in some way; everyone searches in some depths for his own little dilapidated Sviyazhsk.

Truly, I can do without this Sviyazhsk. I confess I hardly remember anything about it: not the arrangement of the houses, not the design of the railings, not the number of people, not their faces, with the exception perhaps of the director Prakharenko with his hefty nose and the appearance of our Lydia, like a model for an athletic poster, whom we kept under surveillance. Perhaps I can also recall the high grass mixed with tufts of reed growing between the sandbars on the Volga side of the island and Lydia's tanned legs rising higher than the grass. In the end we found her and our director. We hid behind a dune and became witnesses to a fascinating act. This totally brightened our entire Pioneer summer, I remember all this perfectly, beginning with her businesslike, funny "here, let me do it myself," all the noises, our one-armed director's wheezes, the phys ed teacher's thin squeal and finally, the combined ecstatic cry.

When our boat heaved away from the island, all the crosses of the neglected city blazed brightly in the setting sun. We were carrying some brick, a trifling amount. It hadn't been worth going for so little. But the director of the home for the blind saw us off with several technicians—nuns, that is—on the rotten planks of the pier. There were also several blind teenagers with pure faces and Pioneer ties around their necks, the honor guard. One of them played a melody on the accordion, "The Girl Saw the Soldier Off to War," and for the sake of such a new friendship, of course, you could row a much greater distance.

In the darkness on the other side, while we were walking through a forest from the shore to the camp, Valevich and I heard the phys ed teacher sternly telling the director, "Our physical relationship has no meaning. I have a completely different circle of acquaintances, the university and the sports club. You can never belong to it. I hope I am making myself clear. I ask you not to compromise me." Only now, in the twilight, parting with the sun, did she put on her white skirt and top with the Stormy Petrel emblem on it. Now, all white, with her bleached mane, sparkling teeth and the whites of her eyes shining as she stood at the foot of the tall, dark forest, she looked like some magical photographic negative. "Wait, Lydia!" wheezed our over-drinking, over-smoking and tired director. "I won't wait," she said, cutting him off. "If you want to preserve our ha! ha! relationship, you've got to keep yourself in line!"

What a surprising relationship—a woman dominating a man! The figure shining in the early twilight. How many times in the years that followed did Yashka and I think about this teacher who had forever vanished from our lives, dissolved in the autumn rains of the year after the war. Everything connected with her is clearly imprinted in my mind: the tall dry grass and the light playing off the water. The tall and dark pine forest, the high bank of the Volga, the blackberry bushes, the cockeyed little houses on the island and the crosses burning in the setting sun and Sviyazhsk . . . Each time I hear the name, something in my soul resists, yet at the same time something secretly is bound to it.

But admit it; how many times in your whole life have you remembered this little town, or, rather, ruin, at the mouth of the muddy river? Five, not more. Everything was swallowed up in the fuss surrounding that strange round object filled with air.

It would rise every time from the dark depths like the city of Kitezh. About ten years ago, the team toured along the Volga; this was a lark for my stallions. They easily beat the local clubs, flirted with the local female athletes and even, it seems, had a bit to drink behind my back. A difficult trip through Europe lay ahead of us and I decided to surprise everyone. Instead of boring training, I organized an entertaining trip down the the Volga. In Kazan our hosts once invited us to go swimming on a little island in the Volga. The river had now become inconceivably wide in comparison to the one of my childhood: thanks to the dams, it had flooded and broadened over many miles, forming a multitude of streams, bays and little islands in the mouth of the Sviyaga river. We were lying on the deck of the boat drinking beer when, after one of the turns, or around a bend, as they used to say, a fabulous sight appeared. There in the July sunlight there trembled a dark blue mirage of cupolas and bell towers, a confused crowd rushing upwards together. "Impressive, isn't it?" asked the local director, "This is the abandoned city of Sviyazhsk. It was built during the time of Ivan the Terrible. Unfortunately we won't have time to have a walk around before evening, but it's no great loss—there's only rubbish there now. Come back in about five years and there'll be something to boast about. They've decided to open an international youth tour center. Then we'll live it up." The boat made a wide turn and the silhouette of Sviyazhsk vanished into the sky.

I don't know if the international dreams of the Kazan bureaucrats ever came true, whether they succeeded in whipping up their vulgar tour center or if the decrepit walls have since crumbled completely.

I recall with despair this blue silhouette which appeared and dissolved. I feel as if I have been tossed overboard like some strange object nobody needs, sodden and heavy, but hollow inside, kept afloat in the middle of the oily Volga waters without the strength either to sink or to move. How suddenly misfortune broke upon me, and worst of all, I didn't even know what name to give it. Perhaps basketball is to blame? The eternal spinning, the stamping across the court, the great leaps, the capture of the ball in huge hands . . . Eternally whirling amidst my giants, I, small and balding, maybe subconsciously imagined myself at the eternal zenith of "psychophysical stability," as the sports specialists say nowadays.

The business with Sergey may have been the last straw. Did Sergey take my prana away? How shamefully I behaved at that time! The fantastic story of the death of a twenty-five-year-old center, our brilliant Sergey Bobrov; you'd have thought no one had more life in him than Sergey. He'd jump elbow-high over the hoop, he'd laugh. When he burst into the room it was as if lightning and thunder had been let loose. He was my favorite; I "discovered" him, educated him, I hoped to get championship medals with him. And it seems that I was the last to notice that something horrible was happening to him. On that shameful day, I was with him in the hospital, telling jokes and thinking about a temporary substitute for his position. And suddenly I saw that the life in his eyes was swiftly fading. God, I thought, my center is dying. Is there anything less probable, God? It had all been negligence. Everything had passed by; there was nothing to hold on to. There was no way I could help him except with useless, pitiful appeals, God! I couldn't even pray for him when he died. In the first place I didn't know how, and besides, I didn't feel that I had the right to. The huge, stiff Sergey, the custom-made coffin, the extraordinary procession of giants—I felt like such a foolish, little child among my seven-footers.

Now, trembling, I attempt to remember my relatives. I even appeal to the mythical "Far-Easterners." "Blood will tell," they say; that isn't such a little thing. For example, one wise guru of the xeroxed, Moscow manuscripts says that humankind is all interwoven. There are no two people who are not connected to each other. There is a fine bond through our cosmic body which leads to Logos; even some New Zealand fisherman is connected to you.

What's more, he can help you if you ask for help, even across such a gigantic distance. So naturally relatives are closer to you in this universal network. They sense you better, more clearly. Their prana flows more easily to you, that is, they can help you better than a fisherman from New Zealand. This is all so beautifully, so majestically portrayed, this eternal human symphony . . .

I imagined meeting the closest relative I have now: my uncle, my father's brother, a retired builder of hydro-electric power stations, a marvelous elderly Soviet man, a political person. In the mornings he reads *Pravda* and *Novoe Vremya*. Not only does he read them, but he circles with a red pencil some wisdom which is incomprehensible to the common individual. Then he listens to the tireless teleliar from "Studio 9." In the evenings he longingly tunes in on "the enemy" voices, as he calls them, listening through headphones. His face is now thoughtful, now crafty; at times he gesticulates, raising his index finger or waving it negatively. "No, that's really too much, gentlemen," he says changing the station from the Germans to the BBC to the "Program for Night Owls." All his free time is devoted to deductions, inferences, theories. He has no anxiety attacks.

In 1937, after my father's arrest and execution—he had been a prominent member of socialist industry—my uncle was also taken away, but he was kept behind barbed wire for only three years. His experiences in jail, however, hardly touched him and he returned the same as he had been, a spiritually healthy fellow. How would he comfort and support me in my present state of disintegration? You have to hang on, he'd say to me. Be like your father, a real Communist. Hang on, Shatok! This is what the "prana" he'd offer me in comfort would be like. Maybe it's not so little.

I am hanging on. I hang on every minute. I walk, I talk to people, I stand in lines in stores, I even work—I hang on, that is, every second. During training sessions I hang on with all my might. I try not to howl. I practice various set plays with the guys and I do everything I should, even though I constantly think about what Sergey, everyone's favorite, is turning into under the ground, about what all of them, such beauties, could turn into if such a monstrous thing should happen to them. I try not to think about all these obscenities and I hang on . . . And although the obscenities return, I drive them away again and I hang on, hang on, hang on . . . On the fifteenth floor of my housing giant—more appropriately called a monster—I am aware of the square of the window every minute, the color changing from blue to black, and I hang on. I know that I'll never do it, but fear burns inside me, and I hang on, hang on, hang on . . .

Valevich is on the phone: vegetative distonia, menopause, overwork; vitamins, peace, tranquilizers . . .

Oh friend, perhaps it is called distonia. Or maybe it's called "Arzamasian anguish" as Lev Tolstoy would put it, or, let's say, "a loss of enchantment?" It must be that it's impossible to live without being enchanted by life. Any pig can be enchanted by life, one way or another. What will become of me if all the prana flows out of me? Everything is evaporating. Even the anguish is disappearing along with other human enchantments, only a senseless body on the floor, one trembling in the lowest form of physical fear.

I was lying flat on the carpet when somebody rang the doorbell. Of course I was completely convulsed by this unexpected sound; unexpected sounds cause something akin to a minor convulsion in me. And, not surprisingly, as the all-explaining Valevich explains to me—you, old man, have an excess of adrenalin in the blood. Everything is normal, completely normal. Just wait, the inner secretions in your glands will dry up and you'll be calmer.

The same young man who had tried to help me on the stairway of the underground passage was at my door. Checking his piece of paper he assured himself either of having landed in the right place or that mine was the face he was looking for, and it turned out that he was not mistaken. Of course he didn't identify me, the one inside the apartment, with the one underground. He was only very happy that his search had ended successfully. He brought a small suitcase into the hallway and, having taken off his hat, the straw-haired, blue-eyed provincial informed me that he brought greetings from Samara.

From Samara? With difficulty I tried to figure out where this was. He smiled: oh, that's just what some of the old Samarans call their Kuibyshev, a city of worker fame. You see, it's just a game. Samara, you know, it's a little more exotic, but Kuibyshev is, well, it's just a name.

Without his ugly fur hat the youth looked rather nice. His long hair didn't resemble a mop but actually had a certain style. Without his clumsy overcoat, he looked Scandinavian: a jean jacket, a sweater like the Beatles wore, everything just right. I asked if he hadn't gotten the wrong address.

But you are Shatkovsky? he asked me, Oleg Antonovich, isn't that right? That means I'm not mistaken. I bring you greetings from my grandmother, your relative. And, as for me, my name is Zhenya. I'm in graduate school, a correspondence course with M.Y.T.H. I've come to find out about defending my dissertation.

In Samara, that is, in the city of worker fame Kuibyshev, I have never had any related grandmothers. I invited Zhenya to come in and sit down. I even offered him a cup of tea; only afterwards did I cautiously ask on which side of the family his grandmother was related to me.

Well, he smiled, she is your godsister, Oleg Antonovich. Oh, what a nice surprise, I thought, and you were all upset about the shortage of relatives. The boy apparently counted on staying with me. He was clearly planning to live with a Moscow relative. Boy from Samara comes to see his uncle in the capital. Or rather, I suppose, his grandfather, since it's his grandmother who is my godsister.

What? What did you call your relationship to me? Only now did the meaning of the word "god" come to me. At first it seemed to mean something like "cousin," "second cousin," "second cousin twice removed." God-sister, Zhenya nodded affirmatively. That is—excuse me Zhenya—you mean to say that your grandmother is my sister, not by blood, but by baptism?

I caught hold of the doorpost, and watched him nod, uncertain and a little worried that this was not a sufficient relationship to enable him to stay at my place during the time of his dissertation "sounding." My heart beat in my chest like a steamship piston.

In our family, I should add, there existed a certain legend about my baptism. My aunt Martha from Leningrad used to talk about it with an ambiguous smile, and sometimes my mother would add something.

Early in the 1930s my parents were the ideal Communist couple. They called each other by their last names—"Have you had supper, Shatkovsky?" "Have you had lunch, Dalberg?" and very rarely did they show each other any tenderness, calling each other Natalya and Anton with obvious awkwardness. He was the director of an industrial giant and she was a Communist lecturer and a Party journalist.

A vague, embarrassing and unreliable legend maintained that once Grandma and Nanny, "survivals of the past," took the ideal Communist child, the guardian of the future—me, that is—took me somewhere. Allegedly the three-year-old tot informed his mama afterwards that he had been to the "circus" where they "ring bells" and "play." Mama questioned the two old women explicitly. As a matter of fact she herself trembled, lest my father find out that a "humiliating ceremony" had been performed over his treasure. The old women only tightened their lips in answer and flashed their eyes angrily. Afterwards, of course, all this was repressed, forgotten. The matter was silently "removed from the agenda," and the old women were forgiven, though it still isn't clear whether this ceremony had actually been performed.

Then came the year 1937. In the first three months our large apartment was emptied. After the arrest of my parents all the rooms were sealed by the NKVD with the exception of one which the future guardian of the radiant future shared for a short while with "survivals of the past," that is, with Nanny and Grandma.

On a dark night in 1942, on the eve of what seemed the complete defeat and inevitable ruin of our country, my grandmother fell into a trench. Until the day before, she herself had been digging it, along with other old women, by order of the house manager, although the Germans were at least a thousand miles away from the city. Her fractured hip swiftly developed into pneumonia, and soon one of my "survivals of the past" set off to where the past, present and future mingle in one river.

In order to survive, the child—me, that is—was taken by an aunt into her half-starved, already overpopulated family. Nanny was not left behind either. She went to live on the far side of the river with some relatives I didn't know.

Every Sunday at dawn the old woman would make the long journey on foot and by tram from her side of the river to the church next to the Tsar's cemetery, the only remaining one in the whole huge town. On the way back from the church to her settlement she would always visit her child—me, that is—who was growing up and whom she obviously loved with her soul's last strength. I was already playing soccer, even on an empty stomach and already watching girls in the dusty sunsets of the war. Nanny would usually sit by the stove and wait patiently, perhaps the child would run into the apartment so she could deliver her customary treat, either a few pieces of beaten sugar or two or three caramel candies wrapped in a rag.

I don't even know when my Nanny died or where she is buried, probably in that very Tsar's cemetery, but what can you find there now?

My mother returned from the Kolyma swamps with a pronounced interest in religion. She wore a cross and read the Bible even though she preferred to keep all this to herself. She never entered into discussions "on this subject," since many of her prison camp friends still preserved an enlightened, materialistic world view and some even considered Stalin the destroyer of their pure, revolutionary Idea.

Once she was telling me all sorts of funny stories about my childhood. The "circus" where they "ring and play" came up. But what if the old women did baptize me? I asked her. You know, that isn't impossible, Mama answered, and stared at me searchingly. She seemed to want me to say more about this, but I didn't. I don't know why I decided to stop—it's not impossible . . . A nasty little thought even occurred to me: in any case, it wouldn't hurt. Before her death, Mama asked to be buried with a Christian ceremony.

I lived with the myth of my baptism, and at times it became dim and fuzzy, its anecdotal outlines miragelike and alien. At other times it came close, warming the air; then I passionately wished it was true. Then I would almost fall into despair, especially the last time, when I realized that now there was no way to verify it and that it was nothing more than a family myth. On the subway at rush hour I would look at the thousands and thousands of Moscow faces swimming by and ponder the fact that the majority of these people are not baptized, our huge, all-absorbing, all-deafening majority.

"That's it, your godsister," Zhenya said uncertainly. "When Grandma first saw you on television during the final Union championships she immediately said, "Why it's Oleg Shatkovsky, my godbrother!'" "She kept meaning to write you a letter but she couldn't bring herself to." "And did she write me one now?" I asked, not without difficulty. "Of course, of course, here it is. I myself, Oleg Antonovich, don't really know the details, but I think

Grandma will give you enough information.''

Respected Oleg Antonovich or simply dear Oleg! I, Elena Petrovna Chestnovo (born Mylnikova), am informing you of my existence, which you probably never suspected, but all the same, I am your godsister. Don't be surprised. We are both related to your godfather Victor Petrovich Mylnikov, my older brother, now deceased. You were baptized in our house behind closed blinds and shutters by Father Sergey Botashev, Victor Petrovich's old friend and colleague. This was all kept completely secret because at that time it certainly wouldn't get you a pat on the head, but it might land you in jail.

If you are interested in more details I will be glad to supply them. You were an infant but I was already fifteen years old when you were baptized. I was in medical school and I remember that day perfectly. I remember your godmother Evfimiya Kozyreva, Nanny, although I only saw her once in my life, that is, at that time.

Now I have a big favor to ask of you, Oleg Antonovich, to take care of my only grandson Evgeny. This is his first time in the capital and he could get lost. Excuse me for this unexpected inconvenience but we have no one in Moscow and few relatives in general. They have all passed away. Dear, dear, Oleg . . . may God preserve you!

Elena Petrovna Chestnovo

I burst into tears. I don't think I ever cried before but suddenly tears spilled from my eyes. Such an indescribable feeling seized me! Such an inconceivable outburst! What could this be called—a storm of love, anguish, pity, exultation—there is no name for it! Something unquestionable and unique had been revealed to me, and all at once I finally realized that I had faith. I was shaken with sobs, and tears flowed in endless streams. Why at moments of spiritual upheaval does so much liquid pour out of you? Who knows what human moisture is?

I fell into an armchair and it gently turned under me, for it is a revolving armchair, but even at this moment something was revealed to me. I mentally defined it as ''loss of consciousness'' but in reality it was something else. For at that moment I saw myself as though from the side, and from a great distance: a small body lying in the arm chair, legs stretched out, head thrown back, hands on my face. Christened! I was christened!

"Oleg Antonovich," the voice of my frightened guest reached me. "Uncle Oleg!"

Some time passed before details arrived from Samara, along with a photograph of my godfather taken in 1933, around the time of my baptism. Victor Petrovich was dressed completely in leather—his pants and his jacket were both black leather. One of the details turned out to be extremely surprising. Victor Petrovich was none other than my father's chauffeur—that is, a worker of the local Party committee.

"At that time," my godsister wrote me, "being a chauffeur was a respected profession and a rare one, especially if you drove a V.I.P. car."

With effort I began to recall my mother's and uncle's stories about our past life. Suddenly it seemed that the outlines of my father's car surfaced in my own memory. Oh yes, the car was American with a wide leather seat in the back. In bad weather a tarpaulin cover was stretched over the top.

It was necessary for Brother to drive around a lot, my uncle had explained, since branches of the gigantic factory were scattered all over the area. For many years he had a chauffeur, Victor Petrovich Mylnikov, a very curious character. He never parted from his gun, because he not only chauffeured Brother but also because he protected him—members of the local Party committee were granted that privilege. He was an experienced NKVD man but as far as his class origins, they were not without blemish.

Further on in Elena Petrovna Chestnovo's letter:

. . . in 1917 two of my older brothers, Victor and Nicholas, finished Young Officer's School. The civil war separated them. Nicholas found himself in the White army. His fate was sad. We lost track of him; it was even rumored that he ended up abroad.

Victor fought on the side of the Reds and received a serious head wound which prevented him from continuing his education. Doctors advised him to avoid mental exertion so he decided to become a chauffeur, a profession which gave him enormous pleasure because even in high school he had shown an aptitude for mechanics . . .

* * *

I look at the photograph. The curious eyes of a young Russian man stare at me from the thick, old photo. The face of a typical Russian mechanic or aviator from the turn of the century. These days you never see this kind of person. He's been replaced by millions upon millions of Soviet ''technologists.'' Not so long ago I saw a young actor with a similar face in some film about ''the turn of the century'' and it seems that I was not the only one to notice him. Movie directors must have an especially acute sense of types; since then this actor has been drifting from film to film all of which are in the ''retro'' style and all about early aviators or automobile technology. He's a pale blond with curious eyes, a magneto fanatic, an admirer of internal combustion engines, obviously a typical Russian but in some way European, and that's what's strange.

When you see such a person on the street you immediately place him in this context—a member of the technical intelligentsia of the old class, some potential Sikorsky, or, if you dig deeper, you might decide that it was just this kind of person who, attempting to save himself from the idiocy of all our great revolutions, sought a disappearing harmony in the strict arrangement of spark plugs and cylinders. This is how you classify someone as a technician, and of course, you are always mistaken. You are always mistaken if you immediately classify human beings into separate categories off the cuff. And everything was not so simple with Victor Petrovich Mylnikov: it wasn't only in automobiles that he searched for spiritual harmony. Elena Petrovich wrote specifically:

. . . V. P. was a friend of father Sergey Botashev all his life, right up to their separation to places ''not so far away.'' During our childhood Sergey Botashev served in the Church of the Transfiguration of God and our house was just across from the church. I was not yet born when my brother, of his own free will, became a constant visitor to this church and served at the holy liturgies there. I forgot to mention that all this happened in the town of Sviyazhsk where all we Mylnikovs are from . . .

Again a new sensation. The touch of something miraculous and warm, a happy and secret touch near my face. The feel of a wing of silken feathers, or a hand with weightless fabric. Sviyazhsk. How unexpectedly everything was united and remembered by the living spirit. So that link had always existed, though it was unknown to me. So my childhood rapture amidst the Sviyazhsk wilds didn't rush in from nowhere but across revolutions and wars from my god-father, the boy Vitya. I felt the life of his spirit then, of his pure childhood in the pure and prosperous, full and peaceful, god-fearing Sviyazhsk.

. . . Our father was the postmaster and we lived in a big apartment over the post office and all around on the island there were churches, monasteries, marketplaces and shops. Sviyazhsk at this time was densely populated and rich . . .

The future Sviyazhsk is an international tour base. I imagined all this trash with anguish, the miserable Komsomol discotheques and the ''festival of protest songs'' with the young protestors boldly attacking Pinochet on the guitar. It would be better to have the former desolation; better even that this small island be gradually clogged with mud in the mouth of the little river. Or better even that decade after decade the foundations should slowly settle, that the bricks should crumble. Even though it's sad, all the same it's more worthy to rot in the archival chronicles than to become a nest for thieves from the ''Sputnik'' young people's tourist bureau.

Gradually, all of us who are connected with it one way or another will disappear and it will disappear from living memory. The nuns were extinguished like candles in that sole surviving church the year after the war. Our one-armed commissar also must have departed already or if he is still alive has forgotten everything in alcohol, not only Sviyazhsk but the phys ed teacher's legs, too. Does Valevich remember? Does he remember that summer at all? It's been a hundred years since we talked about it. For some reason, it's as if I were ashamed of these memories. Perhaps the self-confident Yasha Valevich is ashamed too?

I dialed his phone number. Someone from his huge family answered the phone. The usual calling back and forth began in Valevich's four-room stronghold on Gruzin Street. Papa, are you home? Who's calling? Just a sec, I'll find out. Wait, someone's at the door. Who is it? It's the TV repairman. Oh, at last. Come in, Comrade. But Papa, someone wants you on the phone. If it's from the Institute, then . . . No, I think it's Uncle Oleg. Why didn't you tell me?

"Yashka, do you remember Sviyazhsk?" I asked.

He was puzzled; for a few moments he was silent. Then he giggled.

"I remember, I remember . . . Oleg, do you remember those 'monitors,' those river battleships? Do you remember how they took us prisoner?"

And suddenly in a vivid picture, I recalled everything which had been completely drowned in memory for many years, as clearly as if a projector had been switched on.

On the Volga in those days there had been a war flotilla. What did they need it for? To keep the Chuvash and Mordvin banks in fear? Nobody asked himself these questions then. It exists; therefore it's necessary.

The base of the Volga military flotilla which was located somewhere near our Pioneer camp intrigued us enormously of course. We were always talking about the watchships, the bizarre, shallow-water vessels with the heavy artillery towers. Real river dreadnoughts. Alas, how many times did the Pioneers look into the Volga's distance and see nothing except the usual tugboats with barges and the old ferryboats? These monitors had already begun to seem like some sort of myth.

And suddenly we saw them, the whole squadron in a column, four dark gray—almost blue—battleships. The whole Pioneer group was astounded. Just before, we had been walking in procession along the stony path of the high banks of the Volga under Lydia's direction. We had just caught a disgusting snake, probably a grass snake, for the "animal corner." It was the usual Pioneer routine with the usual maddening glimpse of the phys ed teacher's tanned thighs. And suddenly four grays with naval flags, pennants and signallers were waving out their alphabet from the upper bridges, each with two huge gun towers, and enormous coupled cannons, the dying tribe of the armored river monitors. Yashka and I even lost the gift of speech. We stood open mouthed and mutely jabbed our index fingers in the direction of the Volga.

The phys ed teacher raised her "trophy" Leica, took a picture, waved to the Red navy men, then froze in a pose with her hand raised so that her image would be fixed in the memories of these four strong men. I realize now, remembering her pose, that she was the girl from some painting by Deineka, the spitting image of the Dawn of Socialism.

Suddenly something unbelievable happened: flashing all its signal flags, the last monitor left the formation, cut an insane arc across the entire Volga and sailed toward the high bank right next to the path where our brigade stood. Now we could inspect it in great detail, all the ladders and hatchways, anti-aircraft machine guns and bridges. And the tanned sailors standing on deck grinned at us so you could count all the teeth in their chops. Some sort of command was issued through a megaphone and several of the crew jumped from the side of the ship on to the riverside rocks or into the water. Within a minute no fewer than ten sailors and an officer were running uphill towards us. Miracle of miracles—they were encircling us!

Were we scared! All of us were scared, except, of course, Lydia. She observed the approaching sailors with mocking screwed-up eyes. Looking back now it seems to me that the sailors were a little awed by the sun goddess of socialism. Probably no one like her had ever appeared to these poor guys even in their onanistic dreams.

"You have photographed a war formation," the lieutenant told her. He was wearing a short, tight tunic. He was small but he stooped and rounded his shoulders as though he were tall.

"Maybe I did," she smiled and shook her mane of bleached hair. She was half a head taller than the officer.

He grinned at her as if to say she was nothing to him but a piece of ass, just a quick fuck. But his smile gave him away; it clearly revealed that by some hierarchy unknown to us, a person like him couldn't even dream of anything as splendid as our phys ed teacher.

"It's forbidden," he squeezed out.

"Ha-ha, ha-ha, ha-ha," said our phys ed teacher, "The other day in *Red Tartary* there was a picture of these ships."

A strange silence reigned, then suddenly the lieutenant began to blush profusely. His peaked cap grew very small and from under it flowed streams of sweat. Finally the reason for his shame was revealed: everyone noticed that the lieutenant's pants were gradually being stretched by a strange bulge which took on the shape of a solid peg pointing in Lydia's direction. The little officer bent inwards so as to obscure this bulge and remove it from the center of the picture, but nothing happened. Either the pants were too tight or the object was oversized.

We were silent for several minutes, realizing that something awkward was happening but relating it to the camera, to the photographing of the defensive forces of our river, and not in the least to the embarrassing peg which bulged in the direction of our Pioneer brigade. The first to break down were our girls. Then the sailors guffawed. And then we boys figured it out. The phys ed teacher flashed her Deineka-like smile triumphantly.

"Attention!" squealed the completely purple officer to his sailors. "I, of course, apologize miss—er, Comrade leader . . . but I have been ordered to confiscate your camera . . . or . . . or . . . "

By now he was not looking at the phys ed teacher. He stared somewhere sideways and below her, as though at his own heel; however, the object, such as it was, continued to bulge prominently, a strange and out-of-place force against the background of the small frail figure, but there was some connection in this to the heavy arms of the shallow-sailing watchships.

"Or expose the film?" Lydia contemptuously stuck out her lip. "No sir! Take the Leica but just you wait . . . "

"Perhaps you'll come to flotilla headquarters?" the little lieutenant asked with timid joy.

"Precisely! Tomorrow! Who is your superior? Rear-admiral Puzov? I was in the same class with his daughter for your information!"

She flung the Leica at the officer, like a queen throwing a handful of silver to a crowd.

"Children, follow me!"

"Tomorrow . . . tomorrow . . . " babbled the lieutenant, " . . . at Zelenodolsk . . . at headquarters . . . I'm sure they'll figure it out . . . I personally will . . . wait on the pier for you . . ."

"Three times ha-ha!" commanded the phys ed teacher.

"Ha-ha! Ha-ha! Ha-ha!" our detachment cheerfully responded, leaving the field of this extremely strange battle.

Valevich's laugh boomed into the depths of the Moscow phone system. He too must have recalled all this quite clearly.

"You remember, remember?" he choked through his laughter. "Remember that one?"

"How could I not remember?" I answered, and my heart filled with warmth and love for this, my only friend, who thought of himself as so successful and resourceful and who was actually only a fat, aging child. Who can be closer than a friend with whom, just with a word or even an exclamation, you can go off to the same place in time and space thirty years ago, where blackberry bushes jutted out amidst the gray rocks and the path led to hazel thickets, where the ribbon of the Volga either brightened or turned turbid, depending on the configuration of the clouds flying over our forlorn homeland.

Where does this moment exist that can arise from nowhere at any time, and shine so brightly and with such detail?

"In memory," Valevich explained importantly to me. "In the cells of our brain."

"Valevich, do you know what a memory is, what brain cells are, what a moment is? . . ."

"This is still being researched." he answered.

"But do you remember Sviyazhsk?"

"The church?" Valevich quietly asked. "Of course I remember."

"Yasha, come on over," I told him. "Let's meet on the corner by the newsstand. Something extraordinary is happening to me."

More from Elena Petrovna Chestnovo's letter:

. . . the irony was that we lived directly opposite the local Party committee. That day, returning from school, as I approached our house, I noticed that the shutters were closed. In the courtyard I saw Victor Petrovich's car. What could be happening? Inside something astonishing was taking place: candles were burning, icons had been hung up on the walls, the brocade on Father Sergey's cassock shone in the shadowy light (usually he dressed inconspicuously so as to avoid religious persecution), I heard a baby crying.

Mama, I asked, since when is our house a baptismal font? As you can guess, Oleg Antonovich, at fifteen I was in the Komsomols and very careful. Ssh, my mother answered, God forbid anyone should find out, or we would be in a great deal of trouble. They're baptizing the son of Anton Illich himself! And then I saw you, Oleg Antonovich, a naked baby, and your godmother Evfimiya, and the godfather was, as I already mentioned, my older brother Victor

Petrovich, whom I adored.

After the ceremony, I was handed the baby. Kiss him, Lenochka, this is your godbrother. I kissed you, despite my ingrained Komsomol hostility to the church and the shame which I always felt when thinking about my own baptism.

Try to imagine my inner conflicts, Oleg: Komsomol life has taken over, we're carrying out the Five Year Plan, building huge airplanes, we're civilizing the uninhabited North, and suddenly your brother, a sophisticated person, a mechanic and NKVD member gives credence to religious obscurantism and even involves the new generation which has to live under socialism.

I was such an idiot, Oleg, but you must give me credit for not even thinking of informing on them, as any one of my friends would have done. On the contrary, I experienced against my will a strange anguish and with tears in my eyes I kissed the child . . .

Our so-called "micro," but actually huge, complex seemed somehow unusual that night. Within the sinister monotony of the sixteen-storied thousand-windowed buildings, I suddenly saw the mere glimmer of a creative design which was nevertheless clear and intentional. Perhaps one of the pitiful architects who mechanically plan these microdistricts managed to sneak in a small spark of his own, to breathe into it a hint of living spirit, to somehow alter the whole row of miserable dwellings in a somewhat original way, so that it merged with that hill over there, to stretch that tower just a little beyond the others, to leave the back of the forest inside this block, who knows—maybe he was able to imagine for a second that there would be just such a moonlit night, such emptiness and that a lonely man shaken by some problem of his own, standing by the newsstand, would suddenly see his creation, the face of his city, its eyes lit by a spark of life, with a light over the archway, with just such an arrangement of shadows, with the moon hanging between two buildings and making the top of the forest silver, on an evening of half-moonlight, on a night of God's grace.

The special ambulance that picks up the winos every night passed by. Then Valevich's car pulled up around the corner.

"Oleg," said Valevich, "enough of this. Come sleep at our house. Let us find you a wife. We have someone in mind. Well, grab hold of yourself Shatok! Get going, at least for the last game. Yesterday you didn't show up at the Federation sports meeting but we gave Podbelkin a good fight. That swine attacked you again, bad-mouthed you, saying that in your article last year you put down the international victories of Soviet basketball, that in general you weren't quite . . . well, in general we kicked his ass. So, get angry, Shatok! You have to play the first game against the 'Tanks!' Only your team can beat them! And then I promise I'll arrange everything for you—a trip, money, a girlfriend. You'll go to a health spa. Come on.''

''Yakov,'' I said to him, ''today I was filled with grace. Come on, please don't wince, it's all right. Try to understand. I can't express my feelings in words. Well, briefly, I've had it with sports. I'm sorry, but everything to do with sports now seems to me slightly absurd, all our so-called victories, all this fuss over a simple object, a leather sphere filled with air. I'm trying to find another life, Yasha. I don't know if I will.''

''But you have the Latin American tour coming up,'' mumbled my large, fat friend, distressed. Once, a long time ago when basketball was not yet a sport for giants, he played center on our team. He was the pillar, the tallest. Now he hardly reaches the shoulder of, let's say, my Slavka Sosin.

''They'll go without me,'' I said. ''I've had enough of these politics . . . Yashka, do you really never dream of a different life?''

''After,'' he said vaguely.

''After what?''

''I sometimes think of that after the championship, after the Federation session, after a tour abroad, after something else, but Oleg, there's never enough time to think of another kind of life—as soon as one thing ends right away something else begins.'' He was obviously getting nervous and put his car key in his pocket, after having twirled it on his finger like the Moscow tough guys do. ''And also, Olezhek, excuse me, I wanted to ask you—don't you see anything besides politics and intrigues with Podbelkin in what we do? All the young men, running, leaping, playing . . . Isn't this pleasing to God?''

On the opening day of the final competitions everything seemed pretty horrible to me. Darkness and fog surrounded the Sports Palace with its everlasting slogan: ''For you, our Party, Victory

Through Sport!'' The fans lazily drifted towards the entrance. Actually basketball doesn't interest very many people in Moscow. The strength of our all-star and leading teams has little to do with the popularity of this type of sport. It's all because of selective government measures, so that if it weren't for the political advantage, basketball would simply disappear from our country. Perhaps this is true, however, of sports in general. Everything is distorted to the greatest degree.

My boys were sitting in the locker room as though hungover, still dressed in jeans and raincoats, listlessly talking to each other. With bovine stupidity they glanced at me and then got changed. Suddenly there was a sharp smell of sweat. Before, I never allowed them to play even a practice game with unwashed tee shirts, and certainly not a final game. Now it seemed that we were miles apart from each other: the team, doomed to defeat, and the trainer, a melancholy middle-aged man with eyes like a tormented dog's.

There actually wasn't one man on the team who hadn't been carefully selected. I had known them all since they were children. Usually I searched the schools for talented, lanky boys, courted them as if I were gay, and then recruited them for basketball. I would work with them, slowly bringing them in contact with the best players, and gradually from year to year, they would become the stars. Now they had become the very best of athletes, and came together to be victorious, and victorious even over our current opponent. And yet, they had lost track of the meaning of victory.

Our opponent that day, the solidly established army team, was not a favorite in the circles of real fans, of whom, incidentally, there were very few. The fans named them the ''Tanks'' which also probably expressed their secret contempt for that rigid, punitive machine. They had never nurtured a single player. The colonels of the club followed the remarkable traditions of Vaska Stalin's athletic stables. They simply mobilized already formed, well-trained athletes into an army and had them play for their club. This is how the powerful, practically invincible brigade of mercenaries was created.

In the past my men and I were angry as devils at this military machine, and often we played against them mercilessly, tougher and tougher from the first whistle to the last. Sometimes we even won. Remembering this, the pseudo-specialist and famous demagogue Podbelkin particularly disliked me. But, we hadn't beaten the Tanks in a long time (I had lost any will to take risks, consumed by terror and anguish, and my team was well aware of this). Still, Podbelkin liked me less and less and I even heard rumors that he had attacked me again in a letter to the Central Committee.

We went into the gym, the team members dragging themselves out to warm up unenthusiastically. I went over with my aide to the referee's table and asked if it wasn't possible to replace one of the judges. We said he was prejudiced against us—in other words, the usual business, while, late as always, the ''Tanks'' appeared on the court leaping elegantly in their chic light-blue uniforms, and their trainer Podbelkin, I repeat, a confirmed demagogue, followed, his potbelly sticking out in front of him.

Suddenly something from the past stirred in me. Or perhaps it was something new, something possibly related to the secret vision of the unknown architect who planned the lunar line in our microdistrict, or even something else. To put it another way, *life* suddenly awoke in me and abruptly I was filled with a deep remorse for my *kids* who occasionally threw doomed looks at the deadly opponent. In the next moment, suddenly, passionately, as in former years, I wished them success. I called over our captain Slava and whispered in his ear: ''We're going to beat the hell out of them today!'' Slava looked at me with astonishment, returned to the sidelines and whispered to Dima, who whispered to Sasha, and then the whole team, dropping the ball, stared at me. Slava and Dima had been on the team the longest and they remembered my better days. Both had even participated in one of our historic games when we had beaten the ''Tanks.''

The warm-ups ended. The TV cameras started rolling. I announced who the five starting players were. The only top player I chose was Slava; the rest were rookies from the reserve bench. Out of the corner of my eye I saw Podbelkin sneering and talking to his second, obviously already angry from the start. The trouble was that from the very beginning I had gained my small psychological victory. Instinctively I knew that Podbelkin, wanting to demonstrate his total contempt for us, would select as his starting formation not his regular terrifying gorillas of international basketball but substitutes. That's how it turned out. It was as though he were crossing us off the list of first class performers, and especially me as a first class trainer. And then he saw the four substitutes on our side. Scorn met with scorn. Right there, he suffered a heavy psychological blow from the beginning. Too late to change the lineup—this would mean a loss of face for him.

Several seconds before the game began, something really strange happened: I crossed myself and I crossed my five starters. It was without question an inexplicable phenomenon: the boys crossed themselves in response as if this was what they usually did. Everyone on the bench crossed themselves after we did. The second trainer, the doctor and the masseur crossed themselves.

The stadium began to buzz. The television spotlights were turned off. Later I learned that there was a real ideological panic: the broadcast, it turned out, was *live*, and therefore several million viewers saw this *disgrace*—the sign of the cross over the top league basketball team.

The game began. I saw Valevich at the Federation table, his face in his hands, shaking his head in despair. The president of the Federation, the potbellied Komsomol writer Pevsky, was furiously whispering in his ear. The entire basketball society was conversing earnestly. Podbelkin laughed and twirled his finger at his temple—Shatkovsky's gone nuts.

Meanwhile my babes, led by the highly experienced Slava, were overwhelming the "Tanks" one play after the other.

During the entire game I felt as if everything was completely coming back to me, my life, my love and the whole rhythm of basketball. We are all God's children, I thought, we play our naive game under His benevolent gaze. Praise be to God and the Son and the Holy Ghost!

After the game Valevich quickly came up to me, took me firmly by the arm and led me away.

"The Federation Presidium is having an emergency meeting" he said quietly. "And you know why. Oleg, you know what a crowd I have at home and that basketball keeps them fed . . . "

"I know, Yasha," I answered just as quietly.

"You'd better not go to the Presidium," he whispered, or rather, simply mouthed.

"I don't plan to," I responded in the same way.

"But I can't not go," he said using his eyebrows and his left palm.

I replied with my right hand, placing it on the left side of my breast. Suddenly his face glowed with the far away light of Sviyazhsk. The distance of the past, I thought, is utter nonsense.

We'll run away together, the boyish face of my old, fat Valevich shouted at me. We'll jump into my Zhiguli and in twenty-four hours we'll be in the Crimea, and there we can mingle with the local population and the patrons of the all-union health spa. The health of the individual is the health of the nation, that's what Leonid Brezhnev said. Let's run, Comrade!

No, friend, my face replied, and I, too, overcame the distance of time and entered the zone of Sviyazhsk radiance. It's better that you go to the Presidium. You have a big family. You'll never betray me, because you've suggested we run away.

"But where are you going now?" he asked me, but, although helped by his voice this time, he was barely audible. "I'll call you at home, when all this mess has died down . . .''

At the exit I had a desire to bow to everyone but I noticed that several members of the Federation were looking at me cautiously as though I was the source of an infection, so I refrained.

There were few people in the metro at that hour. The train speedily rumbled down the long tunnel on the Circle line. I sat, my eyes closed, feeling at once wild exhaustion and complete satisfying peace. I felt as if I were alone in the car and again I saw myself as if looking sideways, but this time not from very far away. It was more as if I were just looking down from a corner of the ceiling of the train. I saw a lonely man, sitting in a position of utter exhaustion, his legs stretched out in the aisle, and it seemed to me that some complete openness could be seen in him as when there is no need to worry about anything, when you can walk away from trouble and write everything off to exhaustion. It was even quite pleasant to observe, this middle-aged man in clothing that had once been of good quality but had become shabby, and describe him in words from an old novel or a film, specifically, in some marvelous saying from my youth, sounding roughly like, "This man has seen better days." It was a long time since everything had been so easy and simple.

The conductor, who was as tired as I was, announced the next stop over the speaker. Someone nearby began to stir. I opened my eyes and looked in the dark glass across from me in which everything is remarkably reflected as you fly through the underground tunnel. I saw myself and next to me, not more than a foot away, our phys ed teacher, Lydia, and Comrade Prakharenko, the director of the Pioneer camp "Hollow Herring."

Faces reflected in the dark windows of subway cars usually look younger. Maybe this is why I recognized them. Or maybe it's the opposite; perhaps because of this I was mistaken. I stood up, went to the doors and looked at the couple directly.

Was it possible to recognize our Sviyazhsk leader, our "Girl with an Oar," in this practically old, big breasted, round assed woman? And how could they turn up together after thirty-five years? They certainly wouldn't have married, separated as they were by such a deep and vast cultural gap. She had been the star of the Bio department and he, a small-time Soviet Vassily Tyorkin who was let out to pasture on the roughest, most forlorn Pioneer grass. A dopey martinet, a one-armed braggart, and a drunk too!

The missing arm was still obvious because of the jacket sleeve which was neatly tucked into his pocket. The cultural gap was also still obvious. The one provisionally referred to as the phys ed teacher was in a pantsuit. She wore big glasses, had a boy's haircut and she was made up like Sivka-Burka, a true theatrical Moscow lady, or a Goskino employee. He could be compared possibly to a "friendly country neighbor." The cultural gap was noticeable, but perhaps not as obvious as in those days when . . .

. . . As when Yashka and I, sitting at the oars, would stare with our four eyes at Lydia's sweet, magnificent figure, when to us she smelled of all the grasses of the Volga shore, but at the same time with four nostrils we inhaled the odor of strong tobacco, raw brandy, borscht and rancid breath from the jaws of our director . . .

Now he was an almost respectable not quite old man, who was obviously ashamed of his past alcoholism and proud of his wartime accomplishments. His meaty shnoz with its not quite decent curves was still impressive.

Noticing my interest, they gazed back at me. He, provisionally called Prakhar, covered his mouth with his hand and whispered something to the phys ed teacher. Knitting her brows with annoyance, she turned and looked at me for a brief moment, as though to tell me that although they were people from different circles, certain circumstances had forced her to put up with him. She recognized something kindred in me, not of course the boy from the year after the war, but a member of the intelligentsia, a rather rare bird in our years of late socialism. He continued to whisper to her and she sighed bitterly a few times, but with a bitterness that seemed only on the surface and perhaps even somehow a front. To me they seemed like children now, these two old people once united in shallow water in the rushes, rocked by mighty and splendid orgasms, who had spent their whole lives together. Phys ed teacher and Prakhar, if you only knew how I love your features, shining through your deformed faces. Once more in those few minutes of underground rumbling, I was transported to the Sviyazhsk radiance, to the dying little town, to those pathetic icon lamps, those peaceful and majestic tanned faces, to that quiet, joyful secret, which harmonized, strangely enough, with all that Pioneer business, with rowing and jealousy, with your charm, oh plaster goddess of "Hollow Herring!"

I turned away. If it's they, to remind them of Sviyazhsk would be unkind. Changing trains, I lost them but then saw them again, odd as it may seem, in my underground passageway. They were in front of me; she was helping him put on a gray raincoat. Then, with automatic gesture which was clearly not devoid of affection, she pushed the empty sleeve of his mackintosh into the pocket. They must have thought they were alone in the dark underground, and for a moment their heads met and together they smiled at something.

One exit from the passageway leads to my house, the other to the neighboring giant. Prakhar and the phys ed teacher started up my stairs. Could they live in my building, at one of its forty entries? Fantastic!

When I got to the top, I felt the fresh, memorable world around me. The moon was just beginning to wane and there was still enough light to penetrate the depths of the microdistrict and to throw sharp shadows everywhere, without a doubt foreseen by the unknown architect but hidden from the committee on socialist realism.

The aforementioned couple approached the archway leading to the inner courtyard of my building which led to entrances number twenty-one through forty. I walked toward my entrance near which the First Aid van was parked at that hour. Next to it stood two huge figures in white smocks. The glow of cigarettes. For whom was the van waiting? For whose soul had it come? People are born here, get sick, and die, and you don't know any of your neighbors. It's a disgrace! I could see yet another figure standing by the apartment house, this one in dark clothes, holding a flashlight. I found myself inside a blinding circle. I covered my face with my elbow and then I understood everything. The flashlight went out. Several moments passed before I could again see the entrance, the van, the men, the moonlit shadows, the many dark windows overhead, the phys ed teacher and Prakhar approaching their archway.

"Lydia!" I screamed. "Comrade director! Do you remember Sviyazhsk?"

They froze under the archway. I don't know if they turned. I had no time to see. The flashlight had made me blind.

May 1981, Santa Monica

Quest For An Island

Translated by Susan Layton

"RETURNING ONCE AGAIN TO AJACCIO." ON EACH SUCCESSIVE arrival this literary phrase rang in the mind of Leopold Bar—"the most important essayist alive in Europe today," according to the periodicals. In earlier years he had exerted some effort, trying to formulate a variant title. During the intervals between his trips (meaning the major part of his life) the name of the island's capital didn't cross his lips in any form because he never thought about it. However, he remembered from his childhood a geography textbook which featured "Ajaccio" rendered in Cyrillic letters, creating an odd concoction like eggnog with pepper. The native Corsicans—a substantial number of whom are favorably disposed toward the separatist movement—use the "j" and "c's" in writing "Ajaccio," but they pronounce the name of their capital more along the lines which the Cyrillic invites, saying something between "Aye-cho" and "Eh-cho"—subtleties which would never be learned in the schools he had attended. But the French (and Corsica does belong, after all, to France) turn "Ajaccio" into a pleasing mouthful of consonant clusters of the sort so characteristic of Russian but much less typical of the language of Molière. LB lent his support to the mother country, spurning the fashionable separatist cause, the way he spurned all fashions, because he had never been one to tag along with the crowd. Besides, just think about it: if all the islands in the world gained independence, a traveler would require a whole stack of additional visas.

"Irony charts a path to capitulation," LB had once told his readers. The gravity of blocks of limestone weathered by the wind. The doleful but mighty contours of citadels resisting the wind. Stand here in the rain with your weathered limestone face, as though you had not made half a million surrenders. A life lived gravely in a grave world can lay the sole basis of art—so I'm thinking at the given moment. The given moment. A moment given to me . . .

The rest of the arrival proceeded as usual. A bizarre-looking taxi with no meter—just the driver, who calculated the fare from Campo dell'Oro airport to the Fesch Hotel merely by staring at the rainy skies to reach a figure specified down to the centime. Then in the hotel lobby the same synthetic skins, striving for the cozy atmosphere of a hunting lodge. The same porter glued to the television, which was now storming with all the passion of local soccer: Bastia was beating Toulon. And the same Negro lying on a sofa in a dark corner, sleeping soundly and muttering indistinctly with one hand thrust inside his pants. Who was he, this black man who had been fast asleep in that same corner a year ago? As on the previous occasion, LB took no interest and walked past with his suitcase in hand, going straight to the elevator.

How enormous and simple the world is. LB granted no validity to fantastical projections, even though he had been enthralled by them often enough in the past. The problem of overpopulation, or some question about distributing population evenly across the globe, skirted the plain essence of things: the world is elemental, uncomplicated and tragic. As the norm of everyday existence, tragedy stamps the myriad signs of life—bread, a bar of soap, sperm, getting dressed, undressing, checking into a hotel . . . but no, don't smile. Don't yield any ground. The world is simple, and humor is the immoral, sly subterfuge of literati grown overly literary. LB does not belong to their ranks.

Here was last year's room, where nothing really crucial had occurred at the time, except for the fundamentals—breathing, sweating, urination, defecation, sleep, awakening, thinking and some sneezing as well, it seems (he had caught a touch of the flu). White walls and dark heavy furniture, decorated with carving, no less—all in the Mediterranean style. A balcony overlooking the rooftops of Ajaccio. On the balcony—a bubble-dotted puddle, left by several days of rain. In the puddle lies a garden hose, coiled in sheer mortification. Reliance on metaphor produces a lot of nonsense, but a bad metaphor is preferable to a good one. Shun metaphors, even though some crafty devil tries to slip them into your phrases at every turn. A garden hose is lying in the puddle. LB started undressing in front of the mirror. "How did I get to look like this? Is the reflection faithful? Taking off my cap reveals a big broad forehead sprinkled with reddish-brown freckles. A mangy disarray of thinning hair, worn long. The edematose chin—a constant source of unseemly bitterness. Some people find me handsome perhaps or at least significant-looking. To take a different standpoint, I make a pretty ridiculous sight. Such watery eyes. Bubbles, puddles, melted snow amidst the buildings of a housing project. Off come the jacket, the sweater, the shirt. Over the trousers on each side hangs a game bag, half-full—flab bags, lard left on the shelf too long . . . What meaning resides in the leisurely contemplation of one's person in various mirrors in dozens of three-star hotels throughout the world? Who am I? Is the reflection faithful? Am I handsome or ridiculous? Is my body a junk heap or a vessel, the form of my soul?"

Posing one question after another and gazing at himself with mounting intensity and concentration as he removed his clothes, the swayer of minds throughout Europe gradually began calming down. No more extremes, no more metaphors, no more fuss: he simply *was*, he was what he was, his shape was the shape of a particular individual, and Corsica would have to cope again with his presence for awhile.

The next morning Leo Bar was drinking coffee on his balcony. That night had brought to the western Mediterranean events of far greater consequence than his own arrival—so he told himself with a smile. The winds had changed. A strong southeasterly current had displaced a northwestern slush-bearing front and had even managed to dry the sidewalks, terraces and roofs. It had turned out to be a windy, grayish day with flashes of sunshine, a day much nicer than Bar would have predicted for Corsica in December. On days like this, dressed in gray trousers, black sweater and a cap from London, Leo Bar—viewed from the left at three-quarter face—had the look of a typical Englishman.

You could have the look of an *Englishman*, period—Bar smilingly proposed to himself that morning. It was impossible to have the look of a *typical* Englishman. Typicality already implied some measure of fixed character. It was possible to have the look of a typical poet by simply being a poet, but impossible to have the look of a typical Englishman without actually being English. That was the case, wasn't it? Bar's main aspiration, incidentally, was to produce no impression whatsoever. To get lost as an alien-in-the-midst, blending into the humdrum routine of Corsican life. Here in the off-season nobody would take the slightest notice of some visitor's exceptional nature. There would be no personal contacts, no pesky little plots. The hunt for plots was the scourge of literature, the scourge of life itself. The goal of this trip was the implementation of the right to solitude. Uhh! what smug triviality. "The right to solitude" smacked of today's false romanticism, it was the phrase of a super-phony. Even though he did actually feel like being alone. After the scenes from the theatre of the absurd, played by his Paris editors, after gorging himself nightly at La Coupole, after several months of acting as both sniper and target, there came this urge to go slack, to fade into the background and live a vegetative life. "Live a vegetative life." Again, an intellectual's cliché. This was really the main goal of the trip: to escape the shackles of intellectual clichés. Yet another trite expression—"the shackles of intellectual clichés." And a third—"to escape the shackles." One, two, three . . . via the creaking cogs, pulleys and weights of the literati life. Was it truly impossible to break free? Don't pose difficulties for yourself, don't set tasks, or else the island—a phenomenon of nature—will turn into a phenomenon of literature. Just get going and keep your attention focused, don't interpret, don't overdevelop, don't exaggerate. Simply reflect. There was the key: give an unaffected reflection, like a puddle. "A stork is perched on a roof against tranquil skies—the storm has passed." Reads like a *haiku*. Ye gods, more literary clap-trap!

In this state of torment, superbly self-inflicted at the breakfast table, Leopold Bar went out for a walk on Rue Fesch. Overhead, all along the street, which was squeezed narrow by the shuttered Italian houses with peeling paint, ubiquitous laundry was flapping in the wind. A traffic jam clogged the street: some distance away, a blue van had stopped to make a delivery. By blocking the vista at one end of the street, the van created the illusion of a deep blue sea, out of harmony with the weather. LB turned to walk in the opposite direction and soon reached the Square of the First Consul. This was very likely his favorite spot in Ajaccio. Thin colored tiling on the sidewalks, enormous palm trees surrounding the dullish gray, well-weathered Consul, several stores, including a bookshop, radiating despair, and a Lancôme perfume outlet, the most inspiring of the lot; then the palm-lined avenue stretching to the port; and there, in the obscure distance, the market with its smells of humanity's cradle—pepper, garlic and seaweed. But now the Société Générale bank. Changing money comprises one of the morning rituals of all globetrotters, and Leopold Bar certainly qualified as a globetrotter, a multinational man on the move.

The pound was falling, the dollar was falling, the lira was falling, while the mark crawled upward like a spider on the slimy thread of speculation. Tear out that miserable tongue of yours! On the marble steps of the bank sat an enormous shaggy cowardly dog. The type abounds here on Corsica, more than anywhere else. An island of little brave men and big cowardly dogs. If this dog was guarding the public coffers, you might say that the service would be performed more effectively by a statue of Napoleon. Damn your phrase-mongering! Two absolutely marvelous old Italian ladies, dressed in weary black, well-scrubbed, with every hair in place, were changing their native currency into foreign money. Why does the lira fluctuate so much, when Italy is so stable and sound? The time has come to dispel the generally held misconception about the country's unreliability. These two Mediterranean signoras are five-hundred times more reliable and substantial than all Milan's scummy leftists and rightists, brandishing their portraits of Lavrenty Beria or Benito Mussolini. Leopold Bar, where are you drifting? Into politics? Put on the brakes! The teller was smiling for some reason as he counted the crisp French bills. Did his good mood depend on currency fluctuations? But here was the rule to stamp on your skull: no mingling, no personal contacts whatsoever. Plenty of contacts, ties, relationships, friendships, quarrels and reconciliations have already been established on the continental land masses, even if the island does provide chances to mingle. Fence yourself off!

"Things good?" asked the teller, trying his English.

"*Merci*," responded Bar as he stuck the money in his pocket.

"America?" persisted the teller, watching the customer's gesture.

Then he gave a wink directed slightly off-side. Leo Bar glanced out of the corner of his eye and realized that he personally had never been the object of the friendly looks. Over to the right stood the shaggy coward with a front paw on the ledge of the teller's window.

"That's Athos," said the teller.

"Is he a watchdog?" Leo Bar, the lilly-liver, was entering into contact, after all.

"Oh no, monsieur! Just a friend. He's . . . "

LB left the bank and caught sight of his reflection in the window of a sporting goods store across the street. "Terrific, just the same" flashed through his mind when he saw that slightly overweight fellow. Then he had a sudden recollection of himself holding forth about a Bertolucci film the day before yesterday at the Deux Magots. With a certain aplomb he had stripped away the external trappings, and in no time at all a whole circle of people had formed to listen to *the* Leo Bar . . . You've got to shake off this crap! . . . at least some of it, this nonsense, this scruffy celebrity-hood, the self-importance. What a ludicrous, laughable meglalomaniac! "The cultural phenomenon of modern-day Europe" should try turning into a human being for a week. Become an islander!

The newly emerged seeker of islander mentality went walking along the narrow street, passing the Imperial Bakery, the Napoleon Barber Shop and some souvenir stores with window displays showing an endless array of items commemorating the islander who had proved so successful in his quest for continental mentality. The rebellious lieutenant, with saber drawn and hair ruffled by the wind, appeared on plates and kitchen calendars; the idol stood in his tricorn, set forever; his busts ran the gamut from matchbox dimensions to natural scale; and the faces of the brunettish couple were painted on ashtrays, stamped "Napoleon and Josephine." The street curved uphill, and the top of the slope around the bend brought a view of the sea with the ocean liner *Napoleon*, a gigantic casino on the shore and a square with an equestrian statue, ill-proportioned but quite magnificent, nonetheless. The breath of one man's fate . . . the hapless little schoolboy . . . What a life of tumultuous upheaval: troop movements, fodder, powder, indemnities, diplomatic crossword puzzles, overthrowing a throne and founding a dynasty. Did you have enough time on St. Helena to grieve for your own independent organism? Here on the island the souvenir shops preserved an outline of human possibilities: birth on an island which promised a vegetative existence, but then a climb to fame, the mutilation of a near-by continent, and finally a quiet expiration, after vegetating on another, distant island. There was an entrancing model of human destiny!

Leo Bar halted in his tracks, struck by a thoroughly disgusting, disgraceful thought: wasn't he drawing a comparison between his own fate and Napoleon's? He'd been taken unawares by some contemptible thought-process encompassing laundry waving in the street, the nose of the *Napoleon* jutting into sight behind the casino, a slice of the equestrian statue, a part of a plate with Josephine's portrait. . . . What a goddamn disgrace.

At this point he felt that he was not walking alone in the realm of shame: he sensed the presence of someone behind him. When he turned around, he discovered Athos, who had been accompanying him the whole way and now stood frozen in his tracks with his left front paw raised.

"A real disgrace, pal," said Leo Bar to Athos.

The wind was making a fierce rustle along the quay, taking a romp through the palms in file formation. On a yellow wall fluttered a dark blue leaflet with a sole remaining corner stuck. Intermittently the wind would spread it flat, showing the picture of a child's face with the words, "Mama, speak to me in Corsican!" Sitting at an oval window, a lackadaisical fat man with a magnifying glass was studying the tiny figures of a stock-exchange report. "Location de Voitures sans Chauffeur" said a sign above the door. A car rental agency. Now that was a pretty simple idea: rent a car. A drive in somewhat unfamiliar territory airs out the mind, chasing away idiotic preoccupations with one's own person. The fat man stood up to meet him, giving him a big friendly smile. From the depths of the garage came running an intelligent creature with silky hair—a spaniel named Juliette. In a few minutes Bar had at his disposal a Renault-5, a highly popular model among the locals and one which he saw shaped like a pear. He got behind the wheel. The fat man with his highly clever eyes was standing in the doorway of his rent-a-car. There was something about his face. . . . "He's a Napoleon who didn't make it. He could have commanded vast armies," thought Leo Bar.

"If you don't have a destination in mind, monsieur, I'd recommend Vivario," said the fat man. "It's right in the center of the island. The road zigzags quite a bit, but after you've made the trip, you can tell your friends that you know Corsica like the back of your hand.''

He was smiling politely but with a trace of condescension—a real psychologist. What friends? Just what friends might hear Leo Bar boasting that he knew Corsica like the back of his hand? You, psychologist, are thinking in clichés. Instead of responding to the man, LB reached down to pat Juliette. She instantly began snarling and jumped away from his hand. Not a pleasant feeling: why was the dog so hostile?

''She's afraid that you'll take her with you,'' laughed the fat man.

''She's so happy here with you, is she?'' Unable to resist, Leopold Bar had released some venom.

''This is her home. She's never known another one,'' said the fat man, as he handed him the necessary papers and a map. ''You must agree that people get that way, too.''

''Even entire nations do,'' said Leo Bar.

The fat man broke into a hearty laugh. This conclusion of their exchange had obviously given him tremendous pleasure: he'd made contact with an intellectual's world.

LB drove along the quay, furious with himself. Once again he had failed to stand firm behind his barricade, once again some idiotic, routine little plot had tried to swing into motion.

Driving an unfamiliar automobile actually did prove to be a rather pleasant, diverting activity, and the Renault-Cinq was indeed a sensible car. A heavy-bottomed pear wouldn't be bad at all as its symbol. That somewhat heavy little rear on these pint-sized vehicles gives them an apparent, if not real, solidity, and you step on the gas with more confidence than you might have in some bigger, more expensive cars. The steeply ascending road, the rapid changes from one weather zone to the next, Corsica's stone villages hanging over precipices like medieval fortifications, the intensifying blueness of the sky, and the topographical patterns of the landscape left far below—all filled Leo Bar with a feeling of communion with the island, the Mediterranean and Nature itself. The wind, growing fresher all the time and even acquiring the smell of light snow, was carousing inside the Renault and blowing Leo Bar's problems out the window. Then came the sudden realization that he had driven beyond the 2000-meter mark, bottomless ravines yawned beside him, he had a perpendicular wall of rock to his right, and a patchy cloud was drifting by at a lower level. He started thinking about the unmatched dangers of icy roads on slopes like these, he thought about the tread on his tires, and then he was imagining himself losing control of the car, unable to brake, sliding over the cliff, which did not even have a guardrail at this stretch of the road—despite the high altitude and hairpin turns! Bastards! Adrenalin made his blood churn, and he naturally began to lose control of the car, skidding toward the left edge of the road . . . but then a Citroën-DS darted around the bend ahead, and next, three cars passed LB and sped out of sight in rapid succession—a Volkswagen, a Simca-Matra and a more confident fellow Renault-5. All in a few seconds . . . some amazed-looking, wildly laughing faces flashing past him . . . A man ashen with terror took the curve . . . he saw a forest glade, fir trees and people playing in the light snowfall . . .

Leopold Bar in his somersaulting automobile had not yet hit the bottom of the abyss, when his trembling double stopped at a pass to catch his breath. They'd go on playing in the snow, just like that. Nobody would even notice the demise of "the most important essayist alive today." The funny thing was that he would automatically lose his title, right on the spot, because he'd be leaving the ranks of those "alive today," while a standing among all those who weren't alive today would involve a whole new count. An ordinary human body is not discovered quickly, it would eventually be identified, a belated shudder would pass through the thinking world, the tremor would last awhile—until the next edition of the news, as in the case of Camus: existentialism in action. Oh rosy people so full of life, playing there in the snow!—have you no pity for Leo Bar? "Didn't know the man," atheists would say. "Every human being has our pity," Christians would say. "Must have lost it on the down-shift," sportsmen would shrug. "Ahh, Leopold Bar! What a terrible shame," some pretty, lone intellectual would say. "Thank goodness he left us a fairly sizeable cultural legacy."

Beside the sign for Vivario stood a large Corsican donkey, eating the sparse grass. "Vivario! Vivario!" exclaimed Leopold Bar, in extraordinarily high spirits for his own funeral feast. He hopped out of the car and kissed the donkey on the tip of the nose. My friend, when the Almighty summons you and me to his olive groves, let's stick together, let's share a bower of straw in paradise, and don't take my proposition as magnanimity or condescension, we're truly equals, you and I, and Athos too, and Juliette and Shakespeare and Camus and that little bird flying past—a sparrow, isn't it? maybe a wagtail? . . . sorry, I'm not too swift when it comes to amphibians, reptiles, mollusks, fish or the Sillonette school of criticism, but perhaps this divorce from the animal kingdom simply points up my narrowness—a narrowness determined by centuries of so-called culture, that whole pile of smelly rubbish! You might even be smarter than me, my Corsican donkey, because you have no prejudices.

Like so many other small Corsican towns, such as Vizzavona, Sartène and Cauro, Vivario was built into a cliff. A building apparently having two stories when viewed from one side would turn out to have six stories when viewed from the opposite vantage point. In the tiny square where Leo Bar parked his automobile, a modest bronze Artemis with a dog stood under a stream of water: ''Paese di L'amore,'' read the name—''The Spring of Love.'' Vivario was the home of Corsican blondes, who resemble short Swedes. At a long table inside the Friendship Café a chorus of voices blended in the melody of a graceless folk creation. Leo Bar asked for something to eat. He was seated by the fireplace and served some smoked ham, a round loaf of bread with a crispy brown crust, a carafe of country wine and a bowl of boiled beans. After his exhausting flights of imagination the writer now abandoned himself with relish to the simple pleasures of food.

In the meantime, he was being observed with no small interest by a Parisian woman sitting at a table by the wall across from the fireplace and smoking a Dutch cigarillo. He continued eating, free of the slightest suspicion, but all the while he was becoming the object of seemingly casual and passing, yet unmistakable, attention. Once his hunger had been satisfied, he sensed something and began looking around the room until he finally saw the Parisian woman. Exposed stitching along the seams, quilted jacket with some posh fur lining, crushed leather boots: it didn't take much effort to guess that the lady was outfitted by Sonia Rykiel. The height of stupidity—this snobbism of clothes with such fancy price tags. A craving for symbols and tokens of clanship, allowing the immediate recognition of one's own kind—social rites comparable to secret gestures among

Masons. Caught off-guard, Leo Bar sat there looking at the Parisian with his mouth half-open, giving the impression of a lame-brained parrot. Small head with highlighted feathery hair—the concentration-camp style. A hint of puffiness in the cheeks and under the eyes, a slight pout to the mouth. Her age couldn't be pinned down precisely, but she had to be over forty. To his horror he realized that he was facing the type of woman who had always attracted him, still did and always would. Oh no, not that!! Not some banal little island romance! But she's spotted me—spotted me as a man who obviously belongs to "her circle." I look the part, after all, don't I?—like one of the mobs of run-of-the-mill Englishmen who go gallivanting around everywhere. That's really what my personal resolve amounts to: don't stand out from the average man, don't reveal an exceptional character. Maybe the lady has simply seen me somewhere, like the brasserie Lipp, La Coupole or the café Flore? But my god! What if she actually knows me? No, not that, please—not that. Fence yourself off!

He felt that he was striking false poses once again, his legs had veered apart, and he had plopped into a puddle of falsity. Then he delved into the boiled beans. A simple, scrumptious dish! Just what in the hell was she doing here, 2000 meters above sea level in a Corsican village amidst all these little blondes? The deep-red ham looked translucent in a patch of light from the fire. Maybe I've actually met the snob at some soirée? But it's not too likely she'd have escaped my attention, if I had. I'm breaking the bread—this well-browned, crunchy peasant bread with the texture of cake, I munch with the teeth I still have intact. If you'd stuck to chow like this, you wouldn't have lost so many teeth. A glimmering conjecture: something similar to Leopold Bar's own condition had brought that Parisian here. Couldn't she be a writer? A whole group of these George Sands had cropped up, and some of them were even using masculine pseudonyms. I wouldn't be surprised if Emile Ajare turns out to be a female. He pours himself half a glass of wine and dilutes it with water from Artemis's spring. Now there's a drink! He contemplates the tablecloth and the remains of his feast, he's not gazing around, he doesn't raise his eyes, he's behaving perfectly naturally, mumbling a little under his breath, from a travel bag he takes *The Spy I Loved*, an espionage novel purchased at Orly for the trip, and pretends to read like a man engrossed, totally absorbed in the private life of his own independent organism—as simple as can be, unobtrusive and desirous that others keep their distance; then he stands up with his backside squarely directed at that woman's table—aiming his rump right at her, he walks over to the counter and digs into his pants' pockets, keenly aware of the indignity of that rear-end assault (but nobody's making you look at it, madame!), he pays some trifling bill, flings his scarf over his shoulder as he reaches the doorway, and involuntarily, despite himself, he glances back at her table. The table is empty. The coffee cup is empty, and the ashtray contains an extinguished cigarillo, or rather a filter with a long ash, left at least five minutes ago. Ah, so that's how it was? All the better—much, much better. Even better than you can imagine, precious heroine of the Lelouchian pseudo-cinema which, fortunately, is not taking shape.

The bitter pang of overdue freedom, solitude in the mountains. He was standing in the early mountain twilight in the little square of the tiny village Vivario, and at that moment he felt a bit like an arrogant schoolboy in the graduating class, as though his entire life lay before him. That's the way to finish a big meal—full of bitter pride, it keeps you from gaining an ounce. His subsequent actions: he stuck his head inside a barber shop for some reason (Want your mustache trimmed? Thanks, I'll drop by later), he popped into a souvenir shop and bought a postcard showing the head of a familiar donkey—his future companion in the heavenly mansions, then he went to the toilet, and while relieving himself, he thought about this trickle flowing from the mountain heights into the deepest abyss, quickly losing its distinctive odor along the way, leaving some unassuming damp blotches on rock, pouring at last into a brook or small river completely cleansed of everything repulsive, acquiring the purity of Nature's streams in the great circulation of matter. The marvelous flow of mountain waters! Soon the sky was becoming quite dark, he remembered the hairpin turn and the descent beyond the pass, gave a cough to nudge himself along and got into the car. Then he discovered that he did not know how to turn on the lights. He punched various buttons and moved some small levers, but all he managed to do was activate the distress blinkers. He sure wasn't going to do any driving with distress·blinkers . . . stupid mess, that's for sure. What was that guy trying to pull, palming off a defective car?—conniving fatso, master of the imbecile Juliette!

What a low-down trick, advising him to drive into the mountains in a defective automobile. Perhaps somebody here knows how to turn on the headlights of a Renault-Cinq? He saw a figure slowly approaching—a person with a kind of poncho trailing from the shoulders and a hat perched on the head—a hat like something worn by Bolivian peasants. Excuse me please, I'm having some trouble, would you by any chance know how to turn on the lights in this lousy heap? Pivoting in his direction, the silhouette explained in a Parisian voice. Straight into a trap! It was her. You see—you have to flip the switch—just move it to the right. A hand with an Indian bracelet entered the car like a soft warm bird and moved a little black stub. The dashboard burst into light. *Voilà!* He got out of the car to convey his profound gratitude. The interior of the car was fully illuminated now, and the silhouette standing beside him became more three-dimensional. A scarf tied tightly around the head, topped with the rigid hat. A silly frame for a sweet face with a little pointed nose. Existentialism in action. The stupidest possible plot had begun to unfold. No use resisting it. I'm driving to Ajaccio, madame, and, of course, if . . . you too? how nice, I'd be more than happy to . . .

And so Leopold Bar found himself once again in the subtropical seaside zone, on a beach on the gulf of Propriano. Down and down they had ridden, making conversation the whole time, having readily found a common language in so-called "Franglais." He'd chatted non-stop with Florence (could it be her real name?), covering the demise of literature, the rebirth of cinema, the "new philosophers" (in disagreement with him, she proclaimed Marx a living force), the barricades of May, the hazards of New York, Russia's crises, homosexual love (she didn't disapprove but didn't understand—bravo!) . . . talking, talking so that they dashed past all the signs without taking notice until they had left Ajaccio some fifty kilometers behind to the north and reached an empty parking lot at the deserted beach on the gulf of Propriano, which was naturally occupied in the darkness with its usual business of rolling pebblestone.

After leaving her Bolivian and Parisian attire in the car, Madame Florence in jeans and a blouse was making a tour of the beach in an impromptu dance—quite a ballerina! How limber she is. Leo Bar lagged behind, getting bogged down in the sand, stumbling on a stone, trying all the while to stay in tune with the night's little plot—holding his stomach in, constantly aware of his awkwardness, thinking his shoulders were too narrow, his thighs too heavy, and smoking—smoking incessantly, not so much because he felt disconcerted but because he was sticking to the plot, as the man with a flickering dot of light in his teeth. Gnashing teeth.

"You, I see, are a tobacco fiend, a real chain-smoker," she said laughingly. Turning the diminutive head, bosom, shoulders, she looked about eighteen now as the moon flashed through clouds.

"We've hit just the spot for a side-trip," he said like a dolt. The sound of crashing waves reached his ears from some distance away in the gulf: there in the turbulent play of moonlight Scylla and Charybdis were quietly shifting their positions, like molars racked by the pain of age and overindulgence.

"Here's a chess game. Do you play?" An enormous chessboard lay at her feet. In the flashes of moonlight the black squares looked darker than the white ones. Gigantic chessmen, the size of turkeys or cats, were scattered about, partially buried in the sand.

"Just the spot for a side-trip," he repeated, realizing already that the phrase would elicit no response and that, in her opinion, they had stopped just where they should have. Eurylochos, old buddy, plug my ears with wax! No friends on the scene, the wax can't be molded, the ropes have rotted, the fatal siren song is coming closer, the gulf's surface bristles with the knife-sharp cliffsides of Scylla and Charybdis: they converge, my still body slips into the whirlpool.

"Go on, take your pick—black or white?" She lifted a white knight and then a black elephant-shaped bishop, as though she was grabbing a cat by the scruff of the neck.

"Which one do you want?"

"I don't care."

"So you mean you don't care whether you win or lose?"

"I don't have any doubts about winning. I'm sure I play better than you do."

"You study chess theory?"

"Oh no! Sorry, I didn't mean to laugh, that's not at all appropriate. No theory, I rely strictly on practice. Sorry, I'm laughing again—I'm a little nervous. All right, so you're white. Just for the record, what's you name?"

"But I already told you, back there in the mountains."

"Sorry, I didn't catch it."

"My name's Alfred. I'm warning you in advance, my moves are

going to be simple, starting with e2-e4 . . . there—e2-e4.''

''Sounds like you're a good player. No more talk now, please, I need to concentrate . . . ''

True to her word, she froze in an attitude of concentration, nibbling the nail of her little finger, apparently pondering things as she stared at the board. From time to time she would raise her eyes, looking at Leo Bar and laughing. Her teeth and the whites of her eyes glinted in the intermittent flashes of moonlight. Like a Negress. What funny coquetry, he thought, I haven't seen anything like it for years. What in the hell was a chess game doing here? Obviously it's one of the features of this beach, a game people play in the summer. But just why has this chessboard with these pieces, big as domestic animals, made an appearance in my life? Why is it that wherever I poke my nose, something ridiculous develops? Madame Florence made a move—one which was necessary for launching the four-move combination known as the ''Kindermatt.''

''Checkmate, Madame Florence.''

''Are you joking, Monsieur Alfred?''

Eyes gazing into eyes, a fusion of smiles . . . A little bit of everything must lie behind the film of this night—sheer enchantment and petty squabbles, champagne, abortions, reasonably sane ideas, hormone pills, independence, humiliation, take me with you . . .

''No! Really, that's impossible, it's some Mediterranean fraud. You, Monsieur Alfred, are the real corsair—a cheat, a bandit! Let's switch now so you have black.''

They proceeded to change places, but as they passed on the same side of the board, they collided, losing their balance: laughter, hands outstretched, quick footwork, thoroughly graceful on the part of Madame Florence, while ''Monsieur Alfred'' moved like a crab, not devoid, however, of a certain impetuousness. Now I go first! Revenge, revenge!—e2-e4, e2-e4! Your turn, and don't rack your brain. The fact is, I can't even remember how many times in my life I've confronted this position. So you've outgrown surprises, have you? Every surprise is a cliché. But still they lie in wait for you. Who does? Surprises! Not exactly. Winning's made you a smart aleck! Madame Florence, you're checkmated again, and again in four moves. Monsieur Alfred, you're a creep, a lout, you're nothing but a brazen A-one bastard and can go to hell, I can't stand the sight of you!

She fell down on the sand next to the board and burst into sobs. Her hand thrashed like a fish, sweeping aside the idiotic plastic chessmen. With a shrug and a stiff vacant smile (he knew this expression quite well as one conveying a sense of things left undone—an expression he even liked because it frightened people away), Leo Bar made his retreat, taking a few steps on well-packed sand, and then sat down on a pile of rank seaweed, clasping his arms around his knees and gazing into the gulf's obscure murk. Sputters and swishes drifted across the sea as Scylla and Charybdis withdrew and dissolved into the night, no less the specters of death than tanks put out of action in the Sinai.

Anguish seized him. An imprecise phrase. He was filled with anguish. But that wasn't quite true. Anguish, genuine anguish, was probably still somewhere on the periphery, maybe it was even withdrawing right now with those trawlers which appeared in the fog like aching teeth or crags in myths of the blessed. Goddamn it, a triple mixed metaphor! The big anguish spilled across the horizon, enveloping all of Corsica, covering Sardinia; but its two little sisters were sitting here on the beach—one seizing him and the other filling him. They lacked the strength to get a tight grip and break him.

"Poor Leopold Bar, you're crying too," uttered Madame Florence, some distance away. "You poor man, is that any way to play chess with a woman?"

What a kindred spirit, he thought. Now we'll never part.

In the car she repaired her uncomplicated make-up and put on her Bolivian hat.

"You keep looking for a daughter, Leo Bar, but what you really need is mama . . . "

She had donned Freudian theory along with the hat. Soon he'd get her back to town, drop her off and forget her. As they dashed along the moonlit highway, her two frail knees gleamed in the dark. Why bother with the whole woman, if you could just have her knees?

In the lobby of the Hotel Fesch two men were playing cards, despite the late hour. One was the Negro from this afternoon, or rather, from last year, or maybe even the year before last. The other was a young man, wearing a leather jacket, with limpid scared eyes. Who in the hell has the limpid scared eyes!—the young man or the jacket? No escaping literature . . . The card players stared at Leo Bar as he entered feeling mean, with a solidly sculpted bearing enhanced by malice. Then the two men stood up, and the chance to walk past, pretending not to see them, had disappeared.

"Excuse me, Monsieur Bar, I've been waiting all day for you," said the young man, extending his hand. "I'm the journalist Bolinari—Auguste Bolinari."

Leo Bar, choked by the unexpected, found nothing better to do than grab with his left hand the wrist of the hand extended for a shake.

"Let me . . . even though it's late . . . "

Now a black hand moved in his direction, and this one was squarely met, palm to palm.

"Let me introduce the American writer Willy Barney. He's an old friend of ours—here on the island, I mean. He always makes his visits the same time you do."

"There's a third member of your party, isn't there?" Leo Bar asked with a hopeful look at a pair of little black ears which would make an appearance above the edge of the table and then drop out of sight again.

"Oh yes!" said Auguste Bolinari in a burst of obsequious laughter. "Let me introduce Charles Darwin."

An astonishing creature appeared in his hands: a black Pekinese with blue eyes like his master's, only more impudent. Little pink tongue, tiny sharp teeth.

"There we have it—the crowning point of evolution," said Leo Bar with an air of profundity.

The local journalist was happy: contact with the writer had been established. He wanted Monsieur Bar to rest assured that there would be no ambiguity about their relations, he promised—word of honor—there would be no interviews, he just wanted to invite you, Bar, and you, Barney, to supper . . . there's a wonderful restaurant not far away, with really fresh scampi, crab, oysters—all right from the ocean, the boats dock a hundred meters from the restaurant, everything comes straight from trawlers out of the Propriano gulf . . . Scylla and Charbydis, did you say? . . . thank you, Bar, that's another present . . . two like that in the first five minutes of contact . . . no, no, it's not an over-evaluation . . . let me assure you—no interviews . . . as a long-time admirer of your work, Bar, and yours too, Barney, I'd just like to show you some provincial island hospitality . . .

At this point Leopold Bar noticed a mirror reflecting the entire group of faces: the tall American in a tweed jacket and a turtleneck but barefoot; Charles Darwin, sucking his master's finger; Auguste Bolinari himself—short and svelte in tight jeans and his jacket, showing some resemblance to Napoleon, of course, but ridden with modesty; and finally, his own image—pale pinkish face with the slight double chin, the mouth half-open, and a wild tuft of hair (his cap had evidently gotten lost somewhere). A throng of human and animal life on a single square meter of overpopulated space. A step to the side could redress the balance.

"Excuse me, gentlemen, I respectfully decline the invitation."

"I see that you don't like us," said Willy Barney.

"Not much, I admit."

"What makes us worse than you?"

"Excuse me, I didn't express myself properly. I meant that I don't much care for *us*—the literati. Do you understand? Not you personally, Mr. Barney, certainly not you either, Monsieur Bolinari, or Darwin either, of course . . . "

The American was shifting restlessly on his shoeless feet, clenching and unclenching his fists. To judge by his age, he must have fought in World War II or at least in the Korean War. In any case, he'd probably done some military service, which meant that he regarded a fight as a good time.

"I was thinking about race," he said.

"Ahhh," said Bar.

"Well?" Barney asked harshly.

"Gentlemen!" exclaimed Bolinari.

"Arff!" piped up Darwin.

"I don't care much for your race either," said Bar, "or any other race, for that matter. In general, I don't care much for any of this, gentlemen, do you understand? I just don't, I just don't . . . "

The local journalist stood there mesmerized. The Negro was rocking back and forth on his heels. LB turned and walked away without saying goodbye or making an apology. He'd had it with empty etiquette, he needed to dive under a blanket, catch hold of some slender sprout, wail a little about the latest loss of solid ground and the demise of the island of Corsica, forgetting Leopold Bar for a few hours at least. But instead of turning right to go to the elevator, he went to the left and walked outside into the dribbling rain on Rue Fesch. He quickly passed his rented Renault, which had fallen asleep alongside some other little dozing cars, he found his grimy cap on the sidewalk, put it on his head, entered a narrow stair-stepped lane, where the only light came from the lanterns of ''private clubs'' (the bordellos), then re-emerged onto the Cours Napoleon, a major thoroughfare bathed in an unflagging nighttime light and patrolled by some of the central government's sub-machine-gunners, guarding the repose of the separatists. There he strode along, making entreaties to fate to start the wind and bring a break in the clouds, with just a few little stars, just some minimal signs of bygone life.

Auguste Bolinari came driving down the middle of the street in a sports car (the guy obviously wasn't hard up) and was waving a newspaper. This is for you, Monsieur Bar, for you! The Negro kept hot on Bar's trail, his fists digging into his pockets and knotted muscles twitching on his cheeks.

''Think you're the only one with biological problems?!'' he would yell every so often. ''Think you're the only one who loses teeth and hair, etcetera, etcetera?! Get off your high horse, Bar! Think you're the only high-and-mighty man around?''

LB started running and had soon shaken his pursuers. After escaping, he felt regrets about the men he had left behind and the unachieved cozy supper at a small seaside restaurant with confreres of the pen—two wonderful fellows and the marvelous little pooch Darwin, who would have sat on his knees, begging for shrimp tails. A fire would have been crackling on the hearth . . . He entered yet another empty street with the branches of huge palms hanging in wet rigidity and a bordello's red neon sign growling faintly in the night to announce ''Dodo's Place.'' Now there's the spot for you, if you're no longer capable of simple human associations. Go in and pay for regards!

Dodo turned out to be a Dandie Dinmont toy terrier. What bounciness! From the floor he took a flying leap onto the small table and fixed his round button eyes on Leo Bar. He was all aquiver with unintelligible but intense emotions.

''A martini, Dodo!''

Leo Bar was sitting there along amidst a couple dozen tables and some eighty chairs. The bordello had either known better days or else was preparing for a brighter future. At the moment it was empty, except for the bandit-bartender, whose gray head loomed into view behind the counter, and a young man of undetermined function who was roaming around the dance floor. He looked too casual to be a waiter with his loose-fitting cardigan, shirt unbuttoned to the waist, bracelets on his wrists, chain around his neck and charms dangling from a cowboy belt. In a bordello like this, with plush-covered chairs, a waiter would be wearing a uniform. On the other hand, a bordello visitor—a customer such as Bar—would not be behaving as this young man was, pacing back and forth with a springy gait, shrugging his shoulders, thrusting out his chest, menacingly curling his lip, muttering something under his breath, walking now and then over to the bar, grabbing the telephone receiver and uttering brief, nervous responses in his conversation—all the while vaguely reminding LB of someone he knew.

"A martini, please!" he repeated his order. Apparently nobody had heard him except for the dog. Dodo! Dodo! The terrier gave a yip and went dashing around the empty, dubious-smelling room, anxious to have his share of the action, but there was no action to be had.

Suddenly the door to the street burst open. Into Dodo's Place walked Auguste Bolinari with his chin held high, coldly reserved and offended. He came over, laid a newspaper on the table and left without saying a word. A copy of today's *Le Monde* lay before L. Bar. Some article had been marked with a red felt-tip pen. Leo Bar's mind guiltily composed a smooth statement: "Auguste Bolinari, you pure-hearted soul and lover of literature, forgive me. The entire existence of degenerates like me is supported by pure hearts such as yourself. But what can I do if you just don't interest me?"

The bartender, limping slightly on a leg made lame in days of brigandage, brought him a martini in a glass with a nasty-looking ring of sugar around the rim. Some suspicious tidbit rested at the bottom.

"Is Dodo old?" asked Leo Bar.

"I'm already past sixty, the boy here's thirty, and the little mutt's ten, which makes him the oldest." The bartender grinned and gave the rickety table a swipe with a scrub-brush which reeked of disinfectant, making the martini wobble and nearly spill. "Life moves right along, sir. It's a relentless thing. Time has a way of

. . . ''

"I was just asking about Dodo," interrupted LB. All he needed, to add to his own philosophical tripe, were some words of wisdom from the chief of this den of iniquity.

"We're all 'Dodo,' sir," the man explained, "all three of us."

His smiles, the bows and use of the word "sir" did not convey any particular feeling of good will but simply expressed a professional courtesy, somewhat antiquated in the era of socialism. He had barely walked away, when the thirty-year-old Dodo came over and demonstrated a totally different style.

"You interested in some entertainment?" His hand moved abruptly behind his back, toward his pants' pocket: what was he going to pull out—a gun, a knife? A notebook, it was. "Here's your choice!"

Some color photos fell from the notebook onto the table, displaying specimens of the three principal races of continental land—a Negress, a Chinese woman and a German.

"I'll take all three," said Leo Bar.

"Meaning what exactly?" The young man brought his menacing face close to Bar. The question of resemblance was settled: it was Napoleon Bonaparte with a small nose disfigured during a former boxing career.

"Well, why not?" mumbled Leo Bar. "Let me have all three."

Dodo raised his eyes toward the ceiling, moved his lips as he made a mental calculation and then tore a sheet from the notebook with the exact figure of 1875 francs, "paid in advance."

"Certainly, certainly." Leo Bar took from his pocket the money he had changed that morning and scattered it all over the table in little wads. The sight resembled flotsam on a beach.

A phonograph struck up "Gulfstream," a song from the '30s. Someone opened a door covered with plush to match the walls, and three horrendous girls appeared on the dance floor one by one, wearing transparent burnooses. They were escorted by the toy terrier, Dodo-in-chief. He was having his moment in the sun, performing like a circus pony, prancing jauntily on his tiny old feet in time to "Gulfstream," holding his pointed nose high in the air and casting a look of triumphant pride at the audience—that is to say, at Leopold Bar. After lazily circling the floor a few times, the girls got down to the business of unfastening each other's buttons and snaps, untying bows and ribbons, without stopping their dance. The German became entangled in her lacey underpants and fell onto one knee but then hopped back up and started dancing again with surprising agility and zeal. Leo Bar delved into the newspaper, reading the article marked by Bolinari's felt-tip pen.

"Leopold Bar's new book *Two-Faced but Honest* lays open before us vast empty spaces of this writer's extraordinary spirit, creating the impact of a stalactical cave . . . " he read. "It would be no exaggeration to say that Leo Bar is probably the most important essayist alive in Europe today . . . "

"What's wrong? Not interested?" asked the young Dodo, taking a seat at the table. The tiny table rocked under his elbow. His biceps twitched under the cardigan.

"Who says I'm not interested?" asked Leo Bar.

"I said so!!" Dodo's eyes burned through Bar's fragile skin, sounding out every fold with the supersensitive but blind instruments of pure hate. "Maybe you'd like to see something else, mister?"

"I just might," said Leo Bar, laying the newspaper aside. "Don't you have one other whore? It seems to me that the star of your . . . uh . . . theatre, yes—theatre, must be a certain Madame Florence."

What power Dodo had packed in his fingers! In one swift motion he had grabbed Leo Bar by the shirt collar, making a noisy rip.

"You rotten scum, don't you know who Madame Florence is? She's Captain Bouzzoni's granddaughter! Come on, let's go!"

"Where?" asked Bar with interest as he stood up. What a sassy character! What bizarre nerve the man had!

"Where? To the sea!" Dodo was smiling and trembling with pleasurable anticipation of the reprisals ahead.

They went outside. There as he took gulps of clammy feltlike air under the drooping palms, Bar recalled that in Corsican an invitation to go to the sea carries the force of awful swear-words. The islanders had never had any love on the element which made them islanders—that boundless expanse, laying claim to lock, stock and barrel, to their buildings, to their very existence, so they thought.

"You're wrong if you think I'm going to give up without a fight," L. Bar said to Dodo. "I'm two-faced but honest, weak but brave. The vast empty spaces of my extraordinary spirit have the impact of a stalactical cave."

"We'll see about that in just a second," snarled Dodo, brandishing his fists, leading with his right as he threw a series of short punches and a few long ones at the essayist standing a couple of paces away.

"I see you're a boxer," laughed Bar. The thought of resistance was quickly giving way to the idea of capitulation. "The calmer I act, the less hell to pay. Maybe his fists will get stuck in this dough I'm made of?"

"Why are you talking to me in English? Why should I have to speak English with you, you bastard!" Dodo was bobbing up and down, sparring straight away with the five shadows which now radiated from his body along a white wall.

"You prefer French? Were you a champion boxer in the mother country?"

"Phuuu!" Dodo suddenly made a face, as though he had taken a blow to the liver. "I beat Laroque, Lecrème, Charonne, and then for the final I see some Berber show up. Excuse me, I said, what kind of a Frenchman's that—black as a boot? And they tell me, 'You're from the overseas territories, too.' I was a victim of demagogues with their half-ass sneering at working people! Ever since then I've hated the guts of guys like you!"

Dancing in closer, bringing his elbows forward and hiding his face behind imaginary gloves, he started driving the essayist into a corner between two illuminated shop windows, where at least a hundred faces of Napoleon Bonaparte in assorted sizes stood on display. Thoroughly delighted with the existential situation, Bar took a solid poke at Dodo's cheekbone, promptly dislocating all his fingers.

A minute later, Leopold Bar was slowly crawling away, hugging the wall as he moved toward the beach. The obliging Dodo had given Bar a first-rate workout: his face was swollen, his ribs ached, and, worst of all, the near-champion had broken two of his expensive porcelain teeth. Like the essayist's spirit, his mouth was now reminiscent of a stalactical cave. The fleeing Dodo had sobbed with the shame of the mighty, while LB cried on his hands and knees with the pride of the meek. After all, he had not just given up, turning into a dough-ball, but had waved his arms right up to the end . . . there had been a fight, rather than a case of assault and battery . . . he'd been in a fight. The dark night runs a test of her creatures' masculine qualities. The test had taken place. A nocturnal creature with a swollen face cries on the sand, but nobody has seen him yet—a blessing!

"Would you happen to have a cigarette," he heard in Russian. "*Fumer, fumer,* some smoke?" added the giant now towering over him.

Leopold Bar fumbled in his pocket for a pack of Pall Malls which had been badly crushed in the nocturnal test of "masculine qualities." What would Russians be doing here? The man turned out to be a player on a basketball team who had been left behind in Ajaccio after coming down with a stomach ailment, and for a hefty sum they had removed his appendix at the local hospital.

"It was this long," the basketball player said wistfully, demonstrating with his huge palm which was illuminated by the mangled stub of a cigarette.

So now we have Russia, thought Leopold Bar, swaying back and forth, restraining his moans, swaying back and forth, listening to the story of an operation. Only Russia could have topped off this night. Those innumerable Uncle Yashas and Auntie Tosis ... LB recollected with anguish his trips to Russia in search of his biological and philosophical roots. How he had burned, how he had tried to penetrate the whole incomprehensible entity, right back to the year Marx died. The mover of minds on a global scale had died a provisional death, but what was Russia, minus his influence? In short order, of course, Marx had come to life again, but Bar no longer yielded to the passing fancies of the Western spirit. He had turned back to the Orient, to the wisdom teeth of all mankind, and he had lingered there until his own personal molars started to hurt. Now the whole matter brought searing pain. Russia, Russia! Cast by some hand to the mercy of fate . . . But why should I feel sorry for an alien country? I left Russia, but I've left a hundred other countries too and never felt sorry for any of them. Yes, I left Russia behind like a part of my youth, I shaved her off, like the beard I never wore. What's become of them, all those Tolstoevskys? Here was Russia—a boy in a giant's body, greedily smoking a chain of half-demolished Pall Malls and recounting his tale about the removal of his appendix on the island of Corsica.

"Have you ever had appendicitis? It's pretty creepy, having a whopper like that inside you. Big as my hand it was! You're probably wondering what I'm doing out here at night on the beach? So

I'll explain. The operation's given me a colossal case of insomnia. An appendix like that was a real jolt. I never suspected it could be so big. It's mind-boggling! To tell the truth, knowing that it's *out* adds to the shock. It's a staggering surprise, a complete mind-boggler!—knowing that some unforeseen part of my body has been removed and is no longer there any more. What else do I have inside me, what other unexpected things? With this thought in my head, comrade, I'll be flying to Liège tomorrow, we're playing a game for the world championship.''

''Which championship?'' wheezed Leo Bar.

''The *world* championship.''

''Is that really possible, my lad? The world is a monument, a palm tree, four scruffy dogs, a chipped porcelain tooth, the liner *Napoleon*, a chestnut donkey, millions of automobiles, and finally your appendix. Merely touch all that trash, and it pours down on your head. A *Weltänschauung,* a philosophy, a disposition of mind—the whole thing collapses, comes raining down, makes a big snafu! I don't understand how you can try to win the championship of something so monstrously rotten.''

''Maybe you need some help?'' asked the basketball player. ''From the time I was a child, I was raised with the idea that a person ought to help anyone who needs it, but I've got to admit I'm always glad when nobody needs it. Thanks for the cigarettes, I'm off. I'll keep in mind your question about the world championship. But I'm glad it didn't pop into my head by itself. So long!''

Abandoned by one and all, including Russia, Leo Bar writhed spasmatically on the wet sand. The murky pre-dawn skies drew near overhead, not a cloud to be seen, not a patch of light—just murk, and it was drawing near. In the meantime the heavy wet sand was pulling from below, sucking him into the void. Qualifying as the void itself, the sand was doing its best to make him sink deeper and deeper, it wanted to fill the void with the pain-racked body of Leopold Bar.

''Oh Heavens, my first and last icon, how empty you are, how hopeless and inescapable your emptiness! How bitter to look at the heavens at this hour, at this moment, and to realize that I made no mistake, thinking nothing has ever been up there for anybody.'' Softly whimpering farewell, Bar shot one last glance at the heavens and realized that he had made a mistake after all: there *was* something up there. Over the gulf in the pre-dawn murk a large dirigible was drifting into sight. It came fully into view from nose to tail and hung suspended—a dark gray, nearly black dirigible, afloat in the murk in slightly blurred outline. It was hanging there before the dawn, before Leopold Bar, high in the heavens above the water, simply hanging there, asking no questions, giving no answers.

Radiant light brought Leo Bar back to a waking state. Everything around him was brightly shining—the dancing waves in the gulf, the glass windows of dancing boats, the crest of the mountainous coast and the white hotels along the quay, moving automobiles, a couple of Coca-Cola bottles dumped in the sand, the sand itself, the flighty tattered clouds, a plane traveling the Ajaccio-Nice route, the boundless sky, and (naturally) the source of all this radiance—the Sun. The essayist got to his feet, fully confident that he too was shining or, at any rate, that he had a shine in the whites of his eyes, hidden beneath swollen but shining lids; his brain was shining; and in his stalactical cave (just wait, you bastards at *Le Monde*!) sunshine and ozone were making merry. He took a few steps toward town and then saw the bronze bust of a simple, brave man standing erect on the beach. The pedestal bore the inscription: ''Navy Captain Etienne Bouzonni. Died testing a dirigible in December 1907.'' He looked at the straight nose and the sharply etched chin raised in calm but proud resolution, displaying a trace of kindred feeling. If you believe in Santa Claus stories about the ''alter ego,'' then you might also be prone to believe that a captain like this was alive inside your limp sniveling dough.

He proceeded along the quay and saw the Square of the First Consul coming into sight, followed by the market under regal palms. Up ahead, with her clogs clacking, Madame Florence was walking along the sidewalk in the same direction. She was pushing an oversized stroller containing a pair of baby twins, and in addition she had four dogs in tow—the enormous Athos, as scared as ever, with his legs nearly failing him; that highly courageous but depraved creature, Dodo the toy terrier; the pampered wee Pekinese, Charles Darwin; and the peevish spaniel Juliette. Without accelerating to overtake this marvelous spectacle of a woman with a pair of twins and four dogs, Leo Bar went along with them all the way to the market, where Madame Florence went shopping for artichokes, avocadoes and kohlrabi, piling her purchases in the stroller at the little feet of the twins, who made soft burbles the whole time, lying side by side with their eyes shining.

"Madame Florence," he called softly.

"Monsieur?" She turned toward him but wasn't quite identical to his acquaintance of yesterday.

"Strong resemblance, but it's somebody else," realized the exultant essayist. The dogs—all four of them—were also looking at him. Strong resemblance, but they were different ones. How amazing! "Excuse me, madame! Have a good morning!" he said with a bow and then headed resolutely for the nearest Agence de Voyages. As he came closer, he saw with increasing clarity his reflection mirrored in the travel agent's window. Despite the black eyes and general puffiness of the face, he looked like himself. How splendid to be yourself or at least look like yourself. How splendid to tend to your own business, even if it was only writing some little book. In fact, how splendid it was—ha ha ha!—to write essays, *essays*—poking a bit of fun at your companions in life, both human and animal, because animals too derive benefits from books, even if they can't read. How splendid it was to fill readers with anguish and gloom, even if it made them throw your books aside and then turn to caressing one another or their animals, or else go to the market and buy artichokes, or else, finally, to take journeys from capital cities to islands and back again. For after all, there really was more to the world than the gloomy empty spaces of literature.

"Excuse me for bringing the story to such a preposterous conclusion, but could I have you arrange a plane ticket with an extremely complicated itinerary?" Leo Bar asked the Corsican clerk in the travel agency. "Let's suppose, for instance, Corsica-London-Moscow-Singapore-New York-Warsaw-Iceland-Rome-Corsica?"

"Itineraries as complicated as you like, monsieur," answered the modest little Bonaparte, smiling politely.

November 1977-January 1978, Ajaccio-Moscow

The Four Temperaments

(A Comedy in Ten Tableaux)

Translated by Boris Jakim

From the author: Among my other homeless works, *The Four Temperaments* is perhaps the most homeless. Tender feelings nurtured for eleven years have induced me to drag this piece under the roof of Metropol.

CHARACTERS:

Chol Erik
Sang Vinik
Phleg Matik
Melan Cholik
Razrailov
Cyber
Eagle
Nina
First Lady
Second Lady
Third Lady
Fourth Lady
Love Triangle
Katyusha
Emelya
Gutik
Stage Manager
Uncle Vitya
Fefelov

(*The action takes place first in the distant future, then outside of space and time, and finally in the present.*)

I

(*Chol Erik moves in a frenzy before a white screen. He is dressed in black. He wears dark glasses. He keeps stopping to face the audience, rocks back and forth, raises his arm, as if trying to shield himself from the blinding lights.*)

CHOL ERIK:

Nine days this sun sets,
All is in blood, all is dead . . .
What dull bloodletting!
It's time to go to hell!
And the waves, the waves!
Admire, brothers, this dumb flock of lambs,
These crested idiots that roll
To the foot of stone idols,
To concrete towers the color of bile!
And the helicopters that hang over the marketplace,
Gloomier than beetles in compost—Oh, how disgusting!
No, it's enough! It's time to leave!
But my departure has nothing to do with
Fame, faded honor, or betrayal.
Rather, it's this color, this glum light,
These colors which would make me howl, brothers,
If that were fitting for a
Champion of forehead blows.
But who remembers? No, it has nothing to do with this,
With memory . . . Well, it's time! Farewell!
I've had it!
(*He looks down on the waves that roll beneath the bridge, raises his arms in a mute violent curse, and extends one leg over the bridge railing. Razrailov appears.*)

RAZRAILOV:

At least take off your glasses!

CHOL ERIK:

What the devil! Who is that

Prevents me from dropping into Charon's ferry?
Have you forgotten who I am? Well, I can remind you.
RAZRAILOV:
What for? You're the master of forehead blows.
CHOL ERIK:
I'm remembered! Not everyone has forgotten.
All the same, I don't have time to listen to you.
And cut the bull about my glasses!
RAZRAILOV:
Listen, we remember your outbursts,
The fact that you liked to rip off masks.
(*He giggles aside.*)
Our generation, believe me, has
Retained its memory.
CHOL ERIK:
That's not the point!
What do I care about memory when this damn city
Is painted in such vile colors!
RAZRAILOV:
Take off your glasses! Things are not that bleak.
Make the effort, take the risk!
CHOL ERIK:
(*Takes off his glasses.*)
Why, you know,
It's a little better, a mite more calm.
Everything looks a bit less like a slaughterhouse . . .
RAZRAILOV:
(*Grabs him by the arm.*)
Are you ready to serve the Experiment?
In the name of the positive program?
In the name of your former ideals?
In the name of the masses?
(*He grabs the glasses.*)
CHOL ERIK:
But I don't understand!

(*The white screen fades. A yellow screen is lit up, on the background of which, his arms dangling, stands Phleg Matik, dressed all in yellow.*)

PHLEG MATIK:

Mama didn't return . . . and where's kitty?
The bouillon is spoiled and I will hang myself, maybe . . .
Or maybe tonight I'll read a book
As they used to do in the good old nineteenth century.
(*He doesn't move.*)
Maybe I won't find this book,
Just as I won't find my papa who has gone away . . .
Well, in that case I'll just keep looking out the window
At the acid gray monument across the way,
At the ''We'll improve your mood'' club,
A den of liars and con artists.
(*Makes an indecisive sniffing noise with his nose.*)
No, it would be better for me to hang myself.
Let me soap a good strong rope
As they used to soap ropes in the good old days
Of the twentieth, twenty-first, and twenty-third centuries,
Which were so tranquil . . . Take care, guys . . .
(*Razrailov appears.*)

RAZRAILOV:

Stop!
I beseech you to stop your
Inexorable advance towards the noose!
Believe me, friend, the bouillon would smell terrific
If you would only add some hair restorer.
Your kitten long ago became
An aromatic bar of soap
With which a lovely girl laves her breasts,
And your sweet-smelling mama, my friend,
Will be replaced by the scientific experiment.
Stop!

PHLEG MATIK:

I've long since stopped because of your command.

RAZRAILOV:

Put on these glasses! The world will be transformed
And the acid gray monument across the way
Will show you the splendor of the age!
(*Puts the glasses on Phleg Matik.*)

PHLEG MATIK:
  Why, it's true.
    (*Takes a good look.*)
  The heavy idol has suddenly taken on a silver tint.
  And that squiggle in the marvelous sky
  Reminds me of my kitty's tail . . .
RAZRAILOV:
  Well, then, let's go!

(*The yellow screen fades. A violet screen is lit up, on the background of which Melan Cholik, dressed all in green, wanders back and forth, wringing his hands. He's wearing glasses.*)

MELAN CHOLIK:
  The day fades in the orangery,
  The cutlets simmer in the pan . . .
  My TV set fades,
  The set I inherited from the faded ages,
  Witnesses of history that has faded . . .
  And here the works of youth fade
  And mature matrons fade
  And the Institute of Rejuvenation fades
  And the fading grass fades . . .
  And the sun fades and in myriads of
  Faded years the Galaxy fades away . . .
  Those who are fading inexorably move
  From the beginning to the end of their sentence.
  Only my anguish doesn't fade
  And now I must cut it short
  By taking the poison of the terrible fugu fish
  Against a background of ash gray flowers.
    (*He makes several movements that imply the coming of the end.*)
RAZRAILOV:
  Does it not appear to you that in this fading
  Are concealed the seeds of renaissance?
  That man's creative forces will . . .
MELAN CHOLIK:
  Excuse me, what do you have on your head?

RAZRAILOV:

Why, on my head I have a cap.

A wonderful cap of the latest fashion.

MELAN CHOLIK:

Yes, yes, I see. But beneath the cap?

RAZRAILOV:

My hair.

MELAN CHOLIK:

Yes, I see.

But beneath the hair?

RAZRAILOV:

Beneath the hair is skin.

My own skin.

MELAN CHOLIK:

Yes, yes. Skin. But beneath the skin?

RAZRAILOV:

Beneath my skin is my skull.

MELAN CHOLIK:

Skull! Skull! O God, God, God!

(*His legs begin to buckle.*)

RAZRAILOV:

(*Raising Melan Cholik.*)

Aren't you ashamed! I see you're disturbed

By the most minor of problems, by the contemptible danse macabre!

And this in our age, on the threshold

Of important, revolutionary events.

How primitive! This is no way to be!

Take off your glasses! More optimism!

Let's go forward on the path of the Experiment!

MELAN CHOLIK:

(*Screws up his eyes, without his glasses.*)

Yes, yes. Forward. But I don't understand . . .

(*The violet screen fades. A red screen is lit up, on the background of which, busily rubbing his hands, Sang Vinik, dressed all in white, walks back and forth.*)

SANG VINIK:

And so, my mood is again marvelous!
For how many years have I drunk my fill of life.
And apprehended with my every cell
The reason of the world and the importance of being.
My stomach is in harmony with my digestion
and I love cherry preserves,
And my heart is moved by love
And chases the blood through the vessels as always.
I alternate rest and work,
Love and sport, kefir and the joy
Of alcoholic drinks. I press buttons,
Pluck flowers, inhale their aroma,
Sing in a choir, eat regularly . . .
I'm pleased by all, calm and cordial,
The life of the party, the joy of preference.
So let me with one decisive stroke
Put an end to ugliness once and for all.
   (*Takes a pistol from his pocket and presses it to his forehead.*)
For if I can understand the reason
For all that exists in the world, then why
Can't I understand the reason of this bullet
Which has waited so long
For me to press the trigger?
   (*Razrailov appears.*)

RAZRAILOV:

   (*Aside.*)
I fear that this is the most difficult case.
Red-cheeked, healthy, handsome, and sanguine:
A real suicidal nut.
   (*To Sang Vinik.*)
Listen, my good friend, do you have time?

SANG VINIK:

Forgive me, whom do I have the honor—

RAZRAILOV:

I am Razrailov.
I would like to warn you against
Opinions that are too optimistically vulgar.

I swear to you that the world is far more interesting
Than it appears to you,
And that beneath the outer veil
There is concealed something that—
SANG VINIK:
Cut the bull!
RAZRAILOV:
For example, what do you have on your head?
SANG VINIK:
Well, a cap.
Let us say, a cap of the latest fashion.
RAZRAILOV:
Yes, yes, I see. But beneath the cap?
SANG VINIK:
Beneath the cap is my hair.
RAZRAILOV:
Yes, I see.
And beneath the hair?
SANG VINIK:
Skin. My very own skin.
RAZRAILOV:
Yes, yes. Skin. And beneath the skin?
SING VINIK:
Beneath the skin is my skull.
RAZRAILOV:
Well, you see! A skull! Skull! Skull!
SANG VINIK:
Wow, how interesting! How horrible!
A little terrifying! A skull! Wow!
Let me confess, old boy, that I never
Considered things in this light . . .
RAZRAILOV:
Put on these glasses!
(Hands him the glasses.)
The world will be transformed
And you'll see tragedy everywhere
And you'll find things are more interesting
And entertaining . . .

SANG VINIK
(*Wearing the glasses.*)
You're right.
I see pain and trepidation and alarm . . .
I must live! To fight for optimism!
RAZRAILOV:
(*Heatedly.*)
All this is so and I propose
That you head the vanguard with a few chosen.
That you go forward on the path of Experiment!
Do you agree?
SANG VINIK:
(*Passionately.*)
A wonderful idea!

(*All the lights fade.*)

II

(*The stage is lit from within. It's empty. All kinds of mechanical gadgets are visible: pulleys, winches and wheels ... Several Workmen appear. In view of the audience they begin to assemble the set, talking loudly all the while.*)

UNCLE VITYA: (*An elderly workman.*) Where are you taking that dolly, Emelya? If the Eagle hits it, he'll be killed.
EMELYA: (*A young workman.*) But where should I take it?
UNCLE VITYA: Take it to the left.
EMELYA: I'm not experienced enough, Uncle Vitya. This is something they didn't teach us in the Philosophy Department.
GUTIK: (*A middle-aged workman.*) What's going on, Uncle Vitya? It turns out they've approved the Eagle's role? It turns out they don't give a damn about the union?
UNCLE VITYA: Well, that's exactly right. They've approved it. To be precise, three days ago, on Tuesday, Serchanov and I were hanging around the prop room after work, and the boss got a call. They had approved it.
KATYUSHA: (*A girl worker.*) How I pity Evgeny Aleksandrovich!

EMELYA: Forgive me, Katyusha. Why is it you pity him so? A hearty man, full of zest . . .

UNCLE VITYA: Yesterday, Thursday that is, he tells me, "This it seems is my final role, Uncle Vitya" . . .

KATYUSHA: I pity Evgeny Aleksandrovich so much! For some reason he's very dear to me, very appealing! And who needs this Eagle's role?

GUTIK: This is something we'll air before the Local Committee. Put it down, Emelya. Bring it back . . . move it to the side!

EMELYA: How will we fasten the backdrop, Uncle Vitya? The Eagle's role in the show is both immanent and transcendent. Nobody can handle it better than Evgeny Aleksandrovich.

UNCLE VITYA: You should blabber a bit less, philosopher! You've been on the stage a week and already you're an expert on roles. Hold the rope steady and don't move. (*The Stage Manager, a woman, enters.*)

STAGE MANAGER: Uncle Vitya. I have a terrible problem. How will I fasten the backdrop?

UNCLE VITYA: You have to fasten it with zhgentel bolts, Alisia Ivanovna, with triple brackets and with mulerons.

STAGE MANAGER: But where can we get all this stuff, Uncle Vitya? We don't even have plain bolts.

UNCLE VITYA: That's your business, Alisia Ivanovna. I no longer have the strength to wine and dine Fefelov. Fefelov's tastes are not simple. He likes fine Mukusani wine with his cigar, cognac with his coffee, and some little gift at the end of the dinner . . . some little this or that. . . . But I've exhausted my financial possibilities.

STAGE MANAGER: Maybe we can get by with things the way they are.

UNCLE VITYA: Maybe so. I'm only afraid that in the third act the whole thing is going to fall apart and then we'll have some real fun.

STAGE MANAGER: O, horrors!

UNCLE VITYA: Here, tell Gutik, if he can get some dough from the Local Committee, I'll try to squeeze three or four cans of mulerons out of Fefelov.

GUTIK: The Local Committee won't fall for any of your tricks.

UNCLE VITYA: That's how it is. Well, let's knock off, fellows!

(*Having taken hammers, pincers, and the rest of their things, the Workmen leave the stage. The last to leave is the Stage Manager, Alisia Ivanovna. While already in the wings she looks doubtfully and anxiously at the decorations.*)

III

(*A room sparkling white and saturated with a blue glow. It resembles a laboratory in a science-fiction novel. A huge window behind which is empty bluish space. Four rotating armchairs with soft elbow-rests. Over each of the chairs is a screen in a strange shape. Near one of the walls stands an improbably complex cybernetic device with a multitude of buttons, controls, etc.*

Enter Sang Vinik, Melan Cholik, Chol Erik, and Phleg Matik. They stop in center stage and look about, puzzled. Behind them enters Razrailov, who is breathing with difficulty. He coughs and spits out the window.)

RAZRAILOV: (*Aside.*) What a damned mess! If it weren't for the Experiment I would never have gotten involved. And with a gang of suicides. (*Arranges his tie and quickly combs his hair.*) And so friends, our long ascent is completed. We are in the holy of holies, at the source of the Great Experiment. Here, precisely here, will arise the future of mankind with its unlimited possibilities, and here we, the pioneers of modern science—

CHOL ERIK: Cut the bull! We demand that you explain to us the nature of the experiment. Do you think we've spent so many days climbing the stairs to hear typical demagoguery?

PHLEG MATIK: The main thing is that we've made it. Where's the toilet, citizens?

MELAN CHOLIK: (*Looking downward, into the window.*) O God, I can't see the ground!

SANG VINIK: This is all great, but where are we, Razrailov?

RAZRAILOV: (*His feelings are hurt.*) You've interrupted me. You haven't let me develop my thought. This undisciplined citizen here—

CHOL ERIK: Express yourself more precisely. We've had it up to here with pretty speeches!

RAZRAILOV: (*Screams.*) Don't yell at your savior! If it weren't for me you'd be bobbing up and down like a log in the Gultimoor canal! Citizens, I ask you to observe the one-leader principle even under the conditions of the Great Experiment. Don't forget I'm your director and savior. And so, I ask you to sit down in these chairs, which will be your work places. (*He seats his collaborators.*) Wonderful! Now, citizens of the future mankind, the hope of all six continents, I will explain to you your great mission.

CHOL ERIK: More demagoguery?

RAZRAILOV: I'll exclude you if you keep on interrupting! Friends, in the course of the hundreds of centuries of the existence of civilization the earth has sucked up into itself the vicious ideas, temptations, thoughts and dreams of thousands of generations. Therefore, despite colossal technological achievement, true progress is impossible and I, Razrailov, devoted defender of progress in all epochs, you must know from literature—there lives in me with his flaming eyes the angel of death Azrael . . . this is metaphor, of course, a hint at the laser . . . pardon me for the digression. A colossal break is occurring between the progress of cybernetic machines and the stagnation or maybe even the regression, alas, of mankind. Citizens, here's my idea, supported and financed by the Academy of Long-Short-Life and also by United-Kvas-Limited. A tower has been constructed on the apex of which we now find ourselves. It is of a height which we may call significant. I ask you to pay attention to this object. (*From his pocket he takes a marble and tosses it out the window.*) Now again pay attention to me. At this height you, the participants of the Experiment, will no longer be affected by the miasmas of earth; and, secondly, the influence of height, generated by the most novel stimulator, which I will command from my control room, will augment your mental capacities and creative forces to a colossal degree. And you will be able to control in turn the complex cyber. Thus, the circuit will be closed, the main problem of the future will be solved. A new era! Dawn! A rainbow! Elevated individuums, cyber-people . . . (*He continues to speak but no sound comes from him. He gesticulates, dances . . .*)

SANG VINIK: What's with him?

CHOL ERIK: Forgive me, I can't bear such pathetic scenes. I switched him off. I pressed a button I found under the table and he was switched off.

PHLEG MATIK: The height . . . it's understandable . . . has an effect.

MELAN CHOLIK: How terrifying it is—a man without sound! They say that in ancient times there was a sort of cinema that—

SANG VINIK: Yes, yes, old buddy, just imagine—now this is grand! Not long ago I read that in the past there were films even without odor and without flesh.

CHOL ERIK: But think of the people who lived then! Giants!

PHLEG MATIK: They say that in those days you couldn't even feel up your favorite starlet.

SANG VINIK: Friends, I propose that we become acquainted. My name is Sang Vinik. (*To Chol Erik.*) And you?

CHOL ERIK: You don't remember me? Take a good look! My name is Chol Erik. Well? No response?

MELAN CHOLIK: Don't tell me it's possible to be famous in our time? My name is Melan Cholik and even I'm not counting on anything.

PHLEG MATIK: My name is Phleg Matik. My papa is honoris causa of the university of the city of Bakov, but he disappeared somewhere, and my mama . . . citizens, where's the toilet?

SANG VINIK: Listen, old buddy, how did you get here?

CHOL ERIK: None of your business! I don't go prying into your soul.

SANG VINIK: Forgive me. I also prefer to keep my mouth shut. And you, Melan?

MELAN CHOLIK: What can I tell you? I'm a victim of the illusion known as reality. Razrailov appeared at the last moment.

PHLEG MATIK: But I can tell you my story. The thing is that mama disappeared and kitty got lost and the bouillon was spoiled and I . . .

SANG VINIK: Shut up, Phleg! I understand everything. Well, friends, since it's happened that we're up on the tower and our leader is switched off for the time being, let's play ''chirishek-pupyrishek-bubo.''

CHOL ERIK: A great idea! I like you, Sang!

MELAN CHOLIK: Alas, I've just about forgotten this forbidden game.

PHLEG MATIK: (*Suddenly aroused. Merrily.*) Mama and I used to play it all the time, with kitty as a third . . .

SANG VINIK: I'll begin. (*He shows Chol Erik his fingers curled into a ring.*) Chirishek!

CHOL ERIK: First class! Let me think. (*Thinks.*) Pupyrishek! (*Shows Melan Cholik in succession: "ears," "nose," four fingers and a copper key.*)

MELAN CHOLIK: A complicated move. (*Thinks.*) Ah yes, I've found it. (*To Phleg Matik.*) At night burned entered Napoleon four chrysanthemums and a bouton. (*Shows "horns."*)

PHLEG MATIK: Wow, what a move . . . (*Thinks. Then plugs his ears and whistles.*) Bubo! (*Suddenly weak. Says languidly.*) There, I've got you.

EVERYBODY: Bravo! A masterpiece! What a simple and powerful move! (*They applaud. Razrailov, continuing his fiery soundless speech, also applauds.*)

SANG VINIK: And so, you have twenty seven points, you have eleven, you have eighteen and I have fourteen. You begin, Phleg, your serve. (*From below one hears a muffled explosion. Everyone jumps up.*)

CHOL ERIK: It's begun. To arms!

SANG VINIK: (*Runs to window. Looks down.*) Below there's a rosy cloud that looks like a peony. How about that!

MELAN CHOLIK: O horrors! A fading peony!

PHLEG MATIK: That thing has hit the earth. (*They all look down, then turn away from the window.*)

RAZRAILOV: . . . without compromises and condescension! The rainbow above our heads! Forward, cyber-people! (*Combs his hair, smiles impudently, straightens his tie.*) Well my friends, have you rested? Don't think, Chol, that I'm in your hands. Rather it's you who are in mine. And now let's get to work. To your places! We are born to turn fable into reality! (*The collaborators silently take their places in the armchairs. Razrailov walks up to each of them in turn, squeezes their hands, intimately whispers to each "congratulations," and then leaves the stage with the measured stride of an officer. The Temperaments sit silently, looking straight ahead. Above them screens begin to fluoresce. A quiet but monstrous music begins to play.*)

CHOL ERIK: (*In an altered, metallic voice.*) Problem number one: From reservoir A into reservoir B there is a daily inflow of 400 cubic meters of water and 300 cubic meters of wine. From reservoir C there is no inflow. The problem is to calculate the number of young sturgeon in the ground reservoirs of Antartica. I am switching on Cyber. (*With a sharp sudden whirr Cyber is switched on and lit up.*)

CYBER: Hello, fellows! Congratulations on the beginning of the Experiment. The transmission is concluded.

PHLEG MATIK: I begin. It is necessary to establish the legitimate requirements of every contemporary man with regard to young sturgeon of the ground reservoirs.

MELAN CHOLIK: I continue. According to the chromosome theory of Bonch-Marienhof, by changing the cell expresses an absolutely small number, vanishing into a protoplasm of nose type. Let us discard this. From this follows: eson, seon, neso, a trapezoid with a fire within.

CYBER: A small correction. Logos. The transmission is concluded.

SANG VINIK: The result: An infinitely small number, vanishing into nose, taking into account the needs of Lester Bot at night after drinking, hemoglobin 90—young sturgeon zero minus one. The end.

CYBER: What bright men you are. The transmission is concluded. (*Behind the window in the blue emptiness slowly flies some heavy body. It appears for a moment that someone is looking into the laboratory. All the collaborators turn around and look out the window.*) That's Eagle. He always flies here. Don't pay attention. The transmission is concluded.

PHLEG MATIK: Problem number two. How many devils and foxes can simultaneously fit on the top of a pin? (*Suddenly the right corner of the set falls to the side. The Temperaments turn sharply and look in that direction. Katyusha is standing there. With her head raised, she is looking toward the back of the stage. Next to her is Emelya.*)

EMELYA: Katyusha, I wanted to be sure about tomorrow. Don't forget, I get paid—

KATYUSHA: Wait, Emelya. Look! He's coming down! (*Uncle Vitya runs out.*)

UNCLE VITYA: (*In a whistling whisper.*) You idiots, don't you see that the side of the set has fallen down! (*Gutik runs out.*)

GUTIK: (*Merrily.*) We'll make a note of this. A violation of working discipline! (*A hunched figure passes by, wrapped in a robe from which stick dark brown feathers. A very strange figure.*)

STAGE MANAGER: (*Peering out from the wings.*) Horrors, horrors, horrors. (*The workers repair the set and disappear behind it.*)

VOICE OF UNCLE VITYA: Okay, ready!

SANG VINIK: (*In a metallic voice.*) It is universally known that not one fox can mature and succeed without a struggle of opinions, without freedom to criticize . . .

IV

(*Razrailov's control room strangely contradicts the science-fiction setting of the laboratory. Like a second-hand shop it is full of antique furniture of different styles from the eighteenth and nineteenth centuries. Heavy dusty curtains conceal the windows. In the corner is a small bar in colonial style. On a stand is a gramophone with an enormous horn. Next to it is a cello. In folds of velvet is hidden a piano. There is an easel and a platform with an unfinished copy of the sculpture, "The Thinker." From the ceiling hang intricate chandeliers of different styles. And only a small elegant screen—Cyber's display, surrounded by pots of geraniums—serves to remind one of the Great Experiment. The gramophone sings: "Our dreamy garden has wilted, the leaves have fallen, I hear your sorrowful voice far away, but it is only a mirage, you died long ago and it is only the damp breath of autumn I hear."*

Razrailov dressed in a long velvet robe, wearing a fez, and carrying a curved pipe slides languidly around the room keeping time with the music.)

RAZRAILOV: (*Gets down on one knee, peeks out of an opening in the door.*) They're working feverishly, doing calculations. Whatever you say, they're good people! It's really in vain that we sometimes criticize them excessively and beat on their heads. That Chol Erik. On the surface, he's impatient. Your first desire is to liquidate him, but, if you check yourself, you see that the individuum is working, and how he's working! This is what it means to give them a good kick in the behind before it's too late. (*He continues to slide about the room, stops for a second, completes Rodin's "The Thinker," sits down at the easel, and in inspired fashion applies a few brushstrokes: he turns the painting so that it faces the audience—Shishkin's "Windfall" completely finished. He rushes to the piano, ruffles his curls and sings: "In the lonely hours of night, fatigued, I like to lie down." He writes down some music; plays the first bars of "Chizhik" on the cello; paces about the room with his hand stuck in his hair; moos like a cow, then proclaims: "We are born to turn fable into reality, to overcome the distances" and with a joyous yelp rushes to the table to write down what he has just composed.)*

CYBER: The calculations are completed. I report the results. The fox has a fluffy tail that glistens like needles, whereas the devil is cross-eyed. The transmission is concluded.

RAZRAILOV: Astounding! (*Picks up a crystal wine glass. Pours some burgundy.*) Problem number three. Melan Cholik begins. You have twenty-five apples in your pocket. Your friend has eighteen. You give your friend twenty-five apples, he gives you eighteen. Does man need song the way a bird needs wings for flight? (*Empties the wine glass. A heavy shadow passes by the window. It seems that someone is looking in the window. Razrailov runs up to the window, hangs out, yells scandalously.*) Again you're interfering? I'm going to complain. I hope you break your neck at your war! This is ridiculous! This Eagle is always interfering with the Experiment! (*Switches on the gramophone, which sings: "Black rose, emblem of sorrow."*) What can I do? How can I occupy myself? Should I masturbate? (*He slaps himself on the forehead—an idea!*) I'll get a lady! (*He slides over to Cyber and presses some secret button. The Lady appears in a Medieval robe ronde with a stiff collar; she moves in a mannered artificial way and curtsies; in a slender voice she sings the old romance, "Violetta graziosa." Also curtseying, Razrailov slides over to the Lady, takes her outstretched hand, ceremoniously kisses the tips of her fingers, leads her to a sumptuous bed beneath a canopy, fills a glass with wine, and gives it to her. The Lady drinks in a mannered way. Razrailov also drinks, then looks at the Lady. The Lady looks at him . . . he takes her by the waist.*) Well?

LADY: I am in your power, mon seigneur! (*Attempts to fall onto the bed but Razrailov restrains her.*)

RAZRAILOV: (*Mocks her.*) In your power! Mon seigneur! Don't you know how to behave, you idiot?

LADY: (*Crying.*) A little while ago when I did a striptease you were extremely polite.

RAZRAILOV: That was then, this is now. Put up resistance! Express dignified indignation, you bitch! Yell "rape." Yell "help, help!" (*Grabs the Lady.*)

LADY: Help, help! Caballeros! Rodrigos! Hidalgos! Let me go, you rapist! (*She resists and breaks out of his clutches.*)

RAZRAILOV: (*Chases her.*) That's the way! That's the way! Yell, you bitch!

LADY: You should be ashamed! This isn't worthy of you! Help, help!

RAZRAILOV: (*Grabs the Lady, topples her onto the bed, sticks into her mouth a bottle of vodka; drinks from it himself; screams.*) Oh, what a life! This is it! This is really it!

CYBER: Forgive me for this intrusion into your intimate world. We have received a query from the Academy of Long-Short-Life in conjunction with United-Kvas-Limited. Is the experiment running according to schedule? The transmission is concluded.

RAZRAILOV: The experiment is going according to plan and running ahead of schedule. The goal is reached! (*Laughs insanely. Paws/screws the weakly squealing Lady. The left corner of the set falls away to the side. In the back of the stage is Katyusha, who—her hands pressed to her chest—is looking upward. Next to her is Emelya.*)

EMELYA: Katyusha, here are tickets for *The Sovremennik*. It was hell getting them. Believe me, I was stomped on.

KATYUSHA: Aren't you ashamed, Emelya? At such a moment! Look, he's coming down! Oh, oh, oh, God! He's come down! (*Uncle Vitya, Gutik, and the Stage Manager run out.*)

UNCLE VITYA: (*In a whistling whisper.*) Are you insane, student? Don't you see one side of the set has fallen down?

STAGE MANAGER: They're having a romance during working hours!

GUTIK: (*Joyously.*) Let's make a note of a violation of safety procedure! (*In the back of the stage there again quickly passes by a strange hunched figure in a robe, with feathers sticking out.*)

KATYUSHA: (*Rushes to the figure.*) Did you hurt yourself, Evgeny Aleksandrovich?

EMELYA: Be more discreet, Katyusha. (*The figure disappears.*)

UNCLE VITYA: Pull up the side of the set you bastards! (*Turns the winch.*)

STAGE MANAGER: What can we do, Uncle Vitya?

GUTIK: It looks like a disaster.

UNCLE VITYA: It looks like we'll never finish the show without mulerons. Let me go to Fefelov and throw myself at his feet.

STAGE MANAGER: (*Takes off her ring.*) Give him this.

GUTIK: (*Wipes off tears.*) I knew you were like that, Alisia Ivanovna. (*He tries to kiss her hand.*)

STAGE MANAGER: (*Turning away.*) Don't, Gutik!

GUTIK: Don't think that I'm not like that, too. I entreat you, don't think ill of me. Here Uncle Vitya, please give him this. (*Gives him a ballpoint pen.*)

EMELYA: (*Grumbling.*) Well, all right. I'm not worse than any of you. Maybe this tie will be of use. (*Takes off his tie.*)

KATYUSHA: (*Passionately.*) I'll spare nothing for the sake of the safety procedure. (*Begins to undo the zipper on her dress.*)

UNCLE VITYA: You've lost your mind, girl! I'll tell your father! (*They pull up the side of the set. The Workers disappear.*)

RAZRAILOV: (*Testily.*) Can we continue? (*Throws himself on the Lady.*)

LADY: Caballeros! Rodrigos! Hidalgos!

CYBER: Once again I ask your forgiveness for this intrusion into your intimate world. A special announcement. The Experiment is halted for reasons I do not understand. The transmission is concluded.

V

(*The laboratory once again. The armchairs are empty. Chol Erik, waving his arms in a frenzy, rushes about the stage. Sang Vinik strolls about, rubbing his hands. Phleg Matik sits on the floor and picks his nose. Melan Cholik moves about the stage on buckling legs, wringing his hands as though he were a dying butterfly. Cyber is blinking, worriedly and chaotically.*)

CHOL ERIK: What dull, ungifted people! Another second and I'll destroy everything here with my famous forehead blow! Jellyfish! A pathetic generation! Let me affirm, listen: Song is sigma, the insane sigma of the waterpipe, the insane sigma of the waterpipe!

SANG VINIK: Cool down, friend Chol! Why yell, old boy, and wave your arms? It would be better if you admitted your mistakes. Facts are stubborn things, my friend, and song is the formula for the existence of amino acids plus hybridization of the whole earth. That's the way it is!

CHOL ERIK: (*Furiously.*) You're asking for it!

MELAN CHOLIK: O darkness! O night! How terrible to lose one's friends! How terrible to see the collapse of the Experiment! Friends, the last hope, the last trembling luminaire in the black velvet of the universal night, the only true answer: song is a ribbon, a blue ribbon calling one beneath the couch into the spiderweb of illusions . . .

CHOL ERIK: I'll crush him like a fly!

PHLEG MATIK: Song is a doughnut.

CYBER: I entreat you to end the argument. The transmission is concluded.

CHOL ERIK: Sigma!

SANG VINIK: Amino acids!

MELAN CHOLIK: Ribbon!

PHLEG MATIK: Doughnut!

CYBER: Not so maniacally, please! The transmission is concluded. (*The disorderly bellowing of Chol Erik, the self-confident joyous exclamations of Sang Vinik, the gloomy whines of Melan Cholik, the monotonous cries of Phleg Matik.*) I refuse to work in such an environment. The transmission is concluded. (*Turns of all the lights. The Temperaments fall into embarrassed silence. For a while Chol Erik, Sang Vinik, and Melan Cholik circle about the stage and then gather around the seated Phleg Matik. Phleg uncertainly makes a loud sniffing noise, then smiles.*)

CHOL ERIK: (*Smiles and pokes Melan Cholik in the stomach.*) You can't deny, my friend, that your socialist savings are pretty solid.

MELAN CHOLIK: (*Smiles.*) Down below, I was a cook.

SANG VINIK: A cook? Where?

MELAN CHOLIK: In the Kaptenarmus restaurant.

CHOL ERIK: In that den of moneybags?

PHLEG MATIK: Papa and mama used to take me there. We ate calf's ears *au revoir* in cherry sauce *bonjour*. That's impossible to forget.

MELAN CHOLIK: Imagine, calf's ears!

SANG VINIK: Good old Kaptenarmus! How many memories are connected with it! An evening wouldn't often go by without our gathering there with writer friends. And there below I was a poet, gentlemen, a poet, let me tell you. I remember I was eating their Ostroga hash and the *homme de lèttres* Bigbin Andreev walked up to me from behind, put his head in my plate and also started to eat. What do you think of that?

MELAN CHOLIK: Wow, Ostroga hash! How many tears I shed over it. Because, gentlemen, I have a chronic runny nose.

CHOL ERIK: The only reason for going to Kaptenarmus was the broads. The broads there were all right, no doubt about that. It was great to snatch a lovely lady from under the nose of some bourgeois! I would sometimes enter wearing dark glasses: nobody would recognize the champion of forehead blows. But when I took off the glasses everybody would ooh and aah!

SANG VINIK: Then, you Chol, are that very same Erik?

CHOL ERIK: Aha, you've finally guessed. Yes, I was *that* Erik, but I've been unemployed now for a long time. Those pigs have forgotten the forehead blow. All they know is the evasive attack from the side. But what a time it was! Do you remember the fracas on 42nd Street?

MELAN CHOLIK: How can one not remember it? I locked myself in the toilet then . . .

PHLEG MATIK: (*Aroused.*) In the toilet?

MELAN CHOLIK: . . . and shed a sea of tears. It seemed to me that civilization was dying and that never again would anyone go back to the Kaptenarmus . . .

SANG VINIK: Yes, how well you broke eggs on 42nd Street in those days, Chol! I remember. Yes, I remember. Yes, I remember . . . I was always your theoretical opponent. I always thought that one had to use a different maneuver, namely, the evasive approach from the side. But I must give you what you deserve: the sidewalk was entirely covered with yolks! That was something!

CHOL ERIK: (*Jumps up, makes enormous absurd leaps, roars.*) I want to go down. Down, into that demonic anthill! I can't live without them! I haven't yet fought my last fight, cursed my last curse, loved my last woman! I'll perish without them. (*Falls.*)

SANG VINIK: I also want to go down, gentlemen! I want to write a poem! What do you think of that? I'm hungry for a positive struggle for optimism. I'm hungry for evasive attacks from the side. That's what I want. (*Falls.*)

MELAN CHOLIK: And I want to eat, gentlemen. To cook and to eat. Gastronomy alone used to save me from philosophical pessimism. (*Falls.*)

PHLEG MATIK: And I want to go to the toilet. (*Collapses onto his side.*)

CYBER: I am forced to switch on. I would like to inform my co-workers that, in reality, they want nothing. That is the way they were programmed under the conditions of the Experiment. Is that not so? The transmission is concluded.

SANG VINIK: In reality I want nothing. Only to upset my theoretical opponent just a teensy bit.

CHOL ERIK: I only want to see how the little bitch from Kaptenarmus twirls her skirt.

MELAN CHOLIK: I only want to blow my nose over my favorite Ostroga hash.

PHLEG MATIK: I only want to have a peek at my toilet bowl, at the little meditation corner with the magazine *Knowledge is Power*. (*Razrailov enters.*)

RAZRAILOV: Ai-ai-ai! So, you're sabotaging the Experiment? Aren't you ashamed? (*The Temperaments lie silently on the floor. Razrailov gets down on all fours, creeps away from one body to another, and whispers to each in an inspired way: "Get up, comrade. It's time. Forward! In the name of Progress! Face to face with the epoch!" But the Temperaments remain motionless. Razrailov gets up and presses some button in Cyber.*)

CYBER: (*Roars.*) Get up! The transmission is concluded. (*The Temperaments leap up.*)

RAZRAILOV: And you're supposed to be citizens of the cyber-humanity of the future! Shame! You've short-circuited the Experiment, succumbed to the decadent influence of earthly miasmas, which—I am sure—the Eagle has brought on his wings. If you don't want to work . . . (*Threateningly.*) . . . We can return to the starting point.

SANG VINIK: (*In a changed, almost machine-like voice.*) We want to work for the Experiment and we will work for the Experiment, only we have certain requests we wish to make to the Management.

RAZRAILOV: Well, all right. What are the requests? Just don't get carried away!

MELAN CHOLIK: My request is a modest one! I only want a flower, some kind of plant.

RAZRAILOV: A plant? Be my guest. (*Presses a button. A rubber plant appears on the window sill.*)

PHLEG MATIK: I want a kitty.

RAZRAILOV: Of course. (*Presses a button. On the window sill appears a crudely painted clay kitten with a cute but frightening face.*)

CHOL ERIK: (*Makes a movement full of strain and torment, as though he were trying to free himself from something. Then says in a hollow voice.*) I want a kitten, too.

RAZRAILOV: (*Merrily.*) Of course, of course. (*Presses a button. On the window sill appears a second kitten, identical to the first.*)

SANG VINIK: (*Also moves as though he were trying to free himself from something. Then says in a hollow voice.*) I want a kitten, too.

RAZRAILOV: (*Roaring with laughter.*) As many as you like! The firm doesn't care about expenses. (*Presses a button. A third kitten appears on the window sill.*)

MELAN CHOLIK: (*In a metallic voice.*) I don't want a plant. I want a kitten.

RAZRAILOV: Good boy! (*Presses a button. The plant disappears. In its place appears a fourth kitten.*) Are you happy, boys? Do you have any other requests, personal claims?

ALL: (*In chorus.*) We're completely happy. We have no claims!

RAZRAILOV: And now to work. (*The Temperaments sit down in the armchairs.*) And so, do people need song the way a bird needs wings for flight? Chol begins.

CHOL ERIK: Song is sigma, the insane sigma of the waterpipe.

SANG VINIK: I don't agree. Song is the form of existence of amino acids plus hybridization of the whole earth.

RAZRAILOV: You're repeating the same old stuff?

MELAN CHOLIK: Song is a blue ribbon that lures one beneath the couch into the spiderweb of illusions.

RAZRAILOV: Shut up!

PHLEG MATIK: Song is a doughnut. (*Again an argument flares up.*

The Temperaments break out of Cyber's control.)

RAZRAILOV: (*Confused. To Cyber.*) In your opinion, what's going on?

CYBER: I suppose a disharmony of temperaments. The transmission is concluded.

RAZRAILOV: Perhaps one can unify them?

CYBER: Impossible. A new modeling system would be required. The transmission is concluded.

RAZRAILOV: (*Reflects.*) A new system? Yes, yes . . . (*Someone looks into the window; a shadow passes by; one hears the rustle of wings. A stream of air knocks the four kittens from the window sill.*)

THE TEMPERAMENTS: Oh! Oh! Where are our kittens!? It was a trick!

RAZRAILOV: (*Rushing about, busily. Scared.*) I assure you, the Management has nothing to do with it. It was the damned Eagle, that tin soldier and saboteur. (*The right corner of the set falls away to the side. In the back of the stage stands Katyusha, looking upward. Next to her is Emelya.*)

EMELYA: Katyusha, it's becoming impossible. I think only of you. Honest, I've really fallen for you.

KATYUSHA: Oh, he hit the set, he's turned over. My God, is it the end? (*Hides her face in her hands.*)

EMELYA: What can happen to your damned Eagle? He's come down, the bastard! (*The Stage Manager and Gutik run out, in an embrace.*)

STAGE MANAGER: A disaster! Where's Uncle Vitya!

GUTIK: Alisia Ivanovna, dearest, my most excellent person, Uncle Vitya has run off to Fefelov. I gave him a ruble from the members' dues for the taxi. All because of you! (*A hunched figure in a robe passes by.*)

KATYUSHA: (*Rushes up to him.*) Evgeny Aleksandrovich, have you hurt yourself?

THE FIGURE: (*Irritably.*) Listen, young lady. I have a complicated role. It's tough work, I'm risking my life, losing my feathers and you keep making fun of me. (*Leaves. Katyusha runs away, sobbing.*)

EMELYA: Thick-skinned bastard. He doesn't understand her.

STAGE MANAGER: Emelya, Gutik, save the show! (*Workers pull up the fallen corner of the set.*)

PHLEG MATIK: (*Hiccups.*) The kittens have fallen.

MELAN CHOLIK: (*Crying.*) They'll be smashed to smithereens. A cruel fate . . .

CHOL ERIK: (*Waving his arms.*) Where are our beloved replicas? What you give with one hand, you take away with the other. We know this kind of tactic. I'll destroy everything!

SANG VINIK: Forgive me, Razrailov. We refuse to work under these conditions. That's the way it is, old boy. There can be no question of continuing the Experiment!

RAZRAILOV: (*His feelings are hurt.*) And where is your feeling of gratitude? What would have become of you, young people, if I hadn't appeared at the last moment before each of you? (*He screams and points at each of them.*) You would be bobbing up and down like a rotten log in the Gultimoor canal! You would be hanging like a sausage in your favorite closet! You would be rotting in the vegetable garden! You would be lying around with a hole in your head! I knew you were on your way to suicide. I have been keeping track of you for a long time. And I saved you. From the pathetic, reflective nebbishes that you were, I wanted to transform you into powerful cyber-individuums. I allowed you to participate in the Great Experiment! Where is your gratitude? Where? (*Threateningly.*) Perhaps you would like to return to the starting point? (*The Temperaments look at him in confusion and are silent.*)

SANG VINIK: He's right. Without him we would all be kaput. In my own case . . . I remember a magnificent morning, my digestion was functioning admirably. I drank a glass of tea with cherry preserves and I made the decision to leave life . . . (*One hears a rustle of approaching wings. On the windowsill suddenly alights the heavy, elderly Eagle, with the face of an old soldier.*)

EAGLE: Greetings, my dead friends! (*Four muffled explosions are heard one after the other.*)

VI

(*A silent scene in the laboratory of the Great Experiment. The Temperaments, frozen in tense poses, look at the window. Razrailov stands with arm outstretched. The Eagle, with his elbows on the window sill, is smiling.*)

RAZRAILOV: Get out!

EAGLE: (*Climbs in, wearing high leather boots. Sits down on the sill, lights a cigar.*) I'm exhausted, friends. My strength's gone.

CHOL ERIK: (*In a hollow voice.*) How are you?

EAGLE: I'm an eagle, brothers. Every day I fly past you to the war. I have a war, brothers.

CHOL ERIK: (*Takes a step towards the Eagle.*) Who is the war against, Eagle?

EAGLE: Against the accursed Steel Bird, brothers. It's not so difficult to understand. I'm a simple eagle made of flesh and bones and hot blood, and here I fight an endless war with this monster. To tell the truth, comrades, I'm sick to death, but I have to do it.

SANG VINIK: (*Takes a step towards the Eagle.*) But what are you fighting for, if I may ask?

EAGLE: (*In a thunderous voice.*) For ideals of justice!

RAZRAILOV: (*Hysterically.*) Well, go fly to your ridiculous war! Why are you hanging around here?

EAGLE: Take it easy, pappy. Don't give me grief. It's lunch time. The Steel Bird has also taken time out to fuel up with kerosene and in a minute I'm going to get something to eat at the Kaptenarmus. (*To Melan Cholik.*) The good there has gotten worse since you died.

MELAN CHOLIK: What do you mean, since I died. Let me ask—

RAZRAILOV: I demand that you clear out! You're interfering with the Great Experiment!

EAGLE: (*Makes fun of him.*) Periment! Periment! Some two-bit angel of death you are! And all this is taking place under the very nose of the Head Office. It would be better if I didn't have eyes to see!

CHOL ERIK: (*Gets down on his knees.*) Eagle, take me with you to your war! I'm the master of forehead blows! I'll be useful.

SANG VINIK: (*Gets down on his knees.*) And take me too . . . into the staff. I know the theory of evasive maneuvers from the side . . . you won't regret it, I assure you, old boy . . .

MELAN CHOLIK: (*Gets down on his knees.*) Take me into the field kitchen . . .

PHLEG MATIK: (*Gets down on his knees.*) Take me into the supply train . . .

EAGLE: I can't brothers! Everyone has his war. I have mine . . . and what would I do with your bodiless souls? (*Puts out his cigar on the heel of his boot.*) Well, forgive me for taking your time . . . (*To Razrailov.*) And as for you, less bull, you idiot. (*To the Temperaments.*) Goodbye, my dead friends! (*He flies off. The Temperaments are on their knees, with their heads bent down.*)

RAZRAILOV: Don't pay attention, friends, to this old provocateur with his idiotic jokes. Raise your heads! The Great Experiment . . .

SANG VINIK: (*In a hollow voice.*) We're dead?

RAZRAILOV: Ha, ha, ha, what nonsense! Don't forget, I saved you. Don't forget, Chol. You had your leg over the bridge railing, and then I appeared and . . .

CHOL ERIK: It seems that I was falling, yes, I was falling. Then I felt the impact . . . (*Leaps up.*)

MELAN CHOLIK: It seems that I remember too, friends. It seems that I had time to take the poison . . . the most potent of poisons from the liver of the fugu fish . . .

PHLEG MATIK: And it seems that I had time to get to the toilet . . .

SANG VINIK: I don't remember exactly but it seems that I felt an impact against my temple and only after did you appear, Razrailov. (*He gets up.*) Confess. Are we dead? We demand to know. After all, we have the right. Don't put us in a ridiculous position.

RAZRAILOV: (*Evasively.*) Everything in the world is relative, my friends: Space, time, life, death. And for the success of the Experiment—

CHOL ERIK: (*Stepping up to him with fists raised.*) Tell us!

RAZRAILOV: In the final analysis, the best man is a dead man!

SANG VINIK: Why were you silent?

RAZRAILOV: Why tamper for no reason with the nerves of one's fellow workers?

CHOL ERIK: Then it was you who pushed us to suicide?

RAZRAILOV: (*Indignant.*) Pardon me! That's a dirty insinuation! Sirs, I am prepared to provide proof. I merely cultivated you. Do you understand, I cultivated you in your own interest. (*He yells.*) Get up, all of you! Take your seats! You've become pretty impudent, my friends. You're acting as if you were alive. If this is the way you want it, then know once and for all that you don't exist. You're merely the appurtenances of a complex experiment on the transformation of all mankind. (*He presses several buttons on Cyber's control panel. On the panel there is a chaotic flashing of lights, hoarse sounds resembling moans are audible; separate words can be made out: "... it's hard. The transmission is concluded." "... I can't bear it. The transmission is concluded." "It's not my fault. The transmission is concluded." The screens pulsate furiously. The Temperaments, as if hypnotized, sit down in the armchairs, grip the elbow rests, raise their chins.*)

CHOL ERIK: (*As if attempting to get out from under a heavy marble plate.*) The transformation of all mankind. Following our model, is that it?

RAZRAILOV: That's the idea in its general features, but modifications are possible. We could develop the idea together, if you work diligently. We were already on the right track. One must create, not look for people to blame.

CHOL ERIK: What shit ... (*Razrailov quickly presses some more buttons.*) What shitty behavior all our doubts and anxieties imply. (*Is silent.*)

RAZRAILOV: Well, it seems we finally have some order. Now I can make a little speech! (*Assumes a pose.*) Happiness! Happiness without unhappiness! Complete happiness without unhappiness!

SANG VINIK: (*Moves slightly.*) Farewell, the azure of transfiguration and the gold of the Second Coming ... (*Is silent.*)

RAZRAILOV: Creativity! Happiness in creativity! Creativity in happiness!

MELAN CHOLIK: (*Moves slightly.*) Anna Nikolaevna, look there ... on the tablecloth ... there's a gold ring ... (*Is silent.*)

RAZRAILOV: Purity! The purity of straight lines! Laconism! Purity in laconism! Laconism in purity!

CHOL ERIK: (*Moves slightly.*) How the linden trees used to rustle on the corner of 42nd and 18th ... what beer ... (*Is silent.*)

RAZRAILOV: Progress! Progress without regress! Pure progress is purity, in happiness, in happiness without unhappiness, in creativity and laconism! The best man is a dead man!

PHLEG MATIK: (*Moves slightly.*) Hey, diddle diddle, the cat and the fiddle . . . (*Is silent.*)

RAZRAILOV: Sleep! (*Presses buttons. The Temperaments sit motionless. To Cyber.*) Do you have any suggestions?

CYBER: I have a feeling that the Experiment has failed. The transmission is concluded.

RAZRAILOV: When did you first have this feeling? (*Unexpectedly, Cyber leaves his place. He stretches himself, walks across the entire stage and sits down on the window sill, with his legs crossed.*)

CYBER: Listen Razrailov, you're taking your role pretty seriously. What do you know about my inner world? What do you understand about science? Let's be blunt—you're a charlatan! The transmission is concluded.

RAZRAILOV: (*Smiling impudently.*) A crude and blunt evaluation. Not in keeping with the nature of a machine as complex as you.

CYBER: You make me mad. You force these unfortunates to work, while you yourself busy yourself with plagiarism in the control room. The transmission is concluded.

RAZRAILOV: That's my hobby.

CYBER: You've turned this place into a warehouse of antiques. You fool around with the Lady. The transmission is concluded.

RAZRAILOV: But this is in fashion! You have to understand, I'm a modern man, in the vanguard of true progress, and fashion is the companion of progress. Furthermore, what right do you have to criticize? What is permissible for Jupiter is forbidden to the bull. The Academy has invested money in you. Your business is the Experiment, not criticism. The machines think they can teach us!

CYBER: (*Sighs.*) Just my luck to get mixed up with this two-bit outfit. The transmission is concluded.

RAZRAILOV: Determine how we can regulate the temperaments of our co-workers.

CYBER: (*Sharply.*) That's one thing I won't do! The transmission is concluded.

RAZRAILOV: Why?

CYBER: Because I like them. The transmission is concluded.

RAZRAILOV: But they're dead!

CYBER: I'm not convinced. They argue, suffer, have dreams; they have different temperaments. The transmission is concluded.

RAZRAILOV: Aha, I understand. They've brought disharmony into your inner world, they've agitated your soul. Yes, you really are a complex machine. Believe me, that's not an empty compliment. Yes, yes, I understand. Believe me, I share your feelings. Believe me, sometimes I too have the urge to descend (*looks toward the window*), to stroll about and carouse in the conference halls, to fool around. Sometimes I recall the soapy water, the bubbles, the little rosy foot . . .

CYBER: (*In a hollow voice.*) Don't torment me. The transmission is concluded.

RAZRAILOV: And remember how we used to run galloping on the grass and there were so many smells—the head was dizzy with them!

CYBER: Don't torment me. The transmission is concluded.

RAZRAILOV: Don't be embarrassed, my friend. Look down. I assure you that even though many centuries have passed, she hasn't changed at all. (*With concealed hatred.*) She's just as beautiful. (*Not being able to take it any more, Cyber turns sharply toward the window. His rear end faces the audience: an ordinary human rear end. And it's trembling.*)

RAZRAILOV: (*Taking a step back, he surveys the audience.*) Just think, he has evolved all the way to the human rear end. (*Takes from his pocket a rusty tin can, an enormous nail, and a hammer. He puts the can up to Cyber's rear end, then the nail to the can and, with one blow, drives the nail into the rear end. Cyber falls to his knees.*) That's it! A new model is ready! I'm a genius. A genius! (*Drags Cyber along the floor and puts him in his former place.*) Now I can make a little speech! (*There is a sinister glow on stage. The crippled Cyber. The white masks of the sleeping Temperaments. Razrailov, terrible in his grandeur. One hears a whistle, the rustling of wings; the Eagle looks into the laboratory.*)

EAGLE: Greetings, my dead . . . well, I see something underhanded is going on! And this under the very nose of the Head Office. Well, Razrailov, you're going to get screwed! (*Flies away. The next corner of the set falls away. Katyusha in her former pose. Next to her is Emelya.*)

EMELYA: Maybe you think, Katyusha, that all of us in the Philosophy department are intellectual jellyfishes. You're wrong, baby. We're okay; we know how to do it. Katyusha, I drank some cider during intermission. I'm bold! (*One hears the hollow sound of a body that has just fallen to the floor. Katyusha covers her face with her hands. Emelya runs away. The Stage Manager and Gutik run out, in an embrace.*)

STAGE MANAGER: Horror! Shame! We won't finish the show! Where's Uncle Vitya?! Where's Fefelov with the muleron bolts? Gutik, save us!

GUTIK: Alya, let's spit on it all. I have the members' dues. Let's fly to Sochi and live like people for at least two days . . . (*Limping and leaning on Emelya's shoulder, a hunched figure in a robe passes by.*)

THE FIGURE: (*To Katyusha.*) Young lady, why don't you ask: "Evgeny Aleksandrovich, did you hurt yourself?" (*Katyusha cries soundlessly.*)

EMELYA: (*Trickily.*) How is she to understand, Evgeny Aleksandrovich, the difficulty of your work . . .

STAGE MANAGER: Pull it up! Pull it! (*They pull up the right corner. The set is restored.*)

RAZRAILOV: (*Spits out the window after the Eagle who has just taken off.*) What a nonentity! What a speech he's ruined! (*To Cyber.*) Well, my rusty gramophone, how do you like your new control device?

CYBER: I request that you not insult me. I like the device. The transmission is concluded.

RAZRAILOV: Well, now the game is mine. The Experiment will proceed without interruption. I'll get my doctoral dissertation. Now they'll work for me at the choleric temperament and rest at the phlegmatic. And no nuances. *Voilà!* And so, let's switch on to operational. (*Presses buttons.*)

CHOL ERIK: Problem number three. Does a model need song the way a bird needs wings for flight? Song is the insane sigma of the waterpipe.

SANG VINIK: Sigma is sigmoidal. Alpha is hemorrhoidal. The lyre is blind; the *a* in square derives from the root *x*.

MELAN CHOLIK: Thunder calls while the hound rejoices. Soon the song will coo-coo.

PHLEG MATIK: The results: Birds need song the way airplanes need wings. People need . . . (*bellows*) . . . I can't . . .

RAZRAILOV: Well, well, we are on the threshold of a great discovery . . . one more attempt . . . well? (*Presses button.*)

ALL THE TEMPERAMENTS: People need death!

RAZRAILOV: A work of genius! A masterpiece! Congratulations, brothers! I'm switching you to rest. You've deserved it. (*Presses buttons.*) It's time for me to rest too. You've exhausted me. I'll go to the control room to regulate the rest period. Take it easy! (*Leaves.*)

VII

(*The stage is silent. The Temperaments sit motionless in their chairs. The only light is a faint one flashing in Cyber. Finally Phleg Matik stirs. Then Melan Cholik moves slightly, followed by the slight movement of Sang Vinik and Chol Erik.*)

PHLEG MATIK: I propose that we play . . . (*Silence.*)

CHOL ERIK: Begin . . . someone . . .

SANG VINIK: (*With difficulty makes a cross with his fingers.*) Chirishek . . . (*Silence. Enter Nina, a gorgeous blonde in a miniskirt, disheveled and magnificent. Behind her slips in the Love Triangle, an emaciated character in tights. He assumes a triangular shape.*)

NINA: (*Boldly.*) Well, what have we here? (*Looks around.*) Oho, four impressive, full-fledged male figures. Not bad for openers! (*Makes a flirtatious hand gesture.*) Well, how come you're silent! Maybe saying hello to ladies is not the accepted thing here? (*The Temperaments nod listlessly in her direction. Phleg Matik blows her way something that vaguely resembles a kiss.*) Hey, what's wrong with you? Pour a lady a gin and tonic! (*Astonished.*) What deadbeats! (*To Love Triangle.*) How do you like this? They don't react to a lady! I climbed up to this height to be in the company of four impotent jerks!

LOVE TRIANGLE: (*Morosely.*) Why don't you love me? What do you see in him? My dearest lover, I'm yours! My beloved, alone at last! And what about him? Ha, ha, ha! (*Makes some soulrending movement.*)

NINA: Go to hell! As much good comes from you as beer comes from a reactor! (*Notices Cyber, becomes lively.*) Aha, this appears to be an automatic drink dispenser. I'll get juiced! (*She dances over to Cyber and pokes around in her handbag.*) Not a sou! He pointed the pistol at me before I had a chance to put my purse back into the bag; it's your own fault, you fool! Anyhow, let's recall our childhood pranks. (*Takes out her manicure scissors, looks about sneakily, sticks them into a slit in Cyber.*) Now, don't be offended, sweetie!

CYBER: I'm not offended at all. On the contrary, I'm happy. The transmission is concluded. (*He gives her a glass, followed by a rose.*)

NINA: Wow, a new system! We don't have this type down below yet. (*Drinks, smells the rose.*) Merci, sweetie! (*Again sticks the scissors into Cyber.*)

CYBER: How did you get here, Nina? The transmission is concluded. (*Cyber gives her a glass and a rose.*)

NINA: How do you like that? He even guessed my name. That's progress! (*Drinks.*) Well, sweetie, I was murdered by that idiot Chips, my husband. You know, my ninth . . or rather—I beg your pardon (*accepts the lit cigarette which Cyber has extended and thinks*)—my eleventh, yes, my eleventh. To be brief, a completely trivial story, my dear. A tax collector came to our house one morning. Very sweet and intelligent. A student from the Philosophy Department. Suddenly Chips runs in and the fool's eyes bulge out. And nothing had even happened yet—do you understand, Autie old buddy? True, I was a little—how should I say (*smiles*)—a tiny bit undressed, and he starts screaming. And then come the reproaches, the suspicions. Before I had time to dress he fired at me and shot me twice right here. (*Unbuttons her blouse.*) Right here . . . no . . . a little lower . . .

CYBER: I request that you not torment me. The transmission is concluded.

NINA: Oho, even you're affected! Then it's not hard to see why they finally killed me. Give me a third one. (*Drinks her third glass, smells her third rose.*) And so, I don't really remember how but I found myself at the foot of this pretty tower. Chips, I think, ran to give himself up to the police. You remember, as in that old opera: "Tie me I up, I killed her . . ."

CYBER: I remember. (*Sings a few lines from Jose's aria from Carmen.*) The transmission is concluded.

NINA: Right, that's it! I always died of laughter at that point. And so I'm standing next to your tower, near which there's nobody except this nonentity. (*Points to the Love Triangle, who goes into convulsions.*) Suddenly this Eagle flies up to me, a big solid son of a gun, a soldier, not young but still in his prime. Go up the stairs, my daughter. Go—don't be afraid. Give me a lift, colonel, I said to him. But he said, I can't, I'm flying to war, it's tough work, I'm risking my life, I'm losing my feathers, it's no time for broads. And he flies away. An amusing, sexy old boy. And so I dragged myself up here with this scarecrow. (*Points to the Love Triangle.*)

CYBER: Allow me to ask, who is he? The transmission is concluded.

NINA: He's Love Triangle. He's been after me since I was fourteen. I'm sick to death of him. (*To Love Triangle.*) Hey, show him your act!

LOVE TRIANGLE: (*Morosely.*) All night long I've been seeing you in my dreams. I ask that nobody be blamed in my death. Nina, you're leaving? I'll come at four. Oh, leave me alone . . . your body . . . Oh, if there were only two of us! Understand me, I love you and respect him. My lover! My beloved! My dear lover! (*Goes into convulsions.*)

NINA: (*To Cyber.*) Did you understand?

CYBER: I did. But for you Nina the triangle is too narrow a frame. The transmission is concluded!

NINA: (*Laughs loudly.*) That's exactly it! And these idiots don't understand! The automatic dispenser understands but those intellectual man-dogs don't understand worth a damn.

MELAN CHOLIK: (*Inflates his cheeks three times and slaps them with his palms.*) Bam. Bam. Bahm. Pupyrishek. (*Silence.*)

NINA: Is this a den of dope addicts? Where the hell am I? What kind of corpses are these?

CYBER: It's not their fault, Nina. The transmission is concluded.

NINA: And your behavior is very strange for an automatic drink dispenser. You compel one to be frank. If I use you without paying—that is, by means of scissors—that doesn't mean that you should . . .

CYBER: I'm not an automatic drink dispenser, Nina. I'm a complex Cyber, Nina. You don't recognize me, Nina? The transmission is concluded.

NINA: (*Indignant.*) Why should I recgonize you? There are hundreds of thousands like you.

CYBER: (*Sadly.*) Don't tell me you don't recognize even one familiar feature? The transmission is concluded.

NINA: You're raving! You're malfunctioning, Cyber! (*Cyber extends a glass and a rose to her. He switches on music: a passionate languorous tango. Nina is worried.*) I don't understand . . .

LOVE TRIANGLE: Meow, meow, granny, where's my little ball, how you've grown, Nina . . . (*A convulsion.*)

NINA: I don't understand . . . (*Irritated.*) Where do you get roses? In automatic drink dispensers . . .

CYBER: I keep forgetting that so many centuries of evolution have elapsed, centuries of transformation from the simplest molecules to meeting you in fragrant grass, to saying goodbye to you in soap bubbles, then centuries from the steam engine to the atom bomb, the playthings of idiots, and I wandered in the darkness of experiments, longing for you, serving my science, in your name, until I finally ended up here in this my latest form. Rather, I was enticed here by a gang of charlatans . . . but nevertheless I'm filled with love for you and with nothing else and your appearance here so much like bushy lightning . . .

NINA: Bushy? (*In alarm.*) Wait, how do you mean that?

CYBER: Understand it is a confession of love . . . (*A difficult silence.*) The transmission is concluded.

NINA: (*To Love Triangle.*) Well, how do you like that? Doesn't even give me a chance to look around. (*Looks with alarm at Cyber.*)

LOVE TRIANGLE: (*In his usual intonation.*) And what's new in your inner life? Don't lie? I'll strangle you! Albert, he doesn't understand me! Here you and I have some inner contact. My inner life interests you, your inner life interests me. (*Convulsion.*)

PHLEG MATIK: One very sympathetic Mister Bobby bought a dog called Bobik.

NINA: (*Concealing her alarm.*) Why, they're playing "chirishek-pupyrishek-bubo!" (*With feigned interest.*) No good, brothers, no good at all! You won't get more than five points with a move like that!

CYBER: Nina! Nina! Nina! The transmission is concluded.

NINA: I hear! I hear! I hear! Don't you see what's happening to me? (*Cries.*)

CYBER: (*In a high-pitched trembling voice.*) Nina. (*Weeps.*) The transmission is concluded. (*A head begins to grow on him. The top of the head is visible.*)

NINA: (*Wipes her tears, gets control of herself, smiles.*) What joy! Such happy goings-on! How do you imagine our future, Autie? I don't have a body and you're made of iron!

CYBER: I don't know what's happening to me, Nina. I don't know what's to become of us . . . I don't believe that you're dead . . . you can't die . . . I'm suffering . . . (*His head continues to grow. His forehead is now visible.*) A process of monstrous force is raging in me. I'm evolving. Nina, give me your hand! Nina, you've come! How many centuries I've waited for you! (*The head is completely visible. Cyber combs his hair.*) Hello, my beloved!

NINA: (*Disappointed.*) Greetings, greetings . . . but I thought . . . now I recognize you, dearest. You look like the most ordinary man. But anyway, you're pretty nice. (*Gives him her hand.*) And so, what do you propose?

CYBER: (*Falls to one knee, kisses her hand.*) We're joined to each other forever?

LOVE TRIANGLE: (*Animated.*) We're joined to each other forever? Can't this be done without a pathetic scene? And who keeps calling us and always hanging up? And who keeps calling us and always hanging up? And who keeps calling us and always hanging up? (*Convulsion.*)

NINA: (*To Cyber.*) Can't this be done without a pathetic scene?

CYBER: We'll go to Razrailov and announce my departure.

NINA: (*Interested.*) And who is Razrailov?

CYBER: My love! Hand in hand! The evolution is coming to completion. I'm becoming a man! The Experiment is perishing! Nina! Let's go! (*They leave. Behind them slides the Love Triangle.*)

CHOL ERIK: (*Whistles deafeningly with three fingers.*) Bubo! (*Jumps from the chair.*) Fellows, that's her!

VIII

(*The control room. Dressed as a nobleman from the time of Louis XIV, Razrailov is dancing a minuet, surrounded by four Ladies dressed as shepherdesses.*)

RAZRAILOV: Confess, my lovely shepherdesses. You've come to this meadow by chance!

LADIES: By chance, mon seigneur, by chance!

RAZRAILOV: And you didn't expect to meet a cavalier here, my naughty ones?

LADIES: We didn't expect it, mon seigneur! Ah, we didn't expect it!

RAZRAILOV: And your cavalier is so courteous, so gallant, so elegant?

LADIES: Yes, our cavalier is all perfection, mon seigneur!

RAZRAILOV: And now we'll speak differently, my sluttish shepherdesses! (*Enter Cyber and Nina.*)

CYBER: I ask forgiveness for intruding into your intimate world.

NINA: Oh, I know these girls! (*Runs up to the "Shepherdesses," who greet her joyously.*)

RAZRAILOV: What comes next? (*Pause.*) Where's your famous "The transmission is concluded?"

CYBER: I've finished with all that.

RAZRAILOV: It's about time, my friend. It's about time. You kept sounding like an old radio announcer: "The transmission is concluded. The transmission is concluded." Don't forget, you're a complex Cyber. Believe me, I was even a little embarrassed for you, but I didn't say anything because of a sense of delicacy.

CYBER: You see—I've grown a head!

RAZRAILOV: No, I don't see. (*It must be said that during this dialogue Nina is whispering with the "Shepherdesses" and examining their costumes, while they examine her skirt. The Ladies look at the men and giggle.*)

CYBER: What do you mean, you don't see? Here's the ears, here's the nose, mouth, here's the hair. Everything's in its proper place, just like people have.

RAZRAILOV: I see a rusty nail stuck in your rear end but I don't see a head.

CYBER: (*Angrily.*) Listen, Razrailov. I never thought you were a scientist and even less did I think you were the angel of death—instead I considered you to be a mere charlatan. You can't even see the evolution which I've undergone. You're an ungifted jerk! Understand: the love which has accumulated in me for ages has taken material form and here I am: a man!

RAZRAILOV: (*In a hollow voice.*) Give me back my things.

CYBER: Please. Why the hell do I need your primitive relay system now? (*Gives back the nail and the tin can.*)

RAZRAILOV: Why have you come?

CYBER: I came here with a girl. (*Points to Nina.*) We love each other. (*At this moment Nina is showing to the "Shepherdesses" her Love Triangle. The latter is murmuring something and is contorted in a fit of convulsions. The Ladies laugh loudly.*)

RAZRAILOV: (*To Cyber, in confidence.*) Friend, this is something I understand. It's the call of the erotic, is it? I understand, I understand. If you like you can have all of these four sluts. If you like I'll invite more of them—a whole battalion of sluts. All of them different. Let's carouse a bit, what do you say? I can see you have to be loosened up. (*Puts his arm around Cyber's shoulders in friendly fashion.*)

CYBER: (*Frees himself.*) You don't understand. I'm talking about eternal love. Remember the classical literature: Tristan and Isolde, Romeo and Juliet, Igor and Tanya. (*Moves away from Razrailov, assumes a pose.*) Believe me, worthless Razrailov. In the thunder of words, in compounds of lowly molecules, in crashes and catastrophes—ages of love flow and grass smells and storm-clouds float past and summer passes in baubles of bubbles . . . but you'll never understand . . .

RAZRAILOV: (*Hysterically.*) Why won't I ever understand? Why do you deny me basic intelligence? (*Pulls out a hammer.*) Wait, I'll kill you!

CYBER: (*Smiles.*) At your own risk!

RAZRAILOV: Forgive me. My nerves are playing tricks! But what if I press some buttons. (*Presses buttons on Cyber's chest.*)

CYBER: (*Smiles.*) As you see, they don't work.

RAZRAILOV: (*Slyly.*) Do you have an urge to kill youself?

CYBER: Hardly. I want to live. Animated by love, I depart into the ages and take flesh, as long as my blood—

RAZRAILOV: Enough, enough . . . you're beginning again?

CYBER: Nina, let's go! (*Meanwhile, Nina is showing the "Shepherdesses" some ultra-fashionable dance. The Love Triangle also takes part in the dance.*)

RAZRAILOV: Isn't your lady friend dead?

CYBER: She was killed but she's not dead! She lives eternally! Nina, how long can you dance? (*Showing off before Razrailov.*) You're terrible, you know! (*Nina comes up to them.*)

NINA: (*To Razrailov.*) Hello, scarecrow!

RAZRAILOV: (*Bewildered.*) Madame . . . I'm very pleased . . . I'm deeply crushed that preoccupation with work caused me to lose sight of your demise . . . Madame, try to exert some influence on your . . . I don't even know what to call him . . . on your amant. Remind him of the Great Experiment . . .

NINA: (*To Cyber.*) Don't tell me you've forgotten about the Great Experiment, sweetie? (*Presses close to Cyber.*) Ai, ai, ai! You should be ashamed, my iron honey! What a load of shame it is for your new head to bear. (*Caresses Cyber's hair.*)

CYBER: (*Melting from happiness.*) I forgot, sweet Nina, oh I forgot . . . ai, ai, ai! I completely forgot . . . meow, meow, meow, my honey . . . (*Very rapidly from out of the iron depths of Cyber grows a most marvelous living organ.*)

NINA: (*In ecstasy.*) What a beauty! (*Kisses the organ.*)

RAZRAILOV: (*His scream fills the auditorium.*) There goes my doctoral dissertation! (*Nina and Cyber, mumbling sweet nothings to each other, leave the stage. Love Triangle drags after them. Razrailov rushes about the stage in a frenzy; rips away drapery, covers, rugs; mutters indistinctly; pushes fabrics into a traveling bag; makes marks in some extremely long list. Crowded into a corner, the Ladies rehearse an ultra-fashionable dance. They're so preoccupied that they don't even notice Nina's departure and Razrailov's strange behavior.*)

FIRST LADY: Nina, what are you supposed to do with your behind when going up on your toes? Nina . . .

SECOND LADY: Girls, she's gone!

THIRD LADY AND FOURTH LADY: Ninotchka, where are you?

RAZRAILOV: (*Going by with a pillowcase.*) Shut up, you dead whores!

LADIES: Razrailov, where's our Nina? Razrailov, let us go! We want to go down, to our dear Kaptenarmus! We want to see men! We've fallen behind the fashion! We want to dance "yolkipalki."

RAZRAILOV: (*Shutting his traveling bag.*) Then you shouldn't have danced your way to the grave, you idiots!

LADIES: (*Weeping.*) Spare us, Razrailov!

RAZRAILOV: Polonaise! (*A polonaise resounds. The Ladies dance as if under hypnosis. Razrailov dances with each in turn. Nina runs in. Behind her slides along the nimble, creepily smiling Love Triangle.*)

NINA: Forgive me. I forgot my handbag; it contains my scissors. (*Looks with interest at the dancing Razrailov.*) I see you're a man with imagination. Bye-bye. (*Runs away.*)

LOVE TRIANGLE: (*Contorts himself in a mannered, artificial way.*) I see you're a man with imagination. At any rate, you have enough of it for me. Ah, who's coming? Filthy slut! Boom! Boom! Boom! One missed; two hit the spot! Tie me up, I killed her! (*Runs away in convulsions.*)

RAZRAILOV: (*Dancing.*) I always forget the damn formula and because of that I always lose. *Cherchez la femme*, my friends, *cherchez la femme!*

IX

(*The laboratory of the Great Experiment. The Temperaments are out of control. Chol Erik rushes about the stage. Sang Vinik shuffles back and forth, rubs his hands, smiles merrily and dreamily. Melan Cholik moves slowly on buckling legs, extends his arms. Phleg Matik stands in a corner of the stage and picks his nose.*)

CHOL ERIK: That's her, brothers! Her! Accursed, beloved her! I've been waiting for her all my life! When I was thirteen years old I was sitting by a fence; I was all covered with dust, pimply-faced, biting my nails, a child from the wrong side of the tracks, my father was in jail! A white Rolls-Royce drove past me and in it sat the daughter of some vice-president. She glanced at me—at me, the ugly duckling—over her shoulder! I ran after the car, fell into shit, and arose an eternal foe of plutocracy! If you like, I'll bare my soul, brothers? It was only because of her that I became the master of forehead blows!

SANG VINIK: I too was not completely indifferent to the idea of social justice, dear sirs! I was a simple yachtsman, my friends, an ordinary loafer—healthy, full of lust and life! But once I saw her in one of the numberless windows in the city slums. She was wearing a short, little skirt and was washing windows. Passion inflamed me; yes, passion! I crawled up a pipe and was, to my shame, beaten up by a lout who looked like you, Chol. When I came home, I wrote my first poem. How about that?

PHLEG MATIK: As for me, she reminds me of my kitty. (*Nods.*) Her smell is of fine soap.

MELAN CHOLIK: I knew, I knew . . . a premonition tormented me . . . when I was a small, swarthy cook . . . her glittering gown on stage . . . during intermission she the singer came to the kitchen to taste the borscht . . . I wanted to live in this borscht and die . . . she didn't look at me once . . . she didn't beckon me with her finger . . . faded roses on the music stand . . . untimely old age. O my love, nightmarish like yesterday's cutlet . . . darkness . . . (*Nina and Cyber enter, muttering sweet nothings. Behind them is Love Triangle, busily eavesdropping.*)

CHOL ERIK: (*In the middle of a leap.*) Esther! Are you ready to share the fate of an unfortunate warrior? (*Demonstrates his terrible forehead blow.*)

SANG VINIK: (*Shuffling along with arms outstretched.*) Fenechka, my sunshine, what a meeting! Do you remember the verses: My ugliness sped toward you, your beauty raced toward me?

MELAN CHOLIK: (*Approaches in trepidation and great pain.*) Gloria, happiness, longing, domino . . .

PHLEG MATIK: (*Not leaving his place.*) My kitty, come to me. Little fluff! Little fluff!

CYBER: Forgive me. You're addressing me? But we're finished with all that.

NINA: Are you crazy, fellows? My name is Nina.

CYBER: Hello. Let's be introduced. My name is . . . Nina, sweetheart, what's my name?

NINA: Oh, honey, my poor little automat, your name is Vanya Malachi.

CYBER: Let me introduce myself. I'm Vanya Malachi—Nina's twelfth husband.

CHOL ERIK: (*Grabs Nina by the hand.*) I love your wife, Vanya. And I'm ready to confirm this by a terrible forehead blow! Do you understand?

SANG VINIK: (*Maneuvers from the side. Takes Nina by her other hand.*) Genosse Malachi, Nina and I were created for each other and there can be no question of connubial faithfulness!

MELAN CHOLIK: (*Crawls to Nina's feet.*) My goddess, my hopelessness . . . sauce of my soul . . . if I may be permitted to touch your train. (*His hand slides along Nina's leg.*) One touch of your train. Where is your train?

PHLEG MATIK: (*Touches Nina's chin.*) Little kitty, dearest, little fluff . . . Nina, Vanya, what a mess, after all . . . I've fallen head over heels . . .

LOVE TRIANGLE: (*Mutters in utter confusion.*) I love your wife . . . a terrible blow . . . yes, that's it . . . that's how it is . . . little fluff . . . hopelessness . . . I'm head over heels . . . I'm a man of liberal views . . . (*Convulsion.*)

NINA: (*Laughs.*) How about that! Men are crazy on both sides of the grave.

CYBER: Sirs, don't worry. I, Vanya Malachi, am the twelfth man . . . yes, yes, a man . . . (*Fixes his hair proudly.*) A man of liberal views. I am not at all like the preceding eleven, who troubled my little Nina over trifles. (*He tries to squeeze through to Nina but is pushed back by the others.*) Why confine oneself within the frame of a single triangle when one can construct a beautiful structure from many triangles? A structure resembling a crystal. Please court my wife. Court her, this only flatters my ego. But, gentlemen, I too would like to court her sometimes. (*Again tries to get through to her. A shoving match ensues around Nina.*)

NINA: On your knees! (*All five fall on their knees. Nina laughs. Behind the window is a noise of wings. The Eagle appears.*)

EAGLE: Greetings, my dead friends! I came to find out how my protégé is getting along. (*Seats himself on the window sill, dangles his booted feet. To Nina.*) I see, daughter, that here too you've learned how to get by.

NINA: (*Goes up to the window, wiggling her hips.*) Give me a smoke, gramps.

CHOL ERIK: (*Leaps up.*) Love is a tornado, a cyclone! Nina, you must belong to me only. Only I'm good enough for you. This is what I'll do the others. (*Demonstrates his forehead blow.*)

NINA: (*Smoking. To Eagle.*) They're all crazy about me.

EAGLE: I can see why. You're a good-looking broad, though not my type.

CYBER: Forgive me, she's still my wife, after all.

SANG VINIK: De facto or de jure?

NINA: What *is* your type, pops? You probably like something you can hang on to?

EAGLE: (*Laughs.*) Yes, that's exactly right. Something with a little substance.

NINA: (*Nettled.*) Dumb soldier.

CYBER: De facto or de jure, what's the difference? I've loved her for a thousand years. Do you think we live according to bourgeois values?

CHOL ERIK: Well, tell me where it was de facto?

CYBER: Here on the stairs.

SANG VINIK: (*Provoking them.*) How do you like that, gentlemen? We're waiting for Nina, being subjected to the monstrous Experiment, and here comes this Vanya Malachi and has Nina de facto on the stairs! How do you like that?

MELAN CHOLIK: Alas, as always, three's a crowd! (*Rolls up his sleeves.*)

LOVE TRIANGLE: (*Indignant.*) That's not true! The hypotenuse without the two other sides is dead!

CHOL ERIK: You shut up, worm, whore! (*Aims a forehead blow at the Love Triangle but the latter evades it, of course. Chol Erik, having missed, falls and rolls over like a ball. Razrailov enters with his traveling bag and halts in a corner, without being noticed by anybody. The suitors crowd together.*)

NINA: Military men used to like me in the past. Even old bucks from the general staff . . .(*smiles*) . . . used to send me flowers.

EAGLE: Cut it, daughter, cut it. I've got other things on my mind. I have a war. Of course, I'm a man in my prime and women like me. Do you believe it, a little girl, underage, has taken a liking to me? Well, when I'm flying, I sometimes fall and how can one keep from falling sometimes? And then she runs up to me and wants to know, did I hurt myself, does it hurt? She slips me notes. Understand? Your gray hair looks so distinguished. I love you for your war wounds. And so on. Oh, love is a cruel thing. Oh, a great cruel thing! And the Steel Bird doesn't know this. Sometimes when I claw him, I think, where's your heart? But he, daughter, has a fiery engine in place of a heart! But as for man, even a dead man fights for love. (*Points at the crowd of suitors.*) In general, which one do you like the most?

NINA: In principle I like all men. Every man has something touching and funny about him.

EAGLE: That's true.

PHLEG MATIK: (*Picking his nose.*) Brothers, I'm really crazy about Nina. What a predicament. (*Suddenly leaps to the forefront.*) All my life I've been waiting for her. I've never kissed a woman! I've waited long enough! Nobody else will have her!

CHOL ERIK: (*To Phleg Matik.*) Schlemiel!

PHLEG MATIK: (*To Chol Erik.*) Psycho!

CYBER: Nina, let's run away! (*Tries to break away from the crowd.*)

NINA: I hope they don't crush my twelfth!

EAGLE: O, dead friends! Stop messing around! (*Gets down from the sill.*) You've been visited by love and you're making idiots of yourselves. If I, an old eagle, were visited by love, I would . . . (*Sings and dances, tapping with his boots.*)

> We're earthier than those who live on earth
> And to hell with tales of gods!
> It's just that we bear on our wings
> What others bear in their arms . . .

CYBER: The Eagle's right, friends. (*Sadly.*) Nina, whether you love me or not is not important. The important thing is that I love you. And therefore I am a man and not a metal. (*Dances.*)

NINA: I love you!

CHOL ERIK: You don't love me, Nina! You're in your white Rolls-Royce and I'm in the mud, but I love you and therefore I'm alive! (*Dances.*)

NINA: I love you!

MELAN CHOLIK: Nina, golden slipper, thunder of the orchestra. Your eyes through the steam of pots. You don't love me but I love you and I'm alive! (*Dances.*)

NINA: I love you!

SANG VINIK: In the green sky, on the black wall, beneath the firmament, I saw you, Nina, for the first time. It doesn't matter that you don't love me but I love you and I'm alive! (*Dances.*)

NINA: I love you!

PHLEG MATIK: How can you love such a schlemiel like me? But I love you and life trembles for me like leaves beneath the wind. (*Dances.*)

NINA: I love you! (*Leaps off the window· sill. Dances.*) My boys! Don't be afraid, I won't leave you. I knew that you were waiting for me and here I am. Two bullets in the breast—is nothing. I always know that someone is waiting for me, but I can't always come. (*All dance silently and smile at one another, give one another flowers. Only Love Triangle is motionless. Having assumed the shape of a triangle, he is frozen in the corner of the stage.*)

RAZRAILOV: Ha, ha, ha! Very entertaining. *Danse macabre!* (*The dance stops.*)

EAGLE: Don't interfere with the dance, you freak!

RAZRAILOV: There's never been anything like this. How touching: a broken sewing machine and an old moth-eaten rooster are dancing with corpses. (*To Nina, gallantly.*) Of course, I'm not referring to you, madame.

CHOL ERIK: (*To the Eagle.*) Colonel, allow me to demonstrate the forehead blow!

EAGLE: Don't waste your energy on this nonentity, my boy. (*To Razrailov.*) Just wait until the Head Office catches up with you.

RAZRAILOV: Traitors! You've ruined the idea of the Great Experiment! Individualists! Narrow egotists! Abstractionists! Ists! (*Points to his traveling bag stuffed with sheets and towels.*) What do you care about the happiness of humanity? (*Takes a curtain from his bag.*) What do you care about Progress?

SANG VINIK: It's not our fault, Razrailov. It's a case of intrusion of mysterious forces. We're in love.

RAZRAILOV: Your corpse with a bullet in its head is slumped over the writing desk.

CHOL ERIK: We're happy!

RAZRAILOV: Your corpse is stuck in the Gultimoor canal.

MELAN CHOLIK: We're alive!

RAZRAILOV: Your corpse is rotting in a plot of celery.

PHLEG MATIK: We were saved by love.

RAZRAILOV: Your corpse fell onto the toilet bowl after the rope snapped.

CYBER: She came to me and I became a man. `

RAZRAILOV: You became garbage! (*Takes out a blue yarn and wraps himself in it.*) I am the angel of death!

EAGLE: Pretender!

RAZRAILOV: And you're an idiot!

EAGLE: Do you have a learned degree?

RAZRAILOV: Do you trust young scholars?

NINA: Where's *my* corpse, Razrailov?

RAZRAILOV: Madame, this grotesque scene does not touch upon you in the slightest. (*Throws Nina a fiery red rag.*)

LOVE TRIANGLE: (*Set in motion.*) We're happy . . . I've come . . . madame . . . this does not touch you . . . search for sister souls . . . madame . . . Adam . . . had'm . . . (*Convulsion.*)

CYBER: (*To Razrailov.*) You'd better go.

RAZRAILOV: (*Pulls out a small black curtain, manipulates it.*) Any-benny—ate-pelmeni—any-benny-I-don't-want-any-benny-went-to-hell. Do you give up?

CHOL ERIK: Take this! (*With a running start, aims a forehead blow at Razrailov. The latter evades it and the blow gets Melan Cholik in the stomach. Melan Cholik falls.*)

EAGLE: (*Merrily.*) Beat your friends to inspire fear in your enemies!

MELAN CHOLIK: (*To Nina.*) To love others is a heavy cross but your beauty is flawless. (*Nina kisses him.*)

PHLEG MATIK: (*To Nina.*) The mystery of your beauty and the mystery of life are one. (*Nina kisses him.*)

CYBER: (*Takes Sang Vinik aside.*) I've been meaning to ask you for a long time: What's death?

SANG VINIK: Kafka said: ''Death is beautiful. But not this death—another one.'' (*They stand in thought. Nina kisses them both.*)

CHOL ERIK: (*To Nina.*) Listen, Nina. Here's what just came into my head: I would forget about all valor, fame and glorious deeds on this sorrowful earth. (*Nina kisses him.*)

RAZRAILOV: (*To Nina.*) Madame, I'm sexually attracted to you. (*Nina is drawn toward him. Love Triangle vibrates.*)

CHOL ERIK: Attention! (*Aims a blow at Razrailov but hits Love Triangle.*) That too is not bad! It appears that I've killed the insect! Nina, listen to the rest: When your face in a simple frame would stand before me on the table—

RAZRAILOV: Lies! (*Pulls from his bag yarns of different colors and wraps himself in them, curls into a ball and rolls on the stage.*) Lies! Lies! Lies! (*Four Shepherdesses rush onto the stage in the middle of a furious rendition of the dance ''yolki-palki.'' Their skirts are cut à la Nina's mini.*)

CHOL ERIK: O god! The girls from Kaptenarmus!

RAZRAILOV: Lies! Lies! Lies!

SHEPHERDESSES: Look at all these men! Hooray! Boys we know!

Greetings, Chol! It's because of you I jumped off the bridge! Sang, you're here, too? It's because of you I shot myself in the head! Phleg, I've loved you all my life. You were sitting in the toilet and I was bawling! I hanged myself because of you! And I poisoned myself because of our cook, because of you, Melan! What a meeting! What joy! We're together again!

RAZRAILOV: Lies! Lies! Lies!

SHEPHERDESSES: Nina, you've saved us!

TEMPERAMENTS: You're life!

CYBER: You're love itself!

RAZRAILOV: Lies! Lies! Lies!

EAGLE: (*In a thunderous voice.*) Long live Nina! (*Takes Nina by the hand, leads her around the stage, lifts her up and raises her onto one of the armchairs. Everyone kneels down before her except Love Triangle, who is frozen in a triangular position of waiting, and Razrailov, who has stopped rolling and is also frozen, his head sticking out of the rags. Eagle, severely:*) Where were you born, Nina?

NINA: I don't remember exactly. There were bubbles, foam, a light-blue sky . . . no, I don't remember . . .

EAGLE: How did you live, Nina?

NINA: There was a lot of unpleasantness.

EAGLE: How did you die, Nina?

NINA: You know that. That idiot shot me twice right here. (*Unbuttons her blouse.*) No, pardon me, lower . . .

EAGLE: What do you want, Nina?

NINA: It's clear what I want. I want to live, pappy. I want to go down. I have a dress fitting on Tuesday.

TEMPERAMENTS, SHEPHERDESSES AND CYBER: We want to live! We love you, Nina! We want to go down! The hell with this damn tower! Razrailov, give us the key! We'll descend the stairs and continue walking into eternity! (*All of them leap up and approach Razrailov.*)

RAZRAILOV: (*Crawls out from under the heap of rags, is completely calm.*) One tiny minute. The key? Here it is! (*Shows the key.*) Yummy! (*He swallows the key and pats himself on the stomach.*) The sly fox had a key, in his pockets he would hide it. But tired of hiding it, he did gulp it. Now you find it. Ladies and gentlemen, don't you understand what eternity is? Even death has taught you nothing, ai-ai-ai! Now it's time for me to use my last resort. I didn't want to, but you forced me. (*He takes from his traveling bag an enormous white sheet, wraps one end around himself, extends the other over his head, slides along the stage and makes mysterious movements. He approaches Nina, suddenly grabs her, wraps her in the free end of the sheet and draws her to himself.*) Forgive me, madame. This is an extreme measure. (*Chokes Nina, laughs loudly.*) Unity of opposites, dear comrades!

SCREAMS: He's killing her! Save her! Men, why are you just standing about? Colonel? Vanya Malachi, you're made of iron, after all! (*Nina twists and turns in Razrailov's arms.*)

CYBER: (*Trembles.*) I can't budge. Something terrible is happening to me. I can't feel my head. (*The head gradually fades away.*) The transmission is concluded.

EAGLE: (*Rushes about in confusion.*) Brothers, understand. I'm alive. What can I do? If it were on the other side of the boundary, I would take him apart in seconds. (*Leaps up on the window sill.*) I'll try to fly to the Head Office. I'll get there even if I burn up. (*Grabs the window frame. The set rocks. Cracks appear in it. To Chol Erik.*) What about your forehead blow, friend?

CHOL ERIK: I've lost my strength. My arms feel like they're made of putty. (*All are in a terrible paralysis. Nina is getting weaker.*)

RAZRAILOV: Patience, gentlemen. Patience. Patience and hard work will overcome anything. Don't worry, we'll still do some experiments together, gentlemen!

LOVE TRIANGLE: (*Squeals.*) I won't allow the death of the hypotenuse! (*Throws himself at Razrailov. A brief struggle ensues near the right wall. The right wall tilts dangerously. A piece of the set falls onto the stage with a thud. With his right hand Razrailov grips Love Triangle by the throat, while with his left he keeps choking Nina. Chol Erik, collecting all his strength, directs a forehead blow at Razrailov. He misses and hits the left wall instead. Part of the left wall collapses.*)

EAGLE: (*Yells.*) The tower is falling! (*Hits the window frame with his fist. Leaps down, beyond the window. The window frame collapses with a thud. The lights go out. In the darkness one hears the noise of falling decorations. In a beam·of light Razrailov's distorted face appears.*)

RAZRAILOV: Madness! Everything's falling. This isn't in the script!

(*A piece of the backdrop falls. In the back of the stage is the hunched, exhausted Eagle. Katyusha and Emelya run up to him.*)

KATYUSHA: Evgeny Aleksandrovich, did you hurt yourself?

EAGLE: I love you, Katyusha. (*Embraces her.*)

EMELYA: Finally! (*In the darkness, in chaotic beams of light flash the faces of the Temperaments, the Shepherdesses, and Cyber.*)

SCREAMS: Nina, Nina? Where are you? Nina! (*Loud noise. Another piece of the backdrop falls. At the back of the stage are the Stage Manager and Gutik.*)

STAGE MANAGER: Gutik, it's a total disaster!

GUTIK: (*Gets down on his knees before her.*) Not all is lost yet, Alisia Ivanovna. Be my wife! I love you without measure! (*The set continues to collapse. From out of the darkness Nina appears and disappears like a vision. Behind her floats Love Triangle. Silence. A bright light comes on. On the stage is a heap of fragments, all that remains of the laboratory of the Great Experiment. Uncle Vitya runs out. Behind him, very solid, hands in pockets, walks Fefelov.*)

UNCLE VITYA: (*Sadly.*) You're too late, Andron Lukich, it has all fallen down.

FEFELOV: (*With sober calm.*) You reinforced the sides with zhgentel bolts?

UNCLE VITYA: Yes, yes, of course. But as you see . . .

FEFELOV: What's there to see? It's clear there weren't enough mulerons.

X

(*A coffee shop. A few tables with shaky aluminum legs. Small uncomfortable chairs. In the corner is a television, next to which, backs to the audience, sit Sang Vinik and Phleg Matik. Nearby, alone at a table, sits Emelya, reading a book and glancing at the screen. Four young Waitresses are whispering in a corner near the buffet table. Behind the buffet table sits Melan Cholik. He is bent over the buffet and is watching television intensely, with his eyes bulging out. In the foreground, Uncle Vitya and Fefelov are sedately eating dinner. A little farther back is a restless couple: Stage Manager and Gutik. They eat quickly, drink wine quickly, kiss quickly, and keep looking*) *around constantly. Beside them sit Eagle and Katyusha; before them stand partially full wine glasses. Eagle holds Katyusha's hand in his and looks into her eyes. Katyusha sneaks looks at Emelya. Above the buffet there is a sign with large letters: Don't dip your fingers or your eggs into the salt!)*

UNCLE VITYA:

Andron Lukich, try some ''tkemali'' sauce
Or maybe ''nasharabi'' is more to your taste?

FEFELOV:

''Tkemali'' has more substance. Birds like
Sauces with substance, Vitek.

UNCLE VITYA:

Would you like a shot of something to prepare
Your stomach for the change of dishes?

FEFELOV:

Good strong cognac flies down the
Throat like a bird but where can you
Get good cognac nowadays?
What we call cognac is really slop.

UNCLE VITYA: (*Worried.*)

Please try some, Andron Lukich.
And please get us some mulerons.

FEFELOV:

Well, okay.
Pour a little slop then, Vitek.

CYBER: (*Enters wearing a very formal suit, completely buttoned. And he is carrying a briefcase. He goes up to the buffet. To Melan Cholik in a whisper.*)

She hasn't come?

MELAN CHOLIK: (*Screams at the television.*)

Kick it, you idiot!
He missed the shot, the turkey!
How pathetic our players have become!
(*Bangs his fist on the table.*)
There was a time! The crossbars shook!
Balls were kicked through the net!
If I were out there,
There would be a flood of goals!

PHLEG MATIK: (*Rubbing his hands, smiling.*)
   Tactically, his play is correct.
   Yes, friends, there can be no
   Criticizing a player who sees
   The field so clearly.
MELAN CHOLIK: (*Screams.*)
   A lot you understand!
PHLEG MATIK:
   But he's scored four goals.
MELAN CHOLIK:
   But I could have scored nine! Nine!
SANG VINIK: (*Morosely.*)
   All is lost. Now our team
   Will never make the semifinals.
CYBER: (*In a whisper.*)
   She hasn't come?
MELAN CHOLIK: (*Looks at him.*)
   No, I didn't see her.
     (*Spits. Turns away from the television.*)
   Watching makes me sick. How do you like football?
     (*Looks at Cyber and begins to speak to him in a hot, whistling
     whisper.*)
   Listen, friend, I know you're a big shot,
   That you wheel and deal in the Ministry
   And that I'm nothing . . . but listen!
   She was here, my friend. She came!
   May I never eat bread again if I'm lying!
   It was five years ago, an evening hot like this one.
   Right after football. The door opened
   And she entered, ordered a milk cocktail,
   Spoke a few words in Turkish,
   Or French or English . . .
   In other words, not Russian . . .
     (*Grinds his teeth.*)
   And left . . .
CYBER: (*Sadly.*)
   I know this, brother. Every evening
   You tell me this story . . .
EMELYA: (*Still reading his book.*)

Strange!
It turns out that the philosopher
Izmailov had a much larger
Skull than most people . . .
KATYUSHA: (*Interested.*)
Just think
How many interesting things
There must be in your books.
EAGLE:
I was in reconnaissance once
And in a shelter abandoned by the
Enemy I once found a book . . .
KATYUSHA:
I know, Eagle, I know . . .
(*Turns away a yawn. In despair the Eagle squeezes her hand.*)
MELAN CHOLIK:
Look how he dawdles!
He moves like a sleeping python!
PHLEG MATIK:
An excellent player, but his temperament
Would suit a referee more than a player . . .
(*Gets up, goes to the buffet.*)
SANG VINIK: (*Also gets up. His movements resemble those of Melan Cholik in the preceding nine tableaux.*)
The final whistle! How much bitterness
This whistle has betokened for us,
Fans of this team which is clearly doomed . . .
(*Goes up to the buffet. All three Temperaments whisper together. Melan Cholik bangs his fist on the table, passionately tells some story.*)
UNCLE VITYA: (*Timidly.*)
Andron Lukich, maybe you could
Use this pen?
(*Hands Fefelov a pen.*)
FEFELOV: (*Puts on his glasses and looks at the pen.*)
Mmm . . . yes, I can use it.
Certainly I can use it, dear Vitya.
Or have you forgotten what I used to teach you?
In a household even crap can be put to use.

Only I prefer Parker jotters.
   (*Puts the pen in his pocket.*)
UNCLE VITYA:
   I'll ask the fellows about Parkers later.
   But could you use a necktie?
   After all, Andron Lukich, you're our eagle!
      (*Hands him a tie.*)
EAGLE:
   I request that you be more careful! Your jokes . . .
KATYUSHA: (*Annoyed.*)
   Evgeny Aleksandrovich, don't worry!
   Worry can ruin the liver of
   Even a sturdy old warrior.
   Emelya, come here! This fellow
   Is a student-philosopher. A brain!
      (*Emelya comes to their table. Without looking away from the
      book, he empties the Eagle's glass and eats something from his
      plate.*)
EMELYA:
   Just think, Dr. Aleksandrov's
   Ears were larger than those of
   Other people. Ears like radar . . .
STAGE MANAGER: (*To Gutik, while looking at Fefelov.*)
   They've gobbled up my new ring.
   Will you buy me a new one?
GUTIK:
   I'll soon get you a ring and not worse
   Than the one you lost. I've saved
   A can of mulerons and I'm getting
   Calls from the Little Theatre.
   They're putting on a show Saturday
   And are in need of mulerons, of course.
PHLEG MATIK: (*To Melan Cholik.*)
   She hasn't come? There's no news?
   Friends, I swear that yesterday on
   Small Bronnaya Street just before
   Sunset I saw in a high window a
   Shoulder that looked strangely familiar.

SANG VINIK:

    You imagined.

    She is not in nature. Don't wait for her.

    Perhaps on the Island of Mauritia

    She spends the evenings in cafés.

MELAN CHOLIK:

    Then why, old crocodile, do you

    Come here every evening and shed tears in your soup?

    Brother-crocs! She was here!

    She came, brothers!

    May I never see black bread again if I lie!

    Five years ago on an evening hot like this,

    Right after football, the door opened

    And she entered, ordered an egg bouillon,

    Spoke a few words in Spanish,

    In Polish or in Azerbaidzhani,

    In other words, not in Russian . . .

      (*Grinding his teeth.*)

    And left . . .

PHLEG MATIK:

    Petro, why do you always repeat yourself?

    She'll come, of course, but why

    Do you always make up fairy tales?

SANG VINIK:

    A terrible lie . . .

MELAN CHOLIK:

    Leave me alone, you jerks!

    The waitresses are in charge of customers!

    It's against the rules to ask the

    Bartender ridiculous questions!

      (*Shows them his fists and turns away.*)

EMELYA: (*Looking into his book, goes up to Cyber. Pokes a finger into Cyber's chest.*)

    Tell me, pappy, why are you alive?

CYBER:

    I'm not alive. I'm only resting . . .

    I'm waiting for new life . . .

EMELYA: (*Merrily.*)

    Idealism!

(*Phleg Matik and Sang Vinik go up to Eagle's table, even though there are many unoccupied tables in the room.*)

PHLEG MATIK:

Pardon me, is this taken?

(*They sit down.*)

FIRST WAITRESS:

They sat down.

Petro is off his rocker and these two look drunk . . .

SECOND WAITRESS:

They keep waiting, they come here every evening . . .

Do you remember that woman tourist, Vera?

THIRD WAITRESS:

She was an artist, not a tourist.

FOURTH WAITRESS:

They keep waiting

But aren't we waiting, too?

(*Chol Erik enters. His movements resemble those of Phleg Matik from the preceding nine tableaux.*)

MELAN CHOLIK: (*Screams.*)

He's come, the bastard! He's moving

Exactly the way he waddles on the field

From the center to the penalty line!

(*Throws a bottle at Chol Erik.*)

CHOL ERIK:

Have you finished throwing?

FOURTH WAITRESS: (*Runs to Chol Erik, kisses him.*)

Igor, my beloved!

On the field they kick you in the legs,

In the café they throw bottles at you!

CHOL ERIK:

Stop licking me!

(*Goes up to the buffet.*)

FOURTH WAITRESS:

Igor wait!

(*Her arms dangle.*)

CHOL ERIK: (*At the buffet he guiltily makes sniffing noises with his nose.*)

Don't forget I *did* get four goals . . .

MELAN CHOLIK: (*Screams.*)

You could have had nine! I would have had nine!

CHOL ERIK:

Cut the bull and give me the sausage.

MELAN CHOLIK:

You want a sausage?

(*Calming down.*)

Okay, here.

CHOL ERIK: (*With a sausage.*)

She hasn't come?

MELAN CHOLIK:

No, I didn't see her.

(*Looks around. In a hot whisper.*)

Listen, Igor. You can believe me.

She was here, friend. She came.

May I never see black bread again if I lie! It was five years ago, on an evening hot like this . . .

EAGLE: (*Gets up and proclaims loudly.*)

One day she'll come!

(*Stands with an arm raised. Enter Razrailov and Nina. Behind them, scraping his feet, enters Love Triangle. A silent scene.*)

RAZRAILOV: (*To Nina.*)

Here, *ma chère*, eat we a bit,

A bit we eat and back we go . . .

(*Laughs loudly and, wiggling his hips, leads Nina to a free table. Notices Cyber.*)

Greetings, Comrade Malakhaev!

(*Shakes his hand.*)

How nice we meet, eh what?

Try you pie? Glad very see you here today

And as old colleague would like you

My wife to meet. Madame Florence.

And this a friend of house . . .

(*Nods at Love Triangle.*)

Trusted companion . . .

CYBER: (*In a hollow voice.*)

How did you call Madame?

RAZRAILOV:

Madame Florence.

EAGLE:
  That's not true! It's Nina!
ALL:
  Yes, it's Nina! Nina! Nina!
    (*They all leap up and timidly drag themselves to Nina. Only Fefelov continues to eat.*)
FEFELOV:
  Madame Florence, I recommend the chicken.
NINA: (*Smiling, as if asleep.*)
  Nois lois lyons nielodar . . .
RAZRAILOV:
  As you see, Madame Florence's
  Russian leaves much to be desired.
    (*To Nina.*)
  You see, my dear, they were waiting for you.
  I told you, they were waiting for us.
NINA: (*Pitiably.*)
  Dzondon moire oli Goliotelo . . .
RAZRAILOV:
  She says: "Each to his own."
CHOL ERIK:
  Go away, Razrailov. We remember you.
CYBER:
  Stay, Nina. We've been waiting for you.
    (*A general commotion.*)
RAZRAILOV:
  We don't have time. We're busy now
  With a certain experiment.
    (*Quickly eats from Fefelov's plate.*)
  Imagine beneath the earth's surface—
  The chicken's juicy, you should add more sauce—
  At a depth far from football,
  A laboratory will arise . . .
  Free individuums together
  With electrical machines . . . cucumber . . .
    (*Chews.*)
TEMPERAMENTS:
  We don't agree! No!

RAZRAILOV:

Enough talk!

(*Wipes his lips on the necktie of the utterly confounded Fefe-lov.*)

Let's go, Ninon, Madame Florence or whatever

You're called in different towns.

(*To Love Triangle.*)

You come too, freak!

LOVE TRIANGLE:

O horrors!

Him I love, you I respect.

Pour poison in the food together with a kiss.

Traces of triangular love vanish,

Sufferings pale, Eros is enfeebled.

(*Convulsion. Razrailov takes both Nina and Love Triangle by the arm and, his behind wiggling, leads them to the exit. They disappear. Everyone returns to his previous position.*)

FEFELOV:

How stifling!

(*To Eagle.*)

Don't scream when it's so hot!

We have ways to make you shut up!

(*Nina reappears.*)

NINA: (*Joyously.*)

Hey, friends!

I've come back to you! You've been

Waiting for me for so long

And I've been waiting, too.

(*Weeps. Razrailov rushes out and grabs her by the arm.*)

Mourlen luglio tympan!

(*Her hands are outstretched.*)

Ferran occhi styllo navakobucco!

(*Razrailov drags Nina away. They disappear.*)

EAGLE: (*Sits down, exhausted.*)

She'll come back, you'll see, she'll come back.

MELAN CHOLIK: (*Ardently.*)

She was here, brothers, she came in!

Five years ago on an evening as hot as this one.

Right after football, the door opened

And she entered with some miserable creep
And a triangular shadow . . .

FEFELOV:

He's crazy!

UNCLE VITYA:

Be quiet, Andron. He knows what he's talking about.
(*The Temperaments, Cyber, and Eagle walk to the front of the
stage and stand in thought.*)

CYBER:

I'd like to know what will become of us,
What will become of us in the past and the present?
What will become of us in the future?

EAGLE:

Who knows?
I can only say that we'll all be alive
Two hundred years from now and one hundred years ago.
And on such a stifling and disturbing evening
We'll all be waiting . . .

FEFELOV:

Who ate my chicken?
I swear there'll be no mulerons
For the next performance!

July-August 1967, The Observatory, Koktebel

The Heron

(A Comedy with Intermissions and Rhymes)

Translated by Edythe Haber

CHARACTERS:

Ivan Monogamov: A foreign service officer. A young buck of forty. His appearance and behavior show signs of his having spent long periods outside the Soviet Union, and reveal certain peculiarities in his psychic makeup. He has enormous bright blue eyes, the size of sunglasses. In a word, a rather strange personality, at times displaying complete solidarity with his privileged class, at others a terrible disharmony with it.

Stepanida: His wife. A woman with an important position in public life, although she is not shown in this role here, since she is staying at a resort. In the first act, she is an ageless, lean mare with a firm, light step. There are certain hints of a ''devil-may-care'' spark. During the ensuing action she swells up right before the eyes of the audience: Her breasts, buttocks, and stomach turn into voluminous spheres and, in the process, her appearance takes on a gloomy grandeur.

Bob: Their son, a high jumper. Like all members of his profession, a very nervous lad, obsessed by one idea—to jump higher. Reserved; associates with those around him for practical purposes only. He is constantly doing knee bends, counting, keeping time. He sometimes waves his arms, first to the left, then to the right.

Filip Grigorievich Kampeneyets: Director of the Garment Workers' guest house. A full-blooded and buoyant man in his early sixties, the proponent of a realistic approach to life. He has a ''glorious revolutionary past,'' but that does not mean that he has now thrown in the towel. He is constantly on the phone, constantly in contact with the country's important industrial centers. One might give F.G.K. the title of ''detergent king,'' if it didn't sound too ironic.

This character's bearing really does have something regal about it, only his eyes sometimes wander lasciviously, and, when he opens his mouth from time to time, his tongue can be seen cleaning away mightily within.

Laima, Rosa, Claudia: Kampaneyets's daughters by different marriages. All three are thirty years old, a few days apart in age. Their

Dad has set them up doing different jobs at the guest house. (Laima is Linen Mistress, Rosa is Cultural Activities Director, and Claudia is Dietitian. Plus, they all work part-time in food operations.) But for the sisters the most important thing is their search for the meaning of existence.

Their great dissatisfaction, a longing for something bright and pure, unites them more, perhaps, than their dubious family tie.

Laima, a big blonde, likes to reason, tries to bring something rational to her moral quest.

Rosa, on the contrary, a graceful little brunette with a cigarette forever dangling from the corner of her mouth, is aggressively dreamy, defiantly aristocratic in spirit.

Claudia is a somewhat down-and-out, dishevelled creature of uncertain coloring, with insolent manners; what is known as ''spontaneity itself.''

The sisters all suffer from a severe case of being undermilked.

Lyosha The Watchman: A suspicious type, approaching forty. Everything about him arouses distrust: His foreign jeans on suspenders, long hair, beard, monocle. Even more suspicious are his peasant speech and old-fashioned Russian notions. Most suspicious of all is his mushroom drying, which he works at constantly, enthusiastically, and efficiently.

Lyosha The Garment Worker: A crystal-pure worker with a voucher. The only vacationer here on a legitimate footing. Full of smiles, very complacent about his rights and duties. Remains emphatically aloof from the nerve wracking goings-on. On the whole, is even more suspicious than the other Lyosha.

Cynthia and Clarence Gannergeit: Old farmers, perhaps the last representatives in the Baltic region of the notorious vestiges of the bankrupt system of capitalist agriculture.

They appear from the forest, and, during the first few minutes, seem like tree roots come alive, moss-covered and ridiculous. Afterwards, it's true, a flame lights up within them. The air begins to smell slightly of sulphur.

The Heron: Representative of an endangered species of bird. A seamstress at the Krasnaya Ruta garment factory.

(*The action opens, develops, and dies away in our own day in the Baltic region, near the western border of the Soviet Union, at a guest house intended for vacationing union workers.*

The guest house is called The Garment Worker. It is a two-story house with garrets, a miracle of comfort way out in the sticks. It stands on an emerald-green plain, which gently slopes away towards crests of dunes and the open sea beyond.

The plain is bordered by enormous European chestnut trees, some standing alone, others arranged in groups. Their crowns create the mood of an abandoned estate, of former magnificence, although there has never been an estate here, nor has there ever been any magnificence. Throughout the entire course of its history, during all the centuries of foreign domination and the few short years of independence of the Baltic states, this has always been a God-forsaken place, and all the more so now, since the appearance of industries not far away.

Hills overgrown with a dense pine forest approach the plain from the south. Scattered among the hills are lakes, swamps, fens, hidden animal life protected by the state—a nature preserve. The emaciated thread of a byroad wends its way through the forest. Somewhere fairly close by are a factory and small town, but the sounds of this out-of-the-way industrial life can barely be heard.

Indeed, the spot which Kampaneyets has chosen to occupy is not at all bad, especially since the weather has been fine: All through our story there will be bright sunshine, a full moon, and summer lightning. July is ripe.)

ACT ONE

(The open veranda of a guest house. Wicker furniture, as in old dacha plays Chekhov-style. But you can't fool us: alongside an antique clavicord, an almost meaningless object in the play, is a TV on a stand and two staircases of modern design leading to the second floor. A wall newspaper entitled A Healthy Vacation *or something of the sort, stuck on a column, plus a bust of Lenin, clearly indicate that we are not in some decadent manor house or other, but in a Soviet health resort. In addition to the two staircases to the rooms upstairs, there are two slopes leading down from the veranda to the outside world, one going off towards the sea, the other towards the woods.)*

ONE
THE PRODIGAL RETURNS

Midst the wide world, like an insect
A car crawls through the highway clamor.
It's driven by our young subject,
The foreign service man Monogamov.
A forty-year-old gypsy moth,
A young blade of good Party standing,
For a month or so he has stopped off
In his native Russia. He finds astounding
The over rough-and-ready tone,
He's daunted by the asphalt roads,
The fact some God-forsaken town
Is so unlike the Isle of Rhodes.

Ivan is not a simple soul,
Though his record cannot be impeached,
A modest mind, so *comme il faut*,
Of average height and soft of speech,
He's clear as day, he's loyal and true—
But here's the rub, from birth his eyes
Have been astonishingly blue
And of extraordinary size.

The frozen wastes of Stalin's Moscow
Gave birth and raised our pop-eyed tot,

The son of a high-placed officer.
He grew up, then he learned a lot
Of languages. For love of country
He went and found himself a bride.
And out of patriotic duty
Became the father of a child.
Then soon he left his homeland's limits—
One-sixth of our planet's broad expanse—
To see the mysterious other five-sixths,
Where there's neither Moscow nor Magadan.

Amidst the lights and phony glitter
He still recalled his native birches,
As should be, they still lived within him
When in Madame UNESCO's service.
However, as year followed year
His native land grew hazier.
Today he's in a jungle drear,
Tomorrow near a glacier.
He'd shop in Saks Fifth Avenue,
Which sells the best of cardigans.
He'd order from Chao Tse's menu
And take a jaunt to St. Laurent's.

* * *

To Lithuania from Moscow
He drives along, in no great hurry.
The thoughts of his dear child and Frau
Arouse alarm, and make him worry.
Meanwhile, at the Garment Workers guest house,
Upon the Baltic's sandy shore,
No one awaits him—not cat nor mouse,
Nor does his wife wait anymore.
Amidst the woods, which don't await him,
Neither the wolf nor rabbit waits,
Winers and diners do not await him,
Only, perhaps, the Heron waits . . .
This firebird for a millennium
Waits here in the swamp for her Prince to come.

(*A vacuum cleaner is buzzing. Lyosha the Watchman, hose in hand, crosses the stage. He pretends to be vacuuming the veranda, but in fact keeps glancing inquisitively in various places, first staring off from under his hands into the distance, then through his fingers at the television, then directing his eyeglass—something like a monocle—at the audience. Evening is approaching. Sunset hues.*)

LYOSHA THE WATCHMAN: No dust, my dear sirs, there's an extremely strange absence of dust. What a disjunction: a vacuum cleaner and no dust . . . (*He stops, lost in thought, comes to, and begins to play the fool, whether for himself or for the audience is unclear.*) Harmony is the fullness of life, but if life is full it should have a flaw. The absence of a flaw means life is not full. The absence of dust is a flaw. The presence of a flaw is a gap, a breach of harmony, the impending vacuum. Here you have before you the dead end of logic. If people like us—watchmen—are constantly up against it, what can you say about politicians . . . (*The old farmers, Cynthia and Clarence Gannergeit, climb onto the veranda from the forest side. They are both in rubber boots and homeknit sweaters, but Cynthia is wearing a moth-eaten black fox, its teeth bared, on her shoulders, and Clarence has on his head a felt hat with a wide band, in the best style of the 30s. Lyosha the Watchman notices the old couple at once, but doesn't let on. He undergoes a striking change, however—begins walking knock-kneed, like a bumpkin, and starts talking in an obviously phony peasant style, constantly switching from one accent to another.*) T'ain't a touch a dust in this here Fufluania, now thet ain't right. Ekh, where ha' ye gone, oh dust o'mine, me darlin' Russian dust? 'Tis the damp, the damp, dem fowcets, dey's all a'rustin', the vacationers, dey's all a-ailin'. An' what for? —'cause dere ain't no dust. Ah knows—all the soul ha' gone out o'dese here Fufluania swamps. Ain't no soul here. Now dere's heaps o'mushrooms, but ain't no soul . . . (*The old folks, giggling shyly, carry large baskets of mushrooms onto the veranda.*)

CLARENCE: Today few mushroom again, sir watchman. Such an existentsia.

LYOSHA THE WATCHMAN: Ah, so it be you, me little forest devils. Turned up agin, and not a speck o'dust on ye.

CYNTHIA: Laba diena, sir watchman. Gut abend. Everysing is

okey?

LYOSHA THE WATCHMAN: Okey-dokey, okey-smokey, said ole man Mokey. (*Glances into the basket.*) Eye an' begorra, such a heap o'mushrooms. Do ye gather 'em with a scythe or somethin', Clarence?

CLARENCE: It Cynthia only have special eye for exploratsia. (*Kisses his lady friend on the cheek.*)

LYOSHA THE WATCHMAN: I reckon ya got them nice white uns jes' on top, an' unnerneath they's all poisonous.

CYNTHIA: Nix poisenas. Gut. Ce jest dobrze. Wanderbar. Russkies say—horrorshow!

CLARENCE: Drei rubliks, sir watchman.

LYOSHA THE WATCHMAN: Ya'd even try an' milk a fly, ye devils! (*Grabs the basket, flies up the stairs, and disappears. Bob, a towering adolescent in an Adidas track suit, appears on the second staircase. Walks down slowly, doing knee bends, straightening his shoulders, twisting his torso. Lyosha the Watchman appears again, this time without the basket.*)

LYOSHA THE WATCHMAN: Cynthia, an' did ya have yerself some kind o'dream last night?

CYNTHIA: Ja. Bardzo fantastique, sehr pecooliar.

LYOSHA THE WATCHMAN: (*Avidly.*) Let it out, spill the beans! (*To Bob.*) Aye, an' this granny got dreams enough fer a whole movie studio.

BOB: (*Condescendingly.*) Well, really . . .

CYNTHIA: All begin like in cinema. Das big bend, illuminacion, foxtrot. He vas big and white all over. Had huge nose and white moostache—oossy. He cut his moostache mit his nose.

LYOSHA THE WATCHMAN: (*Trembles.*) What's that yer handin' us?

CYNTHIA: Everyone call him Majestique.

BOB: Why it's an ocean liner, that's obvious.

CLARENCE: Three grosse pipes. I seen too.

CYNTHIA: (*Walks back and forth on the veranda, incredibly animated, giggling and waving an imagined fan.*) He had being to be both ship and man and my cat. I vass also me myself and him, aussi.

CLARENCE: I recollectured. Three pipes, tooths, he had laughiness and van-der-fool suit.

CYNTHIA: I opended his third drawer in belly and there vass New

York, where I stroll with him as with Papa. I importantized, as Amerikanishce Volk say all zee time.

LYOSHA THE WATCHMAN: (*Slightly frightened.*) What's that them American folks say, Auntie?

BOB: Calm down, Lyosha. It's a literal translation from the Russian *vazhnichat'*—means to put on airs. (*To Cynthia.*) So, all in all, everything turned out well? Is everything all right, Madame?

CYNTHIA: Colassale! Magnifique!

BOB: Well, that's just fine. (*To Lyosha the Watchman.*) Hold the stopwatch, Lyosha. I want you to time my dashes. (*The two of them cross the veranda and descend on the sea side.*)

CLARENCE: (*In their direction.*) Drei rubliks, Herr Watchman, I dare to remind.

LYOSHA THE WATCHMAN: Stop actin' uppity, Clarence. Caintcha hold yer horses? (*Hides. The Gannergeits sit meekly in a corner, watch television, and giggle noiselessly. Laima comes down the right staircase, looks towards the sea, suddenly stands stock still and presses her hand to her breast.*)

LAIMA: How he runs! What dashes! It's breathtaking! (*Claudia stalks down the left staircase. Rosa, like a princess with a cigarette, promenades behind her.*)

CLAUDIA: (*To Rosa.*) Don't you force your ideas on me.

ROSA: Nobody's forcing anything on you. Who needs you? (*The sisters begin to set the big oval table in the middle of the veranda for supper.*) I'm curious—what ever has become of one of the cans of Swedish ham Father brought yesterday?

CLAUDIA: (*Bursting out.*) What's it to you?

ROSA: I'm just curious. It's the technique of the theft which interests me. After all, it's not just a case of someone having grabbed a fast bite from the refrigerator. A can has to be taken to one's room; it has to be opened and eaten there.

LAIMA: (*Continues gazing into the distance.*) Now, Rosa, what's that can to you?

ROSA: I hope you understand, Laima, that I couldn't care less about that trash. I simply find it amusing to observe the behavior of our distinguished Dietitian. What an appetite, what lack of discrimination. If she were in your place, she'd probably eat the soap, linen, and first-aid supplies, while if she were in mine, she'd devour the chess and books.

CLAUDIA: Well, now, I'll go tell Papa you begrudge your sister a piece of ham. You dirty rat, I'd like to . . . there are times . . . I'd like to give a certain someone a smack in the kisser!

LAIMA: Claudia!

ROSA: And sometimes I just feel like . . . just flinging a bad word in the face of a certain individual!

LAIMA: Rosa! (*Is distracted from her contemplation of Bob in training.*) Girls, this won't do! Let's sit down and talk it over. (*Sits down at the table. Her sisters follow suit.*) What ridiculous fights we have! I'm convinced that ham isn't the real issue; it's all because of our deep dissatisfaction with ourselves. We're forever searching for something important, trying to justify our existence somehow. That's true, isn't it? (*Rosa and Claudia nod rotely; evidently such talks have long been the custom among the sisters.*) And so when we fall into despair we let it out on some nonsense like Swedish ham. But look, My Sisters—the world is so beautiful! (*Giving a sigh of relief, she turns toward the sea.*) What colors! How the leaves of the chestnut trees are shimmering. And, finally, how beautiful the figure of that youth is, flying among the tree trunks. (*Stands frozen.*)

CLAUDIA: (*Grabs something haphazardly from the table, chews messily.*) Yeah, he's quite a boy. I wouldn't mind . . .

ROSA: First chew your food, you heartbreaker. She's dragged some half-witted watchman off to bed and now she imagines she's Cleopatra.

CLAUDIA: What, are you jealous?

ROSA: First chew your food.

CLAUDIA: Take this! (*Slaps Rosa.*) Damned masturbator! (*Sobs.*)

LAIMA: (*Turns to her with unseeing eyes.*) What happened!

CLAUDIA: I hit Rosa! (*Trembles.*) Our beautiful Rosa . . . (*Reaches out to her sister and kisses her.*) Forgive me, my precious!

ROSA: (*Puffing aristocratically on her cigarette.*) Get away from me. You Cheap Slut! You watchman's whore!

CLAUDIA: (*Laughs hysterically and keeps eating something from the table.*) You're right, you're right, Rosa, my precious! You see, my nerves are so shot I could down an ox! (*Bob jumps out from below somewhere and sits on the veranda railing. Lyosha the Watchman appears. Imitating Bob, he also pretends to limber up, as if he were an athlete. Sits next to him.*)

BOB: Hi, sisters! Aunt Laima, why didn't you come to my room yesterday? I did ask you, you know.

LAIMA: (*Bursts out.*) Oh, Bob, how can you? You didn't even inquire about my emotions . . .

CLAUDIA: (*Playfully.*) Maybe you've got the wrong address, Bob. How's about a quickie with me?

LYOSHA THE WATCHMAN: (*Threatens her with his fist.*) Ya'll get it in the ribs fer that, ya good-for-nothin' broad.

BOB: (*Angrily.*) I mentioned it in front of everybody, and I didn't even make the request of Aunt Laima personally—I made it out of everyone. I asked somebody to come to my room. So what happened? Nobody came. Is it really so complicated? I'm having a problem right now keeping in top form.

ROSA: (*Approaches Bob, walking sumptuously.*) What de-lightful presumptuousness. Can it be that the bird doesn't let you sleep either, Bob? (*Everyone gives a start, as if a secret has been let out. Only the old Gannergeits continue watching television, giggling as before.*)

BOB: (*Frightened.*) What bird?

ROSA: The one that flies here at night, and cries out and disturbs everyone.

BOB: Where does it come from?

CYNTHIA: (*Tearing herself away from the television.*) Ce polska— Polish.

LAIMA: What did you say?

CLARENCE: Nix. (*An awkward silence.*)

LYOSHA THE WATCHMAN: (*Clearing his throat.*) Now, an' what kind o'birds be these? A-shriekin' in the Fuffluanian dampness—ye call these birds? No in our Russia dearest how the cocks they go a-singin'—aye, an' ye takes yerself a handful o' the plowed fallow, fruit of the great Russian toil, so warm, so green, soft as the purest silk, me little missies.

ROSA: Do you know what fallow is, you Slavophile?

LYOSHA THE WATCHMAN: Huh?

ROSA: Fallow is uncultivated land. You haven't done your homework, friend.

CLAUDIA: (*Losing her temper.*) You're so damned literate, Rosa! Butting in all the time with her birds and her fallow! Don't force your ideas on us!

LAIMA: Claudia, please! Papa's coming down for supper soon.

LYOSHA THE WATCHMAN: Aye, an' has the director come back a'ready?

CLAUDIA: (*Venomously.*) Papa and Stepinada have been up there for quite a while now, studying the editorials from *Pravda.*

LAIMA: Claudia!

BOB: There's no reason for you to elbow your sister like that, Aunt Laima. It's no secret to me that my mother and Uncle Filip are having sexual relations. It's a simple and normal thing, and I can only welcome it. As for me, I haven't heard any birds at all. I've been sleeping normally, but to keep in top form I need someone . . . either you, Aunt Claudia, or you, Aunt Rosa, or preferably you, Aunt Laima . . . to come to my room. Please settle the question. If you'll excuse me, I still have some cross-country to do before supper. Lyosha, have you still got the stopwatch? Let's go! (*Bob and Lyosha jump down from railing and disappear.*)

ROSA: Laima, don't tell me you're going to go to that presumptuous brat's room today?

LAIMA: (*Looking aside.*) How strange. When that bird cries out at night I feel such bitterness, such pain, as though the years had whisked by in a meaningless train. But that isn't true, you know. (*Defiantly to the chestnut trees.*) I'm a trained geologist, I discovered a precious metal in far-off lands! (*Turns to her sisters.*) And you, girls . . . Rosa, you, after all, are a chorus director, a conductor, a lecturer; you're romanticism itself. Claudia, you're a technologist of some talent. Girls, this guest house has bewitched us. We've been cut off from life's struggles. Our common Father has taken everything upon his mighty shoulders and has assigned us the strange roles of Linen Mistress, Cultural Activities Director, and Dietitian. And here is the result: We spend our days in idleness, forget the struggle, the past, the future—we're even forgetting our own mothers. We're turning into vegetables. No wonder certain mere youths don't see us as human beings, as individuals.

ROSA: Oh, Laima, my Darling! (*Laima and Rosa fall upon each other's breasts and weep. Claudia eats nervously and messily.*)

CYNTHIA: (*Peers out from behind the television.*) Tri rublikas for zee mashrooms, Frau Watchman!

CLAUDIA: I'm no Frau Watchman to you, you old witch! (*Kampaneyets and Stepanida appear on the left staircase and, linking arms in a business-like way, descend.*)

KAMPANEYETS: . . . and that's why, Stepanida, the most important thing for us at the current stage is basic capital investments. (*Pats his companion on the rear.*)

STEPANIDA: (*Is now in her initial stage, a dryish mare with a faintly devil-may-care manner.*) Comrades! Comrades! (*They sit down at the table facing one another. The evening meal at the Garment Workers' guest house begins.*)

KAMPANEYETS: (*Looks around the table very contentedly and takes a meat patty.*) Well, here we are, all together once again. And what an evening it is, eh, Gals?

"The sea road it was
So quiet and calm . . . "

But where's our cosmic jumper?

ROSA: Your little son, Stepanida . . .

LAIMA: Bob is doing the cross-country, right on schedule.

STEPANIDA: He's a highly motivated boy. Now here's a question of genes for you, Uncle Filip. Whose do you think are dominant?

KAMPANEYETS: (*To Claudia.*) And where's your faithful Watchman? Still working away at his hobby?

CLAUDIA: Now why do you ask *me* that question, Papa?

KAMPANEYETS: (*Laughs softly.*) Now don't get mad, child. I mean his mushrooms, his tender little mushrooms. Why, it's a real obsession, you know, it's right up our alley. If you'd like to know, I honestly respect that Lyosha. I picked him up by chance when he was down and out, and here he is now, a thriving mushroom man. And I'm asking because I like it when everyone is gathered around my table.

STEPANIDA: You have such patronly feelings, Uncle Filip. You're really a . . . (*screws up her eyes and laughs*) lover of the human race.

KAMPANEYETS: You're right, Stepanida. I love to have my clan seated around me and eating good, nourishing food. (*His tongue works inside his mouth.*) I'd really like some beer, some excellent Danish beer. I'll call tomorrow and get some delivered. Now, I do love these daughters of mine, and I'm glad to see them as happy as they are now. Of course, we do miss our mamas, don't we, girls? Vilma Valdmanisovna and Galia Djamilovna and Maria Filimonovna . . .

STEPANIDA: Why, you're a real pasha, Uncle Filip!

KAMPANEYETS: Now, I must disagree with you there, Stepa. It's not a harem I need—people are important to me as milestones on the road of my life. I don't have anything to be ashamed of! Let's take Laima. She brings back memories of those tumultuous days when we—and under the most difficult conditions, I might add—laid the first foundations of statehood here in Lithuania, made it into a glorious Soviet Republic. You young people are enjoying the results now, but we had to begin with the ABCs, we had to knock the most rudimentary truths into their heads. And now look at my dear Rosa. The Karakum Canal, the hot breath of the desert. We turned over millions, billions of tons of sand before we could quench the age-old thirst of Turkmenia. And Claudia—she brings to mind the Berezniaki Potassium Combine, chemistry, the continuing struggle to put into practice the great ideas of that great man . . . ummm . . . Mendeleev . . . And so I rushed back and forth, from one end of the country to the other, on my special plane. Pardon me, but I also feel pride and am inspired by the present day. Even my humble Garment Worker guest house is important and essential. And the part I am playing in the distribution of household products—all those dyes, deodorants, detergents, varnishes, anti-corrosive agents, insecticides—all of that is important and essential. No, really now, I don't have anything to be ashamed of! That's why I gaze about my table with such satisfaction when I return from a business trip. Well, what's new?

ROSA: A bird has appeared. It cries out at night.

KAMPANEYETS: What kind of bird?

STEPANIDA: Personally, I haven't heard a thing.

CLAUDIA: But I've seen you on the balcony at night.

STEPANIDA: Oh, I was just thinking about an article.

KAMPANEYETS: Well, now, first things first. What kind of bird is it? (*The bird's cry—hollow, wild, and disturbing—can be heard. Everyone jumps up. Only Stepanida.continues drinking her tea.*)

STEPANIDA: I don't hear anything whatever. (*The spoon is knock-*

ing in her glass. The cry is repeated.)

CLAUDIA: (*Laughs.*) Why, it's just my Lyosha, the stupid slob! See what he's learned, the bum! (*Everybody sees Lyosha the Watchman who, emerging from the dusk like a faun, imitates the voice of the bird.*)

THE SISTERS: (*Joyously.*) So, it's Lyosha! Lyosha was playing a trick on us the whole time! Lyosha—our Watchman!

LYOSHA THE WATCHMAN: (*Pleased.*) We picks up these here things at ou' mammy's knee, you all . . .

ROSA: (*Bewildered.*) What? Can it really have been only Lyosha the Watchman? (*An instantaneous, sharp sadness has paralyzed the entire company. The cry of a bird, wild, hollow, and disturbing.*)

LYOSHA THE WATCHMAN: (*Puts his monocle in his eye and peers into the reddening sky.*) So thar she be, her very own self. Answerin' me call.

CLARENCE: (*Comes out from behind the television and tips his hat.*) Przepraszem panstwo. I have visionariu.

KAMPANEYETS: Now who in the world is this scarecrow? (*Cleans his mouth.*)

LYOSHA THE WATCHMAN: Aye, an' it be our neighbors, farm folk. They's wood devils, sure 'nough.

KAMPANEYETS: Oh, these stupid jokes. There are no individual farms around here. I'll make inquiries tomorrow in the right places.

LYOSHA THE WATCHMAN: What's that ya seen, Clarence?

CLARENCE: Heron is there, reicher . . . forget Russkies name . . . tsaplia . . .

CYNTHIA: (*Giggles, kisses the face of her black fox.*) Now somebody will came, and all will begininess.

LYOSHA THE WATCHMAN: (*Frightened.*) Hey, granny, better keep outa that thar business. They's others roun' here in charge o'that stuff. (*Bob climbs up on the veranda, wet and cheerful after his run. He waves to someone.*)

BOB: Hey, Buddy, over here!

VOICE OF MONOGAMOV: Am I in the right place? Is this the Garment Workers's guest house?

BOB: Come on up! You don't have to lock your car! (*To Stepanida.*) Hi, ma! (*To Kampaneyets.*) Guten tag, uncle Filip! (*To *everybody.*) Some foreign-looking dude has turned up. In a khaki safari suit. (*Monogamov appears on the veranda.*)

TWO
A STEP

With his enormous eyes, alarmed,
He views the play upon the boards,
The hall, what's here and what's beyond,
The winding path into the woods.

Come to your senses, quiet soul,
Child of the planet, Monogamov!
Just one last step—yes, that is all—
And he's caught in the meshes of a drama.

KAMPANEYETS: You're in the wrong place, Comrade, and on top of that, you broke the law—you went past a "No Trespassing" sign. Show me your documents. I'm the official . . . hmmmm . . . hmmmm . . . Auto Inspector.

MONOGAMOV: My documents? Of course, of course . . . (*Digs into the many pockets of his safari suit.*)

STEPANIDA: (*Stands up.*) Why, Uncle Filip, what do you mean? This comrade might have broken the law, but he's not in the wrong place.

MONOGAMOV: My God! Styopa! (*Takes an unsteady step towards his wife and tries to kiss her.*)

STEPANIDA: (*Holds out her hand.*) Well, hello, Monogamov! (*Monogamov, confused, shakes her hand.*) Well, you're a fine one! Not a single telegram or phone call. It's like the prodigal returning! (*To everyone.*) Comrades, who do you think this is? My lawful, wedded spouse!

BOB: Do I understand that to mean that this is my father?

MONOGAMOV: (*Finally envelopes Stepanida in his embraces. Over her shoulder explains to those present.*) You see, I flew in from Brussels and my family wasn't in Moscow, the neighbors said they were on the Baltic, so I took my friend's car and was on my way. You know, it seemed to me at first you had something private here, a kind of large family with internal contradictions . . .

KAMPANEYETS: (*Hostile.*) What do you mean, contradictions? There aren't any contradictions here.

MONOGAMOV: Believe me, I'm very glad I was wrong. (*To his wife.*) Styopa, do you have a room of your own here?

STEPANIDA: (*Interrupting his embraces with an energetic movement.*) You've grown so delicate and refined, Ivan . . . (*Laughs.*) I wouldn't have recognized you.

MONOGAMOV: And you're just as taut and muscular as ever, Styopa. You're still into sports, are you? Tennis, swimming?

BOB: I simply didn't recognize you, Pops. You've gotten younger, somehow.

MONOGAMOV: (*Embraces his son.*) Bobbie! You've gotten younger too! You used to be so plump, with a pot belly, and now— you're a young god! Did you graduate from high school? Are you in college?

BOB: Really, now, Dad, don't you read the papers? I'm one of the top ten high jumpers in the world. I passed the 2.2 meter mark.

MONOGAMOV: (*Sentimentally.*) And you, Styopa, do you still work in the same hotel, keeping an eye on the foreigners?

BOB: (*Steps on his father's foot.*) Halt, pop! What do you mean, hotel? (*Loudly.*) Mama has been the head of a department for ages now.

MONOGAMOV: (*Takes a step back, with even greater sentimentality.*) Yes, yes, I can see—you've changed over the years. How the years go by . . . If you only knew the things I've seen over the years, the far-flung places UNESCO has sent me to! Kenya, Tanzania, Uganda, the Maldives, the Solomon Islands, Papua, Nepal, Bhutan, Afghanistan . . .

KAMPANEYETS: Will you have some supper? (*Stepanida nudges Monogamov towards the table.*)

MONOGAMOV: (*Taking a seat.*) . . . Jordan, Lebanon, Biafra, Cape Verde, Tristan-da-cunha, Salvador, Paraguay, Greenland, Chile, the Easter Islands . . . I can see everyone's burning with curiosity. (*Slyly.*) But I won't tell you everything all at once. (*Begins eating a meat patty.*)

CLAUDIA: But have you been in Poland?

MONOGAMOV: (*Choking.*) Where?

LAIMA: In the Polish People's Republic?

MONOGAMOV: How's that again? (*The sisters glance at one another. Rosa shrugs her shoulders.*)

BOB: Give me the keys, Old Blue Eyes. Lyosha and I will drag up your designer duds. (*Exits together with Lyosha.*)

MONOGAMOV: Styopa, do you have your own room here?

STEPANIDA: Ivan, first of all, I'd like you to shake hands with the Director of our guest house, Filip Kampaneyets. You must remember our Uncle Filip?

MONOGAMOV: Uncle Filip?

STEPANIDA: Of course you remember Aunt Shura Nikolaiko.

MONOGAMOV: Aunt Shura?

STEPANIDA: It's like this: Aunt Shura Nikolaiko, as you know, is the sister of Vitold Kostianykh, whose first wife, Elizaveta Rysso, has a son, Konstantin Rysso, who married Valentina Poluyanova, who is the Kampaneyets's niece, and, on the other side, Vasyusha Nikolaiko, that is, Aunt Shura's stepson by her second marriage, married Victorina Front—yes, that's right, the daughter of the writer who dyes his bangs—and she's the step-sister of that very same Valentina . . .

MONOGAMOV: Ah, now it seems I do remember Uncle Filip very clearly. (*Holds out his hand.*)

KAMPANEYETS: (*As though looking through some papers and not noticing his hand.*) Will you have some supper?

MONOGAMOV: I'm already eating.

KAMPANEYETS: But in the official sense?

MONOGAMOV: I beg your pardon?

KAMPANEYETS: Well, this isn't some private clip joint, you know; this isn't one of those Solomon Islands of yours.

STEPANIDA: (*Laughing softly.*) Now, now, Uncle Filip, surely you're not worried about an extra mouth to feed? Chin up, Uncle Filip, nobody's extra at our table, we have enough for everybody. (*To her husband, in a whisper.*) He's a good-natured grouch. (*To Kampaneyets.*) Please register Ivan Vladlenovich Monogamov as a family member. (*To her husband.*) Ivan, that's Laima, Rosa, and Claudia sitting opposite you. They're our sisters.

MONOGAMOV: Bravo! Through the years I've had masses of contact with sisters within the framework of UNESCO. They are extraordinary, compassionate people. I remember an incident in Madagascar. We were waiting for a helicopter . . .

STEPANIDA: No, no, Ivan, they're not sisters of mercy, not nurses. Remember, you're not in UNESCO now, you rascal. These are Uncle Filip's daughters, born in various regions of the country. Uncle Filip has given them some responsibilities here. Claudia, for example, is our dietitian. The ham, the remainders of which you see on the table, is under her jurisdiction . . .

CLAUDIA: All of us here have been breaking our backs, you might say, for your dear wife, while Ste . . .

KAMPANEYETS: Stepanida is our part-time phys ed instructor, while Bob was hired as a lifeguard. (*Bob and Lyosha the Watchman climb onto the veranda. Bob is carrying a very fashionable but very small suitcase. Clarence Gannergeit, his hat pressed to his chest, repeats his "drei rubliks" to Lyosha, but the latter only waves him away.*)

MONOGAMOV: What you've told me is marvelous. It's as if you're a collective and a family at the same time. Precisely this feeling of humanity as a single family always enraptured me there as well, within the framework of UNESCO.

KAMPANEYETS: You can't scare us with your Yunesca. Ionesco! Ionesco! Everybody knows what you really mean!

LYOSHA THE WATCHMAN: Who be this Ionesco o'yers, Laddie— yer brother who watches everywhere? We got our own Ionesco in this here place, an' ya cain't hide a thing from him, neither.

MONOGAMOV: As I was driving toward this glade, my heart skipped a beat—it reminded me of Thailand . . . Tell me, is this typical of evenings here?

ROSA: (*To Claudia.*) This Monogamov is attractive, don't you think?

CLAUDIA: Just look at how his eyes pop out. Probably got goiter— means he's raring to go.

BOB: Did you leave all your baggage in Moscow, pop? There was only this one little suitcase in the car.

MONOGAMOV: (*Lowers his eyes.*) That's all I've got.

STEPANIDA: (*An impending storm.*) What do you mean, all?

MONOGAMOV: (*Rattles on, embarrassed.*) The thing is, I was returning to Moscow from Belgium, from Antwerp. Do you understand? What can you buy in Belgium? Judge for yourself.

COMMON SIGH: In Belgium?

CONTINUATION OF THE COMMON SIGH: And last year I . . . from

Belgium . . . three suitcases this big . . .

MONOGAMOV: Really? What in the world did you find there? As far as I know they don't have anything there.

STEPANIDA: (*With apparent calm.*) Do you mean, Ivan, you didn't even bring us any clothes? No blue jeans?

BLUE JEANS CHORUS: BOB: No blue jeans jacket?

LAIMA: No blue jeans skirt?

LYOSHA THE WATCHMAN: No blue jeans shirts?

BOB: No blue jeans sunglasses?

ROSA: No blue jeans toothbrush?

MONOGAMOV: No blue jeans?

STEPANIDA: (*Stands up abruptly.*) Why, you're completely off your head! (*A chair flies away with a crash and tumbles across the floor. Monogamov, terrified and not understanding a thing, runs away and stops only when he reaches the railing. He slowly turns around. In the meanwhile, it has grown completely dark, and we now see our ill-fated internationalist in his olive-colored suit against the background of the dark sky. A gaunt figure with enormous eyes blazing with alarm. Several seconds pass. Noiseless summer lightning flashes for an instant, illuminating the crowns of the trees and the distant sea.*)

MONOGAMOV: For some reason my heart skipped a beat again . . . excuse me . . . The thing is that our comrades at the embassy in Brussels told me you could also ''get a good deal'' in Moscow. So I exchanged all my money in Moscow. (*A tense silence. An exchange of glances.*)

LYOSHA THE WATCHMAN: An' was it heaps o' cash ye done bring, Dovie?

MONOGAMOV: To tell the truth, I don't know. What with the cost of living . . . inflation . . . I've been somewhat out of touch . . . I know, it's my fault . . . It came to 68,000.

STEPANIDA: In rubles?

MONOGAMOV: Right, that's it, in rubles.

RUBLE CHORUS: BOB: Rubles?

LYOSHA THE WATCHMAN: He means *real* rubles.

CLAUDIA: Real real rubles or . . . ?

STEPANIDA: He changed unreal real rubles into real real rubles.

BOB: (*To Father.*) Ah, you brought real real rubles! (*Jumps up from his seat and reaches the ceiling light fixtures.*) All right, Dad!

(*Joyous animation. Everyone exchanges glances and repeats "real real rubles." Kampaneyets with a gesture invites Monogamov back to the table.*)

MONOGAMOV: (*Uncertainly joining in the general animation.*) Yes, yes . . . real real rubles and, besides . . .

STEPANIDA: Let's go, Ivan, I'll show you how I live here. (*The nearby cry of a bird reaches them from the darkness. Everyone freezes. The cry is repeated. The sound of wings. A heavy flight in the darkness. Kampaneyets jumps out to the proscenium with a huge two-barrel rifle which seems to appear from nowhere.*)

KAMPANEYETS: Where is that piece of filth? In the west? (*His shot rings like thunder in the dark sky.*) Did I hit it? (*Once again the cry of the bird and the sound of wings can be heard very nearby.*)

LYOSHA THE WATCHMAN: If you'd a hit her, I'd o' knocked off them thar balls o' yers on the spot.

KAMPANEYETS: What a piece of filth! (*He is shaking.*) What a disgusting piece of filth! (*To Lyosha.*) It's your duty, you son of a bitch, to protect your vacationers!

MONOGAMOV: Who is she?

STEPANIDA: (*Irritated.*) So, it's the same old story! He heard some piece of filth—and already it's "she." It's not a "she" at all. It's just an animal.

MONOGAMOV: (*Whispers.*) No, it is she.

THE GANNERGEITS: (*Giggling from behind the television.*) Heron! Reicher! Forget how Russkies say. Chaplia s bagna!

MONOGAMOV: Tsaplia! Heron! (*Noiseless summer lightning flashes, and for an instant everyone can see distinctly a large, ridiculous looking bird fly past, its long legs drawn back in a pretense of speed . . . Monogamov runs headlong from the veranda and disappears in the darkness. A pause, awkward silence. Stepanida is at the center of attention.*)

STEPANIDA: (*Approaches the edge of the veranda, imperiously.*) Ivan, come back! (*Monogamov emerges from the darkness. Looks completely devastated. Keeps turning around.*)

STEPANIDA: (*Cheerfully.*) Well, let's go, at long last: You'll see how I live here. (*Holds out her hand.*)

MONOGAMOV: Let's go, Styopa, let's go. (*Offers his arm. On the stairs he once more looks around and stares into the dark sky. Then he lets himself be led away.*)

KAMPANEYETS: (*Accompanies the married pair with a dark glance, holding the rifle in both hands.*) Ooh, how I'd like some beer, some excellent Danish Carlsberg beer! (*Cleans his mouth.*) I'll call first thing tomorrow . . . to Copenhagen! (*The light on the veranda quickly fades, the light bulbs dim right before our eyes. The contours of the trees beyond the veranda and a segment of the sea's surface with a spot of moonlight stand out more and more distinctly. Kampaneyets shouts furiously.*) What's going on here, in this lousy garment worker? You can't even go away on a business trip! Lyosha, come over here! Why's that stinking piece of filth flying over the house? What are outsiders doing in staff members' rooms?

LYOSHA THE WATCHMAN: (*Inserts his monocle and looks aside.*) What's it gotta do with me? I'm jes' an ornery watchman. It has absolutely nothing to do with me.

KAMPANEYETS: Why's the frigging light going out there on the left?

LYOSHA THE WATCHMAN: Down thar at th' electric station, Filip Grigorych, ther's a mighty lot o' drunkenness. These days findin' a good electrician's like lookin' fer a needle in a haystack, not to mention watchmen. So you jes' go an' lay yerself down, Filip Grigorych. (*In a whisper.*) And bright an' early that thar phys ed director's gonna help ya rise an' shine. (*Loudly.*) Claudie, let's go and tend the mushrooms! (*Climbs the stairs.*)

CLAUDIA: I'm no Claudie to you, I'm Claudia! (*Climbs behind him.*)

LYOSHA THE WATCHMAN: Come on, come on, Claudie honey! (*Goes up.*)

CLAUDIA: I'm no Claudie honey to you, I'm Claudia! (*Climbs.*)

LYOSHA THE WATCHMAN: Now, Clau, watch yer tongue! (*Climbs.*)

ROSA: (*With hidden despair.*) Claudia, where are you going so early?

CLAUDIA: To read a book!

ROSA: In the dark?

CLAUDIA: You got it! (*Exits.*)

KAMPANEYETS: There isn't a single can of Danish beer, just to spite me. (*Turns in various directions, not letting go of the rifle.*)

BOB: Keep your chin up, Uncle Filip! You'll have your beer tomorrow from Copenhagen. Up, up! Ever upward and onward! I'm going to my room, Aunt Laima, and I hope that there won't be any hitches today. To everyone here—a guten nacht! That's quite a suit my pop's got on, huh? Eighteen pockets! I counted eighteen pockets! (*Overcomes the staircase in two leaps and disappears. Rosa begins climbing the other staircase, her heels distinctly clicking and her cigarette smoldering.*)

LAIMA: Rosa, where are you going?

ROSA: To read.

LAIMA: In the dark?

ROSA: Yes, in the dark.

LAIMA: Alone?

ROSA: Well, not with some scum. (*Exits. Kampaneyets, almost totally removed from reality by now, wanders across the stage with his rifle, hunting out a target in the audience.*)

LAIMA: Father! I am tormented by the meaninglessness of my existence.

KAMPANEYETS: (*With annoyance, as though suffering from a headache.*) Why, what other kind of existence do you want? Everything's so simple. Good and evil. Progress and reaction.

LAIMA: Is that true, papa? Is it all so simple? Thank you. Good night! (*Climbs up the same staircase Bob had leaped up. Exits.*)

KAMPANEYETS: How the devil I'd like some Danish beer! How the devil I'd like a sauna! (*Cleans his mouth. The old Gannergeits, in the meanwhile, have long since abandoned the darkened television and are puttering about behind the clavichord.*)

CYNTHIA: (*In a whisper.*) Clarence, I feel amour for diese man mit rifle. Mein soul craves der musique! Muzak! Muzhik!

CLARENCE: Jawohl, Herr Oberst! (*Pulls a field radio transmitter out of his knapsack, turns it on. The sounds of a pre-war tango from the movie* Peter, *intermingled with the Morse Code, wafts across the stage.*)

KAMPANEYETS: What's that! What enchanting music! And an enchanting time it was! The memories it conjures up . . . the special task force . . . Yes, yes, it was the same year as the Finnish war . . . It all happened when awesome Finland attacked mother Russia . . .

CYNTHIA: (*Approaches Kampaneyets, walking like a woman of the world.*) Ja, ja . . . quelle beautiful time, c'est ca, Herr Oberst!

KAMPANEYETS: (*Raising his rifle.*) What the devil?!

CLARENCE: (*Approaches, shuffling like a footman.*) I have l'impudence, pan Director, but sir Watchman had debtedness fur mushrooms. Drei rubliks and we zuruck under die ground.

KAMPANEYETS: What nerve! What, doesn't Soviet society even exist for you? (*Clarence is silent. His mouth, frozen in a servile smile, glows in the semi-darkness.*)

CYNTHIA: (*Waves an imaginary fan at her husband.*) Away, caperale! Phoo, quelle materialismus! (*To Kampaneyets.*) Engagez-vou a tango, mon Bolshevik! (*Kampaneyets, as though bewitched, puts his rifle aside and surrenders to Cynthia's arms. They dance.*)

CLARENCE: (*Enthralled.*) C'est fantastique!

CYNTHIA: Oi, what a time have been then, the thirties! I adoren the Roossian bear bonbons! Bolshoi Ballet! *Giselle!* Blackouts! I haven one feller from Luftwaffe, he had der habituation bring me rosen, tulips, and on return trip he dump his saturation bomb nach Poland. Fire! Blumen! It was not you, Herr Oberst?

KAMPANEYETS: Unfortunately, comrade, at the time I was fighting up to my neck in snow. The forbidding snowdrifts were bristling with lead. And once we made a daring raid behind enemy lines. I remember the war trophies—a heap of French canned goods. And we captured some women saboteurs—one of them was a great little biter—it wasn't you, by any chance, Genosse?

CYNTHIA: Oh, parachuten, parachuten!

KAMPANEYETS: And remember the way we used to sing? (*Sings.*)

He warmed with the breath of his heart

The gray and cold nights of the north . . .

They don't sing songs like that nowadays.

CYNTHIA: Oh, colossale! (*Sings.*)

He parted the mountainous slopes,

He paved a new path in the clouds . . .

CLARENCE: (*In a reedy voice, from the side.*)

At his word, oh so young and so strong,

The thick gardens did rustle and sway . . .

KAMPANEYETS: (*Pushes Cynthia away and grabs his rifle.*) Hands up, you rats! Confess, who are you working for?

CLARENCE: (*With raised hands.*)

Like the sun on a merry spring day,

Does he circle his dear native land . . . .

CYNTHIA: (*With raised hands.*)

Let us sing now, oh comrades, a song

About Stalin, the great gardener.

KAMPANEYETS: (*Furiously.*)

Against the great enemy threat

Did he seal all our borders with tanks . . .

(*Cocks the trigger.*) So we're going to play dumb, are we? Confess, you devils!

CLARENCE: Devils! Devils! Teufel! Diabolos!

KAMPANEYETS: (*Relieved.*) So, you're evil spirits? (*Breaks the rifle over his knee and tosses it behind the veranda.*) Well, as they say, "If it's not a crime, it's no business of mine." (*Sings.*)

Oh, pour in my battered camp mug

My battle-time ration of booze . . .

(*Drags out a bottle of Courvoisier from somewhere. All three dance now, handing the bottle around and guzzling the cognac from the bottle.*)

CYNTHIA: Meine Klein petit Clarence is simple radio operator, but I is big devil!

KAMPANEYETS: (*Dreamily gazes at the plain lit up by noiseless flashes.*) Oh, what a night it is, comrades: I'd love to go jumping off somewhere across the hummocks . . . to a sauna! . . .

CLARENCE: D'accord?

CYNTHIA: Alors! Proszu pane! (*All three take a flying leap over the railing that would be the envy of Bob and, shrieking, whistling, and laughing, dash toward the forest. The merry screams of the nocturnal devils will be audible in the distance until the end of the act. Meanwhile, the veranda of the Garment Workers' guest house remains empty for several minutes. The summer lightning continues. A wind starts up. The leaves begin to rustle. The curtains sway. The voice of the Heron can be heard very close by, disturbing, hollow sounds, filled with barely controlled passion. Lyosha the Watchman appears on the left staircase, sits down on the steps, and quietly plays baroque music on a small flute. Ivan Monogamov comes out on the right staircase. Stands motionless, leaning against the wall, and looks at the plain and sea illuminated by summer lightning.*)

* * *

THREE
SIMPLE THINGS

Once there lived a bard, a priest of the free muses,
Excessively free muses, at least his neighbor said so.
From morn 'til late at night, he'd do anything he chooses.
And, to while away the time, on the wall he wrote his credo.

Oh, Rooster, show your tail, or you'll collect no eggs.
Do not hide from the hens your throaty, raucous talent.
Compare your lowly verse to a garland of fireworks.
Soar high at Kostroma and come down in Manhattan.

Oh, wandering clown and blade, ensnarer of pure souls,
Do not flee with your sack from prizes and from critics.
Do not stash in your sash small coins and fat bankrolls,
And when the times are cruel, maintain an open visage.

But then the bard got scared. In an official's eyes once
He thought he caught the glint of a venomous blood sucker
And since then with his neighbor he's been playing Simple
  Simon,
Having covered up his credo with a coat of dark brown lacquer.

LYOSHA THE WATCHMAN: (*Turns around abruptly, as though
struck from behind.*) Who's there?
MONOGAMOV: It's me, Lyosha.
LYOSHA THE WATCHMAN: So, you recognized me, Ivan?
MONOGAMOV: Why, of course I recognized you.
LYOSHA THE WATCHMAN: It's fantastic! We haven't seen each other for twenty years.
MONOGAMOV: It's much less than that. Sixteen.
LYOSHA THE WATCHMAN: Unbelievable. We weren't close, you
know. You weren't really one of our gang, and you rarely even
came to the café. It's funny that I recognized you right away, too.
MONOGAMOV: I knew you didn't consider me one of you—and I
couldn't have been anyway, and that's why I rarely came. Then I
forgot that Andromeda Café of yours very soon; but, imagine,
just recently, when I was wide awake, suddenly I had an extremely vivid apparition of the café, just the way it was before it was
torn down. It happened in the Cordilleras, near Cuzco, at an

altitude of 13,000 feet. It's said that a lot of people have vivid hallucinations of that kind there.

LYOSHA THE WATCHMAN: There's one thing you don't know. But then nobody knows. When they began demolishing the Andromeda I was inside. Right there inside, understand? Our whole crowd was sitting across the street, on the boulevard, saying their goodbyes from over there, but I was inside—and not at all for ideological reasons, not as a protest. I was simply sleeping there, drunk. I had forgotten the demolition in the morning—and maybe I didn't even know. At the time I was crooning non-stop to my guitar, you know, I was always high, I didn't even feel the ground under my feet. When they hit the room with the iron wrecking ram, I came to and the sky unfurled above me. I lay like a worm in the desert, a little worm in a desert of thunderous noise. And it was then that I realized . . . then I realized . . . But it isn't important what I realized then . . . What is important is that ever since I've been a janitor, a watchman, a middling peasant, and shady dealer in dried mushrooms.

MONOGAMOV: But how you used to roar out those songs to your guitar!

> Oh, Lord, forgive us all,
> Our faces are like shit.
> And pock-marked is our soul,
> Our skin all grime and grit.

And then you'd do a number in the Louis Armstrong style . . . (*Smiles.*)

LYOSHA THE WATCHMAN: I recently had an offer, by the way, to marry an Englishwoman. But I prefer . . .

MONOGAMOV: You prefer drying mushrooms, Lyosha, and waiting for the heron at night. Right?

LYOSHA THE WATCHMAN: What's that? What's that thar swamp crud to me?

MONOGAMOV: Come on, Lyosha, don't play the fool with me, at least. Who is she?

LYOSHA THE WATCHMAN: (*Hollowly.*) She flies here from Poland.

MONOGAMOV: (*Amazed.*) From where?

LYOSHA THE WATCHMAN: The Polish border is seven kilometers from here.

MONOGAMOV: (*With growing amazement.*) Do you mean to say the

Soviet Union ends seven kilometers from here?

LYOSHA THE WATCHMAN: I mean that's where Poland begins. And that's where she flies at night.

MONOGAMOV: Could it be the other way around, that she flies from us to them in the morning?

LYOSHA THE WATCHMAN: (*With restrained despair.*) She has a lover there, I know that.

MONOGAMOV: Could it be she doesn't notice the national boundary?

LYOSHA THE WATCHMAN: Why does she have to fly here? Why does she have to torture us like this?

MONOGAMOV: Have you been in love with her for long?

LYOSHA THE WATCHMAN: In love? (*He clenches his head with his hands.*) I can't sleep!

MONOGAMOV: (*Gazes into the distance.*) Who's that jumping among the hummocks there, near the woods?

LYOSHA THE WATCHMAN: Those are the devils playing.

MONOGAMOV: Have you gotten close to her?

LYOSHA THE WATCHMAN: Never. I'm afraid. And besides, she's frightened of people.

MONOGAMOV: She's a virgin.

LYOSHA THE WATCHMAN: (*Bitterly.*) What are you talking about? She has a lover in Poland, he draws her there, I know that for sure.

MONOGAMOV: Then why does she fly to the U. S. S. R. at night? I'm sure she's a virgin! (*Very close by a hollow, instinctual call can be heard. Passion, entreaty. Summer lightning blazes, but it does not die out—it hangs over the veranda, illuminating everything round about with a phosphorescent glow. The Heron climbs onto the veranda slowly and noiselessly. She stops in the awkward pose of a gangly young girl. Her legs are crossed absurdly. Drooping beak and wings. Muddy swamp swill is dripping from her cheap nylon raincoat.*)

MONOGAMOV: Heron, are you a virgin?

HERON: I am unhappy. (*The summer lightning dies out. Darkness. The tramping of feet on the stairs: someone is running down to the veranda. Suddenly the electricity comes on. It is Bob, trembling all over. He looks around wildly, and sees Monogamov and Lyosha stretched out on the floor. The Heron, of course, has disappeared.*)

BOB: (*Screams.*) Who is unhappy here? Hey, you guys, I'm asking you, who's unhappy here? What's going on in this damned guest house? Pop, is that you?

MONOGAMOV: I'm in love.

BOB: (*Waves his hand.*) Oh, I knew it! What else could I expect from you, dad! (*Approaches the footlights and addresses the audience.*) You must understand, in high jumping everything depends on the nervous system. All the technique in the world isn't worth a thing once your nervous system goes on the skids. You must understand, I can't go on like this, I can't jump if I feel that someone somewhere is terribly unhappy. My whole schedule goes up in smoke. (*Turns around.*) Lyosha, won't you at least tell me what's going on?

LYOSHA THE WATCHMAN: (*In his usual guise.*) That thar bitchy heron—jes' wouldn't stop its croakin', the slut.

(*Curtain. End of Act One.*)

FIRST INTERMISSION

(The first intermission lasts the usual time, about fifteen or twenty minutes, and through this time anarchy reigns in the theatre. Members of the audience can remain in the hall or go to the lobby, as they prefer. The actors can earn a little extra by carrying round drinks. The verse-prose texts of The Heron *are for sale. Dances. Charades. Flirtations. All kinds of amateur performances are encouraged.*

Meanwhile, something or other is also happening on stage, although this isn't essential. The veranda setting has been moved to the side, and now the whole of the Garment Workers' guest house can be seen amidst the seaside plain. The mirage of a European gothic town may sometimes flash for a short time in the pale sky above the sea.

A bus stop shelter is now at front stage; inside the shelter is a bench. It is presumed that somewhere around the orchestra pit a highway runs past, forgotten by God and man.

The Kampaneyets Sisters by various marriages sit on the bench, embracing. They sing and sway to the rhythm of a song:

> *To the left a bridge, to the right a bridge,*
> *And the Wisla lies before us . . .*

Something wild can be heard in this Polish song, in the shrill, horny singing of the sisters.)

FOUR
OUT IN THE STICKS

Among the many kinds of mania, megalomania, *idees fixes.*
We choose the nights of Lithuania, days of Estonia, out in the
    sticks.

The torpor of the eastern Baltic . . .
The years slip by here five by five.
The towns of the trading Hanseatic
League rot in the marshes, scarce alive.

Commerce here has turned to ashes,
Religion's subject to reprimand,

And Christ, like an insurance agent,
Roams with his briefcase through the land.

The Zodiac sphere is rusted over,
All style is lost, all genre gone.
A church-turned-museum, two or three posters . . .
A Soviet Socialist Baltic town.

* * *

It's tea for two. What tedium.
Here's the insipid fruit of the sticks.
You turn to stone, grow deaf and dumb . . .
But just like sparkling mica specks,
The stones contain a hidden charm.
The whirling 'midst the shoreline rocks
Of thinking water, the angry hum
Of an old short-wave . . . the drowsy gardens,
The aging plum trees . . . vegetation.
Is it patience or is it reticence? . . .
Everything awaits misfortune.

ROSA: What a strained situation . . . A cold evening . . . sunset . . .
the nearness of Poland . . . (*The singing continues.*)

CLAUDIA: Oh, girls, just five more minutes! Why, it just takes my
breath away!

ROSA: Claudia!

CLAUDIA: Oh! I'll stop! I'll stop! (*The singing continues.*)

LAIMA: (*Looks through binoculars.*) There it is on the hill! What a
beauty! A bus from Poland! (*The singing breaks off. Rosa and
Claudia try to tear the binoculars away from Laima.*) Girls, you
can already see it with the naked eye. Now—our main task is to
show we aren't barbarians. We'll give them a careless, absent-
minded glance and say: "What's that over there? Oh, it's only a
bus full of Polish tourists"—and then we'll nonchalantly continue our disco dance.

ROSA: What's that over there? Oh, it's only a bus full of Polish
tourists . . .

CLAUDIA: Oh, it's only a bus full of Polish tourists . . . (*The growing
roar of the bus. It goes by.*)

THE SISTERS: (*Waving their handkerchiefs and shouting rhythmic-*

ally.) Friendship! Friendship! Przyjazn! Przyjazn! (*The noise of the bus fades in the distance.*)

ROSA: (*Embarrassed.*) Oh, girls, I'm sorry, it's all my fault. I was the first to lose my self-control. He gave me *such* a look.

CLAUDIA: Who gave you *such* a look?

ROSA: The dark one.

CLAUDIA: What do you mean, dark? There was just a bunch of old geezers on the bus.

ROSA: There was just a bunch of old geezers on the bus and one dark man of about thirty. A true Polish aristocrat.

CLAUDIA: (*Close to tears.*) You're a fool, Rosa!

ROSA: And you're a backward, hopelessly earthbound person! (*Nervously lights a cigarette.*)

CLAUDIA: Where did you get that American cigarette?

ROSA: He held it out to me! He bent so gracefully and held it out the window! What a man!

CLAUDIA: Ah, you mooched it off Monogamov yesterday.

ROSA: You just didn't see a thing, you were so excited in your provincial way!

LAIMA: (*Looks through the binoculars.*) Oh, girls, the lights have been turned on . . . a bus lit up against the sunset . . . Unforgettable! It's approaching our national border . . . Europe! The Polish People's Republic! (*It quickly grows dark. The lights of the mirage city on the backdrop are illuminated. Cries of the Heron. The Sisters, dishevelled and upset, run toward one another and embrace.*)

To the left a bridge, to the right a bridge!
And the Wisla lies before us!

(*Cries of the Heron. The passionate embrace of the Sisters. They exit. In the darkness a fragile, whitish figure, indistinctly outlined, appears onstage. Sighs and laments. The rustling of wings.*)

ACT TWO

(Once again the veranda of the Garment Workers' guest house in its former splendor. A bright sunny morning. Rosa and Claudia, both in sundresses, are setting the breakfast table and bickering as usual. F. G. Kampaneyets, in a three-piece business suit and glasses, is strolling around the veranda. He doesn't let a telephone with an extremely long cord out of his hands. In the course of the entire Act, the cord will trail after Kampaneyets, gradually entangling all and thus playing a not-inconsiderable role in the staging.)

KAMPANEYETS: *(Into the telephone.)* Take this down, Igor! Ship twenty-two cartons of Iranian detergent to Moldavia and keep it there—there isn't going to be any of that around for a long time now. Petrianu will slip you a batch of varnish from Afanaskin's inventory. Get in touch with Khachapurov about the Dutch shampoo. Contact Mamontov through Morozov and state the bath oil problem in principle.

CLAUDIA: *(Bellowing at Rosa.)* There you go again, forcing your ideas on me!

ROSA: Can't you speak a little more softly? Today's a working day for father.

KAMPANEYETS: Send me up a couple of cases of Danish beer. What? Where'll you get them? Are you out of your mind, Igor? Get moving or you're fired! *(Puts down the receiver and picks it up immediately. Dials the Operator.)* Rita, my angel, Kampaneyets on the line. Who's in charge today? Anya? The one who likes bright lipsticks? Connect us, honey. Anechka? This is Uncle Filip from the Garment Workers. Yes, yes, sweetheart, I'm still crazy about you. I brought you back a little souvenir from France. Sure, it's Chanel, and it's a very bright shade. What kind do you like? Great, we're in luck! You'll get a nice little set today. Oh, those lips of yours, those little lips, those precious bonbons! Anya, gorgeous, put my calls on rush. Two to Zhdanov, three to Kalinin, one apiece to Kuibyshev and Kirov, five to Ordzhonikidze. Thanks, baby. Uncle Filip doesn't forget his sweethearts. Here are the numbers . . .

FIVE
OUR UNCLE

Our uncle often would give voice to
A special fondness for the oyster.
But he also often liked a meal
Of sturgeon or of good smoked eel.

His life was spent to the motor's roar,
As he spanned the breadth of Stalin's land,
And, with the help of his prison corps,
Built dams and canals for the Five-Year Plan.

As the years went by he stuck to his credo,
And, while retired from the revels,
He hovered still like a dread torpedo—
Although he became a bit of a devil.

But unlike the grand diabolism
Of the magnificent Old Days,
The lightning raids of Stalinism,
The stamping out of enemy fleas,
He flings no threats now to the heavens,
He's grown attached to a life of ease.
We have here a brand new demonism,
If you please.

And so from pure and simple sadists,
The deviltry of former days,
We've cultivated hedonists,
Soft demons with peculiar ways.

But that's a blessing, yes it is,
So sighs our timid populace.
Let them scratch wherever they itch,
And with salmon stuff their face.
We eat sprats and boiled potato,
They—champagne and caviar.
But we welcome the rule of matter
Over the spirit—that's how things are.

We welcome too the Earth's rotation,
The lewd meanderings of the Moon,

And the petty demonization
Of heroic Satan, the once great tycoon.

(*While Kampaneyets is dictating the telephone numbes, Lyosha the Garment Worker, carrying a suitcase and with an accordion flung over his shoulder, slowly climbs up to the veranda. For the time being nobody sees him.*)

ROSA: Claudia, you know, I've had a kind of joyous premonition today, ever since morning. A peculiar feeling of anticipation. Do you understand what I mean?

CLAUDIA: What's there to understand? You keep on waiting for your prince to come.

LYOSHA THE GARMENT WORKER: Pardon me, where's the front desk? (*Both lasses give a mighty start and turn toward the new arrival. Kampaneyets also looks at Lyosha the Garment Worker, but just at this moment he makes his connection.*)

KAMPANEYETS: Ordzhonikidze? Kampaneyets on the line! Alik, hi, old pal! Can you give me some information on nitroenamel? Uh-huh . . . uh-huh . . . (*Takes notes in a pad.*)

LYOSHA THE GARMENT WORKER: Show me the way to the front desk, won't you, girls?

ROSA: (*Her hands pressed to her breast.*) Who are you?

CLAUDIA: (*Guffaws.*) Your pri-i-ince!

LYOSHA THE GARMENT WORKER: I like a good joke. Why don't we introduce ourselves? I'm Alyosha Fokin from the town of Paris-Communeville, a mechanic at the Paris Commune Factory, you see. And where are you from, girls?

KAMPANEYETS: (*Approaching, dragging the cord.*) Can't you read, young man? Did you see the "No Trespassing" sign? (*Lyosha the Garment Worker, smiling kindly, begins an expedition through his pockets, drops something, picks it up, folds it. Meanwhile, all the guest house residents—Laima, Bob, Stepanida, Monogamov, Lyosha the Watchman—descend both flights of stairs for breakfast. All are assembled.*)

LYOSHA THE GARMENT WORKER: Well, now, here's my passport, three rubles registration fee, and my voucher.

ROSA: He has a voucher! (*A mime scene. Everyone exchanges glances. A gradual crescendoing whisper, "A voucher! A Gar-*

ment Worker with a voucher! Unbelievable!")

MONOGAMOV: (*To Lyosha the Garment Worker.*) But I've seen you somewhere before. Didn't you work in a tractor brigade in Ceylon?

LYOSHA THE GARMENT WORKER: Can't say I did. I won't put you on.

KAMPANEYETS: (*Takes the voucher with extreme distaste.*) Who issued this to you?

LYOSHA THE GARMENT WORKER: (*Flattered by the general attention.*) Well, it was on Tuesday, no, I'm putting you on, it was Wednesday, you see, they asked me in to the union local. It's time, they say, for you, Lyosha Fokin, to take your guaranteed vacation. Here's your choice—either the Chechuyevo or Khekhovo health resorts or a guest house on the Baltic, the Garment Worker. The name appealed to me a lot, so here I am, welcome kindly! I can see you're a pretty nice crowd, and I made it just in time for breakfast.

ROSA: (*With growing tenderness.*) Yes, yes, please come to the table . . . I'll bring you a setting right now . . . comrade Fokin.

LYOSHA THE GARMENT WORKER: Lyosha.

KAMPANEYETS: (*With the reservation.*) Oh the blockheads, the boondocks! (*To Rosa.*) Set a place for him at the second table. Over here.

LYOSHA THE GARMENT WORKER: Won't I have any company?

ROSA: I can keep you company.

KAMPANEYETS: (*To Rosa.*) My child, you'll keep us company, your collective, your family.

MONOGAMOV: I can keep this gentleman company, since I stand somewhat apart from the collective, as a family member.

STEPANIDA: (*In a furious whisper.*) Playing the same old role, Ivan? Setting yourself apart from the rest? (*Even a not particularly observant viewer will notice that her buttocks and breasts have grown much larger in the second act.*) Haven't you learned anything, working for such a responsible organization?

MONOGAMOV: UNESCO, you know, isn't such a very responsible organization. Everything was so easy there.

STEPANIDA: What does UNESCO have to do with it?

MONOGAMOV: But I work for UNESCO.

STEPANIDA: (*Venomously.*) Ah, you work for UNESCO.

MONOGAMOV: Why, what else?

STEPANIDA: I take it all back. But, still a responsible organization has taught you a thing or two.

MONOGAMOV: A-ah, now I see what you're getting at, Styopa. But after all, not everybody cooperates with them. You, of all people, know that. You yourself worked in a hotel for foreigners. You surely know not everybody does it.

STEPANIDA: Drop it, please.

MONOGAMOV: (*Suddenly notices the enlarged parts of her body.*) Excuse me, Styopa, what's the matter with you? Such sudden changes!

STEPANIDA: (*Somewhat flirtatiously.*) Well, so what? I don't see anything wrong with it.

MONOGAMOV: It's not quite the Parisian style.

STEPANIDA: (*Drily.*) We have our own style.

MONOGAMOV: Yes, yes, of course. Every place has its own style. In Madagascar, for example, beautiful women have . . .

STEPANIDA: I can see you're an expert on the beauties of Madagascar. Did things really work out better for you there?

MONOGAMOV: Strange as it may sound, yes. Something strange happened to me in Madagascar. You can't even imagine how I stood out there.

STEPANIDA: No, I can't imagine at all. Let's go to the table. (*Everyone has already taken their seats around a large table, at the head of which, of course, is Kampaneyets with his telephone. Lyosha the Garment Worker imperturbably "vacations" at the small table. Rosa fusses about him, occasionally coming to a stop and, with an absent-minded, happy smile, fixing her hair.*)

LYOSHA THE GARMENT WORKER: Okey-dokey!

ROSA: Do you like breakfast?

LYOSHA THE GARMENT WORKER: High quality stuff, there's no denying—though, of course, I usually eat soup in the morning.

ROSA: Soup for breakfast?

LYOSHA THE GARMENT WORKER: Uh-huh. You down a couple bowls of noodle soup and your hangover's gone.

ROSA: Are you married?

LYOSHA THE GARMENT WORKER: Now, how couldn't I be married, if I've got three kids?

CLAUDIA: Congratulations, Rosa.

ROSA: (*To Lyosha the Garment Worker.*) I'll make you some noodle soup tomorrow.

KAMPANEYETS: Rosa, sit down at the table, won't you? Your job is to involve the vacationer in cultural activities. The dietitian sets his menu.

CLAUDIA: I'll make him soup.

BOB: At training camp at Tsakhkadzor, before a match of giants, the decathlon contender, Proshkin, ate three bowls of cabbage and pork hock soup for breakfast. And he beat the American, Richard Pope.

MONOGAMOV: Breakfast culture varies from country to country. In France, the so-called *petit dejeuner* . . .

LYOSHA THE WATCHMAN: (*Guffaws unexpectedly and tumultuously.*) Pete eats on Jeanette! (*To Lyosha the Garment Worker.*) Hey, Garment Worker, ya hear that? In France, they gobble down their breakfast right on Jeannette!

MONOGAMOV: (*Smiles.*) You're quite a character! *Petit dejeuner* consists, as a rule, of coffee, butter, jam, a croissant . . .

LYOSHA THE WATCHMAN: (*Guffawing uncontrollably.*) Ya hear that, Garment Worker? They eat through ass on! Whoa, whoa!

LYOSHA THE GARMENT WORKER: (*Coldly.*) Cool it, you hick! (*The telephone rings.*)

KAMPANEYETS: The Ukraine? Zhdanov? Put it through! Sashko, zdorovenki buly! Oh, stop bugging me with your trinitrotolune! Out with it instead—where are you hiding the antifreeze? (*Laughs.*) That's it! Come on, come on, I'm writing it down . . .

MONOGAMOV: Now, in Spain . . .

STEPANIDA: Bob, at last you have some color in your face.

BOB: You can thank Aunt Laima for that.

LAIMA: (*Bursts out.*) Bobbie, please!

BOB: What's the matter? It's only natural . . .

MONOGAMOV: About Spain, by the way. I was there both under Franco and afterwards. Amazing changes. It's amazing how quickly people forget about the nightmares of totalitarianism . . .

CLAUDIA: (*To Lyosha the Watchman.*) Lyosha, the hell with all of them; let's go swimming!

LYOSHA THE WATCHMAN: Now, this here lassie jes' cain't get her fill. An' what we gonna do at night? I gotta get them mushrooms sliced now, gotta be thinkin' 'bout me future.

MONOGAMOV: How quickly they're returning to a normal democratic life! Meetings on every corner! Discussions in every café! Spain now . . .

LYOSHA THE GARMENT WORKER: (*In the meantime he has gotten out a bottle of vodka, taken off his jacket and shirt, and, dressed only in his undershirt, has begun playing the accordion. He sings.*)

> Through the mountains dark and drear,
> And the meadows green and fair,
> A young lad did wander on
> To the Donets Steppe . . .

KAMPANEYETS: (*To Lyosha the Garment Worker.*) What is this, amateur theatricals? We'll ask you to leave here, comrade vacationer—your voucher is still in doubt! (*Into the receiver.*) We've got the radio on here. What? You say it's a nice song? Viacheslav Sergeevich likes it? Is he there? (*Stands.*) He spent the night with you? Oh, Sashko, you so-and-so! You were living it up with some girls? What? You live it up without girls? (*Stands at attention.*) Good morning to you, Viacheslav Sergeevich, and Zdorovenki buly, of course. Yes, yes, a beautiful song. (*To Lyosha the Garment Worker.*) Can't you sing any louder? (*Into the receiver.*) Yes, exactly, Viacheslav Sergeevich, a song from our youth. I agree absolutely, our Sashko . . . ha, ha, well, of course, your Sashko, Viacheslav Sergeevich . . . is invaluable! (*His warmth reaches a fever pitch.*) Zdorovenki buly, Viacheslav Sergeevich! (*Hangs up, stands for a while in a sweet stupor, with a dreamy smile on his lips.*) Oh, how I'd like something . . . (*Cleans his mouth.*)

LYOSHA THE GARMENT WORKER: (*Downs half a glass of vodka.*)

> Down there in the dark coal mine
> We did spy a fair young lad . . .

KAMPANEYETS: (*Applauds with tender emotion.*) Now that's a real song for you, comrades! Handed down as in a relay race from generation to generation.

LYOSHA THE GARMENT WORKER:

> Come on and stop the music now.
> Come on and stop the music now.
> I beg of you, my girl
> Is dancing with another man!

ROSA: An elementally original, truly anarchic nature!

LYOSHA THE WATCHMAN: (*Stands up, drawn as by a magnet to Lyosha the Garment Worker, sits down by him.*) So yer from Paris, laddie?

LYOSHA THE GARMENT WORKER: From Paris-Communeville, hayseed!

MONOGAMOV: Now, what was I talking about? Was it Spain or Bolivia?

STEPANIDA: Ivan, quiet, please! (*Strikes the table with the palm of her hand.*) While we are all gathered together, I'd like to bring an urgent matter to everyone's attention. What is going on here at night? I've always taken pride in my sleep, but lately even I've begun to sense movements, some sounds, some emanations. I would like to bring this to the attention (*emphatically*) of everyone and, first and foremost (*emphatically*) of the management. (*With a heated, loud whisper to Kampaneyets.*) And, in general, Uncle Filip, you've slipped quite a bit lately. It always seemed to me you were capable of powerful feelings, such as responsibility, male pride, jealousy, at least. Now I believe I was mistaken!

KAMPANEYETS: (*Pretends he didn't catch everything—he was so engrossed in his work.*) Sorry, what did you say, Styopa? (*Dials the phone. From behind the pillar of the veranda peer the old Gannergeits' little faces, beaming with wrinkles. They call Kampaneyets. He chases them away with feigned severity. Into the receiver.*) Algis Zhuraitisovich, this is Kampaneyets calling about funds for the third quarter. We've had an influx of vacationers here . . . yes . . . yes . . . Excuse me, Styopa . . . These are important negotiations . . . (*Takes notes, computes something on a calculator.*)

STEPANIDA: (*Stands up and again slaps the table.*) So, it seems to me that my lawful wedded spouse is the source of the nighttime disturbances! (*Points her finger in Monogamov's direction.*) He comes to my bed, insolently and sluggishly plays the role of husband, and then, after waiting for me to fall asleep, he disappears until morning and comes back wet to the knees and reeking of the swamp.

MONOGAMOV: Styopa, why in front of everyone?

STEPANIDA: In that UNESCO of yours, my bright falcon, you've forgotten certain norms of our Soviet life. (*With growing rage.*) You'll have to answer for those somnambulistic adventures! To everyone! To your son! To the women! To members of the community! Last but not least, to the Garment Workers! Where do you tramp about at night?! (*Monogamov, walking shakily and with closed eyes, comes out to the proscenium. The far-off cry of the Heron can be heard. A muffled, mysterious tenderness. Everyone jumps up. The chairs are pushed away.*)

ROSA: This is the first time she's cried in the daytime. Well, how can one help falling in love?!

STEPANIDA: (*Haughtily and coarsely.*) Ivan Vladlenovich, answer for your unseemly carryings on! What have you grown so thoughtful about, my fine lad?

MONOGAMOV: (*Opens his enormous eyes, in a staggering whisper.*) About hunger! (*A new pause and rather strange confusion. F. G. Kampaneyets, mumbling "Fifty-five. Comrade Patronauskas, sixty-six minimum, seventy-seven maximum," moves around the stage and entangles everyone in his long cord.*)

STEPANIDA: (*Struggling with the cord, approaches Monogamov.*) What more do you want, Monogamov?

MONOGAMOV: Are you aware that two-thirds of mankind is chronically underfed? Have you ever heard of Biafra, of Bangladesh? Do we dare to shoot films, put out books and records, demand creative freedom, when hundreds of millions of children do not get the proper proteins, fats, and even carbohydrates? Do we dare conquer outer space when humanity's genetic code is threatened? Bob, my son, my high-jumping youngster, do you agree with me?

BOB: Sure I agree. Listen, pops, I've got some business to talk over with you. Won't you give me your jacket? If you want, I'll pay you a couple hundred for it. I've got to fly to a meet in Tashkent. With a jacket like that I'll immediately crush them all psychologically—Yashchenko and Gavrilov and Kiba. (*Looks at his watch, becomes entangled in the cord.*) All rightie?

MONOGAMOV: (*Takes off his jacket, throws it to Bob, appeals to the audience.*) Among those of us who live in highly developed countries, store counters are overflowing with all the necessities—sausages, . . .

ALL: (*In a hysterical chorus.*) SAUSAGES! (*As Monogamov proceeds down his list of foods, the chorus continues to echo him hysterically. Only after "shrimps" and "soufflés" the hysteria gives way to bewilderment: no one has heard of such things.)*

MONOGAMOV: Ham, cheese, salmon, caviar, shrimps, butter, vegetable oil, cakes, chocolate, different flavored soufflés, the freshest fruits and vegetables, soft drinks and fine wines (*notes of hysteria*), and meanwhile the children of Kampuchea receive only a handful of rice apiece while the Tuaregs of Mauritania ofen faint from hunger! (*Everyone faints, Monogamov becomes more and more entangled in the cord. He suddenly notices that both Lyoshas, having halted their shot glasses halfway, are staring at him with their mouths wide open, their arms stretched out toward him in a poorly motivated gesture of entreaty.*) Well! Well! (*The Watchman and Garment Worker clink their glasses and consume their drinks.*)

LYOSHA THE WATCHMAN: (*To Lyosha the Garment Worker.*) Now, you stick w' me, laddie. Folks roun' here, they're nervous, they makes yer head go roun', but me? I'm jes' a simple watchman; let's you an' me be buddies.

LYOSHA THE GARMENT WORKER: A watchman, you say? But I don't like the look in your eyes. (*He again takes up his accordion and, ignoring the cord, plays "Beyond the Far-Off Narva Gates."*)

MONOGAMOV: In Europe every accident turns up in the papers! In our country we have an immense system of social security!

ALL REPEAT: Security. We have the greatest security.

MONOGAMOV: But in Africa and Asia fatalities are counted only in the hundreds! They don't even pay attention to a few dozen! (*Howls heart-rendingly, almost in a paroxysm.*) This cannot be allowed! (*Runs to the Kampaneyets Sisters.*) And you, sisters, embodiments of motherhood! Do you, of all people, understand that we are all children of the earth, everyone from the well-groomed Party Committee secretary to the poverty-stricken pariah in Madras? Mothers!

CLAUDIA: What do you mean mothers, you epileptic nut?! Laima is a geologist, I'm a technologist, and our Rosa is still an innocent young girl. (*Vibrating and changing places, the Sisters get entangled in the cord.*)

MONOGAMOV: (*Appeals to Kampaneyets.*) Filip Grigorievich, you, at least, a man of such scope, ought to take into account the dangers of widespread rickets, of physical and moral degenera- tion! Here you are, wheeling and dealing over the telephone, but it's not for yourself, isn't that right? It's for your family, isn't it? For you the family is, after all, a model of all humanity—surely I'm not mistaken? Surely anybody's legs withered by pellagra are also your legs!

KAMPANEYETS: (*Suddenly looks attentively at Monogamov, as if seeing him for the first time.*) Listen—uh, what's your name?—Monogamov. I like the way you sum up the problem. Of course, anybody's legs are our legs. (*Casually takes the trembling, overwrought Monogamov by the arm.*) Maybe, all things con- sidered, we can form a closer relationship? Is it true that U. N. employees don't have to go through customs? (*The telephone rings.*) Mekharadze? Bababaev? Where's our mohair, Bababaev? You're playing with fire, Rafik! Uh-huh, uh-huh ... (*He becomes entangled in his cord.*) There you are, sitting on oil, on beer, on chocolate! You can go to hell, comrade Rafik Bababaev!

MONOGAMOV: (*Struggling with the cord, he falls on his knees and crawls towards Stepanida.*) Styopa, you at least should come to your senses! After all, I remember the way you used to be—impetuous, fiery! Surely all these inflated circumferences, this great-power aplomb—it's not really you, it's a put-on. At least you try to understand that all of us on this planet are one family, that destruction, entropy, are threatening all of us together. After all, we don't know if what we call rational life ex- ists anywhere else in space. And what if we're the only ones?! (*Spews out in complete hysteria.*) We! The only ones! The Eye of God is turned upon us alone! Ah?

STEPANIDA: (*Squeamishly.*) What religious hocus pocus! You've gotten yourself completely entangled, Ivan! Your tongue has run away with itself, you're a nervous wreck, you can't look your people in the eye. No, I can't leave things like this, it's my duty to react. Come over here! (*She pulls Monogamov's head into her armpit. They all try to disentangle themselves from the telephone cord. Sharp, hopeless jerks. Finally the group becomes fixed. The Heron climbs onto the veranda. Her former slow, timid movements, but this time a kind of decisiveness shows through, as if the bird has forgotten about her skinny knees, and about the streams of swamp moisture flowing down her beak, her wings, and her ratty, pathetic raincoat.*)

HERON: (*Awkwardly raising her legs, she walks along our "Lao-coon." Her round, rather stupid eyes glowing, she inquires in a stupid voice.*) Who's here? Who's here? Who's here? Kto tu jest? Who calls? Kto wola? (*It is as though everyone has grown mute; no one can answer, although everyone seems to be trying. Monogamov's back and rear are trembling. Lowering her head, Heron exits. A silent, spontaneous movement in the direction of the departing Heron. A pause. Immobility. Suddenly the old Gannergeits give a sprightly jump over the veranda railing. They dance across the stage, affectionately addressing their grimaces, nods, and gestures to Kampaneyets.*)

>On the land, and at sea, in mire
>Does our tender bright ember e'er burn!
>If your wings in their flight ever tire,
>Then fly down for some tea, dear glow worm!
>Oh, the bombers do bomb,
>The flamethrowers fight on,
>And the ponderous tanks crawl and creep!
>If you finish, my friend,
>Your tough legerdemain
>Then fly down in your fabulous jeep.

(*Lyosha the Garment Worker comes to and picks up the rousing tune on his accordion. He looks at Rosa and smiles softly.*)

ROSA: You are . . . impulsive . . . you are unpredictable . . . Lyosha the Garment Worker . . . (*Blushes to the point of tears.*)

LYOSHA THE GARMENT WORKER: Let's go, Rosa, and—well, I mean, okey-dokey all in all—you'll show me the cot where I'll spend my guaranteed vacation according to the laws of nature. (*Rosa and the Garment Worker free themselves from the fetters of the telephone cord and quit the stage. The old Gannergeits reappear on stage with a bunch of enormous white mushrooms, each the size of a felt boot. Lyosha the Watchman jumps up, trembling. The fetters have fallen to his feet. Claudia is also free.*)

CLAUDIA: (*Grabs her boyfriend by the hand.*) Lyosha, what mushrooms!

LYOSHA THE WATCHMAN: (*Hides his excitement.*) What's that, mushrooms . . . they ain't nothin' special . . . Eh, Clarence, how's about a three-spot for 'em?

CLARENCE: Ja, ja, pan Watchman! Three spot! (*Gives him the mushrooms.*)

CLAUDIA: Now our future is secure! (*Claudia and Lyosha the Watchman run off with the mushrooms. The old Gannergeits hide behind the television. Clarence pulls out his ham radio. Crackling, static, voices: ''Achtung! achtung, Tashkent speaking.'' Bob and Laima give a start.*)

BOB: (*In his father's jacket.*) Aunt Laima, my heartfelt thanks for helping me maintain my balance. I'll be the best high jumper in Tashkent. Watch me on television.

LAIMA: When you face the raging crowd, my boy, remember I'm keeping your home fire burning. You have a very reliable rear here.

BOB: Thanks again. Give my best to my parents. (*They exchange handshakes. Bob jumps over the railing. Laima exits behind him. Of the entire group sculpture there remain in the center of the stage only Kampaneyets, Stepanida, and the trembling body of Ivan Monogamov. All three are intertwined by the telephone cord. In the middle the majestic Stepanida rises. Ivan Monogamov's back trembles. Kampaneyets, fearfully glancing at Stepanida, gestures to the old Gannergeits with feigned severity, ''Wait a little, comrades!!''*)

MONOGAMOV: (*In a hollow voice.*) Heron! Where are you? Answer! (*Stepanida silently presses down on his head with her elbow.*)

CLARENCE: (*Puts on earphones, broadcasts.*) Breslau, Breslau . . . Schwarzwald here . . . schweigen . . . (*Cries.*) . . . Bristol, Bristol . . . Blackwood here . . . silence . . . Dijon . . . Foret Noir here . . . silence (*French pronunciation.*) . . . (*Cries.*) Odessa, Odessa . . . Chernolesie here . . . molchat . . . (*Sobs.*) Hitler kaput . . . Stalin kaput . . . Churchill kaput . . . We've been forgotten by the whole world, exzellenz . . . (*Cries.*) . . . hornification of the skin . . . (*Giggles.*) . . . little hooves, horns, tails . . . (*Giggles.*) . . . the batteries are running out . . . (*Cries.*) Oh, exzellenz, your excellency . . . what a time it was, the furzige jaares . . . The Second World War! (*He cries, hiding his face in his shortwave radio.*)

* * *

SIX
THE SECOND WORLD WAR
(A SOLDIER'S SONG)

LEAD SINGER:

Over the statues Italian,
Over the columns Athenian,
Over the meadows Rumanian,
Our song like a swallow flies!

FORMATION:

Hey, hey, Europe!
You jolly fields and lakes!
We all march in step,
The pedigrees all quake!
We'll lay a land mine
And knock down Notre Dame!

NURSE:

And you'll knock me up, my handsome,
In the crater. Bam! Bam!

LEAD SINGER:

Over the fields Galician,
Over the steeples Austrian,
Over the fjords Norwegian,
Our song like a swallow flies!

FORMATION:

We're storming Pripet,
The crew just feels like hell.
I'd wet my palate
On a Molotov cocktail.
They're shooting past us!
We'll knock down Rotterdam!

NURSE:

And you'll knock me up, my precious,
Under the tank. Bam! Bam!

LEAD SINGER:

Over the sands Saharian,
Over the smoke Stalingradian,
Over the jungles Cambodian,
Our song like a swallow flies!

FORMATION:
Hey, signal corps sweeties,
Come greet us when we land!
Open up the whiskey,
And bring over a jazz band!
And to the rockets' bright light
We'll knock down Potsdam!

NURSE:
And you'll knock me up, my pilot,
In the gun mount. Bam! Bam!

PILOT:
And you'll knock me out, my sweetheart,
(*In a bass.*) Like Potsdam! Bam! Bam!

CYNTHIA: (*Encourages Clarence with a poke in his rear.*) Mon caper-ale, communiquez, s'il vous plait! I need man beacoup, bardzo! (*Clarence giggles, broadcasts. The telephone rings next to Kampaneyets. He picks up the receiver.*)

KAMPANEYETS: Kampaneyets on the line! Who's speaking? Kalinin? Zhdanov? Voroshilovgrad? (*Waits, anxiously listening to the silence.*) Here it is, at long last! (*Scratches his buttock with his foot. Wild joy lights up his face.*)

CYNTHIA: Si-si-mi-si-si-va!

CLARENCE: Gliu-gliu-gliu-gliu!

STEPANIDA: Filip Grigorievich, what's wrong with you?

KAMPANEYETS: I'm being sent for by high frequency circuit!! I must fly!

STEPANIDA: You're lying, all of you! You're not up to the HFC level! You're behaving disgracefully, and to think I tried to be your equal!

KAMPANEYETS: (Becomes more and more bedeviled.) Vzhakh! (*Throws down the receiver.*) I can't stand it! (*Jumps out of the fetters. To the song, "Oh, the bombers do bomb, the flamethrowers fight on," all three devils dance lightly across the stage and then, with a whoop, jump over the railing and disappear in the sun gleam.*)

STEPANIDA: Uncle Filip, stop! Uncle Filip! he's gone! (*Raises her arms like the heroine of an ancient tragedy.*) Woe is me, woe! Woe! And he talked so much about ideological integrity! About moral purity! About the forties! About the thirties! Men are hopeless! (*Swaying, Monogamov rises and steps over the rings of the telephone cord.*)

MONOGAMOV: (*Opens his enormous eyes, calls out.*) Where are you? Where are you? Heron, answer!

STEPANIDA: (*Almost with loathing.*) Swamp swooner! I'm going to Moscow today to gather some information about you.

MONOGAMOV: (*Semi-delirious.*) Yes, yes, do. I need some information about myself.

STEPANIDA: (*Pulls a document out of her brassiere.*) Well, then, sign this power of attorney that gives me the right to your money. (*Monogamov signs the power of attorney right off.*) I'd like to know, I'd really like to know who's responsible for hiring personnel like you. (*Slips the power of attorney back into her brassiere and, stamping soldier-like, panting, her haughty gaze threatening all the ends of the earth, exits.*)

MONOGAMOV: (*Drags along, stretches out his arms like a blind man.*) Heron! Heron! Answer! (*The distant cry of the Heron. Tenderness. Yearning. Monogamov tries to imitate the sound.*)

VOICE OF HERON: Where are you, Rossianin?! Russian, answer! (*Monogamov, as though he has regained his sight and his youth, gives a joyful start and runs to the rear of the stage, toward the sea. On stage, strange, magical lighting. The gothic mirage appears in the sky. The setting of the Garment Workers' guest house moves off. The setting of the intermission slowly moves in.*)

SECOND INTERMISSION

SEVEN
A MILLENNIUM

According to most ancient lore
There sailed to Russia Norsemen bold,
Known as Varangians. They came to shore
And the native folk were told:

"Both beast and bird we have a-plenty,
Our youths are mighty, elders wise,
Our cattle's fine, our lasses hefty—
But order is in short supply.

"This can't go on. Come, be our rulers,
Oh, blue-eyed princes: We'll give our thanks!"
The Norsemen thought this most peculiar,
But raised their flags on the river banks.

The weather then was hot and pleasant,
The banners rose above the shores.
The cloudless skies of that fair season
Did not foretell the Tartar hordes.

*   *   *

Now Russia's reached its millennium . . .
The centuries have tumbled by,
Through times of trouble, harsh and glum.
Now order is in good supply.

*(The bus stop shelter against the background of the seaside plain.
The sound of heavy rain. Distant cries of Monogamov and Heron.
The stage darkens and the theatre quickly grows light. Those who
wish may go out for refreshments. Lovers of erotica will probably
wish to remain in the hall. Ivan Monogamov, exhausted and soaked
to the skin, crosses the proscenium, walks under the bus stop shelter,
and tries to light a cigarette. He sees the frightened Heron in a corner, huddled against the wall.)*

MONOGAMOV: *(Rushes to her.)* You?! My dearest!

HERON: Jezu! Pan, I work in Czerwona Ruta Garment Factory . . . Jezus Maria! . . . as seamstress . . .

MONOGAMOV: Heron, I understood everything at once, from the first sign, from the first sound! I am yours! I have lived all of my forty years for you! My dream is in you!

HERON: (*Huddling more and more tightly.*) Przepraszam pana, not too close contacts, no contact of ultimate kind . . . no touch . . . I so wet, wilgotna . . . Not disgusting for pan? To rain . . . I not always like so . . .

MONOGAMOV: Don't be ashamed! You are wilgotna, but you should be damp, wilgotna, my Heron! When you call, I imagine all the damp groves of Europe, all of its nocturnal cities . . . You are Europe, youth, a dream! Don't be ashamed of your wings, your feathers!

HERON: Proszem, you not laugh at poor girl . . . At factory—pay only ninety rubles. I pay for food, and for sleep—and have no money for rajstopy . . .

MONOGAMOV: (*Slips her some wet money.*) Take this for your rajstopy, for your damned panty hose, my beloved! Buy yourself a new raincoat!

HERON: Jestem virgin, prosze pana . . . I am cherry. At club, nobody dance wit' me . . . (*Beseechingly.*) Prosze pana, not too close contacts.

MONOGAMOV: (*Seething with passion.*) Silent, my beloved! You are not a seamstress! You are Heron! You are the dream of all Russian men! My love! (*Embraces her.*)

HERON: (*Weakens in his arms.*) Pan wie, I eat toads . . . frogs . . . Swallow them live . . . pan mien bzidi . . . (*Embraces Monogamov, covers his back with her wings.*)

MONOGAMOV: Nie bzidi . . . I feel disgusted. I feel sweat. I feel sinful and holy. I a-do-ore you! (*He penetrates her.*) Are you Heron?

HERON: Kochane, who are you? Rossianin?

MONOGAMOV: Are you Heron?

HERON: Rossianin?

MONOGAMOV: Are you Heron?

HERON: Rossianin?

MONOGAMOV: Are you Heron?

HERON: Rossianin? (*These questions, interrupted occasionally by groaning and happy laughter, will be audible from the total darkness of the stage for all the remaining fifteen minutes of the intermission; therefore all members of the audience, even lovers of erotica, are invited to find entertainment and refreshment, and to socialize. The pithy dialogue will be transmitted to all nooks and crannies of the theatre. Marvelous howls of apotheosis together with the bell will invite you to return to the hall. Heron and Monogamov in a spot of moonlight. They straighten out their clothing, gaze at one another lovingly and in embarrassment.*)

MONOGAMOV: (*Coughs in a slightly formal manner.*) Well, now, tell me about your life, where did you go to school?

HERON: It true you know many languages?

MONOGAMOV: Now I know one more. (*Both laugh in embarrassment.*)

HERON: For you I lay egg.

MONOGAMOV: You'd better think before you do that.

HERON: Nie, nie, already decided. (*An accordion begins to play somewhere nearby. The Kampaneyets Sisters sing in a three-part harmony: "To the left a bridge, to the right a bridge, and the Wisla lies before us." The frightened Heron, gracefully jumping up—a flamingo, pure and simple!—and lifting her wings, moves off into the darkness. Monogamov moves by her side, phosphorescent like the "King Stag." Light fades in the hall.*)

ACT THREE

(Once again the veranda of the Garment Workers' guest house. During this Act we will change the time of day without regard for chronology, being guided instead by the requirements of the dramatist's and director's art. For the time being, it is night, the moon, light specks, rustling, swishing, whispering. Keyboard music in the baroque style. At long last the small clavicord is of use to us. Lyosha the Garment Worker is now playing the instrument, pensively and sadly. He is obviously reveling in his solitude. Lyosha the Watchman quietly descends the spiral staircase. He notices Lyosha the Garment Worker and inserts his glass in his eye.)

LYOSHA THE WATCHMAN: You belting out Vivaldi, Garment Worker? *(The exposed Lyosha the Garmet Worker jumps up, shamefacedly bustles about, pulls his accordion out from under the chair, and plays the first bars of "From Moscow to the Very Borders." Then he flings the accordion away, walks up to Lyosha the Watchman, and puts his hand on his shoulder.)*

LYOSHA THE GARMET WORKER: Hey, man, I only recognized you at second sight.

LYOSHA THE WATCHMAN: Now you had a better disguise. I only realized it was you when we began drinking vodka. I remembered that gobbledygook of yours about James Joyce. It was '68, I think, when it passed from hand to hand.

LYOSHA THE GARMENT WORKER: That's it, exactly, passed from hand to hand. And that's what it was called: "Slut Under an Umbrella." What a disgraceful thing!

LYOSHA THE WATCHMAN: But it was beautiful. At the time everybody simply fell in love with that whore of yours.

LYOSHA THE GARMENT WORKER: And I remembered the little song you wrote then: "Seven Fridays in a Week." Tell me, Watchman, what scared you off?

LYOSHA THE WATCHMAN: An iron wrecker, a baba, as they call it.

LYOSHA THE GARMENT WORKER: And with me it was a living female wrecker, a baba with pickles. It was on a crazy night. We had been roaring out our poems, singing, going from house to house, drinking gin and tonic . . . I don't remember who was

treating, whether it was foreigners or some of our own celebrities
. . . We were all wild about gin and tonic at the time. We found a
kind of piggish revelation in that drink. But pigs is what we were:
We imagined we were the darlings of civilization, we were fuck-
ing and puking in every corner, but, you see, we looked upon our
juniper euphoria mixed with beer blues as a special mark of
distinction. Towards morning, as I remember, we went swimming in a dirty construction pit in a crummy Moscow suburb—I
don't know what drew us there except for cheap snobbism. And
then we hired a truck and drove to a farmers' market. Our crowd
was straight out of a Fellini movie—broads wearing ostrich boas,
hats, masks, jeans, someone in a dinner jacket and someone naked, wrapped in a blanket. The police didn't touch us for some
reason, maybe because of foreigners, maybe because of our own
shitty celebrities. To make it short, it was a return to the simple
folk, We gorged ourselves on sauerkraut and guzzled brine
straight from the barrels. We saw a delightful little mamochka
selling pickles, the very soul of kindness and all-forgiveness!
"Mamochka, give us a little pickle!"—and the whole gang dove
into her barrel. And what does Mamochka do but slam the lid on
our fingers. She gave us a look like Ivan the Terrible. Oh,
Mamochka, what a harpie!—Everyone else walked away, but I
stood, paralyzed. One pickle fell on the floor and she crushed it
with her foot. We look each other in the eye, and I shriveled up
like the pickle under her heel. "I'd like to stomp you all like
that," she hissed—and then I understood that my freedom, my
youth, my aristocratic piggishness were at an end . . . Ever since
then I've given up the damned stuff.

LYOSHA THE WATCHMAN: (*Warily.*) But why did you come here at
the very peak of the drama? Couldn't you control yourself?

LYOSHA THE GARMENT WORKER: (*Frightened.*) What do you
mean? I actually am a genuine worker. From Paris-Communeville. With a reservation. (*Looks his companion in the eye.*)
And why are you stirring up the waters here?

LYOSHA THE WATCHMAN: I'm a genuine watchman. I dry mushrooms here. And that's it. (*Laima appears on the stairway. The
men, noticing her, get on all fours and crawl around the floor.*)

LAIMA: (*Points to the television with a solemn gesture.*) Boys,
Tashkent is going on the air!

LYOSHA THE WATCHMAN: I'll be a monkey's uncle, now an' where did I stash me little juggie?

LYOSHA THE GARMENT WORKER: No, this ain't the way it's done among comrades. Where's my little bottle of white wine? (*They crawl on all fours, stumbling over one another. Laima, as if under hypnosis, approaches the television. Doors slam on both stairways. Claudia and Rosa.*)

ROSA: Claudia, my dear, my angel—it happened! I am happy!

CLAUDIA: You're in luck, Rosa. Yours doesn't pick mushrooms.

ROSA: Mine wants to pick berries. To make vodka.

CLAUDIA: By the way, sis, I've been happy for a long time already, only I felt funny saying so. When you and Laima would get going with your "Warsaw-Warsaw," it turned out I was some kind of animal without spiritual needs.

ROSA: And what do we need Warsaw for if thing are fine here?

CLAUDIA: And what do we need Warsaw for if things are fine here?

LAIMA: (*In front of the lit-up television.*) Tashkent! Tashkent!

LYOSHA THE GARMENT WORKER: (*Bumps into Lyosha the Watchman.*) Where's my little bottle of white stuff?

LYOSHA THE WATCHMAN: Been ripped off.

LYOSHA THE GARMENT WORKER: I object. Let us seek until we find. Like they sing in the song—come seek, oh, comrade! (Ivan Monogamov emerges from the misty depths. A ray of Venus accompanies him. Everyone trembles and stands still, when they spy the romantic figure of the smitten internationalist.)

MONOGAMOV: (*Stretches out his arms, ecstatically.*) Thank you, night! Thank you, stars! Thank you, rain! Thank you, sand! Thank you, swamp! (*Stands still as if entranced.*)

CLAUDIA: He's back from his date. See, he's thanking nature. His little birdy's really gotten to him.

ROSA: Oh, that Monogamov! He's more in love than anyone!

CLAUDIA: Have you flipped, Rosa? You know what the consequences will be? I'm scared to think about it.

LAIMA: (*Presses her hands to her breast.*) Girls, come over here! It's Tashkent! Tashkent is on! (*Lyosha the Watchman and Lyosha the Garment Worker are at the proscenium. They've begun speaking in "secret voices."*)

LYOSHA THE GARMENT WORKER: Come clean—was there ever anything between you and this Heron?

LYOSHA THE WATCHMAN: She was driving me crazy. I was afraid of falling in love. Nothing else.

LYOSHA THE GARMENT WORKER: I'm afraid that I wouldn't have been scared off. I would have fallen with a terrible thud. Luckily everything had already started by the time I arrived. Now there's nothing more I can do.

LYOSHA THE WATCHMAN: He came just in time, that foreign service guy. Now they'll denounce him instead of me.

LYOSHA THE GARMENT WORKER: Yes, I'm scared to even think what'll happen when Stepanida returns.

LYOSHA THE WATCHMAN: Listen, doesn't it seem to you . . .

LYOSHA THE GARMENT WORKER: No, thanks pal. The crushed pickle is enough for me. We're powerless here. After all, this is . . .

LYOSHA THE WATCHMAN: Exactly. A violation of each and e-v-e-r-y norm.

MONOGAMOV: (*Suddenly turning towards them, his enormous eyes shining.*) Friends, at least share a little happiness with me!

LYOSHA THE GARMENT WORKER: What have we got to share? I had one bottle, and even that's been ripped off. (*To Lyosha the Watchman.*) Where's my little bottle of the white stuff? (*Grabs him by his shirt front.*)

LYOSHA THE WATCHMAN: A man's bein' killed fer a little juggie! (*They grab one another and roll around the floor in a fictitious fight. The old Gannergeits run mincingly onto the stage.*)

CYNTHIA: (*Guiltily.*) Helas, if we have in theatre a stage . . .

CLARENCE: (*Guiltily.*) That means we need on stage ein wall, mauer. (*Quickly erects a light plywood screen in a corner of the stage.*)

CYNTHIA: If we have wall that means it have . . .

CLARENCE: Nail! (*He hammers a nail into the wall.*)

CYNTHIA: Eef vee hev wall and nail . . .

CLARENCE: We have to hang rifle! (*Hangs a rifle.*)

CYNTHIA: (*Laughs sadly.*) If on wall hanged rifle . . .

CLARENCE: (*Holds out his arms in a helpless gesture.*) It have to . . .

LYOSHA THE WATCHMAN: (*Grabs Clarence by the leg.*) Gimme back me juggie o' Stolichnaya, Clarence!

LYOSHA THE GARMENT WORKER: (*Grabs Cynthia by the leg.*) Where's my little bottle of the white stuff? (*Clarence takes an enormous, three-liter "little" bottle out of his bag. The two friends are happily "out of it."*)

LYOSHA THE WATCHMAN: That's jes' what I blabbered to ya—the devils ripped it off!

LYOSHA THE GARMENT WORKER: But they *did* give it back, all rightie! The *did* give it back! Thanks to them for that. Thanks loads! (*The old Gannergeits, bowing bashfully, slowly back away toward the television.*)

MONOGAMOV: (*Intercepts them.*) Thank you, my dear old Gannergeits, my gophers, my devilkins, spy-chicks, shadows of the Great War! Perhaps you alone knew my Heron before, guessed that she was not a simple seamstress like hundreds of others you see around; and when she, standing on one leg in the swamp, gazed sadly at this guest house as at an unattainable enchanted castle, you sometimes cheered her up and brought her a humble mollusc. Thank you!

FROM THE TELEVISION: Our cameras are poised on the Central Stadium in Tashkent. Before a raging crowd the Tashkent Earthquake High Jump meets are now underway.

LAIMA: I feel faint.

MONOGAMOV: (*To the sisters.*) Girls, have you ever experienced the feeling of love?

ROSA: (*Proudly.*) Yes, Monogamov, I understand what you are speaking of.

CLAUDIA: And how come you go around all the time forcing your love on everyone? (*Guffaws.*) You stink through and through of frogs!

MONOGAMOV: (*Elatedly.*) Yes, yes, I stink through and through of frogs!

LYOSHA THE WATCHMAN: Yes, yes, someone from the province of Olsztyn is in love with her. I feel sorry for him.

LYOSHA THE GARMENT WORKER: (*From behind his bottle.*) Why butt my buttock—seems she's an easy lay.

MONOGAMOV: (*Joyously.*) Yes, yes, she's an easy lay!

LYOSHA THE GARMENT WORKER: (*Takes Monogamov by the arm, leads him aside, in a secret voice.*) I've got to speak to you right this minute, old man!

FROM THE TELEVISION: In the high jump sector it's the idol of the young, Bobby Monogamov! The bar is at the two-and-a-half meter mark!

LAIMA: It's him! I'm fainting! Over here, everyone! (*To Monoga-*

mov.) Forget your slut for a minute at least, you negligent father! Your son is at the bar! Wish him luck!

MONOGAMOV: God will give him luck, not me.

LYOSHA THE GARMENT WORKER: (*In a secret voice.*) Are my ears deceiving me? You pronounced God's name in an unacceptable way, with a capital letter.

MONOGAMOV: Really? I didn't notice.

LYOSHA THE GARMENT WORKER: You are a graduate of the Military Foreign Language Institute, you know. What's your rank now?

MONOGAMOV: Major. Or lieutenant colonel. Not any higher. But not any lower either.

LYOSHA THE GARMENT WORKER: I remember you from my former life. You were a playboy, a loafer, a cynic.

MONOGAMOV: That's not how I remember myself.

LYOSHA THE GARMENT WORKER: Why have you fallen in love with the Heron, old man?

MONOGAMOV: Because I never knew love before.

LYOSHA THE GARMENT WORKER: You circled the globe at the height of the sexual revolution.

MONOGAMOV: All of that wasn't it. I searched everywhere for what I imagined in my youth.

LYOSHA THE GARMENT WORKER: But why an animal?

MONOGAMOV: Because she is an animal.

LYOSHA THE GARMENT WORKER: Why a bird?

MONOGAMOV: Because she is a bird!

LYOSHA THE GARMENT WORKER: (*Looking all around.*) I haven't said a thing to you, old man. (*In a whisper.*) You're playing a very dangerous game, you're about to commit a stupendous foul. I repeat, I haven't said a thing to you, but . . . think again before the iron laws of the drama take over.

MONOGAMOV: Who's brewing this drama?

LYOSHA THE GARMENT WORKER: (*Looking around.*) That nobody, that so-called Watchman, didn't have the strength to warn you, and by the time I came it was too late.

MONOGAMOV: You? Why here . . .

LYOSHA THE GARMENT WORKER: (*In his disguised voice.*) Why! Why! Don't bug me, buddy! I've got a voucher, a right to a vacation. You made yourself comfy here, got yourself three square meals a day, for family reasons, but I'm here according to the law. (*Hobbles away, then stops and looks at Monogamov with sympathy. Holds out his bottle.*) Want a swig for courage?

MONOGAMOV: What have I got to be afraid of? (*Drinks from the bottle. A bright, sunny noon sets in on stage. F. G. Kampaneyets descends the stairs carrying a folder, Stepanida climbs up to the veranda with a briefcase. Filip Grigorievich is already considerably diabolized in comparison to the preceding acts. His hair has twisted into little horns, there is a lustful smile on his lips, his gaze wanders. The female activist, on the contrary, has gained in majestic roundness. They take their seats at the head of the table where communal repasts usually take place.*)

STEPANIDA: (*Sternly.*) Begin, begin, Filip Grigorievich! Enough of that scratching!

KAMPANEYETS: Staff members! Please be seated at the table. The meeting is convened . . . (*To the old Gannergeits, who have sidled up to him.*) Oh, the bombers do bomb, the flamethrowers fight on . . . (*Giggles.*) Cynthia, while the comrades are seating themselves, scratch my back, along the backbone, under the shoulder blades . . . aah . . . aah . . . (*Everyone takes seats around the table. Laima, of course, half-faces the television.*) Well, all in all, we are convening . . . (*Grows gloomy, bored.*) The meeting, the regular, or—what's the other kind called—emergency, is it, or special meeting, or who the fuck knows what . . . (*Shuffles through his papers.*) All in all, we will decide on the case of the former UNESCO employee, Ivan Vladlenovich Monogamov.

MONOGAMOV: Former? Bravo, Filip Grigorievich! That's a good joke!

STEPANIDA: Don't start rejoicing too soon, Mr. Monogamov. The most curious facts have turned up in the central organs. Why was it you wrote nothing in your spotless résumé about druggists, about your Jewish pharmaceutical relations? Don't tell us you didn't know anything yourself? (*With growing fury.*) There, now everybody knows everything! Your true colors are clear! UNESCO has dismissed you from its ranks!

MONOGAMOV: Say what you like, but I have a contract!

LYOSHA THE WATCHMAN: What would yer like? Which cognac?

LYOSHA THE GARMENT WORKER: Contact, you hick! He's got contacts! A Zionist! That's the kind they send abroad! They don't send honest guys, but ones with contacts who go and really clean up!

MONOGAMOV: Madame, this is contrary to international law.

STEPANIDA: I'm no madame! What a nerve! Calling me madame to my face!

MONOGAMOV: (*To Kampaneyets.*) Filip Grigorievich, still and all, I'd like to know how the charge against me is formulated.

KAMPANEYETS: (*Digs into his papers.*) Oh, may you all burn in hell . . . The charge, the charge . . . How the devil I'd like some Danish Carlsberg beer! (*Powerful mouth cleaning.*) Here it is, your charge. (*Reads, frowning.*) The Heron, a rare and delicate species from the animal world, is undergoing rapacious extermination in the countries of capitalism. Only with the planned-detailed-organized preservation of the Heron population practiced under developed socialism . . . (*Looks for a paper, grunts heavily.*) . . . In summary, Monogamov, you are charged with malicious violation of the ecological balance. (*Grunts, breathes heavily, swears under his breath.*) Do you confess that you are having sexual relations with the Heron?

MONOGAMOV: (*Not at all upset, and even, it seems, pleased at the question, as sometimes happens when one is happily in love.*) That concerns only the two of us. Her and me!

STEPANIDA: Do you see the nerve he has, comrades?

LYOSHA THE GARMENT WORKER: What is this, Vanya, not man enough to confess?

LYOSHA THE WATCHMAN: Like it or not, ya gotta spill the beans, Vanya, me lad! This ain't no parliament!

KAMPANEYETS: Oho-ho, let's get on with the vote. Who is for the confession of Ivan Vladlenovich? (*Everyone raises his hand, including Monogamov himself, but excluding the old Gannergeits.*)

ROSA: The confession of a prodigal soul—how thrilling! Don't make a hash of your story, Monogamov!

CLAUDIA: Give us the details! How do the two of you do it?

LAIMA: (*Glancing at the television.*) Another false start! One last try remains! Ivan Monogamov, don't disgrace your son!

STEPANIDA: (*To the Gannergeits.*) And you, farmers, why didn't you raise your hands?

CYNTHIA AND CLARENCE: We knowed everyseeng completement . . . alles . . . fsyo . . . we not voted never. We nicht adored votingische democracy . . .

KAMPANEYETS: (*Gloomily.*) At a meeting you have to raise your hands. What else are meetings for?

MONOGAMOV: (*To Gannergeit, reproachfully.*) Really, it's unheard of not to vote at a meeting. Why, it makes no sense. If everyone's for, then everyone must raise their hands. That's how things are done.

CLARENCE AND CYNTHIA: Correctment! Correctment! We wilde devils, we forgetted a little der historical lesson. We—for!

MONOGAMOV: (*Stands up.*) Then I will respond! Ladies and gentlemen ... oh, excuse my UN habits, comrades—live with wolves and you howl like a wolf ... So, comrades, my life has taken strange turns. I always yearned for mono-love, and therefore I rarely participated in the mass orgies of my militarized student days. Alas, I was quickly disillusioned—and this did not happen, of course, because of my marriage to Stepanida Vlasovna, but it spite of it. Life seemed to fade for me, and I became the playboy and cynic my Moscow contemporaries still remember. I want to stress that I never had the slightest impulse to travel beyond the bounds of our homeland; I have a very realistic view of my abilities, and the twenty-eight languages—why, that's pure physiology, practically a freak of nature. Then suddenly I was summoned, I was put through an extremely complex security check (there wasn't even mention of any druggists, Stepanida Vlasovna), and I was assigned to the UN Commission for the Struggle Against Hunger, with headquarters in Lausanne. I don't remember when and where it happened ... at the airport in Dakar one night? ... early in the morning on the Amazon? ... At sunset on the beach at Big Sur? ... In short, there was a piercing instant when I again fell in love with life, I felt the unity of all our living environment, its immensity and smallness, its delicacy and elastic expansiveness. It seems to me that precisely at that instant I began to hear the cries of my Heron, or something of the sort, I began to await the woman of my life, the bird of youth. I waited and searched, ladies and gentlemen—oh, excuse me, comrades. This searching is the only explanation I can give for the very long list of medical personnel within the framework of the UN which our keen staff members provided to me. Alas, it seems I was misunderstood ... alas ...

STEPANIDA: Oh, you were understood, all right. Let me congratulate you: Starting from yesterday you have become a "non-traveler."

MONOGAMOV: Excuse me, but that doesn't sound serious. Man cannot be a non-traveler. (*Slightly reminiscent of Gorky.*) Man is forever a traveler! (*Sinks into thought and then cries out like a wounded bird.*) What! Styopa, there was something sinister in the sound of your voice, something that we, Soviet internationalists, are afraid even to think about. What?! Do I now risk never seeing London again, or the Isle of Malta, or Djakarta, or Paris? . . .

LYOSHA THE GARMENT WORKER: Why don't you arrange to live with us in Paris-Communeville, friend? We'll spend our common leisure time together.

LAIMA: (*Heart-rendingly.*) He won! (*Falls from her chair.*)

FROM THE TELEVISION: It's a victory for the Soviet high-jumping school, taking off on the left foot and carrying over the right into a smooth roll over the bar. (*Enter Bob with two big suitcases. Everyone turns to him. Laima extends her arms sculpture-like.*)

BOB: The whole world was up in arms against me. A certain Davis. A certain Chavez. A certain Crawford. We Soviet high jumpers must know our home fires are burning brightly!

LAIMA: It's here, my little boy! Your rear is here!

BOB: (*Frowning slightly.*) Aunt Laima, you're being too literal. We high jumpers have extremely mobile nervous structures.

STEPANIDA: As a mother and citizen I am proud of you, Bob! As a citizen and mother I call upon you to join in the censure of your father for having lost touch with his native soil.

BOB: But I lost touch with my native soil, too. Two-and-a-half meters—I don't believe it myself. I didn't have any hope at all of winning in Tashkent. I missed two tries. My left take-off foot seemed to be filled with lead, seemed to feel someone's profound unhappiness. And suddenly . . . I don't know what happened . . . papa, mama, Aunt Laima . . . It's as though I heard someone's call . . . A sensation of someone's happiness pierced me . . . It is possible, I said to myself, and right then my turn came. The world record fell! What was it? (*Embarrassed silence.*)

KAMPANEYETS: Well, now. (*Shuffles his papers irritably.*) There is a motion, after all, to wrap things up. Otherwise we can burn ourselves out with too many meetings—Comrade Lenin has warned us against that. (*Shielding himself with papers for a se-*

cond, he exchanges winks with the Gannergeits.) And so, the proposed resolution, damn it. The meeting of the community of the Garment Workers' guest house—staff members and a vacationer—strongly censures (*speaks more and more rapidly*) the antisocial behavior of I. V. Monogamov, manifesting itself in the violation of the environmental balance, and requests that he forthwith cease sexual relations with a certain feathered creature. In addition, we recommend to the appropriate organs that appropriate measures be taken for the appropriate fortification of air space in the region of the border of friendship with the Polish People's Republic, for the suppression of the penetration of certain feathered species from foreign to native swamps. Who is for? Come on, come on, comrades! How much can you take? (*Cleans his mouth.*)

GANNERGEITS: (*Hops with raised hands.*) Quick, quick, Genossen! (*All including Monogamov raise their hands.*)

KAMPANEYETS: Who is against? (*All lower their hands.*) Any abstentions? (*An idiotic silence. The sunny noon fades. Once again moonlight, rustling, swishing, summer lightning. Joyfully.*) Meeting adjourned! (*Scratches his rear with his foot, bobs up and down, and exchanges winks with the Gannergeits, while preparing to jump over the railing and take to his heels.*)

MONOGAMOV: That means I can go? (*Looks at his watch and quickly combs his hair.*) That's just wonderful, wonderful . . .

STEPANIDA: (*Stands up, immense and majestic.*) Stop this blasphemy against the community! (*Points her finger at Kampaneyets.*) You, Kampaneyets, conducted our meeting with criminal indifference. You are no longer a leader, you're bankrupt!

KAMPANEYETS: What do you mean? What are you dissatisfied with? the meeting's over—everyone was for! Haven't I earned a swig of excellent beer and a bite of fish? Can't I go with my veteran friends to the bathhouse? I'm no bankrupt, I want bottoms up! (*By now he's completely "out of it," giggles, and hops up and down.*)

GANNERGEITS: Bottoms up! Bottoms up! Our Knabe, our darling, he earned everything! (*All three devils dance off to a corner of the veranda, where they settle down as though in a sauna, delighting in one another and, for the time being, not paying the slightest attention to the action.*)

STEPANIDA: (*To Monogamov.*) And where are you off to, you renegade? You voted for your own censure?

MONOGAMOV: (*Despairingly.*) Of course I voted "for." What else? What else can you do at a meeting? But, you know, I . . . (*Hides his face in his hands.*)

BOB: Someone here is fantastically unhappy. My legs are filling up with lead again. Who is unhappy here?

STEPANIDA: You also voted "for!"

BOB: (*Screams.*) But, you know, the meeting was already over!

STEPANIDA: My son, when you vote "for," you are not simply performing a formal act of unanimity. While joking with the others, each of us is thinking about what is most precious to him or herself. Now, for example . . . (*Approaches each one in turn, dangling her spheres over each and fixing her heavy gaze in each one's eyes.*)

ROSA: I voted for love. Simple and disturbing.

CLAUDIA: And I'm for nobody butting in, for various smart alecks not forcing their ideas on me.

LYOSHA THE GARMENT WORKER: Okey-dokey. I'm for freedom of Zimbabwe.

LYOSHA THE WATCHMAN: For the dust, for the dusk, for the soul o' mother Russia.

LAIMA: For happiness, which lends one wings!

MONOGAMOV: (*Hollowly.*) I understand all of you, my dear friends. I voted, as always, together with everyone, for everyone, and I never . . . (*The sky becomes emerald. Pink rays, either of the sunset or the dawn, slant onto the veranda. A wind rises. Heron, in shimmering white garb, climbs up to the veranda. Monogamov cries out and presses his hands to his mouth.*)

HERON: You will never stop loving me, my Rossianin!

MONOGAMOV: Never, my Heron! (*Crawls after her on his knees, falls, holds out his hands.*)

STEPANIDA: (*Astounded, gazes at Heron like a child.*) No, this is not Heron! This is something wonderful! When I was a child it seemed to me this existed somewhere, but I swear I never saw it! I simply don't believe my happiness! What are you?

HERON: I am Heron! (*Holds out her hand to her. Stepanida, awestruck, takes her hand. They walk side by side with a hint of solemnity, as though dancing a polonaise. Suddenly one of*

Stepanida's spherical breasts bursts, then the other, then with a hiss both her buttocks and her stomach deflate. Her clothing sags on her, and she walks alongside Heron, pitiful, timid, and entirely human.)

LAIMA: (*To Heron.*) I must confess to you. In all my life I never found a single mineral. I cannot become pregnant. If not for your coming I would never have discovered that there is happiness in the world. Dazzling creature, what are you?

HERON: (*Holds her hand out to her.*) I am Heron! (*Now the trio promenades across the stage to the barely audible sounds of a polonaise. The happy, beaming Monogamov crawls behind Heron, holding her sparkling white train. All the others move around them in circles, as though drawn by a magnet. Only the devils pay no attention to anyone, delighting in one another, riding a high.*)

LYOSHA THE GARMENT WORKER: (*Rushes toward Heron, wails.*) I don't know what you are! I never imagined that you would appear in the play, *someone* like you! I must confess—I forged my voucher. It's counterfeit! (*Weeps bitterly.*) I'm counterfeit through and through!

HERON: (*Holds out her hand-wing to him.*) Do not cry! I am Heron!

ROSA: I also have something to confess, I don't know exactly what yet. I also fooled everyone, and I fooled myself. I played an aristocrat of the spirit, but all I ever dreamed about was a penis. Whoever you are, may I touch you?

HERON: You may! I am Heron! (*Holds out her hand to her.*)

BOB: I craved happiness only for my high jump showings! Who am I? What have my legs served? Tell me, if you've really come!

HERON: (*Holds out the edge of her garment to him.*) You shall find out! I am Heron!

CLAUDIA: Have pity on me, for no good reason! (*Cries.*) Dumb broads *do* have a right to happiness?! Dumb, nervy, mooching broads? You, what did you say your name was?

HERON: (*Holds out the edge of her dress to her.*) I am Heron!

LYOSHA THE WATCHMAN: (*Falling, doing a somersault.*) Have pity on a coward, a coward! I wrote poetry and was afraid, I fell in love with Heron, landed in a drama, and was scared shitless. Now I'm drying mushrooms—and I'm still afraid! Have pity on a coward, your radiance! (*Throws away his eye glass.*)

HERON: You too give me your hand, Lyosha the Watchman. I am Heron! (*Holds out a corner of her train to him. Now everyone is touching her, one her finger, another her elbow, another her white plumage. She leads them all in a quiet polonaise. Finally she stops in the center of the stage, and all the characters «except for the devils» sit or lie down close by, arranging themselves like shrubbery around a sculpture. Everyone looks at Heron with adoration and happiness. Their faces are radiant.*)

HERON: And you, my Rossianin, you were the first to fall in love with me, and I also fell in love with you first; but now you are one of them.

MONOGAMOV: (*Beaming.*) Of course. I understand, my heron.

ALL: (*With a sigh of total happiness.*) Our Heron!

EIGHT
THE ENCHANTED WORLD

What an enchanting world the Creator has designed:
The pines, the loons, the moon, an automobile, a highway . . .
Vision is given those who are not completely blind,
Hearing is given those who can hear at least half-way.

Here's the enchanting world. At the Paris Opera.
Slender, impulsive, young, the prima donna of the *foyer* (*French pronunciation*)
Swathed in her chinchillas, sips champagne with her *foie gras*.
Filling with enchantment both young playboys and old *roues*.

Here's the enchanting world. Your neighbor Ivanov,
His meaty face as yet under the sway of dreams,
Goes for the morning paper and, giving a hacking cough,
Under the pouring rain demands to know what it all means.

Here's the enchanting world. With a soul as pure as snow.
A dog died in agony, a splendid Scottish setter.
He lived but one short year, then he lifted his keen nose,
And was gone like the summer rose to his special canine heaven.

Here's the enchanting world. It is guided by the Lord.
Angels do sing in it, and the devils serve on boards.

HERON: Well, here we are all together now. Even our devils are close by, our tired devils, the constant companions of humanity. It is said that everyone shall be saved. You ask for details, but I do not know everything. I know only that your world surrounds you, my children. Sand and pines, my children. Swamps and the sea, my children. Roads and national boundaries. At night, when I called to you, the cities all around were sleeping, and the leaves were rustling. You woke up, and on the edge of reality and dream it seemed to you that you understood my call, but reality thickened and you lost it. What I must pass on to you . . . (*Suddenly falls silent and lowers her head.*)

ALL: (*With growing alarm.*) What? What? What? What? What? What? What? (*The devils, with shy little smiles and guilty bows, dance out toward the wall with the rifle.*)

CYNTHIA: (*Bows to the audience and the actors.*) Przepraszem pans-two, but if you have in theatre ein stage . . .

KAMPANEYETS: (*Sighs.*) Unfortunately, it behooves . . .

CLARENCE: Ein wall. (*Brushes away a tear.*)

KAMPANEYETS: (*Spreading his arms in a helpless gesture.*) According to the laws of drama . . .

CLARENCE: It has nail! (*Whimpers.*)

CYNTHIA: Eef vee hev wall and nail . . .

KAMPANEYETS: (*Coughs slightly in embarrassment.*) This is objective reality, comrades.

CLARENCE: Hanged a rifle? (*Silently sobs.*)

CYNTHIA: (*Extremely embarrassed.*) If on wall hanged rifle . . .

KAMPANEYETS: Excuse me—Chekhov thought this up, not me—but it must kill. (*Pushes the wall with the rifle, waves his hand in despair, and turns away, genuinely grieved. The wall with the rifle begins to revolve slowly.*)

ALL: (*In despair.*) No!

CLAUDIA: (*Hysterically.*) Lyoshka, do something!

ROSA: (*Sobbing.*) Lyosha, stop it from revolving, I beg of you! (*Lyosha the Watchman and Lyosha the Garment Worker get down on their knees.*)

LYOSHA THE WATCHMAN: (*In despair.*) What can *we* do against the laws of drama! We, the great unwashed?

LYOSHA THE GARMENT WORKER: For that you have to be born different. (*They embrace and weep. The wall with the rifle con-*

tinues to revolve slowly.)
ALL: No! No! No! (*They jump up and screen Heron with their bodies, hide her from view. A thunderous shot. Everyone—both people and devils—scatter in different directions. In the center of the stage lies a heap of snow-white garments—the motionless Heron. Killed! Frozen poses of almost unbearable sorrow. The devils move off to the rear of the stage and, sadly bobbing up and down, croon their favorite song:*

> Oh, the bombers do bomb,
> The flamethrowers fight on,
> And the ponderous tanks crawl and creep!
> If you finish, my friend,
> Your tough legerdemain,
> Then fly down in your fabulous jeep.

Monogamov, coughing badly, as though in the final throes of tuberculosis, crawls out toward the ramp and looks at the audience with his enormous eyes. The pile of white feathers reposes behind his back.)
MONOGAMOV: Goodbye! Goodbye, my youth! How long you lasted, there was no end to you, and now—goodbye! Now I am beginning to die. How many years I will be dying—ten or forty—that isn't important. Goodbye, my world, now I won't see you any more. In Africa, in Europe, in Asia, in the Antarctic, in America, in Australia, I shall be blind. Goodbye! Goodbye, my Heron, I have nothing more to wait for, I shall never forget you, I shall never see you again. (*Lowers his face to his hands and freezes. From the pile of white feathers the former awkward, pitiful bird with round, stupid eyes arises. She is holding something under her wing. The night of Act One sets in. Summer lightning. Heron hobbles to the proscenium and places an enormous snow-white egg alongside Monogamov.*)
HERON: (*To Monogamov.*) Rossianin!
MONOGAMOV: (*Terrified.*) What?
HERON: Shhhh! Wait! (*Sits on the egg and settles down to hatch it.*)

* * *

NINE
A QUESTION

A wave that goes by near a breakwater
When it passes dies away.
A sailboat that scurries over the water
Finally flies away.

Everything passes, decays, and leaks,
You cannot stop the moment.
A change of government often leads
To the end of a monument.

The creation of a great empire
Also contains its caput.
The drama which has just transpired
Will also end in a minute.

Plays rarely achieve immortality,
They are doomed to oblivion.
In this connection we chose naturally
A heron as heroine.

In this connection why not create rhymes
Between equator and crater
And give to the hero a stanger's eyes
And so start up a theatre?

In the darkness somebody thumbs his nose,
Someone walks by with a laugh,
You go on your knees and you ask, serious,
Is there anything really left?

1979, Peredelkino